TUNDRA 37

A NEW DAWN, BOOK 2

AUBRIE DIONNE

Entangled Publishing, LLC
2614 South Timberline Road
Suite 109
Fort Collins, CO 80525
Visit our website at www.entangledpublishing.com.

Edited by Kerry Vail
Original cover design by Kim Killion
Cover art by Heather Howland

Ebook ISBN   978-1-937044-49-7
Print ISBN   978-1-937044-51-0

Manufactured in the United States of America

First Edition February 2012

To Chris

PROLOGUE
THE SEERS

I'm losing her.

Abysme guides the vessel in silence, her blind eyes rolling as she senses our course, two hundred years away from Paradise 18. She's scattered her thoughts among the stars, and her mind drifts farther from the sister I once knew. I fear the machine has engulfed her individuality. She's forgotten the meaning of our goal, the oath we took three centuries ago. Most of all, she's forgotten me, creating an emptiness inside me more profound than the desolation surrounding us.

If I had my arms, I'd reach out to comfort her and usher her back from the black abyss spread before us. As children, I kept her alive through the destruction, signing us up for the *Expedition* and winning two tickets off Old Earth before it succumbed to hell. But can I save her now?

I send impulses through my brainwaves and into the ship. *Bysme, do you hear me?*

Unlike her, I have one operating eye and can see the control chamber we hang from. Twisting my head, I search her features. Her skeletal face twitches. She writhes and the wires holding her in place stretch taut. I wonder what I've done to us, the shock of our disembodiment jolting me. Every input hole drilled into my skull snakes with activity. The ship surges through me, a vast intranet of information, names, status charts, and infinite trajectories. If I couldn't feel the cold, regulated air on the remnants of my torso, I'd be lost in the machine too. I remind myself of our mission and the perseverance flows into my veins.

She doesn't respond and the fear wells up from within me. Can I guide the ship alone? I realize I've left her at the helm for too long while I drifted into memories.

Status of Beta Prime? Bysme speaks in monotone computer speech as she turns to the corner of the main control deck where the orb glistens, tempting us with the mysteries hidden in the cosmic swirls within its core. Sometimes, I wish we'd blasted the ball off the hull after its tendrils attached to the outer frame instead of recovering it for study. We've guarded it for so long, Project Beta Prime has become part of us, yet we're further than ever from unlocking its secrets. All I know is the insistence of my memories, like ghosts that refused to be ignored.

Unchanged. The weight of my voice in our mindspeak reflects my disappointment. *Like everything else.*

Bysme falls silent, and I scan the systems searching for answers that aren't there.

CHAPTER ONE

MATCHMAKER

The Expedition, *2751*

Names trailed in pairs along the wallscreen as the next batch of destinies unfolded. Gemme pulled her hair into a ponytail and sipped her synthetic coffee, reviewing the computer's choices. Beside her, a constellation of stars glittered on the sight panel. She studied the spherical pattern, content to watch the world float by from the safety of the *Expedition*'s computer analytics wing.

She'd live and die on the decks of the aging transport ship. The certainty of her fate comforted her from the black void pressing in. Consistency gave her solace, and in her life regularity reigned. She lived through her work, finding life in numbers.

After another long sip, she gazed up at the screen and read the first pair of names.

Aaron Tixton and Cassandra Smith.

She accessed their profiles with the tip of her finger on her keypad. Both Lifers tested well in energy maintenance and ship repairs. Their personalities were type ISTP and type ENFJ, and their family trees didn't intersect until third cousins in the first generation, providing a promising match. Neither showed any manifestation of the rare hypergene they'd searched for since they left Earth, but no one she'd ever matched had. There were no guarantees the Seers would last until the ship reached Paradise 18. Suppressing a moment of worry, she scratched her chin, then typed an affirmation on the touchscreen.

Ray Ellis and Melissa Stewart. Although they were three years apart, Ray being the senior, their genes were optimally compatible. With resistance to Alzheimer's, cancer, and heart disease, they would produce durable children. The touchscreen flashed as her finger pressed enter.

Molly Fritz and—

The portal beeped, interrupting her work. Who would visit so early on the first morning shift? She'd dragged herself out of her sleep pod for a reason. The Seers expected the next report by fourteen hundred, and she didn't have time for unplanned meetings.

Gemme sighed and clicked off the screen. She couldn't have an intruder spying on the new sets of matches. She pressed the portal panel and the particles dematerialized like falling stars, revealing a stellar beauty.

"Luna?"

"Gemme." Luna shifted and leaned her busty body against the portal frame. "How are you? I haven't talked to you in years."

For a reason.

Uneasiness spread through Gemme's shoulders, making her neck tingle. A vision of Luna's highly mascaraed teen face scrunched up in anger came back to her. *What am I going to do with you, you freckle-faced cybergeek? You make me look bad with all your studying and high test scores,* Luna had taunted before she smacked Gemme in the chest, leaving a bruise that had lasted for two months. Sure, Gemme had pushed her back, but Luna's final shove had landed her in the recycling bin. She'd suffered in that cold, metal container for four hours before a custodian heard her banging for help.

Luna had claimed it was an accident, and as the Lieutenant's daughter, and the descendant of the original founder of the *Expedition*, everyone believed her. Gemme hadn't pressed the issue. No one messed with the Legacys. Since then, she'd stayed clear of the beauty and her bullying tactics. As Luna hovered over her, Gemme sensed where this conversation led, and it made the coffee in her stomach churn like acid.

"I've got a lot of work to do, Luna. What do you need?"

Luna flipped her wavy blonde hair behind her shoulder and stared at her as if she had a right to be there. "I want to discuss my pairing."

"You know I can't talk of future matches." Gemme fought to keep her tone professional. "The computer makes the decisions. I only review the pairings and double-check for glitches."

"You have more power than you let on, Gemme, dear." Luna pushed past her and slinked across her office, tapping her fingertips along the keyboards.

Hot air flared out of Gemme's nostrils. The nerve! Luna asked her to change the bylaws, to risk her job after years of bullying? Her cheeks burned like a supernova. The keys clicked under Luna's long nails in a rhythmic pitter-patter. Thank goodness she'd locked down the system.

The blinking button for the screen stood out like a dwarf star. Luna inched toward it. Gemme squeezed by her and stuck her small body between Luna's ginormous chest and the touchscreen, turning her back on her to protect the machine.

"I can't change the pairings, only approve or disapprove."

"You can disapprove of everyone for me."

The harshness in her voice made Gemme whip around from the controls and stare her down. "You're telling me you don't want a lifemate?"

"You didn't let me finish." Luna's lips slid into a smile. "Everyone, that is, except Miles Brentwood."

Of course. Gemme could've guessed that request from a parsec away. The computer hadn't assigned Miles Brentwood a lifemate yet. Five years their senior, not only was he powerful, attractive, and brilliant, his sweet charm could warm even the coldest reaches of deep space. Somehow, even though Luna was gorgeous, Gemme didn't think she deserved Brentwood, and she reveled in the fact that she couldn't honor Luna's request.

"The computer decides the lifemates, not me." Besides, pairing

Luna with Lieutenant Brentwood would explode the mainframe of the lifemate pairing system. The computer's choices had an excellent success rate, much better than the statistics she'd seen from Old Earth. She couldn't imagine people choosing for themselves.

Luna shrugged as if she discussed tricking a five-year-old instead of defying a centuries-old system. "If you deny every pairing for me, eventually his name will come up."

Gemme held her nose up, but her head only came up to Luna's magnificent plunging neckline. Why didn't her uniform ever look as good? "I'm not going to bend the rules for you."

Luna pulled back and pouted her full lips. "I thought you'd say as much. That's why I brought you a bribe."

She dropped a piece of paper on Gemme's desk. Before Gemme could reply, Luna slipped around her and jogged out the portal. "Think about it. Get back to me." Her voice echoed down the corridor, cheerful, yet tense.

Gemme watched her leave, stunned. What could Luna have that she wanted, besides an apology? She'd already earned a cushy job with a cosmic view. Gemme picked up the piece of paper, feeling the strange thinness in her hands. Paper was only used for formal occasions. What could it be?

Opening the folds of the document revealed a border of glittering gold. The writing was etched in inky cursive. Gemme gasped as she studied the contours of the inscription.

Request granted. Please present this upon arrival on Control Deck 67.

A ticket to visit the Seers. This rarity was one more shred of proof the Legacys had advantages others didn't have.

Why would she ever want to meet them? The Seers had sealed their chamber for the last century for fear of weakening their fragile bodies with germs. People whispered about their transformation from real humans born on Old Earth to skeletons and machines. Just thinking about how they'd severed their arms and legs after the limbs had atrophied to have wires run directly into their torsos made her squirm.

She realized Luna didn't know her at all. Status quo contented

Gemme more than any high position or special meeting. She wanted to live her life on the *Expedition*, drink her coffee, and play matchmaker in space.

Gemme slipped the document underneath her keyboard. She'd have to return it to Luna herself. This couldn't be trusted with interdepartmental mail and she didn't want Luna thinking she owed her anything.

After the portal materialized, she flicked on the button for the pairing system and the list of names blinked on her wallscreen.

Now where was I? Oh yes, Molly Fritz and—

A letter G stole her attention from halfway down the second column. She skimmed the names.

It couldn't be.

Gemme gasped and backed away from the wallscreen. Her touchscreen fell to the floor and rattled.

Gemme Reiner and Miles Brentwood.

Her first thought was of Luna running at her with a laser gun.

But I didn't choose it. The computer did.

She knew the day would come when her name would cross the screen, she just didn't think it would be today or it would be him. Everyone would suspect she devised the pairing herself. She'd look like the most selfish, hypocritical computer analyst in the history of the *Expedition*. She might even lose her job.

She scrambled to the floor and collected the touchscreen. Her hands shook as she replaced it on her desk. Wasting no time, she highlighted their names and the reasoning for the pairing. They both had history of mild high blood pressure, and a few minor propensities for anxiety in their family trees. They weren't incompatible, but they sure as hell weren't a perfect match either. Although, their first names sounded so right together: Gemme and Miles.

Shaking the nonsense from her head, she forced herself to focus. The fluorescent yellow connecting her name and his made her uneasy. Her finger paused over the word *delete*. For a millisecond, she thought of his strong hands touching her cheek, running across the back of her neck and into her hair.

Stop fantasizing!

Why would such a man be matched to her? Obviously the computer had miscalculated. Here lay the one glitch she was destined to fix. Gemme's finger trembled as she pressed the touchscreen. In an instant, their names disappeared, deleted forever in the vastness of deep space. Even the Seers wouldn't detect it in their nets.

A response beeped on the screen.

Pairing denied.

Gemme breathed with relief. She couldn't have people thinking she'd manipulated the system, especially Luna. Besides, attraction shouldn't factor in any of the matches.

She picked up her coffee mug just as a crash echoed above her head. The floor rumbled beneath her feet. Had her deletion wreaked havoc on the whole system?

Two monotone voices echoed in unison out over the intercom. "Comet shower approaching. Collisions imminent. Evacuate the outer levels."

Gemme froze. Danger to the *Expedition?* Impossible! The Seers would have detected any danger from a parsec away. They could never be wrong. The Guide said so.

Another crash shuddered the floor and she fell to her knees. The wallscreen flickered. She gazed out the sight panel at the familiar constellation. Balls of red with trailing tails streaked the sight panel. She fisted her hands. Had the Seers failed? She had no time to ponder the impossible. Her office lay on an outer deck. She had to get to safety.

Her first thought shot to the computers. Could she save her life's work? For privacy, the Seers instructed each matchmaker to store all data on the computer in front of her. The lights flickered out and an alarm screamed down the hall. One of the fiery balls grew larger, hurtling right toward the glass separating Gemme from the void of space.

Forget the data.

Taking one look back at her touchscreens, Gemme sprinted to the portal and slammed her fist on the panel. The second it took for the particles to dematerialize tugged on her nerves. Visions of space sucking her out haunted her more than visions of being stuck to the ship like the Seers. Gemme clutched her hands together and bounced on her toes.

The particles disappeared, and smoke wheezed in. Bending down, Gemme covered her mouth with the sleeve of her uniform and ran. The ship pitched sideways, and she fell into the wall, bumping her knee. Her leg collapsed, but she forced herself up through the pain. The corridors lay empty. Was she the last one on the outer decks? She hoped so. Most of the Lifers slept in their cells at the heart of the ship at such an early hour.

"Hull breach imminent. Congregate to the inner decks immediately."

Was there a hint of fear in the Seers' voices? Gemme refused to believe it. The Seers had everything under control. They always did. They wouldn't let anything happen to her, would they?

She punched the portal panel in front of the elevators, but nothing happened. Fear twisted her stomach, climbing its way up her throat. She breathed in, and the air seared the back of her mouth. Coughing, she slammed the panel harder.

Come on, you aging piece of junk.

The panel light flickered out like a dying sun.

Smoke filled the corridor and burned her eyes. She ran to the air shaft's emergency ladders. Another crash hit the hull, and another. What were the Seers doing? Had they lost their minds? She clung to each ladder rung as she climbed down, afraid another shock would send her plummeting ten levels at once.

As she reached the next deck, the air spiraled over her head. Pressure sucked the breath out of her lungs. A warning buzz sounded, and the Seers' unison voices echoed out, "Hull breach on Deck 86."

Gemme searched below her feet. She could climb down ten more rungs to close the lower hatch, or climb back up five to close the upper hatch. Metal clicked, and the emergency systems made the decision for her. Beneath her feet, the particles of the lower hatch materialized.

Panic rushed up her legs along with the dwindling air. The Seers had locked her out.

Gemme stared at the spinning particles. If she fell too soon, she'd be stuck in the particles of the hatch and the portal would rematerialize inside her. She had to wait for the hatch to become solid.

The air grew thin and she gasped for breath. The force of the suction pulled at her, yanking hair out of her ponytail. Once the hatch formed, she leaped down on top of it. Scrambling in the folds of her uniform, she brought out her keytag.

Thank goodness she'd worn it around her neck. Sometimes the cord irritated her skin, and she took it off, setting it by her touchscreen. Now, she wasn't sure if her touchscreen still existed. The thought of her office pummeled by comets flashed in her mind. She couldn't go back for anything now.

She shoved the keytag into the portal panel and typed *override*. A message popped up.

Please enter your security code.

The temperature dropped and she shivered, sucking in one last breath. Gemme forced herself to type slowly to get it right. One missed touch would shut her out forever.

Her heart raced as she tapped the panel and the particles disappeared.

A wave of hot air blew by her as the hatch reopened. Gemme jumped down and slammed her fist against the panel to close it above her. As the particles solidified, she climbed down to the next level and kicked something blocking her way.

"Whoa! Look out."

Miles Brentwood gazed up from the toes of her boots, his green-flecked eyes piercing the semidarkness. Gemme's heart sped up. To see any person right now made her emotions crumble, never mind the man she'd been thinking of ever since she deleted their pairing. "If you're going up, there's no way out. I sealed the passage."

"I'm not going anywhere." He took the sight of her in, traveling up her cheek to her eyes and she almost lost her grip on the ladder rung. "I'm looking for you."

Miles Brentwood had come to spend the end of the world with her? Gemme's mind reeled. Nothing that morning had made any sense. She felt stuck in some sort of quasi-nightmare turned hot dream. "What?"

Although chaos crashed around them, his hair still looked perfect, the blond wave rising an inch above his broad forehead. "I'm retrieving all the stragglers. I followed your locater number."

"Oh." She looked away, feeling sheepish and small. How could she have ever thought he'd know who she was, never mind go searching for her in particular during this disaster?

He gestured over his shoulder. "There's a safe chamber just down this hall. Follow me."

Gemme collected her scattered emotions just as something crashed against the hatch above them. The screeching sound of crushed metal echoed down the vent shaft.

Brentwood shouted over the din, "This compartment's losing pressure, come on!"

She followed him down two more levels and through a side passage she'd never have found by herself. They crawled through an air shaft, collecting dust webs under their fingers. A metal grating hung missing half its hinges. Had he come all this way just for her?

Brentwood looked back at her over his shoulder. "It's not far. You can jump."

He paused at the hole below them and waited for her to make the first move.

Of course, his valor screamed "ladies first."

Gemme dangled her legs and judged the distance from the ceiling to the floor below her feet. If she fell the wrong way, she'd break both her ankles.

He must have seen fear cross her eyes because he offered his hands. "Here, I'll help you."

The warmth in his voice calmed her racing thoughts. She locked on his gaze. The flecks of green were so pure, they reminded her of the foliage in the biodome. Those eyes could have been hers to gaze into. She damned the pairing program. Why had it ever put such an outrageous idea in her head?

"Take my hands."

Gemme blinked her thoughts away and slid her hands into his. Their palms molded into a perfect fit. His skin emanated heat, warming her cold fingertips. She closed her eyes as the ship crashed around them. She expected to feel pain, but a light-headed ecstasy bubbled over her.

When she opened her eyes, the airshaft remained intact with Brentwood eagerly waiting for her to move. All the crashing had happened inside her, levels being knocked down to reveal surprising emotions she didn't think herself capable of. Yet, the feelings stirred an undercurrent of familiarity. Gemme searched his features to see if he experienced any of the same emotions, but his wide lips frowned. He was more concerned for her than drunk on possibility He hoisted her down and her feet hit the floor with a bounce. The ship pitched again, and she fell against the wall. Brentwood jumped behind her and ushered her forward, his hands along her waist.

"Just a few more steps."

They ran to the belly of the ship, where the structural integrity would hold under pressure. Brentwood slapped a panel and the portal disappeared to reveal a bunch of colonists huddling together. Food rations were stacked against the far wall along with space suits. Panic worked its way up Gemme's spine. If they needed those suits, they were dead already.

"Shouldn't we run to the escape pods?"

Brentwood shook his head. "Not yet. The Seers believe they can salvage the ship. The escape pods would only scatter us into deep space."

Gemme nodded and bit her lower lip. She'd known his answer. Escape pods were useless unless they found a habitable planet. It would only delay inevitable death.

He bent down, his face hovering a breath away from hers, lips slightly parted. Gemme froze in shock, noticing each light hair in his eyebrows and the moisture on his lips. Only lifemates leaned in so close. He pulled back, shaking his head as if recovering from a trance.

"My apologies. I must search for others."

Before Gemme's heart could beat again, he'd disappeared down the corridor, smoke trailing in his footsteps.

CHAPTER TWO
DAMAGE CONTROL

Each comet collision to the hull hurt like a puncture wound to Mestasis's own flesh. She checked on Abysme, but her sister calmly calculated readjustment maneuvers by her side, as if evaluating a math equation. More cyborg than woman, she showed no sign of physical pain or emotional reaction to the threat. Although Mestasis had no more of a claim to normal humanity than her sister, her thoughts battled with which parts of the ship to salvage.

The biodome sat in the center, just above the heart of the ship. She'd instructed Lieutenant Brentwood to secure the majority of colonists beneath it, so that part of the ship took priority over all else. They must preserve the human, animal, and plant life, which meant steering the extremities into the line of fire.

Abysme's head jerked. *Engine capacity at thirty-six percent. Rerouting alternate energy means.*

Mestasis sent out a corresponding impulse. *Harborside capacitors engaged.*

Did Abysme's voice hold a hint of desperation, a fraction of humanity? Or was Mestasis the only one of them to weigh such decisions on her soul?

A comet ten meters across crashed into the main communications tower. She winced as she sealed the bridge, locking out three colonists to preserve the lives of the several hundred hiding below in their family cells. Each life lost was a unique human genome that could never be reclaimed or reproduced. The *Expedition* was losing its diversity, and Mestasis could only gamble so much of it away before their mission failed.

She needed her sister now more than ever. *Bysme, what are we going to do?*

Abysme's cataract eyes flickered like two radiant moons. *Structural integrity will hold. We must fly through the field. Protect the orb.*

The orb was the least of their concerns. What was her sister talking about? *Bysme? Protect the orb?*

Abysme shifted, wires stretching. *Protect the ship.*

The cold, analytical edge to her tone made Mestasis want to cry out and shake her. But Abysme was right. The comet conglomeration trailed too far back to sit and wait it out. They had to navigate their way through or risk further damage.

The engines flared up and she knew Abysme would use their last store of energy to propel the ship forward. Estimating the trajectory with the least amount of exposure took only milliseconds, but to Mestasis it weighed on her soul like an eternity. She chose the course, and Abysme approved it. Together their minds steered the ship within centimeters of collisions on either side.

Ninety-two percent of her mind worked on navigation, while the last eight percent traveled to a memory she thought she'd lost. They'd worked together once before to prevent a disaster threatening both their lives.

ॐ‿ॐ

Old Earth, 2436

The air hung hot and dry with golden swirls of dust accumulating on everything in a thick sheen. The world had turned stale and Mestasis could feel conflict brimming in every molecule. She chipped a piece of old paint off the banister and let it fly into the wind. Leaning over the balcony of her high rise, she peered through the smog clouding the lower levels below.

A piece of tarp rustled as a woman hung her laundry to dry. Children kicked dented containers in a game of soccer on an intersecting corridor between her building and the one next to it. Above her, the roar of engines filled the air. Hovercrafts flew between the buildings stacked like dominoes across the world's surface. The rich had no need to descend to the lower levels.

Until today.

"When will he come?"

Mestasis turned and saw her own face: dark skin, round, velvety brown eyes, and thick lips. Abysme leaned on the edge of the patio door, wearing her best clothes and the one pair of waterproof boots they'd saved up for all summer to share.

"Soon. I thought I heard the engines coming down, but it was a transport ship."

Abysme jutted out her lower lip. "I don't want to leave Mom. She needs us."

They'd had this argument a thousand times, yet Mestasis tried once again to convince her. "With this, we can help Mom more. Just think of the money we could make if we get in, if we graduate."

"I just want the world to stay as it is."

"Everything is going to change, Abysme. I can feel it. The only way we're going to survive is if we change with it."

Her twin joined her on the balcony, clutching the railing as if the smog would rise up and take them away. "That's what I'm afraid of, Metsy."

Mestasis took her hand. "I'll always be by your side. That's one thing that won't ever change."

The air rumbled over their heads and a gust of wind blew back their hair. A hovercraft with the words *Telepathic Institute of New England* lowered between the buildings and hung like a dragon across their balcony.

The hatch lifted and a middle-aged man emerged. His pale skin shone white in the sun. Streaks of gray shot through his curly blond hair.

"Are you Abysme and Mestasis River?"

Mestasis nodded with determination. Abysme shot him a suspicious stare.

"Are you ready to take the tests?"

"We are." Mestasis nudged Abysme and she nodded, studying her boots. If their mom had been home to say good-bye, Abysme would've had more closure. But she had a double shift at the recycling factory, and she'd lose her job if she missed a day. They paid a hefty sum to live in New York City on Level Fourteen above the gangs.

"Jump in. I'm Doctor Jasper Fields. I'll conduct the tests when we arrive."

Mestasis mindspoke, reaching out to comfort her sister. *Bysme, take a deep breath. Don't look back.*

Abysme stuck out her lower lip. *You can't make me.*

Frustrated, Mestasis threw down their only case of luggage. If her twin exhibited a negative attitude the whole time, TINE would never accept them.

Tears dripped down Abysme's cheeks. She mouthed something, but Mestasis couldn't tell what she said over the din of the hovercraft's engines. To her surprise, Abysme jumped first. She settled into the seat next to Dr. Fields and sulked as she clicked the seat restraint.

Mestasis paused at the threshold. If they passed the tests, they'd live at TINE, and she wasn't sure how much they could visit. She ignored her own advice. Looking back to their tiny apartment, she tried to memorize the weave of the rug where they'd played algebra games all night, the shape of her mother's sleeping bag huddled next to the wall, and the antique mirror where she'd helped Abysme braid her hair. Emotion surged up, and her knees weakened. She shouldn't have looked back. Sniffing, she tore her gaze away and leaped into the hovercraft, feeling like she plunged off the balcony to end her life. She settled into the seat next to the doctor.

"Get comfortable. It's a long ride to the coast."

Their tiny apartment disappeared and they rose through the misty clouds. Neither of them had seen the world above Level Fourteen. Mestasis shielded her eyes as they adjusted to the bright sun. The upper levels had windows with real plants, extravagant porch-side gardens, and decks to land hovercrafts. A greenhouse capped each building, shielding the damaging ultraviolet sunlight.

⁊ↄ⤳⥾

A crash against the outer hull brought Mestasis back to the present. She blinked, staring at the comet trails streaking across the main sight panel. How could she loose herself in a memory in a time like this?

Because they succeeded in the past, and she needed the memory to remind herself they'd succeed again. When they worked together, they were an unbeatable pair. Using her sister's ability to stretch her mind ahead of the ship in the vastness of space, she calculated the course, steering clear of the largest comets. *We can do this.*

⁊ↄ⤳⥾

An hour later, someone nudged Mestasis's arm. Her lids flickered open, golden swirls dissipating. Where was she? She stared out the sight panel of the hovercraft seeing sky so blue it looked like paint. Dr. Fields. The tests. They'd left home forever. She decided she'd rather be asleep than deal with her turbulent emotions.

Bsyme, Bysme, why did you wake me?

Something's wrong.

Mestasis was the emotionally stronger twin, but Abysme's talents outdid hers by tenfold. If anything was wrong, she'd know.

What is it?

Abysme grabbed her sister's hand and shoved it against the dashboard. Images flooded Mestasis's thoughts: energy capacitors, system hydraulics, air exhaust pipes. Something wavered beneath the hood, an oval-shaped metal pod. The heat signature surged well beyond normal levels. A drip of sweat ran down her forehead.

What is that?

Abysme shifted on her seat, eyeing the doctor. *I don't know, but it's gonna blow.*

Panic flooded Mestasis's mind. *How are we going to tell him? He'll never believe us.*

Abysme's eyes widened, intense. *Show him.*

Their heads turned to the doctor and they stared, projecting the image of the metal pod. The doctor winced and jerked his head. The hovercraft dipped in the air before he regained the controls. Mestasis's stomach flipped and she gripped onto her sister's arm for support.

"What the—"

Abysme squeezed her twin's hand and they resubmitted the image.

His head turned to them and his eyes widened. "It's coming from you?"

She nodded in unison with Abysme.

"You're telling me there's something wrong with the engine?"

They nodded again, slow and certain.

Looking like a ghost had slipped over him, the doctor brought up the systems with the tip of his finger and eyed the gauges. "You better not be pulling a prank to delay us, girls. It says here everything's fine."

Abysme shouted through her mind. *Don't be stupid.*

Mestasis hushed her twin's words before they reached his ears. She gave her sister an admonishing look. *You could explode his head and make us crash anyway.*

Abysme shrugged as if admitting to cheating on a test. *I'm just trying to keep us safe.*

Don't think you could fly this thing.

Abysme stuck her nose up in the air. *You wanna bet?*

The doctor punched in a landing code. He spoke into the intercom. "Requesting clearance on the next available dock."

A signal from the top of a building below them blinked as a beacon.

He sighed. "We're going to be late to our appointment, but I'll have them take a look."

The hovercraft descended toward the building, clouds parting before them in wisps. As the pressure on the engine lifted, the heat signature dropped and Mestasis breathed. The ship parked on the ridge of a greenhouse, sending up dust and dirt into the atmosphere. The hatch lifted and cool morning air seeped in.

"Don't go far. I'll be right back." The doctor jumped out and signaled a man from inside the greenhouse. Abysme jumped out after him.

Where are you going?

Just looking around.

Mestasis gazed out the main sight panel. The tangle of vegetation spread against the glass of the greenhouse. Vines reached up for the sky as if struggling to break free of containment. Besides their potted single blade of grass, she'd never been close to real leaves. It reminded her of the jungle stories Mom whispered at bedtime. Maybe it was okay to take a closer look.

She caught up to her sister just as Abysme smeared her face against the glass. Mestasis touched the greenhouse, and condensation formed around her fingertips. A tomato, vine ripe and bulging with watery seeds, made her tongue tingle. Beyond that, rows of apple trees stood like soldiers in a formation, dotted white with growing blossoms.

She trespassed in a high-up world where she didn't belong. Pulling a soybean wafer out of her pocket, she crumpled it in her palm. They ate processed food, while the rich enjoyed the last fruits of a dying Earth. As much as she hated them, she wanted her family to be a part of their world more than anything, to live in the final rays of the sun.

Steps sounded behind them. The girls whirled around as if caught stealing. Doctor Fields panted, running a cloth over his forehead as he caught up.

"You're both accepted."

"What?" Mestasis rubbed her eyes against the glare of the bright sun.

"You don't need to take any tests. You're in." He handed them a locator. "Call your mom if you want and let her know before we take off."

"I don't understand." Abysme finally spoke out loud, and Mestasis jumped at the rancor in her sister's voice.

"The hovercraft had a bad ventilator. Rat droppings clogged the filters."

He shook his head in astonishment. "I've seen a lot of telepaths in my career, but never have I seen two bound together in synchronization. You girls saved our lives. You don't have to worry about a single thing again. TINE will take care of you from now on. Be back by the hovercraft in five minutes, girls." Doctor Fields gave them a stern glance before turning around.

Abysme kicked the side of the glass with her boot. Mestasis cringed, but the wall didn't shatter. The tip of her sister's boot thunked and bounced back. Even though Mestasis had secured their future, she couldn't help the dirty feeling she'd also given away their deepest secret and sold their souls for a better place to live.

Abysme crossed her arms. *Don't have to worry about a single thing again, huh?*

Mestasis's skin burned with embarrassment on her cheeks. The situation overwhelmed her. She'd lost control, handing their future to a man her sister didn't trust.

If only what he said was true.

∂∞∽

Engine failure seventy-eight percent.

Her sister's voice brought Mestasis back to the present. She twitched her neck, calculating alternative energy means. They had to fly the ship out of the parameters of the hurtling comets.

Mestasis analyzed the systems still online and prioritized the ones less likely to cause physical harm to the colonists. *Shutting off gravitational rings, rerouting energy from bays 4, 13, and 20.*

No matter what she did, it wasn't enough. The energy gap tore at Mestasis's soul until she could barely stand the pressure. She turned to her sister, pleading.

Bysme, I need your help.

Her white eyes turned down, as if she could suddenly see her. Her cheek twitched, the wrinkles scrunching. *We'll make it, sis. Keep trying.*

Abysme spoke in common speech patterns! A real person still rolled around inside her fragile skull. Her sister's true voice urged Mestasis to focus. In a fraction of a second, she'd figured out enough energy to keep them sailing well away from the hurtling rocks.

Clear space shone on the main sight panel, a sea of darkness sprinkled with twinkling stars. The ship soared free of the danger zone.

Mestasis breathed, feeling cold, regulated air sear her old lungs. She shouldn't have taken so many breaths without her breathing apparatus, but in that moment she needed to feel alive.

Abysme's voiced jerked her out of her relief. *Mission to Paradise 18 abandoned. Seeking alternative colonization habitat.*

Panic rushed right back through the bolts in Mestasis's spine. What? Change the entire course of the mission? She shot a finicky glance at Abysme. Had her sister truly lost her mind? Reviewing the ship's performance and the remaining functioning systems, Mestasis's hopes plummeted. They'd never make it another two hundred days in deep space, never mind two hundred years.

Abysme's calculations were correct. Their mission to Paradise 18 had failed.

Disappointment in herself and hopelessness choked her. Next came emptiness, a black abyss of dire oblivion threatening to obliterate her last pulses of determination. Mestasis hung limp, allowing the wires to stretch dangerously far as her body weight pulled her down. She'd have given up and died in that moment if it wasn't for the shining star shimmering on the edge of her sight.

Compatible habitat found. Abysme drew up a star chart and Mestasis took in another breath.

Tundra 37 lay in the star system they passed. The initial readings reported compatible oxygen and carbon dioxide levels, light gravity, and solar exposure, mostly on the northern side. A category six planet experiencing an ice age; it was not optimal for survival, but certainly adequate, better than drifting in deep space.

Mestasis straightened and the wires pulled her back up.

Change of course approved.

CHAPTER THREE
MESSENGER

Lieutenant Brentwood hustled down the corridor clutching a beeping locator. Already thrown off by the emergency, he questioned his sudden urge to lean in and kiss that woman's cheek. It seemed so commonplace, like he'd done it a thousand times before. But he'd never met her. Was he losing his mind? As a lieutenant, duty always came first.

Smoke filled the adjacent corridor, and he searched for an alternate route. The locator showed three dots on the far side of the running track above the biodome, and the Seers had ordered him to evacuate decks eighty through ninety. He'd only made it up to eighty-four.

He spun around and banged open another ventilator shaft. Did the smoke inhalation distort his senses? He loved people and interactions. Social prowess and charm came as easy to him as simple math. His mother used to call him her little sweet talker. His class had elected him as senior president, and upon graduation, the Seers had chosen him as their personal messenger, delivering their decisions to the congregation in his smooth-toned speeches. But that woman had thrown him off his mark.

Even now the intensity of her presence affected him. His tongue still stuck to the bottom of his mouth. She wasn't a blonde bombshell, or an aggressively sly upper officer. She was the Matchmaker, a shy computer analyst, with freckles speckling her cheeks, sleek nutmeg hair, and smoky gray eyes. Nothing about her screamed intimidation, yet she possessed a subtle draw, pulling him in. Maybe his reaction to her had something to do with her job. She held his destiny in an important way. As the sole matchmaker of her generation, she'd decide his lifemate, his match.

The alarm wailed in his ear. He realized he stood frozen before the shaft, breathing in smoke-clogged air. He shook his head and climbed. She interfered with his job, and this was no time for such thoughts. He had more people to save. The dots on the locator beeped anxiously as far cries for help.

Crawling through the airshaft, he reviewed his options. The Seers had locked off decks eighty-six through ninety, and the locator traced the vital signs to eighty-seven, smack in the middle of the depressurizing zone. Maybe they they'd found an air bubble. Brentwood ground his teeth together in determination. He'd find a way to reach it.

He found a vent to an alternate corridor. He kicked in the metal grating and jumped down. Bringing up a blueprint of the ship on his miniscreen, he studied how to reach them. The main corridor leading to the upper decks had been compromised and the Seers had sanctioned it off, withdrawing air pressure to conserve energy and reroute it elsewhere.

An airtight service shaft filled with cables ran adjacent to the corridor. He could crawl through and emerge in the hydraulics room, which controlled the aerobics pool and the spin cycle bikes. The track lay just beyond that.

Brentwood pulled out his laser gun and fired three shots at the chrome wall. He'd damage the cables, but no one would be using the exercise room any time soon. A hole big enough to squeeze into sizzled in the laser fire. He waited for the metal to cool enough to touch it and climbed in.

The serrated cables, thick as his fist, made for excellent ropes. He brought himself up, silently thanking all the pull-ups his fitness coach had shouted out in his class years. His muscles tightened as he grasped a handhold and heaved. Thankfully, if the three Lifers weren't hurt, it would be easier to bring them down.

The shaft bent at a right angle, and he hauled himself over the edge, catching his breath. The blueprint on his miniscreen shone fluorescent green into the darkness. He'd reached halfway. The cold wire rubbed against his stomach as he crawled over the cables. He used the screen to light the shaft ahead, casting a ghostly glow on old spider webs and rat nests, the offspring of the test subjects taken on the *Expedition* in the first generation. The sides of the shaft pressed in on him. He groped with his arm to judge the distance. Had it been this narrow before?

He checked his locator. One meter separated him and the place where the floor hovered close enough to blast through. The cables dug into his torso as he squeezed himself forward and the cold sank into his bones like a disease. His toes numbed and his fingers throbbed. Only three meters of metal separated him from deep space, and the Seers had cut off all heat to the outer decks. The temperature dropped every second he spent in the shaft.

The Seers' voices came on his intercom, startling him.

"Lieutenant, turn around."

He brought his arm up and squeezed the button on his lapel. "I'm following orders, evacuating the upper levels."

The monotone voices buzzed back. "Deck eighty seven will collapse any minute. Return to the emergency chamber immediately. I repeat: turn around."

Anger formed a boulder in his chest. He growled, "I can save them."

The cold machine-women had no right to shut off human life, no matter what the consequences. Fury turned to determination, burning within him, keeping him warm. He slid on his elbows until he reached the end of the shaft. His readings reported the atmosphere holding stable. He dragged out his laser and fired up into the floor.

A warmer gush of air flowed in. Flashing red lights illuminated the ceiling of the fitness bay. Brentwood pulled himself up. If he read the miniscreen correctly, the upper deck had lost its pressure and the hull buckled above his head.

He moved to run, but his feet rose from the floor.

"Damn." The Seers had shut down the gravity rings. What next? Lower the oxygen levels as well?

Bubbles of water from the pool jiggled in the air like giant amoebas. Brentwood flailed his arms as he floated out of control. He struggled to pull himself together, but the dizziness swimming in his head made it difficult.

Beeps cried out between each pulse of alarm, bringing him back to attention.

The three colonists. He had to reach them and get them to safety.

A pool net floated by and he lurched out his arm and grabbed onto it. He spun under the new weight, but regained balance. Swinging the pole, he caught a wall light. Pulling himself to the wall, hand over hand on the pole, he gripped the bulb. Using handholds along the wall, he worked his way to the distance track.

"Hello? Anyone in there?"

The alarm drowned out his words. He felt like the last survivor of a shipwreck, left to wander alone as it broke apart around him with no anchors to hold onto. The thought of being the only man still alive made his stomach wretch more than the light gravity. He didn't even like working in an office by himself.

He checked the locator, and the green dots were larger.

"Hello?" His voice echoed down the bay.

He ducked as a hoverchair floated by in a meandering arc, sputtering as the thrusters flared out of control. The seat was upside down and vacant, straps dangling.

A screech echoed so loud he thought his ears would bleed. The ceiling warped under the decreasing pressure. Resisting the urge to panic, Brentwood kicked his legs against the wall and floated over the bright orange track.

Three people wearing white civilian jumpsuits floated in the corner next to the sealed portal. Two girls clutched each other, shivering, while a young man tampered with the portal panel.

One of the girls spotted him and waved him over. "Over here. We're trying to get through."

Brentwood yelled back. "You won't make it."

They didn't hear him, or chose to ignore his comment.

Damn it. He kicked his legs like a swimmer in molasses, wishing he could run again. "You have to come back this way with me."

As he drifted closer, one of the girls recognized his navy lieutenant's uniform and pulled the boy back.

"Dammit, Daryl! We're in trouble now."

The boy swatted her away and pulled a clump of wires out of the wall. "I've almost got it."

Brentwood ordered, "Don't open it."

The boy whirled around and glared with defiance. "I'm trying to get us out of here."

Brentwood pulled himself within arm's reach. "There's no atmosphere on the other side. The Seers sealed the corridor."

The smaller of the two girls covered her face with her hands. Her malformed legs hung limp in the air. Even with the Matchmaker's double check on genetic calculations, birth anomalies still manifested. They could only tame so much of nature and the small genetic pool made it more difficult to keep each subsequent generation healthy. That's why they had analysts like Gemme Reiner giving the cold computer analysis a double check with a human touch. Computers weren't always perfect.

Brentwood made a point not to draw attention to her. Thank goodness for the zero gravity. He could never fit her hoverchair down the cable shaft.

He put a reassuring hand on her arm. "What's your name, hon?"

She peeked from under a finger. "Vira. That's my sister, Rizzy."

Rizzy stared at him as if he'd flown them into the comets singlehandedly. "How are we going to get out?"

"Using an energy cable shaft. It's a tight squeeze." He looked at their boney bodies. "Anyone hurt?"

They shook their heads.

"Come on. We don't have much time."

They floated across the track like ghosts in a dead land. His emotions surged when he looked into their young faces. How could anyone leave them to die here? They had parents, brothers, sisters, and friends. They weren't a math equation, not to him. He wondered if the Seers had discounted Vira because of her handicap. Maybe they thought she wouldn't make it either way. Brentwood's chest tightened. He'd make sure she survived, even if it meant staying behind himself. The Seers wouldn't understand. They'd calculate it as an uneven trade. His anger surged, and he gritted his teeth together, focusing his energy on saving them.

They reached the hole he'd blasted through the floor. Brentwood handed Daryl his miniscreen.

"Use the screen to see ahead and watch out for a drop in four meters."

"Yes, sir." Daryl took the device and disappeared into the darkness. Brentwood nudged Rizzy down into the hole next, wondering how he'd get Vira through. He much rather hold her, but the narrow shaft prevented it.

"Hold onto my boots, and I'll pull you through."

"Okay." The determination in her voice made him proud of her courage.

The metal ceiling screeched as Vira's small fingers grabbed his ankles. He plunged into the hole, pulling Vira behind him. Soon the deck would cave under the pressure. He thought of calling on the Seers, but he knew they'd already done what they could. He would have to hustle the kids to the lower decks. Good thing the Seers seemed busy with saving the ship.

"Let's go, guys. Be careful, but crawl as fast as you can."

Rizzy squeaked in disgust. "There are rats down here."

Brentwood tried to console her, "They're harmless, just remnants of old experiments that managed to escape."

She halted in front of him, his head stuck under her feet. Behind him, metal crumbled and a familiar gush of air blew by him as deep space sucked their atmosphere out. He didn't want her to panic, so he tried a technique he used on his little brother to make him eat his vegetables. *Just think of the dessert in the end, little dude.*

"Just think of being down on the safer decks. Being free."

"I'd rather think of not being sucked into space," she called back, half giggling, half crying.

He laughed. "That's true too. Whatever works. Just keep going."

The route back seemed longer than the climb in. The suction of air increased until Rizzy's long hair stood out behind her like a cape, and he could feel his own wavy locks blown back so hard, he'd be left bald by the time they cleared the shaft.

"Vira, hold on tightly."

He felt her unlace his boots and tie the strings around her wrists.

Vira shouted, "What's wrong with the air?"

He whipped his head around, swallowed his misgivings and forced himself to wink. "Just a small leak. We're almost there."

When they reached the angle, the shaft widened, and Vira wrapped her arms around his neck. He pulled himself and Vira down behind Daryl and Rizzy. They emerged from the laser hole into the corridor. The bright fluorescent lights reassured him, but his lungs worked harder to breathe the thin air. A steady gust pulled them backward and he clutched the portal panel, pulling them through against the suction.

"Brace yourselves against the portal frame."

Once Rizzy and Daryl cleared the portal, he slammed his fist on the panel behind them and the particles rematerialized, sealing the remaining atmosphere in.

His ears rang in the silence. He stopped and drew a long breath of relief.

"What were you guys doing up there so early?"

Rizzy and Daryl looked away, but Vira whispered in his ear. "They were kissing."

"Vira! Shut your mouth." Rizzy's neck reddened.

Vira climbed forward on his shoulders so he could see her face beside him. "It's true. I caught them sneaking out, and I came to check on them."

"It's not right being paired up like animals," Daryl spat out, bringing Rizzy close to him. "They never consider love. To hell with the Matchmaker. She can fall into a black hole."

"Daryl!" Vira shouted. "He's a lieutenant. He'll turn you in."

Daryl held onto Rizzy as if the hull puncture could still suck her out. "I don't care. The ship's going to hell anyway."

Brentwood opened his mouth to lecture the young man on the *Expedition*'s manifesto in the Guide, like he'd done so many times in the past: *Lifers don't have the luxury of choice. Our mission is to further the human species, and our survival depends on it. We must sacrifice our rights to provide for the next generation, to preserve the genetic code and prevent inbreeding and mutations.* But he couldn't bring himself to say it. Vira was proof the system didn't always work, and he wasn't about to mention anything about deformities in her presence. Thinking of the matchmaking system and the Seers shot a current of disquiet throughout his composure.

The Seers' voices blared on the intercom, breaking the argument. "Comets cleared. Gravity restored."

All four of them plunged to the floor. Vira landed on top of Brentwood, knocking the air out of his lungs. At least he had cushioned her fall.

Daryl groaned. "Aw, man. They could have given us more notice."

Brentwood gave him a smile. "The Seers don't consider extraneous details."

"More like they've forgotten what it's like to be human." Daryl rubbed his knees and helped Rizzy up.

Brentwood chose to ignore him. Normally he'd call out such disloyalty, but his own misgivings about the Seers had crept into his mind. "Come on, guys, I have to get you to the safe chamber."

He led them down the hall into the chamber below the biodome. When the portal dematerialized, colonists surged forward to take Vira. Daryl and Rizzy disappeared into the crowd. Brentwood searched the sea of fearful faces for the Matchmaker. Her heart-shaped face stood out from the crowd like a lover among strangers. She scrutinized him with a strange, knowing glance. He wanted to turn away, but he stood frozen in place, gazing back at her, memorizing the blue-gray mist of her eyes.

"Lieutenant, report to the control room immediately." The Seers' droning voices roused him from his reverie and he studied his lapel. Hadn't he turned it off?

"Sorry, what was the order?"

"Report to the control room immediately." Was there a hint of annoyance? Surely not. They were more computers than humans.

"The control room?" His skin prickled with the thought of meeting the Seers eye to eye.

"Affirmative."

The silence weighed on his chest before he replied. With all the germs he carried, why would they sacrifice their own safety to speak to him in person? Did they want to reprimand him for disobeying orders, or did the comets damage the ship beyond repair? Either way, he'd best get up there, no matter how much their disembodied voices made him uneasy.

He pressed the communicator button. "Be there right away."

CHAPTER FOUR
MESSAGE

Gemme froze as Brentwood's gaze grasped hold of her, catching her staring like a child with her finger in the sugar crystallizer. Her first impulse urged her to look away, but a tantalizing curiosity arose, forcing her to confront her inner heart. What was his allure?

Brentwood glared down to his communicator. He spoke a few words and disappeared into the multitudes. Gemme resisted the urge to pursue him. Her feelings went against everything she'd ever learned, against her career, and the core of who she was. What was she thinking? Surely her irrational draw to him developed from the stressful circumstances of the comet shower. Her thoughts needed an anchor, and he climbed in, literally, at the right time.

Her logical mind kicked in. She regained her reasoning too late. He must think her some crazed, hormonal delinquent. She certainly couldn't pair him with her now.

No one else noticed. The condition of the ship consumed their every thought. Her mind shot to her office. Deep space had ripped out a part of herself. Was it all gone? Her life's work sprawling like cosmic dust through a black hole?

She noticed a fellow Lifer holding a miniscreen and jogged over to him, cutting her way through the throng. "Excuse me, sir. Can I have a look?"

He pressed his fingertip to the screen to shut off a personal message and handed it over. "Sure. Take a look for yourself if you want to. It's not good."

She'd already received a message on her locator from her parents and her brother. They were safe in a different chamber on the other side of the biodome. She brought up the schematics of the ship and dragged her finger across the screen to her quadrant.

The shaft she'd climbed down remained sealed. There were no readings on the other side, which meant decks eighty-six to ninety-two ceased to exist. There wouldn't be a pairing program now at all. There might not even be enough ship left to save.

Gemme handed the man his miniscreen and sunk to the floor. At least she and her family were safe, but she couldn't tell how much longer the ship would protect them with such extreme damage to the hull. Her small world had changed in minutes, and the next steps the Seers took would decide the rest of her life. For someone who'd held so many people's destinies, her own fate lay with two fragments of human beings, and she didn't like it one bit.

"Don't worry, it's gonna be okay."

The high-pitched voice brought Gemme back from her grieving. She wiped her eyes and focused on a small girl who sat with her back against the wall and a blanket strewn across her legs. Gemme straightened as her cheeks reddened. If such a small and innocent creature could lend so much strength, she could at least mop up her tears.

"I'm fine." Gemme replied, bearing a weak smile. The girl seemed to be alone and Gemme couldn't imagine how scared she must be. The least she could do was keep her company. She shuffled next to her. "Where are your mom and dad?"

"They're in the other safety chamber across the biodome."

"Oh, that's where my parents are as well."

The girl smiled. "I'm glad they're safe."

Gemme settled back against the wall beside her. "Me too."

"Your lifemate saved my life."

"What?"

"He found me along with my sister and her stupid boyfriend. He led us all the way down here."

The girl must have confused her with someone else. "I don't have a lifemate."

The girl's dark eyes stared at her, insisting. A vision of Brentwood breaking through the portal leading survivors came back to mind.

"Do you mean the lieutenant?" A shot of panic ran up her spine. Did this girl know of the deletion? Impossible. She must have caught Gemme staring at him earlier on.

The girl nodded, curls bouncing.

"Lieutenant Brentwood isn't my lifemate." Her voice came out harsher than she'd planned.

"Oh." The girl looked down, but a defiant spark in her eyes told Gemme she didn't believe her.

Gemme changed the subject. "It's okay. What's your name?"

"Vira."

Her mind raced through the computer pairings performed by the last analyst before her. Vira...Vira Pryer. Daughter of Natalie and Jason Pryer. The anomaly. She resisted the urge to glance at the lumps under the blanket. This particular pairing had haunted her boss, the former matchmaker of the generation before her. The parents had excellent genes, no signs of deformities on either side and some special attributes not normally seen in such combinations. They were supposed to have excellent children who'd exceed the norm. Then, they'd birthed Vira. She'd never be able to walk, let alone be paired herself.

Her parents had fought for her to live despite her genetic flaws. Surprisingly, the Seers allowed it, showing a burst of their dwindling humanity. But, it was quite the scandal twelve years ago. To hear about it secondhand and see it on the screen pained her, but to meet the girl in person wrenched her stomach. Since it wasn't her pairing, she didn't have access to the files, but sometimes she was tempted to break into the system and have a look for herself.

Gemme wanted to tell her *she* was the one who was sorry. The system had failed her, but her trembling lips couldn't form the words.

The girl put a hand on her cheek. "It's all right, Gemme."

Words couldn't form, and she touched the back of the girl's hand gently.

The portal to the control deck loomed like a stargate to another universe. Brentwood paused at the threshold, staring at the panel that hadn't been pressed in over ninety years. A shiver crawled across his shoulders as he imagined what lay on the other side.

"Lieutenant Brentwood, reporting."

A green light flickered on and the portal dematerialized. Cool air gushed out, smelling of chemicals, dust, and putrid rot, reminding him of the biosludge recycling all organic decay in the biodome.

"Access granted." Their dual, chanting voices boomed louder at their doorstep than on the intercom, and it reminded Brentwood of their ultimate power. The first Lifers had built the ship around the twins' abilities. Only someone with telepathic talents could fly it, and those specific gifts had yet to manifest in any of the generations of Lifers.

Brentwood stepped across the portal. A sight panel stretched the length of the deck, glittering with stars and cosmic swirls of golden particles. He expected the two women to stand at the helm and reminded himself they were not women any longer, but extensions of the ship.

"Over here, Lieutenant."

He whipped around to the voices above his head and stumbled backward in shock. Two skeletal torsos hung from the ceiling like chunks of humans caught in a mechanical spider web. Wires spread where arms and fingers should have been, and thick cables shot into their waists, like the stems of flowers in an upturned vase. The woman on the right stared down at him with one, intense dark eye. Thick, white cataracts eclipsed the other. Her twin jerked her head in small twitches, her gaze leering blindly around the room as if seeking a dimension beyond reality.

Brentwood pulled himself together and bowed, resisting the urge to shudder.

The one on the right moved as she mindspoke through the intercom system. Her cracked lips were numb, unmoving slabs of flesh. "We've brought you here for many reasons." Behind her, the wires writhed and coiled like snakes.

He nodded in silence. Part of him wanted to scream at them for sealing off the children and another part wanted to hear what they had to say and be done with it so he could get back into the corridor and breathe fresh air. Could these pieces of human beings really protect the *Expedition*?

"You saved many lives, Lieutenant. Your bravery does not go unnoticed. However, you cannot risk your own life for those lower in rank. We cannot lose you. You are far too valuable to us and our mission."

Brentwood stiffened, riding a current of outrage. It took all his strength not to raise his voice. "You left three children to die. If I didn't put my life on the line, they'd be adrift in space right now."

"We understand your concern, Lieutenant." The Seer on the right craned her head and a drip of gurgling liquid seeped into a tube connected to the base of her skull. Brentwood tried not to stare, but the freakish mix of human and machine hypnotized him, burning into his mind to manifest later in his nightmares.

"You must see the larger mission objectives. As you are aware, the Guide is the fundamental doctrine keeping this ship and its operations together. The Guide requires us to protect the mission at all costs. This means preserving the vast majority over the individual."

"Who's to say Vira's not important to us, to the mission?"

"Data, Lieutenant. Statistics."

He growled, "Screw data and statistics, she's a little girl."

The Seers twisted as if talking among themselves before responding. "We're not here to argue, Lieutenant. We've summoned you to show you we are human like yourself. We strive to protect the human race above all else."

Humans like me? They didn't seem like him at all. After so many years connected to the ship, did the Seers truly have the foresight to protect them? Brentwood's head spun. He certainly couldn't steer the ship himself. The Seers were the only hope they had.

They continued as if they sensed his doubts, "Our intentions are virtuous. We did approve her parents' request to keep her despite the rare anomaly in the pairings system."

He crossed his arms. He had his doubts about the pairing system as well. "Go on."

"Instead of focusing on those that perished, we must now face our uncertain future. The ship is in poor condition, and we must take new measures to preserve the mission's goals in the manifesto."

Prickles ran up his arms and legs. He'd had enough of this discussion. "What do you want me to do?"

"We've deviated course. The ship will not hold together long enough to make it to Paradise 18. We must land on an alternate habitat for colonization."

This much he'd suspected. At least they weren't all going to die. "All right. Where are we going? What should I tell them?"

"Tundra 37 is a compatible location for our colony. If we land the ship, we could keep the life systems sustainable until an engineering team constructs a suitable shelter."

The plan seemed too easy. Brentwood shook his head. "There's got to be a 'but' to this."

The Seer on the right lowered herself to look into his eyes with her single dark eye He resisted the urge to back away. The Seer moved her upper shoulder, and the wires nudged him toward a sparkling globe in the distance. "Tundra 37 is a frozen world experiencing a glacial period. Living conditions will not be optimal, but we must learn to adapt in order to survive."

"I see." He leaned toward the sight panel as if spying it closer would help him prepare. "I'll look up the initial scout readings and make arrangements."

The Seer settled back into the framework of the metal grid. "We've sent alternate occupations for the Lifers able to contribute to our colonization efforts. You are to make the announcement of the change and relay our assignments."

Her twin squirmed suddenly, and the lieutenant jerked back. "What's wrong with her?"

"Nothing. While we talk, she senses our course. Each change in trajectory jolts her body."

The lieutenant wasn't convinced, but he didn't want to spend one minute longer in their eerie presence. "I will convey your message."

"Thank you, Lieutenant. We'll send out new assignments soon."

He bowed. "Until we reach Tundra, 37, then?"

The Seer nodded. "Have everyone secured in their personal cells by twenty-one hundred. We expect a rough landing."

CHAPTER FIVE
REASSIGNMENTS

The stems tickled Gemme's palms as they bowed gently in a whispering wind. A radiant sun glowed overhead, warming the top of her head and burning her cheeks. Her sundress shifted in the breeze, embroidered roses winking at her just above her bare legs and feet.

Have I died?

Golden swirls clouded her vision and she blinked against the glare of the sun. The swirls dissipated as her eyes adjusted, scanning the meadow. A winding dirt road circled the grasses. Beyond that, a distant farmhouse clumped next to a silo on the horizon. At the center of the field, a stack of real books lay in a heap underneath a willow tree. She cut her way through the long grass, blinded by the stunning rays of sun. A buzz whizzed by her ear and she flailed her arms as a fat, yellow-striped bee dipped and circled around her. Gawking, she followed its meandering path until it zipped away above her head. The only insects she'd ever seen were flies in the animal cells in the biodome.

A patchwork blanket cushioned the books. She settled down on the crude fabric, crossing her legs and flipped open the top volume. Numbers and calculations filled the pages. She ran her fingers over the thin paper, feeling somewhat at home.

Yes, I know this. Algorithms, proofs.

Her own thick pencil strokes decorated the margins. A sense of dislocation dizzied her. Had she ever written with a pencil? She performed all her calculations in keystrokes. How did she recognize her writing in the book? The thoughts just turned in on themselves and she snapped the binding shut, searching the sun kissed meadow for answers.

Have we reached Paradise 18?

The thought was preposterous. Paradise 18 wouldn't come for another two hundred years. Her bones would be dust, and her great-great-great grandchildren would be standing here instead.

She spoke aloud out of habit, "Computer, location and time?"

No response. Her fingers ran over the spot on her arm where her locator clung ever since she was born. Her fingertips smoothed over fine hair and naked, tan skin. Tan skin? Her arms were pastier than tooth gel. Panic bristled the hairs on her neck. How long had she been missing? How would anyone on the *Expedition* find her?

"Jenny."

A woman's voice carried on the wind.

"Still working on your precious numbers?"

Gemme ducked underneath the tall grasses, her mind racing through her pairing charts and family trees. No one on the ship had that name. She rose up slowly and peeked over the stems. A bobbing head of almond hair, a shade lighter than her own, weaved its way up to the hillside.

A sweet voice sang the name in a taunt. "Jenny."

సౕ

"Gemme, wake up."

Dim fluorescent lights stung the backs of Gemme's lids. She rubbed her eyes and pulled her arm away from the tiny hand shaking it.

"The lieutenant has an announcement."

Gemme's eyes flashed open. She'd never dreamed of Old Earth before, and the jarring difference in realities took her a moment to comprehend. The *Expedition* seemed cold and lifeless, artificial. She hadn't thought of it that way before. The ship was the only home she'd ever known.

"Attention all Lifers." Lieutenant Brentwood's voice jolted her upright. Vira sat beside her, concern watering the poor girl's eyes.

She whispered, "You were asleep for a long time."

"How long?" Gemme rasped back while the Lieutenant reviewed the damage to the ship.

Vira shrugged. "Hours at least." Her small hands held up a container of water. "Here, have some of this."

"Thank you." Gemme struggled to pull herself from the groggy numbness of sleep and listen carefully. The cold water snapped her out of her dreamy haze. When her brain tuned in, Brentwood already spoke of their future.

"Tundra 37 is our only hope. The atmospheric gases consist of 78.09% nitrogen, 20.95% oxygen, 0.93% argon, 0.039% carbon dioxide, and small amounts of others, compatible to Earth. The fourth planet in rotation around the star Solaris Prime, the northern side is mainly exposed to the sun. Plant and animal life has been recorded in small amounts, and the median temperature is negative seventeen point seventy-eight degrees Celsius."

He placed both hands on the podium and stared into the masses as if he leveled with the audience. The way his gaze traveled through the space between them and settled on her captivated Gemme like a trance she couldn't shake. No wonder the Seer's had chosen him for their speaker five years ago. He'd make any dire news turn to hope. Since she'd pressed the delete key, who would the computer have matched him to next?

"It's a damn cold planet, and not a paradise, folks. I'll give you that. But we can survive. I've been doing research on information collected by scouts who first explored this galaxy. Mineral deposits on the southern side would keep what's left of the *Expedition* going until a suitable shelter is constructed. Readings show the planet will warm up in the centuries to come, and our children's children will experience the beginnings of a massive glacial thaw. All we have to do is stay alive until then."

"The Seers usually go through me with everything, but since

time is short, they are downloading new assignments directly to your locators. Each one of you must work together to establish the colony. I know you weren't prepared for anything like this. You thought, like I did, we'd live our whole lives on this cozy spaceship. But life brings surprises, and this one's going to be a heck of an adventure. We're all in this together. Let's get out there and build our future."

The crowd cheered and Brentwood settled back, waving away their gushing applause. Gemme's mind whirled with the news. What would happen to her matchmaking? She looked down to her locator and waited for the message to appear. The screen lay blank, so she refocused on the Lieutenant.

Brentwood raised his arms and the crowd settled. "One more thing. Everyone must report to their personal cells and secure their seat restraints. The Seers plan to land this vessel within the next few hours. No one, I repeat, no one, should be wandering the corridors. The landing will be rough."

Gemme could see why he'd waited to deliver the last bit of news. The mood hushed around her as the reality of the situation sank in. They weren't going to be in deep space any longer, or ever again for that matter. Tundra 37 held the rest of their lives. Her locator beeped.

Incoming message.

A wave of beeps rang around her as the others received their new life assignments as well. She brought up her arm and clicked the button.

Exploratory team Alpha Blue.

An explorer? Were the Seers out of their minds? Gemme had sat at a desk all her life. She scrolled down to read the rest of the message.

Analyze mineral deposit on the southern side of Tundra 37. Formulate best method for extraction and transportation. Compile rough estimate of the size and composition of resources.

Analyzation and numbers. That's why the Seers had given her the job. But on an ice planet in the middle of a glacier? Overwhelmed, Gemme's thoughts reeled. She could hardly bear to walk through the unheated corridors, never mind trek across sheer ice.

Wait, there was more. Gemme scrolled down wondering how it could get any worse.

Team leader: Miles Brentwood.

She scanned the podium where Brentwood stood. His gaze locked on hers and he ignored the people crowding around him with questions. They bumped him sideways and pulled him forward, but his gaze remained fixated on her, his lips parting as if in a question.

Embarrassment and fear swirled through Gemme. Every pining thought in her wild heart lay on display. The computer had said he was hers, and since that moment her emotions had run rampant. But she'd pressed the delete key and comets had shattered the pairing system in pieces all over deep space.

She pulled away, hiding behind an older man pushing his way through the crowd. Sooner or later she'd have to deal with her mixed-up feelings. But right now the ship ushered them forward to land on a new world.

CHAPTER SIX
GOLDEN SWIRLS

Bysme, I need your help with the landing. Please come back to me.
Mestasis repeated her message, calculating the best place to land in a world covered in ice. Bysme had fallen silent after the shower, her mind chanting the coordinates of Tundra 37 as if it skipped in place.

We've reached the damn planet. Now help me land this steaming hunk of junk. Mestasis sighed, surprised by her own venom. She shouted at her disabled sister when she should be using kindness and love to bring her back. The stress played on her nerves like Mozart on the piano. She decided to calm herself and sifted through the data files from Old Earth, choosing an aria from Don Giovanni before trying her sister again.

Bysme, please wake up. Then, she had an idea so twisted, she felt strange even trying it. *Help me land safely to protect the orb.*

Bysme stirred, the wires holding her in place creaking like old bones. *Landing coordinates approved. Initiating landing sequence.*

Mestasis paused, concern nagging the edges of her psyche, but she didn't have time to question her doubts any further. Bysme was talking again, and they had a ship to land.

When Gemme reached her personal cell, Tundra 37 filled the sight panel above her food congealizer. Splotches of cerulean swirled above slabs of endless white. She doubted the frozen rock held any means of refuge. Bleak as velvety deep space, scout ships had deemed it uninhabitable hundreds of years ago while searching for Paradise 18.

She strapped herself into the wall seat with shaky fingers. She'd only used the harness once before when they'd experienced engine turbulence and the gravity rings cycled down. A crash landing was much more serious. Astrophysicists designed the colony ships to land once, and only once on their chosen paradise planets, their heat shields disintegrating as they plummeted through the atmosphere. For the *Expedition*, this was it.

The Seers' voices resonated throughout the ship, "Secure all seat restraints."

She checked her seat restraints and hoped the remainder of the ship would hold. The hull supplied their only means of shelter. For a moment, she wished she still lived with her parents in their family cell so she wouldn't have to be alone. The Seers had spread out each Lifer's personal cells to ensure the majority of them would survive if the landing damaged part of the ship. Gemme realized she hadn't even said good-bye. *Would Lieutenant Brentwood survive?* She blocked the thought from her mind. He was neither a good friend or loved one. She shouldn't even consider him in her thoughts.

"Landing sequence initiated." The Seers' unified voice echoed on the intercom.

Gemme wrapped the straps around her arms and held on as the ship entered the planet's pull of gravity. The engines rumbled underneath her feet as the deck tilted and Tundra 37 blotted out the sight panel. It had looked like a pinprick from her office, and now it loomed in a massive, bloated globe. She felt as though the world would swallow the *Expedition* alive.

The rumbling increased as the ship dove forward, entering the atmosphere. Heat panels fanned out in wings. Fire replaced the stark white and Gemme closed her eyes. Holding on for her life, she should have been in her office, completing the pairing report, sipping her coffee, and nibbling soybean wafers for lunch.

Why did this happen to our ship? Was it a result of an error the Seers made? Or pure chance?

A peek through her scrunched lids revealed bright orange-red light as the heat licked its way through the shields. She crossed her arms against her chest and clenched her rattling teeth. Gemme hated not being in control more than arrogant Lifers demanding lifemate reassignments. Ever since childhood, she'd strived to impose regulations on everything. That's why she loved numbers and analytics. That's why the Seers appointed her matchmaker in the first place. She excelled at rationalization, until of course her chance meeting with the lieutenant skewed everything she'd ever known.

The walls shook and a DNA model crashed to the floor. A memory surfaced though the chaos and Gemme clung to it, as if reliving the instant would save her from the pandemonium invading her life.

ॐॖॖॐ

Gemme's mom stood at the food congealizer, stuffing carrots through the blades. The pulsing buzz covered the trickling waterfall on the wall screen. Golden swirls filled a computerized sun above the falls.

"Mom, you're covering my Gaia music!"

Her mom shouted from the kitchen, "I know, honey. I'll be done soon."

Gemme sighed and threaded another blue bead of nucleotide on the wire.

The food congealizer gurgled to a halt. She waited for the tinkling music to calm her, but Ferris ran into the room, using his fingers as a laser.

"Pow, pow, pow. You vaporized."

"Ferris, stop!"

Before she could lift the structure off the floor, Ferris stumbled through it. His little feet kicked the double helix across the room and the strands fell apart. She'd lost all the evenings spent wiring the structure together. Life felt useless, pointless, like she fought a battle lost many generations ago.

Gemme collapsed on the carpet and lunged for the beads, scraping them toward her with her arms.

"Sowwy, G." Ferris's toddler lisp slurred the words. He bent down to pick up a cytosine and she swiped his chubby hand away.

"Leave me alone."

Ferris wailed like he'd witnessed the end of the world. Her mom ran into the room holding a dish towel and the plastic repository for the food congealizer with goopy mush still stuck to the bottom. Ferris ran over and hid his head in her utility apron.

"What's going on?"

"Ferris knocked over my DNA model."

Their mom kneeled on the floor and pulled Ferris away to look into his red-blotched face. "Ferris, is this true?"

He nodded, "G not lemme help."

"Honestly, Gemme. You're twelve and he's three. It's only a plastic reproduction."

"But, Mom—" To her it was so much more, a means for sanity, the answer to life.

"Don't 'but, Mom' me. Now let him help you pick it up."

She looked down at the carpet where the repository leaked food waste into a puddle. "And after that, you'll help clean up your mess. I don't have time for this. I still have to finish the life system reports and your father will be home soon." She stormed back into the kitchen.

Gemme glared at her little brother. "Don't touch anything."

He sniffed, wiping his nose on his jumpsuit, and she made a mental reminder not to touch his arm.

"Go sit by the air ionizer."

Shoulders slumped, he dragged his feet over to the ionizer and plopped on his synthetic-diapered butt. "Wanna help."

"No." A single strand had survived the accident, and she held it to the fluorescent lights, examining the bent wire. Maybe she could twist it back in shape and all wouldn't be lost.

A bead bounced on the top of the ionizer. Gemme turned around just in time to see it rattle into one of the vents. "Ferris!" Why did she have to watch him every second?

Her brother's face turned red as an emergency light. He fell backward.

"Ferris, what's wrong?"

Had he eaten a section of DNA? She scrambled over on her hands and knees and held her hand up to his mouth, heart racing. No exhalation. She stuck her fingers inside his mouth, but she couldn't find anything in there.

"Mom!" Gemme shouted, but her mom didn't come. Ferris's face drained of color.

Why did she have such a busy mother? Gemme threw him over her knee and slapped him on the back. When nothing happened, she tried again, hoping she didn't hurt him in the process.

An image of a small coffin jettisoned into space flashed in her mind and she squeezed her eyes shut to ward it out. She had so much to teach him, so many games to play. All those evenings she'd spent with her reproduction, Ferris played pretend by himself. Guilt seeped over her until she despised her own fears.

On the fourth squeeze, a chewed-up ester bond flew out of his mouth, skidding across the carpet. Ferris took in a deep breath and slumped into her arms. Relief flooded her senses until she thought she'd melt into a puddle like the congealizer sludge.

"You all right?" She ran her hand over his curly blond hair.

He nodded, his eyes still glazed over with shock.

"You scared the neutrons out of me. Why would you eat that?"

He stuck his thumb in his mouth and mumbled. "Sowwy."

"That's okay. You're all right and that's what's important. You have to promise me you'll never eat one of my models again."

"Okay."

"No, say it: *I promise.*"

He took his thumb out of his mouth. "I promise."

"Good." Finally, the tightness in her chest let up and she could breathe again. "Listen, we'll clean this up later. Let's go play laser fight."

His eyes brightened. "Really?"

"Yeah." She placed him beside her and jumped up, forming a gun with her fingers. "Come and get me!"

Ferris scrambled up with excitement. Giddy with a new sense of freedom, she dashed into the kitchen with him chasing after her. Space didn't bother her any more. There were more important things to worry about, like her brother.

∂∾∾∾

Ferris had smashed her DNA model fifteen years ago. If only she could let go now. Gemme watched the DNA structure jiggle on the floor, feeling as though her own DNA shuddered along with it. Ear-piercing screeches and crashing bangs interspersed with periods of whirring hums. She stared at the winding strand of double helixes and forced herself to focus on the memory and remain calm.

Think of Ferris. With his graduation coming later this year, he still lived in their parents' family cell, so at least the three of them were together. In limbo between family life and married life, Gemme had to endure this landing alone.

Why couldn't the computer match me up when it had the chance?

Brentwood flashed through her mind and she realized the computer had its own plan for her. Too bad the shattered fragments of the mainframe floated in outer space. A life without the comets flitted through her imagination, a life where she'd work on her matchmaking, marry Brentwood, and live her elder years on the *Expedition*.

Why had it seemed so impossible when she pressed the delete key?

What was she afraid of?

Staring out the sight panel at the white sky, the alternative proved much worse.

"Prepare for touchdown."

The Seers' chanted warnings haunted her. Gemme knew too well from her ship schematics class how astrophysicists designed the *Expedition* to land in water. Not on ice. Mountain peaks poked their way into her sight panel. White flakes obscured the landscape. She hoped loose snow cushioned the *Expedition*'s descent.

A jolt racked her body, driving pain up her spine. Her harness pulled against her chest and she bit her tongue, tasting salty blood in her mouth. What if the landing paralyzed her and they hooked her up to the computer alongside the Seers?

Dammit, stop it!

Gemme wiggled her toes, and every digit still moved. The Seers would have to wait for another friend. A series of bumps came next, jostling her until her brain felt like mush. Her fingers throbbed from clutching the seat restraints, yet she gripped harder, digging her fingernails in the plastic.

The main lights flickered out. Warnings blinked around her, illuminating everything for a second, and plunging her into darkness in the next heartbeat. Gemme reached down and pulled a flashlight from her pocket. At least she'd strapped herself in prepared.

Alarms wailed in the corridor. The sound of metal grating and crunching echoed behind her. Gemme clicked off the flashlight, smelling burnt plastic. If her cell caved in, she didn't want to see the walls or the ceiling coming down at her. She closed her eyes and tried to weed out all of her regrets.

I should have gone to Ferris's awards ceremony.

I should have accepted my mom's old badge on my uniform.

I shouldn't have pressed the delete key.

The shaking subsided and the ship ground to a halt. Gemme gasped in a long breath of air. Was it over? She clicked on the flashlight and shone the golden beam across the room. The DNA model sat on the floor, still in one piece. No illumination came from the sight panel. She turned the flashlight toward the glass. A mound of white blotted out any vision of the planet. The Seers must have submerged the ship in a snowdrift.

She released the harness and fell on her hands and knees. The floor felt oddly motionless. The familiar chug of the engines no longer surged underneath her. Ever since it launched, the *Expedition* had moved in a singular path, hurtling through space. Now, for the first time, the ship rested in a final, icy grave.

Her stomach hurt where the seat restraints had pinned her down. She examined her skin, wondering if she bled internally. The metallic taste of blood filled her mouth from when she bit her tongue, and she swallowed it down, waiting for the Seers' instructions.

The intercom remained silent. What if they didn't survive the landing? What if she was the only one alive? Gemme scrambled up to the portal and slapped the panel. The particles dematerialized to reveal more blinking lights and smoke.

"Hello?" Her voice resonated against the chrome in between shrieks of the emergency alarm. "Is anyone there?"

She coughed and ducked under the smoke, using the wall to guide her down the corridor.

Please, someone be alive.

Maybe she could send a message to Ferris. She checked her locator. The screen showed no signal. The landing must have damaged the remaining control towers. She had no way of knowing who survived.

A portal dematerialized down the corridor and a middle-aged man stumbled out holding a woman in his arms. Relief flooded Gemme at the sight of other people.

"Help us." He dragged the woman toward her. A white bandage blossoming red had been wound around her head.

At least Gemme wasn't the only one alive. She stumbled down to reach them, making sure to duck beneath the smoke.

"Is she all right?" Gemme examined the woman's head. She didn't respond to outside stimuli, but her breathing remained steady.

"She hit her head on the wall." The man struggled to hoist her limp body.

Gemme put her arm under the woman's shoulder. Protocol dictated any wounded passengers be taken to the nearest emergency sick bay, but she wasn't certain if any sick bays still existed. "Where should we take her?"

"I don't know." With flighty eyes full of fear, the man looked more lost than she felt. "The Seers have everything under control, right?"

Not.

Gemme's faith in the Seers had plunged farther than their ship. But the crew of the *Expedition* was still alive, whether by the Seers' hand or not. Looking into the man's desperate eyes, she wasn't about to tell him her misgivings, so she changed the subject. "I'm not sure we should move her."

The man jerked his finger up at the smoke. "I'm not keeping her here."

The intercom buzzed on and they both froze, gazing up to the speakers on the side of the wall.

"Everyone remain calm."

Gemme knew the voice better than her own. The sound filled her with relief.

"This is Lieutenant Brentwood. Communications are patchy at the moment, but I'm working on reestablishing contact with the Seers. Until then stay in your personal cells unless you need medical attention. All wounded seek attention on Deck Six, Bay Four. I repeat, wounded must report to Deck Six, Bay Four."

The intercom sizzled off. Gemme hung on to his last words, her spirits revitalized. Brentwood had survived. Not only that, but the ship may be repairable because he was working on it as they stumbled around helpless. Just those two small facts brought her a rush of hope.

"Come on, let's take her to Bay Four."

They shuffled down the corridor to an emergency stairway. Although twenty decks separated them from Bay Four, Gemme didn't see the point in trying the elevators. The man wrapped his arms around the woman's shoulders and Gemme took her ankles, heading down backward. She gritted her teeth, wishing she'd used the workout decks more often. Her calves burned with each awkward step. The man's jitters didn't help. He kept pushing faster, and Gemme struggled to keep his pace. Maybe conversation would calm him.

"What's your name?"

"Ben Harvey. This is my wife, Isabelle."

Oh yes, I remember: Son is Robert Harvey matched to Britt Stone.

Gemme had completed Robert's pairing three months ago. The computers had calculated an instantaneous match, both candidates demonstrating excellent skills in bioengineering and aerodynamics.

Where was their son now? Gemme knew not to ask. Chances are Ben Harvey wondered the same thing. A wave of nausea swept through her. Had her own family survived? The claustrophobic stairway felt surreal, as if she'd trapped herself in a nightmare and couldn't wake up. Gemme shook her head against dizziness. No, this was her reality now, and they had ten more decks to go.

"What's your name?"

"Gemme Reiner."

Ben Harvey's eyes widened as he registered the infamous name. "So, you're the Matchmaker?"

"Yeah, that's me." She expected any number of bad jokes or accusations of mismatched pairings.

"You selected a good match for our Robby. Britt's given him such joy. I'm eternally grateful."

Maybe she *was* stuck in a dream. Gemme couldn't believe his words. "Uh—you're welcome?"

Ben Harvey smiled for the first time, revealing perfect white teeth. "But I bet you hear that all the time." He winked and she decided she liked him more than her initial impression. "Five decks to go."

Numbness plagued her fingers. She moved the position of her hand on his wife's ankle and pins pricked her palm. Her lower back muscles throbbed, so she counted steps to get her mind off the pain.

One hundred and thirty-four.

One hundred and thirty-five.

Why did she always seek solace in numbers?

They huffed down the remainder of the stairs until the number six shone through the smoke in emergency red light. Gemme had never been so happy to see it. With a heave, she elbowed the portal panel to the deck.

Clean air flowed in and Gemme's lungs soaked in the draft. "That's a promising sign."

People shuffled down the corridor in front of them. Some of them hobbled with minor cuts and bruises, but others wheeled their loved ones on make shift stretchers made out of tables and rolling chairs, wearing their own haphazard bandages. Gemme focused on her ward. The red splotches had spread through Isabelle's bandages.

Medics stood outside Bay Four, assessing a line of patients as they waited for admittance. A younger woman brought them a wheelchair, and Gemme helped Ben lower Isabelle into a comfortable position.

"You've done so much for me, thank you." He sounded as if he said good-bye.

"You don't want me to stay?"

He waved her away and she noticed a bruise on his balding head.

"It's unnecessary."

Gemme paused. She'd spent so long helping him with one single purpose in mind she didn't know where to go.

"You must have your own family to attend to."

Gemme hadn't allowed her thoughts to wander to Ferris and her parents. She swallowed a lump in her throat. "I do, yes."

Ben squeezed her hand. "Take care."

"I'll try." As more wounded flooded into the emergency bay, Gemme fought against the tide with her heart racing. She had ten decks to climb to find her parent's cell. Dreading what she'd find, it took every ounce of courage to jog up the first flight of stairs and confront her fears.

CHAPTER SEVEN
THE BEACON

Brentwood's lapel pin lay as silent as deep space. He pressed the button on and off until his fingertips hurt. Frustration boiled up inside his chest. The Seers had no right to ignore him during a disaster.

Unless their old, deteriorated bodies hadn't survived the crash.

His chest tightened. The *Expedition* didn't have a plan B that he knew of. When no others had been born with their talents, the scientists secured the Seers to the ship, thinking they'd last well into the arrival of Paradise 18. They didn't factor in comets pummeling the hull.

"Hello?"

Nothing. He might as well be talking to a cleaning droid.

"Damn." He kicked a dent in the metal wall. As much as he hated the crypt-like main control deck, he had to check on them. Most systems on the ship couldn't run without their mind control, and they needed heat not only for themselves, but to keep the biodome running. He doubted Tundra 37 had a sufficient food source underneath all those layers of ice.

"Lieutenant."

A tense voice nagged him out of his thoughts. The head nurse, a woman in her early fifties, jogged up beside him.

"Yes?"

"We're having trouble with the life support systems."

He exhaled slowly, allowing his frustration to seep away with his breath. So many problems to fix. He'd have to tackle one at a time, and to make matters worse, the other three lieutenants weren't responding to his pages. "What do you mean?"

"The energy supply to Bay Four is patchy at best. The skin regenerators are malfunctioning, and the heart monitors aren't steady. We need a sufficient supply of energy to attend to those with critical needs."

He nodded and spoke with authority in his voice to calm her. "I'll check on it."

"Thank you, sir People are starting to panic."

"There's no need for panic." He gave her a steady look. "I'll get everything under control. Just see to the wounded, make sure they get the care they need."

"Yes, sir." His reassurance seemed to calm her. She gave him a weak smile and jogged back to the emergency bay.

As much as the life support systems needed energy, they'd all freeze to death without the Seers at the helm. He'd check on the fusion core, but first he'd check on the two people who were supposed to be in charge.

Brentwood sprinted to the main artery connecting the control deck to the belly of the ship. The floor pitched up, and his muscles strained as he climbed the ramp. He'd been on duty for two shifts going on three. The crash provided a never-ending slew of problems keeping him busy. Like his father always said, "You'll have enough time to rest in your coffin, floating for eternity in the vast unknown."

Yeah, Dad, reassuring as always.

Hoping his parents had survived the crash, he took a turn and halted in mid stride Part of the ceiling had caved in, and debris clogged the corridor. Wires sparked at his feet, sending him sprawling backward.

"Damn it again!"

Brentwood waited until the cables settled, counted to three, and jumped forward, grabbing onto a pipe in the ceiling. He dangled for a second over broken glass before swinging back and forth like a pendulum. When he swung forward again, he let go and landed in a rolling ball on the other side of the debris pile.

The lights flickered above him, threatening to engulf him in total darkness, and he scrambled up, closing the last few meters between him and the Seers' portal.

He paused at the panel, smoothing his hands through his hair to keep it out of his eyes.

Oh, heck, it's not like they're running around naked in there. He slammed his fist into the panel and the particles spun like crazed dust motes as they dematerialized.

Wires rained down in a curtain of jellyfish tentacles. Sparks flew from all directions, sizzling around him like ill-tended fireworks. Brentwood swiped them away. "Hello? Is everything all right?"

He scanned the debris littering the floor. Old star charts, broken computer screens, and a tuft of gray hair.

Brentwood's heart jumped and stuck in his throat. He kicked through the rubble, fell on his knees and dug out a shoulder and a balding, wispy-haired head.

She was the one with the good eye, the one who'd addressed him at their last meeting. Now the dark eye stared at nothing, or whatever awaited her in the beyond.

"No." He scrambled, running his hands over her thin skin to feel her forehead. She felt like wax and brittle bones. "You will not leave us like this."

Turning her on her back, he found vacant input holes drilled into the bones of her spine. Goose bumps prickled his skin as he ran a fingertip over the cold metal ring, wider than three of his fingers clumped together. What fit in it? He scrambled, pulling up tubes from the rubble.

Feeling way out of his domain, Brentwood inserted anything that looked like it would fit into the hole. Reattaching the Seers didn't fall into his job description, not one bit. If it had, he wouldn't have taken it. Just holding her in his arms made his skin crawl.

A tube spouting gurgling pink liquid stuck out from a pile of broken ceiling panels. He reached over and pulled it toward her, his fingers slipping on the slick substance. The edge of the tube fit perfectly into the ring in her spine. Brent paused, doubting himself. What if he killed her?

She already looked dead.

Pulling his cringing shoulders straight, he stuck the tube in and pushed until the end clicked. The plastic filled with fluid and the Seer's body jerked in small movements, as if pulses of electricity restarted her heart.

He turned her around and looked into her withering face, trying to remember her name.

Mesto? Mesty? He'd read about their impoverished beginnings while studying for lieutenant hood. Plucked from the slums of Old Earth at the ripe age of nine, these sisters were granted a second chance at life. As he looked down into her three-hundred-year-old face, she'd had a third and fourth chance as well. And he'd just given her another.

The name flowed back to him. "Mestasis. Mestasis please wake up."

The eye fluttered. Flaky lips twitched, revealing toothless gums.

"Please come back to us. We need you."

The lights flickered around him. The main intercom buzzed on.

"Computer, status reports."

Her voice filled Brentwood with relief.

"Thank the stars! You gave me quite a scare."

She shivered in his arms and he pulled her closer, feeling her humanity for the first time. She focused on him. Her eye traveled from his face to the rubble behind them.

"Where's Bysme?"

"What? Who?"

"My twin."

Brentwood jerked. He'd forgotten about the other one.

"I'll find her." He placed Mestasis gently on her back and threw himself into the wreckage.

Did the ship need both twins? He hoped not. A chrome panel as large as a desk lay on the floor, propped up by something underneath. Bracing himself for the worst sight imaginable, he hoisted the panel and threw it against the wall.

"What the?"

A globe the size of a bowling ball shimmered back at him. Intricate metal weave work surrounded it, the thread-sized strands thrusting into the floor. Cosmic dust swirled in golden spirals inside the globe, the colors changing from lavender to vermilion, then deep crimson. His ears rang as he stared at the conglomerations, each pattern beseeching him to lean closer. A brief vision of a meadow flashed before him along with a heady scent of animal hides. His hand reached out to touch it.

"Lieutenant." Mestasis's voice yanked him away from the globe. "Leave the orb and tend to my sister. She's still hanging from the ceiling."

He gazed up to see the old machine-woman slouched over, her chin resting on her chest. Confusion shot through him. Why had he put his own cravings first?

Shaking his head, he searched for anything to stand on to reach her. A ladder would have been ideal, but the Seers had no use for such things. He pulled on a cable dangling from the ceiling. The anchor felt solid, so he climbed hand over hand.

"Bysme." He called to her as he dangled just before her ashen face. "Bysme, do you hear me?"

Her skeletal remains hung motionless.

"She's not responding. Mestasis, what should I do?"

Her voice resonated directly in his head. *Use the respirator.*

An oxygen mask hung beside Abysme. Holding onto his perch with one hand, he attached the plastic to her mouth. Her chest rose and fell with the airflow.

He tried again, "Bysme?"

Two blind eyes popped open and stared at him, sensing his presence. He almost lost his grip on the cable. "Jeez." He'd had enough close encounters for today.

Her voice resonated on the intercom, even though her lips sucked at the breathing apparatus. "Location of the beacon?"

"What?" Brentwood had never heard of a beacon.

"The beacon is not your concern, Lieutenant."

It must be if one of the Seers placed it above a falling apart ship with crashing systems. A current of anger rose inside him. Brentwood hefted Mestasis and hung her back on the ceiling where she could see the viewing panel with her one good eye. "Everything on board this ship is of my concern."

Mestasis spoke as if she assured a child. "The beacon is not on this ship and doesn't concern you. I've regained much of the systems control. Please, leave us to sort out the situation on the ship. We'll brief you shortly."

"Yes, ma'am." He lowered himself down and jumped to the deck, eager to get to the ship's core. "Are you sure you don't want any of this cleaned up?"

"All in due time, Lieutenant. You must see to your other duties."

"All right."

The Seers fell silent, and he wondered if they conferred amongst themselves in mindspeak he couldn't hear. Brentwood stepped over the debris and exited, sealing the portal behind him. The encounter made him uneasy, and he couldn't tell if it stemmed from the fragility of the Seers, their cryptic communications, or the strange globe they'd kept hidden underneath their noses. The object looked like something from one of his Old Earth fantasy novels, and he knew the strange globe filled with golden swirls wasn't originally part of the ship. Even now the misty swirls called to him like a song yearning to be vocalized.

•••

Gemme rushed up the emergency stairs to Deck Sixteen. The smoke thickened the higher she climbed. She choked, tasting ash on her tongue. Hopefully the ventilators would kick in soon.

Sixty-seven

Sixty-eight

Sixty-nine

She couldn't remember how many times she'd counted to a hundred; anything to keep her mind off of all the horrible imaginings of what could have happened to her parents and Ferris. Deck sixteen's red numbers shone through the smoke and she slapped the panel, catching her breath as she waited for the particles to dematerialize.

The corridor lay empty as a tomb. She ran six portals down to her family cell on the right, taking steps she'd walked a thousand times in her childhood. Buzzing the intercom, she stared at the blank screen and prayed. *Please be safe.*

Ferris's face flashed back at her in surprise. "G! There you are! I've been looking all over for you."

Relief shook her body to the core. "Ferris, I'm so glad you're alive."

"I walked all the way to your cell, but you weren't there."

"I was helping a man bring his wife to the emergency bay."

"Always helping others before yourself, aren't you?" The screen went blank as Ferris initiated the portal sequence to let her in.

The wall separating them dissolved and Gemme fell into her brother's arms, squeezing him. He towered over her, an entire foot taller. But he still looked up to her in all other ways. "How bad is it down there?"

"Hundreds of wounded overrun the emergency bay. The man's wife had to wait in line for care."

"That bad, huh?"

She nodded. Scanning the room behind him panic jolted through her. "Where's Mom and Dad?"

"You know them. Workaholics like you. Dad's with a team stabilizing the fusion core and Mom's checking on her office. She's compiling a report of the life support systems."

"What are you going to do?"

"I'm staying right here where Lieutenant Brentwood instructed. No use running around when there's nowhere to go but outside on the ice."

He raised an eyebrow. "I'm surprised you're not in your office. That's the next place I was going to look."

"It's gone, Ferris. Everything's gone."

His hazel eyes crinkled. "What do you mean *gone*?"

"The deck's not there anymore. My entire office is drifting in deep space."

"No way."

Gemme nodded and collapsed onto the synthetic sofa. The cold plastic rumpled underneath her as she sunk down. Although she sat in the same seat she'd cuddled in since a toddler, she had never felt more lost.

"You mean there's no way to pair us up anymore?" Ferris shook his head, wiry hair falling in his eyes. "I have no idea how to feel about this." He swiped his hair back. "It blows my mind."

Gemme knew what *she* felt: fear. Their world of predestination had been shattered, allowing the chaotic universe to stream in. Live feed to pandemonium, here we go.

Ferris scratched his head. "Wait a second. You're telling me we have to find our own lifemates?"

"I don't what's going to happen, but I would assume with no program, odds are slim the Seers would work on building another one with so many other problems to fix."

"Woot!" He punched the air with his fist. "I was so worried you'd set me up with Marla Simmons or Reilly Foster."

Gemme covered her face with her hands and groaned. Why was she the only one lamenting the loss of the pairing program?

Because the computer matched you to Miles Brentwood. She gritted her teeth, shirking the thought. *No, because I excelled at my job.*

The sofa crunched beside her, and Ferris put an arm around her shoulders. "I'm sorry, G. I'm such a blockhead. I wasn't thinking about the loss of your lifetime's work. What are you going to do now?"

"I've already been reassigned. Exploratory team Alpha Blue."

"You're going out there?" Ferris pointed to the frosty sight panel. He sounded like the Seers had given her a death sentence. "But you hardly come out of your office. You don't even want to visit Dad in the fusion core."

Gemme pursed her lips. Ferris's points hit home. Some adventurer she'd make, and Brentwood would be the supervising officer to watch her fail. Tears brimmed in her eyes and she blinked them back. She was supposed to be the older sister, the one who had everything figured out.

"Aw, I didn't mean that, G. You'll be a great explorer. You watch; I bet you'll save us all."

Gemme sighed, gazing at the ice slabs sprawling in all directions from the sight panel. "If I'm going to save us all, then we're doomed."

CHAPTER EIGHT
FLUCTUATING SYSTEMS

Brentwood slipped into a white protective suit, zipping the front up to his chin. He pulled the hood over his face, his breath steaming on the plastic visor. The synthetic fabric felt too thin to protect him, but thick enough to suffocate him. Repressing his nerves, he moved in between the portals separating the fusion core from the rest of the ship. Warnings beeped at him. A recorded voice spoke on the intercom.

Caution: Must wear protective gear at all times beyond this portal.

He suppressed the urge to hold his breath as the second to last portal closed behind him and the chamber sealed before initiating the final portal sequence. His logical mind told him it would do no good. Besides, he knew his breath capacity limits from his races on swim team. Although he'd always come in the top three, he couldn't hold his breath long enough to find the supervisor, walk back to the portals, and wait until the defensive sequence of portal panels played out.

Men and women in protective gear scattered on the circular walkway. Some recorded readings on the coolants and pressure gauges while others dragged hoses and wires over their shoulders. A high railing separated him from thirty-foot drop where a gigantic gray cylinder towered up like some poisonous mushroom in a fairytale. The sight always spooked him, like the *Expedition* held a ticking bomb in its belly.

Brentwood grabbed a man's arm, not wanting to spend any more time than necessary down in the dungeon as the other Lifers called it. "Who's in charge?"

"The chief engineer's over there." He pointed to a man holding a miniscreen, punching in numbers with his clumsy gloved hand.

"Thank you."

Brentwood pushed his way through and tapped on the man's shoulder. "Sir, Lieutenant Brentwood."

Usually he flashed his lapel pin, but any identification lay underneath the plastic. The engineer would have to take his word for it. "Can I have a moment to speak with you?"

"Certainly." Misty, blue-gray eyes flashed up in the man's visor, triggering a nudge of recognition. The man gestured toward the portal. "Let's talk without all this gear in between us."

Brentwood followed him to the portal locks and waited until the man pulled off his hood and breathed in before pulling the plastic off his own face.

"You're the Chief Engineer?"

"That's right." He extended his gloved hand. "Joe Reiner, sir."

The name jolted him. He shouldn't be asking during a crisis, but curiosity won. "Wait, you're related to Gemme Reiner?"

Joe paused and his voice softened. "You know my daughter?"

Brentwood stumbled on his words, feeling boyishly shy. "N-not really. Not very well. I found her during the crash. The emergency portals had trapped her on the upper decks."

"Thank goodness she's all right." He braced himself against the chrome wall.

Brentwood wanted to reach out and steady the man, but he thought his gesture would be too personal. "Last I saw her, she was safe in the containment area."

Joe regained his composure, giving him a look of utter gratitude. "Thank you for looking out for her."

"I was just doing my job, sir. The Seers had me scanning the upper decks looking for stragglers."

Joe shook his head, looking away. "That's Gemme for you, always at work, even at the end of the world."

Brentwood smiled, warmth radiating inside him. Gemme's devotion impressed him. So many workers grew disillusioned with the *Expedition's* practices, and she performed her job until the very end, just like him. "You should be proud of her."

Joe's face crinkled around his eyes as he smiled. "I am."

So many questions about Gemme sat on his tongue, but he had a mission to accomplish and didn't want to seem overly intrusive.

Pushing thoughts of Gemme away, Brentwood took a deep breath to prepare himself. "What are the conditions in the fusion core?"

Joe's face hardened as if the last few hours had been the worst of his life. "It's stabilized for now. Only small leaks, and we're working on containment as we speak."

"Excellent." Brentwood settled back on his heels. One less problem to worry about. He moved to the portal, and Joe grabbed his arm, holding him back.

"There's more."

Brentwood had the same plummeting feeling he had when his father told him about the ruin of Old Earth for the first time. He could feel the hair on his head turning prematurely gray.

"The comets damaged several fuel cells. We're conserving energy by rerouting to the emergency systems, but even under extreme conservation efforts, we only have enough hyperthium to operate for another three months at most. After that, the fusion core will begin to shut down."

Brentwood nodded, numbness spreading as the reality hit him. The Seers must have predicted this. That's why they reassigned him to Exploratory Team Alpha Blue. Responsibility fell heavy on his chest. He would have to find the hyperthium deposits on Tundra 37 or the entire ship would degrade.

Although panic ripped through him, he couldn't spread it to the others on board, especially Gemme's father. They needed a leader, and Brentwood was ready to take the job. He straightened up. "I have it covered, sir. The Seers assigned me to head an exploratory team for my next mission. We'll find the hyperthium you need to keep the *Expedition* up and running."

Joe breathed in. "Good. Glad to see someone's on the job."

"I'll assemble my team as soon as possible."

He put a hand on his shoulder. "Be careful; it's a new world out there, and the scout ships only covered twenty percent. Who knows what frozen horrors lurk in those ice mountains."

"Good advice, Mr. Reiner." Brentwood paused as the old man slipped on his containment hood. He had to tell him about Gemme, and the words sat heavy in his mouth.

"Mr. Reiner, sir."

"Yes?"

His stomach hardened as he spoke. "The Seers assigned Gemme to the team as well."

"Andromeda's sake! Why in all the galaxy would they choose her?"

"I don't know, sir. Their actions are mysterious to me."

Joe scanned the chamber as if he'd lost himself somewhere in the particles of the portal. His gloved hands clenched and the plastic crinkled around his fists.

Brentwood put his hand on the man's shoulder to steady him. Breaking a promise to himself, he made a promise to Gemme's father, one that would only bring him closer to her. "I'll take care of her, sir. I'll bring her home safe."

Vira longed for her hoverchair. Without it, people had to carry her everywhere and she became more of a hindrance than anything else. Smoke seeped into the ceiling above her like an evil being convalescing to smother her whole.

"I can't get the damn thing to work, Natalie." Her father's voice echoed from the family room down the hall. She winced, hating when her parents fought.

Her mom yelled back. "You've got to do something! The lieutenant said to stay in our personal cells."

"We're not staying here if the smoke is going to get worse."

The anger in her father's voice soured her stomach. She cringed underneath the blanket and peeked above the seam with both eyes. They'd opened the portal to her room, allowing for fresh air. She couldn't see her dad, but she knew he fumbled with the ventilator panel. Her mom stood in front of the portal to the main corridor, fanning the air with a towel.

"Half the ship is gone. We have nowhere else to go." Her mother flung the towel across the family room. Something shattered and Vira hoped it wasn't the antique globe of Old Earth. She loved spinning it around and letting her fingers rest on a different paradise spot each time.

Her mother disappeared into the family room and Vira slipped off her blanket, slowly bringing herself out of her sleep pod. She dropped to the floor with a plop, bumping both her elbows. Stings jolted up her arms. Rubbing her elbows, she checked to see if her parents had noticed, but they argued in the back of the family room, where they thought she couldn't hear them.

"We could visit the Foresters. Rizzy's there now."

Her mom's whispers carried to Vira's ears. "I don't want to intrude. Besides, I'm not sure what they'd think of us choosing our pairing for our daughter. I don't care if it's the end of the world, we're not going to disobey the Guide. It's meant to protect us. We shouldn't have let Rizzy go."

Vira pulled herself arm over arm, puffing and heaving. She'd have to develop more muscle strength. She wondered how long it would take for someone to build her another hovercraft. Finally, she reached the back wall in the corner of her room. She propped her back against the chrome, catching her breath.

Vira tore down Rizzy's antique poster of some fantasy movie from Old Earth to touch the bare wall. Her ancestors had stored it in thick glass for a hundred years before Rizzy pleaded with her parents to take it out and hang in their room. Rizzy would scream at her, but fixing the smoke was far more important. She'd endure her sister's wrath to keep them safe. Besides, Vira never liked the staring eyes of the white-haired mage and his scepter of lightning. He reminded her too much of her own secret powers.

She double-checked on her parents. They'd have a fit if they suspected anything strange about her. She already had such a great deformity, any additional abnormalities would be too much for them to handle.

Placing her palm against the wall, she closed her eyes. The chrome stung cold as frost under her skin. Feeling up and down, she calmed herself and allowed her thoughts to wander until they grasped hold of the inner workings of the ship. She focused on the cables and wires connecting to their cell, running beneath the wall. She sensed their presence like a nest of snakes just beyond her reach.

In the blackness underneath her eyelids, she identified strings of connecting impulses, much like the threads in her blanket. Some ran to the air ionizer, some to the refrigerator, and others to lighting. Their channels lay empty. The Seers had cut off the electricity.

Vira paused, wondering if the Seers would notice a small deficit in the rechanneled flow of energy. She'd only need to reroute it for a few minutes in order for the ventilator to filter the smoke. The solution lay within her reach. Her parents' happiness meant so much to her, so she took the chance.

Squeezing her eyes shut, she redirected a stream of electricity to the ventilator. The concentration made her dizzy, but she held onto the thread of thought until the connection sparked. She heard the rattling of the air shaft as the vacuum kicked in.

"It's working!" Her dad's voice squeaked with surprise from the other room.

"What did you do, Al?" The relief in her mom's voice made Vira smile.

"I don't know. I pressed the circulation button and voila."

"Thank goodness the Seers are still up there doing their job."

Her dad's voice turned bitter. "Sure, thank the Seers and not your hard-working husband."

Her mom laughed. "I'm thanking you too."

She heard them kissing and scrunched up her nose. *Ew!*

Her mom spoke next. "Why don't you go get Rizzy? I'll start dinner. There must be something we can eat without the food congealizer."

Vira considered rerouting more electricity. Her stomach grumbled, craving hot food. The Seers' presence lurked just millimeters from her fingertips and her thoughts froze in place. Too many adjustments would certainly draw their attention.

"Should you go check on Vira? She's been sleeping all day." Her dad sounded weary.

"Oh yes, I'll do that."

Vira had only seconds to pull her hand away from the wall before her mom slipped in.

"What are doing on the floor, dear?"

Vira shrugged and pouted, looking as sad as she could without producing real tears.

"You poor thing. Your legs must be freezing." Her mom sprinted over to her and scooped her up in her arms.

She lay her down on her sleep pod and massaged her atrophied calves. Vira couldn't feel her mother's touch, but it gave her mom comfort, so she smiled as if rubbing her useless legs made her happy. Really, having all this attention from her mom made her happy. As for her legs, she'd rather just cover them up and forget.

"We should slip on your jumpsuit. Daddy's got the ventilator running, and soon all the smoke will be gone."

Vira exhaled in relief. Not only had her plan worked, she'd pulled it off without her parents' knowledge.

Her mom searched her face. "I know you're concerned about the ship, dear. People are fixing it as we speak. Don't worry, they'll have the systems back online."

"Okay, Mom."

Vira tried to give her mom an assuring smile, but a nagging doubt tickled the back of her mind. She'd left the electric current running, so she'd have to find a way to reconnect to the system and turn it off later. Hopefully, the rest of the ship distracted the Seers enough not to notice.

CHAPTER NINE
QUEST FOR HYPERTHIUM

Gemme wondered how many pairs of polar fleece pants she could fit around her waist and still be able to walk. Looking four kilograms heavier, she flinched in the mirror and tried on a fourth pair. Good thing she had some stashed away just in case the heating systems failed. She was always over prepared.

Better to be warm and plump than sexy and freeze to death. Who are you trying to impress, anyway?

As she stuffed her legs in, she thought of Brentwood and pulled off the fourth pair midway up her thigh. Even she had her limits. She kicked the extra pair off and shoved it into her backpack, along with a beacon light, a first aid kit, and several protein bars. Brentwood would pack enough food for the team for days, but she didn't know how long they'd be out there.

Plugging her last full energy cell into her miniscreen, she flicked it on and checked the time.

Fifteen-hundred and fifty-two minutes, twenty seconds.

Damn!

Why did she never have time to say good-bye? Did her parents even know about her new assignment?

Probably better for them not to.

The portal beeped and she whirled around. Ferris's voice came through the intercom. "Just stopped by to wish you good luck."

She pressed the panel and the particles dematerialized, reminding her of the snowflakes whizzing by the sight panels. He stood in the portal frame, slouching. She wondered if she shouldn't have told him. He would have seen her name on Alpha Blue on the reassignments charts eventually, and she didn't want him to be angry at her. At least she had time for one good-bye.

"It's not like I'm leaving and not coming back." Gemme rolled her eyes. "Come in. I only have a few minutes."

Ferris frowned and dragged his feet. "I've brought you something." Reaching into the breast pocket of his wrinkly uniform, he pulled out a glossy piece of paper.

Gemme took the computer printout in her hands, remembering her graduation ceremony. A pimple-faced teenager stared back at her, his stringy arm hanging around a younger version of Gemme with wavy locks shielding one eye. Worry creased the skin around her other eye. The Seers hadn't chosen her position on the *Expedition* at that point and the endless possibilities had overwhelmed her. Unfortunately, endless possibilities became the story of her life.

She smoothed her finger over the sleek surface. "You'd just passed your algebra test."

"Yeah, you helped me study."

"I guess, but you were always good at math."

"Not as good as you." He smiled, belying his gloomy eyes. "That's why the Seers chose you, Gemme. You're special, and they believe you can do this."

Gemme sighed. "I've never been more scared in my life. I don't even like walking in the biodome, never mind an entire new world."

Ferris shook his head. "You're braver than you think. You saved my life once, remember?"

"I put you in danger by not watching you like I should have." Gemme looked away at the model on the floor. She still hadn't moved it since the crash.

He grabbed her arm so tightly, she met his gaze. "You did what it took and saved my life."

They sat staring at each other until her miniscreen beeped and an androgynous voice buzzed, "Sixteen hundred."

Gemme slipped the picture in her jumpsuit pocket, feeling as though she never had enough time. "I've got to go."

"Always working, aren't you?" Ferris gave her an admonishing quirk of his eyebrow.

Gemme's lips tightened. "It's what I do best."

He stood, walked over to her and collapsed around her, hugging her tightly. "Be careful, G. And remember, there's more to life than busting your butt."

"I'll try."

Gemme pulled away, not wanting to look into his watery eyes. She left him in her cell, cursing him for coming. His presence made leaving the *Expedition* all that much harder.

The ship contained her entire world. She'd never exited the hull. Besides the Seers, no one had. Gemme shivered, the fear creeping across her skin, and forced herself into a jog to make up lost time and improve her circulation to warm her cold fingers.

The corridors leading to the loading docks at the stern lay empty. Although she reached the portal five minutes late, she paused before entering loading dock C, checking her reflection in the glass separating the balcony from stacked containers and cranes below.

Brentwood had to be down there. He led the team. Gemme smoothed over her loose ends, feeling self-conscious. She looked sleep deprived, anxious, and haggard, and nothing she could do now would change her appearance. *Oh, well. It's not like we're matched up anyway.*

She took a deep breath and entered the loading bay, shuffling down the steps to the equipment below. The air smelled like chemicals and the metallic reek of wet iron. A bear of a man in his fifties stood at the bottom, scratching a grizzly black beard.

"Hey there, you must be Gemme Reiner, Cupid's other half."

She shook her head and tsked-tsked in reproof. "You'll have to come up with a new name. I've been reassigned."

He held out a paw of a hand, complete with thick hairy fingers and a scar running from his thumb to his wrist. "Name's Tech. And I know. You're the new analyst for Alpha Blue."

She grabbed his hand and shook it tightly. "You're on the team?"

"Yuppers. I'm the engineer. I work with your father down in the core."

She recalled her dad coming home and complaining about a guy showing up to work with too much wheat beer in his belly. Gemme coughed and then cleared her throat to cover it up. "Oh yeah, I think he mentioned you before."

"Me and him, we go way back. He'll do anything for a fellow core worker."

"Sounds like my dad." Thank goodness her father had covered up the incident. At least she had one ally on the team.

"Good, you're here." Brentwood's tenor voice, refreshing and melodic, echoed down from above.

Gemme whirled around, ponytail flying. The lieutenant stood on the top platform, looking like the digital representation of a Roman God basking on the steps of Maison Carrée in her antiquities text.

Okay, now my imagination is getting out of hand.

She gawked as he worked his way down to them in his prim uniform, complete with a shiny, golden lapel pin of the *Expedition* and a pressed white shirt poking out from a blue polar fleece top stretched across his hard chest. His minty aftershave floated over, tingling her nose.

"Ms. Reiner, I believe we've met before." His fingers wrapped around her hand. Normally she had a firm grip for handshakes, but her fingers turned to jelly in his grasp. The warmth of his skin transferred to hers.

"And I'm Tech Dougherty." The older man chimed in, interrupting Gemme's moment of bliss. Brentwood released her hand to shake the old man's paw.

"Nice to meet you, Mr. Dougherty."

"Naw, just call me Tech."

"Sure thing, Tech." Brentwood scanned the bay, distracted.

Tech followed his gaze. "Missing someone, chief?"

"Yes, one member of the team is late."

"I'm right over here." Luna appeared the same time the ventilators came on, and the air current flung her golden hair over her shoulders like an interplanetary superhero cape. She'd zipped her jumpsuit to the great canyon between her breasts, and each curve popped out like the top of a grapefruit.

Isn't she going to freeze? Gemme shivered just looking at Luna's bare skin. Gemme tugged on the collar of the turtleneck underneath her uniform. Along with the three pairs of polar fleece pants making her butt look like a marshmallow, she had enough clothes on for both of them combined.

Maybe I overdid it?

"Excellent." Brentwood smiled. "Nice of you to join us, Ms. Legacy. Now we can begin the briefing."

"This is it? The whole team?" Tech furrowed his large unibrow. "You'd think the Seers would send out an army. No offense, ladies."

"None taken." Luna smiled and licked the curve of her upper lip. She jumped down the last four steps and landed next to Gemme. "Nice to see you, Gemme, dear."

"Hi, Luna." Gemme swallowed a lump in her throat, feeling mousy and plain. She wanted to reach over and zip the final few inches of Luna's jumpsuit, just enough so the swell of skin didn't pop out and make them all gawk. Why would their mission need a biologist, anyways?

Luna leaned over and whispered in her ear, "I don't suppose you still have my ticket?"

Gemme shifted uncomfortably. "I'm sorry, Luna. It was destroyed in the comet shower. I barely got out of there alive."

"Pity." Her eyes turned frosty and Gemme fought the urge to back away. *Pity that I lost the ticket, or that I got out alive?*

Brentwood cleared his throat to get them to pay attention, and she and Luna turned their heads. "The reason for such a small team stands right behind us." He lifted his arm and pointed to a vehicle with double sets of tires a foot taller than him. "Allow me to introduce our transport."

The massive land truck stood before Gemme like some monster

of the deep ready to barrel through anything in its path.

"What is it?" Gemme circled the tire. The sheer size inspired awe, making her feel a fraction safer than before. As least she wouldn't be trekking on foot.

"A landrover." Brentwood leaned on the shiny silver spoke. "The prototype, the only one assembled on the *Expedition*."

"I heard of these. They were meant for Paradise 18." Tech ran his hands over the bumper. "I never thought I'd ride in one."

"Yes. The Seers had planned for the landrovers to go into production in the next generation. That's why we only have the single prototype. It fits four people comfortably and is capable of lugging the mining equipment behind it."

"How fast can it go?" Luna wrapped her fingers around a spike in the tire. She reminded Gemme of Sleeping Venus pricking her finger on the world's axis. But in Gemme's world, she'd be more like the evil queen of black holes.

Brentwood raised his hand. "Before we explore the landrover's capabilities in depth, I need Tech to tell us about hyperthium, the purpose of our mission and the one mineral that's going to keep the *Expedition* alive."

He clapped Tech on the back. "The audience is all yours."

"Well, lemme see..." As Tech rambled under his breath, Gemme wondered if they'd find anything with such an oddball team. More likely, they'd drive each other crazy and end up frozen in a ditch.

Tech cleared his throat. "Hyperthium is found in igneous rock, with the largest concentration in granite. Other hyperthium containing minerals are spodumene and petalite, but it's mainly the granite that we're after. Due to its alkaline tarnish, hyperthium metal is corrosive, meaning you shouldn't touch it."

He pointed a finger at Luna as if rubbing her hands all over hyperthium was all she dreamed about.

"Got it, Tech." Luna grinned like a panther waiting to strike. Gemme straightened her crooked turtleneck and focused on Tech's words. She felt more like a goose than any type of predator.

"Breathing in hyperthium dust can irritate the nose and throat. Higher exposure can cause a build-up of fluid in the lungs leading to pulmonary edema."

Gemme crinkled her nose. With frostbite, hypothermia, and strange alien creatures, she had enough to worry about. Pulmonary edema, whatever that was, ranked low on her list.

Tech rubbed his beard as if he'd hidden the answers in the rat's nest below his chin. "The first scouts to explore Tundra 37 reported a large amount of hyperthium on the southern side of the planet, twenty five meters below a layer of ice."

Brentwood placed a hand on Tech's shoulder and squeezed. "Excellent warnings, Tech."

The lieutenant looked to Gemme and Luna. "We have the scout's initial coordinates. All we need to do is travel to the dig site and set up the equipment. Gemme, you must analyze the size and composition of the mineral deposit. Tech will set up the mining drill, and Luna's with us in case any indigenous species decide to show up. She's on the lookout for anything we can eat on this ice rock. So if you see something moving, you go to her. All other reports must be filed with me."

"Got it." Gemme nodded and gave Brentwood a serious stare to make sure he knew she'd processed all Tech's information.

Luna laughed, her fingers wiggling in the air. "Come on, let's ride this crazy beast. I call front seat." Gemme looked down at her space boots.

Tech shrugged and glanced at Gemme. "Guess you're stuck in the back with me."

She frowned, disappointment a heavy rock in her stomach. She'd rather sit near Brentwood, but at least Tech provided a pleasant substitute for Luna. Besides, she wasn't supposed to be having feelings for him anyway. She'd agreed to keep far away.

"Sure. You can tell me old war stories about my dad."

He scratched his head and rolled his eyes. "Where do I start?"

"Start at the beginning, we'll have all day." As Gemme stuck her boot on the indents leading to the hatch, Brentwood caught her hand. She turned around, thinking she'd forgotten her backpack or done something wrong.

"I'm glad to have you with us, Ms. Reiner." His eyes gleamed like jewels from Old Earth. She wanted to hold his hand forever, to never face the cold world outside. His grip remained firm, giving her strength. Blood flowed into her cheeks.

Tech watched with a curious eye behind Brentwood. She kept her answer professional. "I'm glad to be of service, Lieutenant."

She thought he'd let go, but his eyes remained steady, staring into hers as if something special existed between them and he only needed to delve a little deeper to find it. "Let me know if you need anything."

Gemme's heart beat fast against her rib cage. *Like a comforting embrace, a passionate kiss, or you.*

She blinked her emotions away. "Will do, Lieutenant."

He released her and her heart tugged as if it had attached itself to him.

"Need a minute?" The corner of Tech's mouth curved.

"No, I'm fine." Gemme climbed into the landrover wondering how her heart would ever survive this mission, never mind the cold.

CHAPTER TEN
SNOWDRIFTS

The portal opened, walls parting into two halves. The metal screeched as it dug into the crevice in the hull for the first time in hundreds of years. This wasn't a chamber lock with dematerialized particles. Gemme watched the ship open entirely, exposing its bowels to the harsh reality of wind and ice.

The brightness blinded her and she raised her arm to block the sheer white. The engines sputtered on and she pitched forward as the wheels turned underneath her. Bracing herself against the back of Brentwood's seat, she prepared herself for the unknown. No one spoke as the landrover crept into the light.

The cold seeped in quickly, settling in the marrow of her bones. Gemme shivered, hugging her shoulders and sticking her fingers underneath her arms. Brentwood flipped a switch and a current of warmer air blew by her face, providing a meager hint of warmth.

Solaris Prime blinded her with unbridled light, reflected off the snow. As her eyes adjusted, the shape of mountains formed in the distance, poking up from slabs of pure, unbroken ice. Brentwood turned the wheel and the landrover skidded right, raining flecks of snow on the windshield. In moments, a brutal wind blew the flakes away. Out of the left sight panel, Gemme saw the outer hull of the *Expedition* for the first time.

Her heart plummeted. All those years she'd drawn the mighty ship in art class in perfect geometric circles and squares. Now her home amounted to a heap of broken metal with chipped paint spelling out *x..pedi..on*.

"Man, we really wrecked it, didn't we?" Tech muttered from behind her. He peered over her shoulder and Gemme sat back, allowing him room to catch the view. She'd seen enough.

"Remember, Tundra 37 is our new home. The *Expedition* is only a temporary shelter. We'll construct new buildings," Brentwood called to Tech and Gemme over his shoulder.

Although he meant to comfort them, deflation spread through Gemme's spirits, as if she found her hero masquerading as an illusion. They rode on an artificial substitute, a dream of the first Lifers of the *Expedition*. The precariousness of life overwhelmed her, and she slumped in her seat wondering if they could build a home out of ice and snow.

"You sure the atmosphere is breathable?" Luna covered her mouth with her hand.

"You're breathing it now." Brentwood's head turned and Gemme saw him smile in profile. "We've breathed it for hours. The Seers pumped it in to run the ventilators in the ship."

Luna coughed as if he tricked her. "No wonder my lungs hurt like hell."

"That's the cold, not the quality of air." Brentwood spoke like a schoolteacher. "Our lungs are used to a regulated environment. We're all going to have to make changes, even our bodies."

He sounded like he mentioned a change of clothes instead of habitat. Gemme knew Brentwood had to maintain a calm demeanor, but she wanted to hear something else from his lips, some sort of complaint, something real to assure her she wasn't the only one having trouble adapting.

Tech grumbled beside her, "I've got goose bumps where the lights don't shine."

"The heat will increase in a moment," Brentwood explained. "The engine has to warm up."

Gemme's teeth chattered and she contemplated pushing against the hulk of Tech's right side for warmth. Luna didn't look cold at all. In fact, she still had the zipper down so low the light shone in places it shouldn't. Maybe all that padding in front provided insulation?

One look at Tech convinced her against cuddling up. Luna would have a field day with more stuff to pick on her with, and she didn't feel right about Brentwood seeing her close to another man.

Not like he was hers or she was his.

Gemme sighed, screaming at her inner thoughts to shut up and waited for heat to spread through the compartment. The *Expedition* grew smaller out of the corner of her visor, her one tie to everything that defined her. Without it, she navigated uncharted waters. No routine decided her life. Cast adrift on frozen tundra, Gemme wondered how much of her true self she'd discover and how many of her fears she'd confront.

She thought of all the people inside the hull: her parents, Ferris, and even Vira. These people counted on them to find the mineral deposit. Gemme closed her eyes and told herself to toughen up.

Hours passed and the frozen landscape blurred into monotony. Luna spoke in hushed tones with Brentwood, like a secret meeting of two close friends. No matter how much Gemme strained her ears to hear enough to join in the conversation, only stray tidbits wafted to the backseat.

Luna was smarter than she let on.

Frustration eating a hole in her stomach, Gemme munched on a soybean wafer from her backpack and dozed off with the crumbs still on her legs. Her head jerked when she fell forward too far. The side cushion of the seat provided a place to prop up her face without straining, but blocked out any chance of joining the conversation. First day on the job, and they'd already left her out. Giving up, Gemme closed her eyes and lost herself to exhaustion.

※

"Jenny, what are doing standing there like a scarecrow? Mikey's coming to pick us up any minute."

The woman standing before her stared through cloudy gray eyes like her own. Her nut-brown hair blew free in the wind, trailing to a white sundress and sandals with daisies painted between her toes. Golden swirls moved within the daisies and Gemme blinked until they disappeared.

"You look like you've seen a ghost."

Gemme studied the woman up and down. Maybe she had. "Who are you?"

She laughed, throwing back her head. "You've been doing too much work. It's time to have some fun." She grabbed Gemme's hand, and Gemme stiffened at her touch.

The woman pulled her forward. "Honestly, why do I always have to drag you with us?"

"Where are we going?" Gemme struggled to keep up with her pace. The earth crushed underneath her bare feet, like she walked on crumbled bread. The sun's rays seared her retinas, but the warmth it offered differed so much from...

"To the party, remember?"

"Where are my shoes?"

"They're in Mikey's pickup truck. You left them last night before skinny-dipping."

"Before what?" Gemme's foot caught on a branch and she pitched forward. The earth came up harder than she thought, knocking her jaw into her head. She bit her tongue, pain exploding in her mouth. Starbursts blossomed behind her eyes and the field darkened as if someone switched off the lights.

❧◈

Gemme regained consciousness to dim light and wondered if she'd programmed twilight mode into her sleep pod. The landrover pitched, suspending her in the air before landing hard, jarring her body. Reality barged in. She wasn't on the *Expedition*. Glancing out the rear sight panel, she watched the flaming edge of Solaris Prime disappear beyond the horizon. The white scenery dulled to various shades of gray, making the world even more alien.

Gemme wiped condensation from the sight panel with her sleeve. She squinted against the foggy glass, trying to make out the shape of mountains in the twilight. The thought of no light switch frightened her. What if their energy cells ran out? Would they have to wait until the next day to see?

A snowdrift shifted, like someone pulled it on wheels and Gemme blinked and stared, pushing her face up to the three-inch thick glass. Her breath plumed on the panel and she wiped it away, searching for the source of the movement. The mountains loomed as shadows on the horizon and the twilight cast every shape in a haze.

"Tech?" she whispered, but he didn't answer.

She glanced behind her, taking the risk she'd miss another strange movement. Tech snored, his chin resting on his chest. Luna typed on her miniscreen, and Brentwood focused on the path ahead.

Gemme whipped her head back to the window and held her breath. Brentwood's words came back to her. *Report anything that moves to Luna.*

What was she going to say? *I saw a snowdrift move?*

She watched the sight panel like a hawk. The landrover crested a ridge, and the plains disappeared below them. Losing sight of her target, she shook her head and sighed. It was the first day of her journey and she was already losing her mind.

"Ride's over, people." Brentwood eased the landrover to a halt. The constant rumbling beneath her feet rolled to silence and the finality of the moment hit Gemme in the stomach. For the first time, her sleep pod on the *Expedition* would lay empty.

His voice sounded cheerful but weary. "Let's make camp."

"You mean, actually go out there?" Luna slammed down her miniscreen.

Brentwood turned and grinned. "That's right. Did you think we'd sleep right here in the landrover?"

"That's certainly better than freezing in the cold."

He laughed. "I brought thermal tents from the ship's emergency supply. Come on, we'll make a synthetic fire."

"And sing good old 'Kumbaya,'" Tech grumbled groggily, shifting his position as if both his legs had fallen asleep.

Gemme slipped her arms back into her thermal coat, tightening the hood around her face. Synthetic angora hair tickled her cheeks as she pulled the string taut. She thought about mentioning the moving snowdrift, but the encounter felt so surreal, she blamed it on her imagination and adjusting eyes.

"It's a balmy negative seventeen degrees Celsius out there. So bundle up and let me know if your fingers and toes turn numb. Everyone ready?" Brentwood's hand hovered over the panel for the hatch.

"Yeppers." Tech had slipped on his own hood. His beard covered his face in a quilt, and Gemme envied his extra facial hair.

The sound of a zipper ripped through the compartment as Luna secured her jumpsuit and pulled a wrap around her shoulders. A fuzzy wool hat covered her head. "You bet."

Brentwood watched Gemme and she nodded. He winked at her before pressing the panel. The hatch lifted and cold air streamed in, stealing every ounce of heat.

Gemme shivered and squinted her eyes against the wind. She thought her retinas would freeze and she'd turn blind as the Seers. Blinking back tears, she held her breath and jumped out. Her boots crunched on snow, wobbling despite the solid footing. The heavy weight of real gravity pulled on her legs as she trudged away from the landrover, seeking the unknown. The frozen plains stretched out in a vast, exposed hinterland. No chamber on the *Expedition* compared to standing in the sweeping landscape, the wind whipping through her as it if could carry her away.

Brentwood unloaded gear with a plop onto the snow. "Any volunteers for setting up the tents?"

"I'll do it." Gemme scooped up a handful of iron rods and nylon. Anything to keep her moving, keep her warm.

"Count me in." Tech gave her a nod.

"Ms. Legacy?" Brentwood paused with his arms full and shot Luna a questioning glance.

Luna plucked a glass vial out of her backpack. "I have to collect samples."

"Samples of what? All I see is blasted snow for miles." Tech waved his arm across the far mountain range.

"Anything that may contain life." Luna stuck her nose in the air and whipped around, disappearing behind the landrover.

Tech raised an eyebrow at Gemme and whispered under his breath. "Ha. 'Samples,' my ass."

Gemme clamped her mouth tight to keep from laughing. She checked Brentwood's reaction. He busied himself unloading energy cells. Here she was, trying to impress him with her tent-making skills, and he probably preferred the way Luna stood up for herself, choosing educated work over grunt labor.

Stop now. You'll never win this battle.

Gemme gritted her teeth, throwing down a rod that didn't match the diagram anywhere. Tech picked it up and stuck in into thicker rod, pulling the nylon across it. "Doing good, Ms. Love Connection."

Someone had watched too many Old Earth videos. "Thanks." *But, no thanks.* She sucked like a black hole at tent building. She couldn't even summon the energy to correct him *again* concerning her job status as *ex*-matchmaker. A sour taste sat on her tongue. Gemme needed to focus and all this jealous angst grated on her nerves. Why couldn't she dismiss Brentwood and be done with it?

Swirls of fluorescent green reflected in the nylon fabric, distracting Gemme from her thoughts. She turned, staring in awe. Violet and vermillion danced above them in waves, radiating in streaks from the night sky. The ever-changing pattern hypnotized Gemme in the same way she stared at a flickering flame. Reverence welled up inside her, making her feel like a little girl seeing the universe for the first time.

"Would you look at that!" Tech dropped the last three tent poles in the snow. They rattled at his feet.

Brentwood rounded the landrover and stood by them, hand on his hips. "I'll be a droid's uncle! It's like back on Old Earth!"

Tech nodded, looking eager to talk about his expertise. "The charged particles, in this case originating from Solaris Prime, enter Tundra 37's magnetic pull. When they collide with the air molecules, the fluctuating current emits light in a magnetic field."

"Thanks, Mr. Scientist." Gemme thought she'd dish out some of his own medicine in their name calling game.

Tech chuckled. "At least my class years are good for something."

Gemme thought she caught the corner of Brentwood's lips curve up and wondered if he found her joke amusing. Any sign of emotion would make him more human and less of an authority figure. She wanted to know the man underneath the uniform. What did he dream of? Why had the computer matched her to him?

Brentwood caught her staring and an electric current passed from his eyes to hers. Gemme's heart jolted and she wondered if the magnetic field shifted to encompass them, making her skin tingle with excitement. The moment surged inside her and she licked her cold, cracked lips wanting to say so much.

Tell him about the pairing.

Tell him before it's too late.

Brentwood's eyebrows rose as if in expectation. He leaned toward her, his coated shoulder brushing against hers. The light reflected on half his face, the other side in shadows. His eyes burned with intensity as if a miniature Aurora Borealis swirled in their depths.

"Why didn't you tell me I'm missing the show?" Luna chimed in from behind them, ruining the moment.

"We just noticed, Ms. Legacy." Brentwood moved away from Gemme and invited Luna into their semicircle with a wave of his arm. Gemme stepped back in relief and disappointment. At least she hadn't said anything embarrassing.

Tech couldn't hide the suspicion is his voice, "Did you find any samples?"

"Maybe. I'll have to take them back to the lab for analysis." She flashed a small test tube with her gloved hands.

Standard snow filled the tube, but Gemme kept her mouth shut, shivering as if Luna made the air colder still.

Tech narrowed his eyes. "Doesn't look like much."

"I'm looking for signs of organic life. She stared at him as if he were a toddler, "Micro-sco-pic or-gan-isms. Aka: too small to see."

Tech grunted. "Yes, those would make quite a hardy meal."

"Ugh!" She shook her head and stormed away. Tech shrugged and glanced over to Gemme. "Must have been something I said."

Gemme decided she liked him more than she initially thought. So what if he drank too much wheat beer sometimes? At least he had a sense of humor.

She watched Brentwood as he set up camp. She wanted to rewind to two seconds ago, when Brentwood gave her his undivided attention. The fire he'd built blazed behind them, warming Gemme's back. She turned and sat on a supply container, raising her feet to the flames.

"Don't melt your boots." Tech collapsed beside her. He'd assembled most of the tents, due to her inexperience with assembly diagrams, and exhaustion shown in the slump of his shoulders.

"Thanks, don't melt your beard."

Tech quirked a fuzzy eyebrow and Gemme laughed, feeling light as the energy in the sky. If Tundra 37 had such beauty, what else did it hide? Maybe the ice planet wasn't such a horrific place to set up a home after all. The possibilities filled Gemme's head with buoyant hopes.

Her backpack beeped, and she reached down and pulled out her miniscreen.

"Looks like someone's been looking for you," Tech said, noticing the incoming message light.

Out of the corner of her eye, she saw Brentwood look up from stacking supply containers as if he was curious. But when she turned his way, he was busy again.

Gemme scrolled down to see a message titled, *How's the snow?* "It's Ferris!" she exclaimed, grinning ear to ear.

Brentwood quirked an eyebrow and she gave him a smile. "My brother."

"Oh." He scratched his head. "Do you want some privacy to write back?"

"No, no, no." Gemme stood up, carrying the miniscreen. No reason for everyone to move because of her. "I'll go into my tent."

Taking the miniscreen back to her tent, she paused at the flap. Why go inside when such a gorgeous sky hung overhead? She'd spent her whole life under an artificial ceiling; it was about time to get in touch with nature. She found an embankment just underneath a hill on the southern side of camp and settled down, her butt forming an impression in the snow. Balancing the miniscreen in her lap, she watched the lights play out in the sky above her, pausing now and then to type a sentence.

Dear Ferris,

You're such a galactic worrywart! Tell Mom and Dad I'm fine. The mission is proceeding smoothly, and riding in the landrover is quite an experience. You should be more jealous than concerned.

Sniffling carried on the wind, following by tiny hiccups of sobs. Luna stumbled down the hill a few meters from her and crumpled to her knees. Gemme closed the lid of the miniscreen to help her, but Brentwood beat her to it, appearing at the hilltop. The wind had lessened, and she could hear every word.

"Ms. Legacy, are you all right?" He slid down the hill and helped her up.

She sniffed. "It's Tech. He doesn't think what I'm doing here is worthwhile."

"Oh, he's just a little blunt sometimes. Don't worry, he'll warm up to you. He knows just as much as we all do that we need an alternate food source."

"I can't find anything, yet. Some biologist I am." Gemme was surprised. Luna had seemed so bold and confident around her, and this was a side of her she'd never seen. She wondered if Luna acted out to get Brentwood's attention, but the tone of her voice sounded sincere.

Brentwood put an arm around her, helping her walk back to camp. "The Seers selected you specifically for the team. They thought you were the best person for the job."

"No, they didn't." Luna scoffed, surprising Gemme. "They picked me because they had to, because I'm a Legacy."

"Nonsense." Brentwood's voice was soothing. "They'd do nothing of the sort."

Her voice dropped low, and Gemme strained her ears. "It was the least they could do. They were supposed to make me a lieutenant, like all the Legacys before me, but my test scores were too low. They wouldn't bend the rules to allow it."

Brentwood remained silent and Gemme wondered what he

thought about this new piece of information. She always suspected the Legacys had special treatment, but to make each generation a lieutenant based on bloodline was utterly wrong.

Luna sighed. "You don't know what's like, not being better than the people that came before you, always failing expectations when *others* got better test scores."

Gemme knew just who the "others" Luna had referred to with such resentment was: her. She brought her hand up to the place where Luna had shoved her all those years back. Even though her entire body was numb from cold, she still remembered the raw ache of the bruise.

Luna continued, "I had planned to meet with the Seers. My family had one more ticket to visit them, as part of the bargain they'd struck with my ancestor, Thadious Legacy. Before the comet shower hit, I was going to try to convince them I was still worthy."

Brentwood's voice was soft. "Why didn't you?"

Luna paused as if considering how much to tell him. "I gave my ticket up for something I wanted more: a favor that didn't pan out. Besides, with the ship crashed, it didn't matter."

Gemme froze, unable to listen further. If Luna had put her pairing with Brentwood before her career, then she wanted the man more than anything.

Gemme collected her miniscreen with shaky fingers. Did she want Brentwood enough to get in Luna's way?

CHAPTER ELEVEN
ENCOUNTER

Emergency bays at full capacity.
Fusion Reactor unstable.
Lieutenants Smith, Levingston, and Kohler unresponsive.

Mestasis fought down an overwhelming wave of panic as she sorted through the upsetting reports. So many problems and Abysme ignored all of them, useless as a baby with her face turned toward the orb. Had her sister lost her mind? Addressing the beacon with the lieutenant present defied the very rule system they'd constructed with the scientists who'd discovered the orb. Either Abysme hadn't sensed the lieutenant's presence, or she didn't care. Either way her sister was losing control.

An incoming message beeped on the mainframe and Mestasis brought up the location of the transmission. Alpha Blue! Thank the stars they were still alive.

Lieutenant Brentwood's sharp features flashed in her mind as he spoke. "First day successful. We've made good time, and the conditions are bearable."

The muscles in his face twitched slightly and Mestasis registered the facial patterns as disappointment. "No sign of life or anything else besides snow. Ms. Legacy is on the lookout and has taken samples. If all goes well, we'll reach the mining site in two days."

Mestasis sent a response. *Good work, Lieutenant. Keep us posted.* She hid the fact that Abysme wasn't responding by amplifying her voice to like both of theirs combined. No need for the lieutenant to know. He had enough on his mind and she needed him focused.

The message flicked off and Mestasis breathed a sigh of relief. At least one aspect of the day was successful. As long as Alpha Blue pushed on, she had hope for the colony and her own salvation. If the team failed, she'd failed them all.

Gemme woke to sniffling. Did Tech snore? How could she hear him all the way across camp?

She twisted in her thermal cocoon and poked her head out. The energy cell throbbed with warmth from the back of her tent, but her breath still blossomed in the air. Sunlight filtered through the nylon, casting a shadow rivaling the size of the landrover on the northern side.

A quick intake of air rode the wind, followed by a watery snort. Gemme shot up on her elbows, wondering if whatever lurked outside her tent could smell her rising fear. Trying not to make a sound, she dug in her backpack for the laser she'd slipped on the bottom.

She pulled out soybean wafers, extra fleece pants, and a skin regenerizer she'd lifted from the emergency bay, then scraped the bottom of her bag. Where did it go? The shadow grew larger, a mound of writhing snakes pressing against the nylon. Her throat constricted as a clamp squeezed down on her heart.

Her alarm beeped, the sound jarringly loud and alien, disturbing the calm of the morning. The beast lurched back, sniffed, and then pounded the snow as it thrust its head underneath the nylon tarp.

A snout, long as an alligator's, poked through the bottom of the fabric. Gemme wiggled out of her thermal cocoon and inched back on her rear. She opened her mouth to scream, but terror sucked the air out of her lungs. The beast pushed itself in farther and a hide of tentacles filled the tent, the jiggling appendages casting strange medusa-like shadows on the ceiling. The beast reeked like the dead salmon in the hydraulics tank.

There's your moving snowdrift.

Gemme scrambled back until the cold zipper pressed against her neck. The tentacles stretched, wrapping themselves around her hairbrush, her boot, and an empty water bottle, the tip wiggling into the spout. Transfixed, Gemme blinked to get herself moving, doing something. She fumbled behind her until her shaky fingers located the bottom of the zipper. She yanked it up, the zipper catching on the fabric halfway up.

The sound lured a sticky tendril across the floor. Suction cups dotted the end, opening and closing like tiny mouths gulping for air. The tentacle curled, feeling around her sock. Gemme pressed her back against the fabric and pushed herself through the hole, rolling backward into the center of camp.

"Couldn't sleep, Aphrodite?" Tech sat by the remnants of the fire, a half-eaten protein bar in his hand. He stared at her with an eyebrow quirked.

"Something—Something's in—"

"Well, spit it out."

She didn't have to. The tentacle poked through the hole in the zipper, rising like a sea monster from the depths of the Atlantic.

"Emergency Code 43!" Tech shouted, "Get out of your tents!"

He pulled Gemme back and they huddled behind the container he'd sat on. The tentacle attached itself to the tent spike and yanked it out.

She grabbed Tech's arm. "Where's your laser?"

"In my tent."

"Great place for it, Mr. Scientist."

Brentwood emerged from his tent half dressed in a rumpled shirt and polar fleece night pants. "Code 43?"

"Over there!" The plastic collapsed on top of the tentacle horde and the beast let out a whirring cry. The beast shook until the tent fell off.

Luna screamed, her voice ripping Gemme's ears in half. Gemme spun around thinking another beast had its tentacles in her hair. But she wasn't so lucky. Luna stood in her running jumpsuit complete with a fuzzy headband and pink leg warmers-violating uniform code. Where did she get that kind of extravagance anyway? She looked like she'd just returned from a brisk morning jog. Her voice startled the beast, and it took off, scampering on a thousand small paws over the snowdrift.

"Don't stand there, catch it!"

Gemme twisted around and gaped. Luna shouted at her, of all people.

Watching the beast skitter away, Gemme noticed the sun glaring off of something on its back. The picture of her and Ferris stuck to one of the top tentacles along with two of her soybeans wafers and her miniscreen, which had her entire life on it, including the mineral analyzer she'd need to find the deposit.

Before Gemme could reason with herself, she bolted after the creature. Snow crunched underneath her socks as she hustled up the mound. The landscape looked puffy and soft from the sight panel, but in reality the white ice crystals had hardened like rock, stinging her soles. She reached the top of the snowdrift, spotted the tentacle horde and skidded down the other side on the glacial surface, ignoring her throbbing feet.

The beast ran in a diagonal line to a crevice in the snow. Gemme careened over the ice and lunged toward it, wondering how she'd ever stop it, never mind haul it back to camp for Luna.

She reached out as she sprinted and grabbed a tentacle. The membrane slipped through her fingers like wet jelly. A gelatinous residue coated her palm. The miniscreen stuck like a fly in a spider's web to its back, the tentacles oozing over it until it sunk deep within the writhing mass. The beast slowed down and she increased her pace, her lungs burning raw. She jabbed her arm into the tentacles. Her fingers brushed against a hard surface in the squiggly mass. She almost had it. Gemme thrust her arm in deeper, but strong arms wrapped around her, pulling her back just as the beast disappeared.

"Whoa there! You almost fell in." Brentwood clutched her against his chest, his breath heaving in her hair. His arms wrapped around her shoulders as her feet kicked over the edge. The crevice had come up sooner than she thought, plunging three meters down into a splash of ice water. If she'd grabbed onto the beast, she'd gone right over the edge with it. Brentwood saved her life.

"My miniscreen, my picture, it took everything."

"None of those things are more important than your life, Gemme."

The way her first name fell off his tongue made her twirl around in his arms. Her hands rested on his chest, grasping his rumpled shirt. His normally combed hair stood up in a massive wave above his eyes. His arms tightened around her, as if she'd slip right from his fingers into the ice waters below. She melted into his embrace, the mingling warmth of their bodies heating up. The feeling of the electromagnetic field returned, stronger this time, sizzling the air around them.

He smoothed back her hair and the gesture resonated deeply inside him, like he'd done it a thousand times before. His warm breath tickled her cheek. Gemme's lips trembled in anticipation. The moment felt inevitable, each second pulsing forward to bring them here, at the edge of this world, at the beginning of their own.

"You lost my specimen!" Luna's voice screeched behind them. Brentwood released Gemme as if Luna had caught them committing a crime. Cold wind blew where he once held her and Gemme shivered, crossing her arms against her chest.

Luna slid on the ice, looking like a figure skater in a winter wonderland. Gemme wondered how she managed to keep her cheeks rosy in just the right place and her lips red as the cherries in the biodome.

"How could you let it get away?" Luna's bright blue eyes seared through hers like lasers.

A hard rock formed in Gemme's stomach and she wanted to spit it out in Luna's face. "I almost fell over the edge trying to catch it."

Luna gazed down into the crevice like an evil stepsister contemplating an appropriate demise for her rival. "You could have at least ripped off a tentacle."

Brentwood stepped between them. "Ms. Legacy, I'll handle this. Get back to camp and inform Tech to start packing. We have another long ride ahead of us." Was Brentwood trying to get rid of her? Gemme fidgeted, feeling ice crystals form inside her nostrils.

"Of course. You know the implications of this don't you?" Luna grinned at Brentwood, batting her eyelashes.

Gemme stared and Brentwood shrugged.

"There must be an entire ocean underneath us, supporting life."

"Very interesting, Luna, but right now I must tend to Gemme."

Luna looked like she'd swallowed one of her samples by accident. "Right. I'll speak with you back at camp."

She cuffed Gemme on the arm. "We're lucky you didn't jump, dear."

Anger rose inside Gemme in a rip current. Why didn't Luna pursue the beast herself? She was the biologist. Gemme wiped her palm on Luna's jogging suit, the pink staining red with gel. "Oh, I almost forgot. Here's your sample."

Luna stared, her eyes wide. She opened her mouth to respond, but Brentwood intervened. "Wonderful! See, you did get a sample."

Gemme couldn't tell if he tried to lighten the mood, or if he truly thought the goop would suffice. Whatever the case, she made sure to slather her with every last bit of it.

Luna clamped her mouth shut, flaring her eyes. Brentwood gently nudged her forward, his hand on her arm. "You should get back to camp before the sample dries up."

"Certainly, Lieutenant." Luna stormed off with no smile this time. Gemme shivered, balancing from foot to foot to keep ice forming on her toes. If she weren't freezing her butt off, she would have enjoyed the scene much more.

"My goodness, you aren't even wearing your boots!" Brentwood offered his arms. "If I may?"

Gemme froze, not understanding what he referred to. Before she could react, he scooped her up, sliding an arm underneath her knees and another behind her neck. He lifted her as if she weighed nothing, and her frozen feet rose from the ground. She molded into his embrace.

"Better?"

"Much, thank you." Embarrassment flushed her cheeks. Here she was in the middle of nowhere with her frizzy morning hair, no coat, and her dirty socks from yesterday crusted with snow. She probably even had bad morning breath. Quite the adventurer, she was.

A brisk wind blew around them and Gemme hid her face in his shirt, feeling self-conscious and more than a little excited to have him hold her again.

His boots crunched in the snow as he hiked back to camp. "I'll have Tech take a look at your feet. His wife's a medic, so he knows more about frostbite than I do."

"Thank you." She heard his heartbeat pounding in his chest with each step each took. Wrapping her arms around his neck, she wished the moment could last forever.

Holding Gemme made Brentwood's skin hot as fire in a land of ice. He forced platonic thoughts into his composure as she wrapped her arms around him, her soft skin brushing against the back of his neck. What kind of lieutenant would he be if he took advantage of one of the members of his team on the most important mission he'd ever had?

Gemme nuzzled against him, and he focused on the remaining steps to camp. Her brave rush to confront the beast both surprised and impressed him, and he couldn't imagine the terror of waking up with a monster in her tent. She had more strength than some of the other lieutenants, hidden under such soft shyness and modesty.

She looked toward camp, her gaze growing distant as if she had something on her mind.

"You doing okay?"

"Yeah. I can almost feel my toes."

"Let's hope Tech can help."

He studied her profile in stray glances down, remembering the curve of her cheek, the delicate bridge of her freckled nose, and the flutter of her long, brown eyelashes. He wanted to ask her what troubled her, but he also didn't want to pry.

Tech met him on the edge of camp, fidgeting with his gloves. "Is she all right?"

"I'm fine." Gemme interrupted him as if all this attention

embarrassed her. "It's just my feet."

"She didn't have time to slip on her boots." Brentwood explained, trying to justify her actions and alleviate some of her embarrassment. "Could you take a look?"

Tech nodded, uneasiness slipping into his features. "Sure, bring her into camp."

Brentwood entered his tent and placed Gemme on his own thermal cocoon. Gemme pulled off her socks. Redness tinged her delicate toes. Brentwood looked on as Tech massaged her feet gently.

His heart skittered. "Will she be all right?"

Tech nodded. "She's fine. When they turn black and blue you have to worry."

"Good." Gemme breathed in relief. "I can't have you hauling me around for the rest of the mission like an invalid."

"We'd do whatever's necessary." Brentwood interjected. "You're an important member of this team."

"You'll have to stay off them for a while." Tech advised, giving Gemme back her socks. "Let us pack up camp. You stay here and rest."

A rip current of frustration came over Brentwood as he saw Gemme so helpless. "You'd think they could have spared at least one medic to go with us."

Tech shook his head. "After the crash, my wife reported to the emergency bay to help, and I haven't seen her since."

Brentwood gave Tech a sympathetic smile. "You must miss her."

Tech waved him off. "Nah, that old witch. It does us good to be apart. No offense, Ms. Reiner, but that matchmaking system must have short-circuited when it paired us together. Why do you think I drink so much?"

Trying to smooth over Tech's remark, Brentwood changed the subject. "She must be working hard. You wouldn't believe what the emergency bay looked like after the crash."

Tech sighed. "Let's hope there's still enough of us left to have a colony."

Gemme put her hand on Tech's shoulder. "Don't worry, Tech. We'll find a way. As the Matchmaker, I know how many people necessary to start a generation, and the *Expedition* had twice as many when it took off. We have more than enough people now."

Brentwood's miniscreen blinked with an incoming message. Work always got in the way in times like these. He gestured toward the tent opening. "Let's allow Ms. Reiner some rest."

"Sure thing, chief." Tech bowed to Gemme, and then ducked away. Sunlight flashed in and out as the tent flap slapped in the breeze.

"Are you going to be okay in here?" Brentwood bent down beside her. She looked up at him with her thin lips slightly parted.

"I'll be fine. Thanks for saving me."

The sudden urge to kiss her overwhelmed him and he swallowed his passion, feeling vulnerable and stupid. He'd trained for his entire life for such a mission, and this was the time to prove himself. He couldn't let a woman get in the way, no matter how beautiful, brave, and intelligent she was.

How would he ever be paired with anyone after this? To think she'd be the one to do it, to make him marry someone that wasn't her. Brentwood couldn't stand the thought of it. The very nature of her job stuck him in the ribs like an uncomfortable pain in his side.

"Not a problem." Pulling away, he grabbed his miniscreen and ducked out before his emotions got the better of him. The brightness of the sunlit snow brought him back to reality, and he squinted, trying to adjust.

Luna slumped over a sample tray, using a syringe to apply chemicals to the gel and Tech loaded the heavy equipment in the landrover. Brentwood chose a spot where he could read the message in private. The familiar icon of the Seers flashed on the screen; a retina with the hull of the *Expedition* at its center.

Jeez, what do they want now? A status report?

He had nothing. A strange tentacled beast, snow, and more snow. What would he tell them?

Brentwood scrolled down to the message and pressed the Enter key.

Alternate mission objective.

Squinting from the glare of the sun, he read further.

Locate and retrieve a biological anomaly with the following specifications:

Collagen forty-five point three percent. Protein twenty-one point seven percent...

The list rambled on, describing no species Brentwood had ever learned about in his classes. He shook his head at all the gibberish. What did this have to do with his mission or their survival on the *Expedition*? He scrolled down.

Specimen location at 90 degrees north latitude. Brentwood checked the coordinates of their first mission. The specimen rested less than a hundred meters from the mineral deposit. Intrigued, Brentwood scrolled down.

See attached picture of corresponding orb.

The strange, mystical ball in the Seers' control chamber eyed him hauntingly from his own miniscreen. Even now, the cosmic swirls and starbursts chanted his name. A voice called to him. *"Miles, come home."*

He blinked and rubbed his eyes. Too much sun and not enough hydration. He must be hallucinating. He cracked open a water bottle and continued reading, wiping sweat from his brow despite the frigid temperatures.

Status of mission is priority one. Top secret. Inquire with Luna Legacy concerning the nature of the beacon: code Beta Prime. All other crew members must be kept ignorant.

Ignorant? How would he keep an alternate mission from the rest of his crew? Brentwood itched with frustration. Did Luna know about this mission all along? He slammed down his miniscreen and walked over to the blonde beauty as she packed up her trays.

"Hey there, Lieutenant. Come to check on me?"

Brentwood kept his voice at a whisper. "What do you know about the 'orb'?"

"What orb?" She clicked down the lid of the tray and gave him a wink.

"Code Beta Prime. The Seers have me in the loop."

"I see." She stuck the trays into a supply container. "Let's talk a walk, shall we?"

"Please."

The way her arm linked around his reminded him of a climbing vine of ivy in the biodome. Her grip tightened around his forearm like she lured him into a trap. She pulled him toward the back of camp, where the wind howled around them, blowing tips of snowdrifts in tornados over their heads. He kicked the snow until he brought feeling back into his toes.

"The second generation of Lifers on the *Expedition* found the orb attached to the ship while navigating near the galaxy of a sun-like star called beta CVn in the constellation Canes Venatici. The device, partly metallic and partly biological life, attached tendrils to the ship. They think the magnetic pulse of the *Expedition*'s energy cores drew it in. Scientists and biologists studied it for years, mesmerized by the golden swirls, but only the Seers truly understood it, making connections none of us humans would understand."

He realized he leaned in too close, his face only inches from her red lips. But he couldn't pull away now. "Why didn't you tell me about it?"

A stray wisp of blonde hair blew between them, tickling his forehead and she tucked it away behind her ear. "Why would I? It's considered a dead case, an old wives' tale. No one's talked about for generations."

Brentwood studied her eyes, cold as the water that almost swallowed Gemme. No deception lay in the depths, only confusion. If the Seers trusted her, than he had to lend her his trust as well. "The Seers just gave me a new mission. Apparently, this orb is picking up energy impulses from a beacon on this planet, a mere two hundred meters from the mineral deposit."

Luna's delicate blonde brow rose so high, wrinkles formed on her pristine forehead. "No way."

"Yes. And they want us to find it. Just the two of us. No one else involved."

She smiled like he asked her to be his second-in-command, or even his lifemate. Brentwood squashed the thought.

"I understand." She pointed a finger into his chest and twisted it against his collarbone. "Your secret is safe with me."

Brentwood didn't like this pairing as much as he didn't like the Seers, but he had no other choice. He longed to get back to camp and check on Gemme. Had she woken up? Did she wonder where he was?

Luna eyed him expectantly as if she guessed who his thoughts drifted to. Brentwood pulled his eyes away from the direction of camp. "That's it for now. Pack your things. We've leaving in an hour."

"Yes, sir." Luna dislodged her arm. "Let me know when our next secret meeting is. I'll be looking forward to it."

The eagerness in her voice made him squirm with unease. He watched her like someone watching a ticking time bomb as she strode back to camp, her hips swaying with each step. What had he stumbled into? A secret alien project? Deception of his crew? A descendant of the Legacys breathing down his neck? Brentwood rubbed his face with his gloved hand, feeling like Tundra 37 lumbered way over his head.

Biggest mission of your life: Day 2.

CHAPTER TWELVE
SPY

Vira stared into the sorcerer's deep violet eyes. Rizzy's ripped poster hung across their room, a large gash running from his shoulder to his staff. She listened as her sister's breathing changed from short bursts to the long intakes of deep sleep. The wires powering their family cell lurked behind those intense eyes, surging with stolen energy she'd directed all by herself.

Plopping out of her sleep pod, she squirmed her way across their bedroom floor. Rizzy's day-old jumpsuit tangled in her legs, and she stopped to pull it off. She wiped her hand on the carpet, because who knew where Daryl's germs touched, before pulling herself forward.

The chrome stood above her like a portal to another land, a place of impulses and charges, a place where she could travel without the means of her underdeveloped legs. She put a hot hand to the chrome, her fingers making mist on the perfect, silver surface. The wires coiled just where she'd left them that morning, and she reached out with her mind, channeling her energy to connect with the charges within.

It took only moments to redirect the stream. She heard the

ventilators sputter out and peeked over her shoulder, making sure the absence of their hum didn't wake Rizzy. Her sister's pod registered deep sleep mode. She was safe from detection. Her mom would be angry in the morning when the air smelled stale, but maybe the Seers would have the energy redirected to their family room soon.

Vira pulled her hand away from the chrome and squiggled her way back, yearning for the warmth of her sleep pod. She stopped halfway, clinging to the carpet fibers. Could she find out what was wrong with the ship? What if she could help?

She scurried back to the chrome and placed her hand in the same spot. The metal still emanated heat underneath her skin. She connected to the ship, scanning status charts. Life support systems functioned at fifty-five percent, biodome humidity levels were normal, and growth rates were slow but steady. The energy capacitors were low.

Another presence gripped her like someone wrapping their fingers around her neck. Vira stiffened at the mental touch and gasped, holding her breath. She felt exposed, as if she lay naked on the congregation floor for everyone to gawk. But this scrutiny was far worse. Her every thought lay on display: her anger with Rizzy for sneaking out late at night, her love for peanuts, her overprotective streak for her mother. Everything.

The presence analyzed her like a specimen in a jar, probing every fold of her brain, poking in every weak spot in her heart. *Please. Let me go.*

This presence had no compassion, no sympathy. It moved as if desperate, searching for answers Vira didn't have. Clawing at her weaknesses, it spread throughout her body like a disease. One thought consumed it above all else: a pulsing orb Vira had never seen.

Like a mini universe, the globe swirled with activity, alive. It smelled of roses, ocean surf, horsehides, and other impossible things that only existed back on Old Earth. Vira wanted to plunge into its golden depths and explore, but the orb's capabilities could not exceed the circumference of its curving world. Just as the orb disappointed her, it hinted at a much larger object very near. She wanted to find the larger object, but the impulses were too faint to track down. As much as the orb and the object it hinted at confused her, Vira embraced it and the presence weakened, loosening its hold.

That's it, think of the orb.

She filled her mind with it, following the cosmic patterns as tiny galaxies came and went and stars died in supernova, only to be reborn in the crux of a black hole. None of it made sense, but holding onto those ephemeral images allowed the presence solace enough to release her.

Vira snapped her hand away from the wall and fell, panting, onto the floor. She squeaked as feeling jolted through her numb fingers in a thousand prickly pins.

The lid of Rizzy's sleep pod rose and her sister's head poked out like a turtle in a shell. She rubbed her eyes and focused on Vira huddling on the floor of their room. Vira gasped, wishing she could become invisible. What would Rizzy think if she knew she spied on the ship? If she found out about her freakish powers?

Rizzy's face screwed up, sour as a rotten tomato. "Are you trying to rip my poster down again?"

"No." Her voice came out weak from relief.

"Yeah, right. I could call Mom and Dad right here on the intercom and then they'd catch you red-handed. I know you tore it down in the first place. I know it!"

Vira cringed, hiding her face in the carpet. It reeked like Rizzy's old socks.

"I'm sorry."

"Yeah, right you are. I know you hate it."

"He's creepy."

"He has magical powers. You wouldn't get it."

Vira bit her lip. She got it all right, more than she wanted to.

"Besides, it's an antique, passed down from our ancestors."

Rizzy jumped out of her sleep pod and crossed her arms. Vira tried to move to the kitchen to avoid her, but her powers had sucked all her energy, and she fell on her side into the carpet.

She expected Rizzy to smack on her head with her pillow, but her sister's arms came under her, pulling her up. Her voice softened. "Come on. I can't have you freezing outside your sleep pod. It's like negative one in here."

Vira hated how her disability unarmed the people around her, making them feel nothing but sympathy and pity. Sometimes, she'd rather have the pillow smack her on the head like a regular sister fight. "You're not going to hit me?"

"No. But don't do it again."

"I won't."

Rizzy tenderly laid Vira back in her sleep pod. She pressed the keypad and muttered, "Nighty night." But Vira's mind still raced with thoughts of the presence she'd met. Was there a mind to the machine behind the *Expedition*?

Impossible. The Seers would have detected it. Besides, this presence lurked beyond the mainframe. Each impulse resonated from one source: a real body behind the consciousness, frantic and weak. She clutched her stomach as the lid of the sleep pod closed. She used to feel safe within its bubble-shaped dome, and now even the darkness inside seemed threatening.

One of the Seers themselves caught her.

Vira had always believed the Seers watched over them with the best intentions for all the Lifers. She held onto that thought late at night when she worried about the blackness of space around her and how they all relied on a ship built hundreds of years ago. At least the Seers hovered at the helm, making sure nothing bad would ever happen. Vira clutched her pillow in her hands, squeezing the fabric into clumps. The *Expedition* suddenly became a more menacing place and even the lid of her familiar sleep pod pressed down on her in the blackness.

She'd seen into this Seer's heart; she'd seen her motives, identified her own fears and triumphs, just as the Seer examined her. She had a name: Abysme. She was a person, just like herself, with wants and needs, priorities and prejudices, strengths and weaknesses. Underneath all her Guide-driven objectives, this Seer just looked out for herself.

Mestasis yearned for the numbness of sleep. Eternally connected to the mainframe, her thoughts moved at light speed throughout the *Expedition*, never ceasing. Each pulse stuck her brain like a pinprick, and with too many holes her mind would turn to mush. Only when the ship terminated would her thoughts be her own again, and she'd be free to rest and, finally, to die.

Pushing away her personal concerns, she returned to the system analysis. The ship sucked energy like a vortex, draining the remaining capacitors at an alarming rate. She regulated the temperature down two degrees and dimmed the ultraviolet lights in the biodome.

The *Expedition* needed an alternative fuel source quickly to maintain their current living conditions. She checked on the status of Alpha Blue. Halfway to their target goal and driving the only working landrover, they provided a decent amount of hope shaded with worry. At least they'd survived the initial exposure. People on Old Earth spent years in arctic conditions, even setting up homes on the poles, but Mestasis didn't know if the children of the *Expedition* were as hardy after a lifetime of light gravity and regulated conditions. Peering deep into their communications, an anomaly caught her attention. She opened her eye and turned her head to her sister.

Bysme, why did you change Alpha Blue's mission objective?

Abysme hung tangled in the wires, reminding Mestasis of the dead pigeons caught in Old Earth's nets. She used to curse the rich who hung the contraptions between buildings to keep them from flying into the hovercraft engines. She'd climb the escape ladders outside the buildings, risking her life to pick the birds out. By the time her nimble hands threaded their bodies free, most of them were already dead.

Bysme?

Her sister's reticence had continued since the landing and Mestasis wondered if a part of her had given up. Abysme's communication with Alpha Blue surprised her, sending jolts of optimism through her veins. At least her sister cared enough to check on the exploration team. But the illogical nature of the message concerned her. Why would her sister put any goal above obtaining an alternate energy source? On top of that, Abysme had given the irrational order without consulting her, thereby defying the Guide.

Bysme?

Her silence reminded Mestasis of when the mainframe froze due to information overload. She waited, each second pulling at her nerves.

Bysme's forehead wrinkled. *The beacon points directly to a matching device. Identification must be made to ensure safety of crew.*

Mestasis thought upon her sister's response. It was a phenomenal coincidence the planet they landed on had a matching alien artifact to the one on their control deck. She calculated the odds with an astonishing conclusion, making her all the more uneasy.

Yes, but we need energy. Alpha Blue's mission cannot be compromised.

Bysme's head jerked, wires twitching. *Negative. Nature of object must be revealed before any colonization efforts are secured.*

Mestasis paused. They'd never argued about mission objectives in the past. But then again, the Guide had set their course in a straight line from Old Earth to Paradise 18. The comets had forced them to break all the rules, and the lines of right and wrong had blurred.

For the thousandth time, Mestasis contemplated the threat level of the alien artifact. The orb illuminated the corner of their control chamber, bathing their torsos in mystical light. She'd never liked it, and her gut instinct had kept her close enough to keep her eye on the sparkling surface, but far enough to form a barrier, blocking its enticement. Abysme had taken control of monitoring the orb, and she hadn't mentioned it in a long time, until after they'd landed, until she thought it was gone.

Mestasis's mind prodded the wires connecting to the orb, traveling the path she'd long feared. She had to learn the nature of what lurked in its misty depths. Her mind crawled toward it, climbing the tendrils it had thrust into the control room floor. The presence of the light loomed like a quasar in her subconscious, its rays reaching to engulf her. Fear crossed her heart in a slash and she fought against it. She forced her mind open, allowing the warmth in.

≈×≶

Her hand reached out, fingers wiggling, all five of them, healthy and pink with heat. They moved in the air, dragging swirls of dust through a patch of sunlight. The golden swirls dispersed and she entwined her fingers in ringlets of dark hair, loosening knots, smoothing, and braiding into three thick strands. Euphoria bubbled through her as she moved again, feeling the world beyond her fingertips. Mestasis smelled the familiar scent of burnt plastic from the recycling factory mingling with a whiff of cheap, synthetic peach perfume. A lullaby drifted to her ears, sung in the alto voice, calming her like no one else ever could.

The stars are too many to count.

The stars make sixes and sevens.

The stars tell nothing—

And everything.

The stars look scattered.

Stars are so far away

They never speak when spoken to.

Regret panged in her gut, followed by a deep wave of melancholy and the urge to set things right. Mestasis ached to exist in the cosmic swirls forever, to forget her fragmented body and her cold existence attached to a computer mainframe. Just as she clung to the memory, her imaginary fingers slipped, and the fabric of light, air, and touch dissolved. The vision faltered, the orb only strong enough to hint at the world it held inside.

≈∽

She pulled herself away, tearing her heart in the process, leaving a primary component of herself behind. The cold ship came back, regulated air blowing on her torso, wires plunging into her limbs. But Mestasis would never be the same.

The orb held a memory of her mother.

CHAPTER THIRTEEN
ICE

Gemme smoothed her fingers over Brentwood's sleep cocoon. The thermal fabric smelled like his minty aftershave mingled with a husky, manly tinge. Curiosity overwhelmed her. She buried her face into the fabric and thought about the warmth of his arms.

Emotions swirled through her in a blizzard. The more she tried to squelch them, the more they raged inside her, and she became more obsessed with him than ever. These feelings were no simple equations to figure out or string of numbers to analyze. They made no logical sense, and that scared her more than any tentacled beast or ice planet. She wanted to dash as far away from him as possible until she regained her rational mind, but she also ached to rush into his arms and kiss the strong angles of his face.

Tech had placed her boots and coat on a container by the tent flap. An hour had passed since they'd left her, and she needed to stand up and do something. Her feet tingled with feeling and some soreness. She reached out for her boots and slipped them on, relishing the way the fur inside nestled her toes. Thankfully the beast hadn't stolen them as well. She didn't know what she'd do without her miniscreen, and she'd miss the picture of her and Ferris. But, thanks to Brentwood, she was alive and not some frozen chunk of ice on the ocean floor.

Gemme emerged from the tent into the brisk wind. The rest of Alpha Blue had already packed most of camp. The remnants of their fire melted a crater into the ice, and footprints littered the site like twisting footpaths to nowhere. Tech stood next to the landrover securing the cables around the mining rig. Where was Brentwood?

"Ms. Reiner, you're up! Feeling better?" He didn't even call her a name this time, which meant his concern outweighed his sarcasm. Gemme would have appreciated his kindness more if she hadn't felt as though she had missed something.

She scanned the camp. With the two remaining tents fluttering in the wind, it seemed so abandoned and empty. She walked up to Tech. "Where's the Lieutenant?"

His eyebrows rose. "I saw him go over that snow mound with Luna."

"Oh." Her chest tightened. What could they possibly have to talk about again? The snow samples? Or was she still complaining about the Seers' choices? Why did they choose such a secluded spot? Part of her wanted to climb the snow to spy, and part of her was too disgusted to care.

She tried to remain logical and conceal her disappointment. "Thanks, Tech."

"I'm sure he'll be back soon. If you want me to get him—"

"No, no, no." To have Tech interrupt their private meeting just because she wanted to know where he was would be momentously embarrassing. She waved him back. "I have to pack up anyways."

"Okey dokers. Let me know if you need any help."

"Thanks."

She dragged her feet to her own collapsed tent. Goop congealed in icicles on the fabric and her possessions lay scattered in the snow. Slipping on a sheet of black ice, she cursed, wondering if she'd ever get used to walking on surfaces that weren't made out of plastic and chrome. She found her backpack under a section of tent and knelt on the ice, pulling her life back together. She kept thinking of how

Brentwood had saved her. Did he merely perform his job, keeping the team safe, or did he act out of a deeper concern?

Trying to remain logical, Gemme waved the rescue off. She should focus on continuing the mission. Ferris and her parents counted on her to find the mineral source, and that's what she'd do. Anything else distracted her from that cause.

As much as she tried to convince herself not to, Gemme stole glances at the snowdrift. Time seemed to drag on and their prolonged absence stirred up bitterness. As she zipped up the top of her backpack, Luna crested the ridge with a flushed face and windblown hair, looking like she'd just won the Lieutenant's heart.

"My goodness, Gemme, darling. You've slept a good a part of the morning away. I hope you've recovered from your near-death experience."

The derision in her voice made it sound as though Gemme had exaggerated the whole thing. Kicking her tent peg out of the snow, Gemme replied, "I didn't see you chasing it."

"I'd been running all morning."

"Running where?" Gemme scanned the monotonous mounds of snow.

Luna gave her a defensive glare. "For samples, of course."

"Of course."

Gemme kicked another peg, sending the metal rod skimming over the ice. She wished there was a whole line of them to take out her frustration on. Her gaze betrayed her, scanning the top of the snowdrift again. Luna caught her staring.

"I sure the Lieutenant will be back to camp soon, dear." She pulled down the hem of her jumpsuit so the fabric squeezed her curves. "We had important matters to discuss."

Like what? How to avoid doing actual work? Gemme wanted to ask but knew better than to provoke her. She focused her energy on folding her goop-coated tent.

"Ms. Reiner, you're up and walking!"

Gemme turned as Brentwood slid down the hill. He seemed thrown off by something, a faraway look haunting his eyes. She wondered what he and Luna had discussed. An illogical current of anger rose inside her and she crushed it down. What he did with his free time shouldn't concern her. They were on the same team, nothing more.

Gemme watched him closely as he approached, trying to spy any feelings he had for Luna in his bright eyes.

"Are you okay?" His voice sounded too familiar as his brow rose with concern. Brentwood's presence ripped a vulnerable hole in her heart and she pretended to be more interested in stuffing the tent into a holding bag.

"I'm fine."

All that time she waited for Brentwood to show up, and now she wished he'd disappear. Gemme couldn't trust her emotions. They changed every minute, fickle as the wind. Right now his overprotectiveness made her feel like his helpless little sister. She could take care of herself. She was an independent, smart, professional woman. She refused to let her feelings for him get in the way, or let this mission intimidate her, no matter how much it fell out of her expertise.

As her thoughts heated up, she struggled to jam the fabric in with blistery, red fingers. Brentwood took up the other end and the length of the tent slid into place.

"How are your feet?"

She wiggled her toes in her boots. Thanks to him she still had toes, but she was too frustrated with him to acknowledge it. "They're swollen, but they're not falling off."

"Good."

She zipped up one side of the tent bag as he zipped the other. Their fingers met in the middle and his hand brushed against hers.

"Sorry." He smiled, not looking sorry at all.

Gemme's heart thudded like a heavy drum in her chest. The snow moved underneath her feet, and she wondered how the meager beat of her heart could cause such a disturbance. The pounding grew louder, reverberating deep inside her gut, and she realized it came from the snowy hills behind them. She whirled around with Brentwood, scanning the horizon.

"What is it?"

His hand still rested on hers and he squeezed, warming her fingers.

"I don't know, but it can't be good."

Shapes dotted the horizon, first a few, and then a whole army. The urge to move bubbled up inside her, but she froze, watching the shapes grow larger with a morbid curiosity as the rumbling grew louder.

"It's more of them!" Luna shouted, backing up to her tent. Gemme wondered which "them" she referred to before recognizing the now familiar hide of tentacles as the first one approached.

She turned to Brentwood. "What should we do?"

"Take cover!" he shouted over to Tech and Luna. Tech jumped into the landrover, and Luna ducked inside her tent.

Gemme looked down at her folded tent. They didn't have enough time to reconstruct it, and she wasn't sure it would deter the beasts anyways. She turned to run toward the landrover just as the first wave of beasts stomped through camp. As first, she thought they'd eat them alive, but as the beasts passed, it seemed they were more interested in escape.

The flow of hides eddied around the two remaining tents and the landrover, blocking them from shelter. Their jaws clacked as they ran, as if to scare away anything in their path.

"There's nowhere to go." Panic rippled out to Gemme's limbs, her fingers shaking. She felt naked, vulnerable, her body fragile compared to their sheer numbers and mass of writhing appendages. Brentwood threw his arms around her and pulled her close.

"Hold on. Don't move."

Together they stood against the horde. Tentacles brushed her back and arms, and Gemme held on tightly, wrapping her arms around Brentwood's torso. She'd faced the end of the world before with Brentwood by her side, and she'd do it again. Wondering how fate always threw them together, Gemme closed her eyes and held on.

At least Tech made it to the landrover. At least someone will continue on toward the hyperthium.

She tried not to think about how it would feel to be trampled by hundreds of paws. Whirring cries droned around them. The beasts plunged ahead and she wondered what they were running from.

The mass passed them quickly, leaving only a few weaker stragglers scrambling through camp. Relief weakened her knees as

Gemme realized they'd made it through. She looked up at Brentwood, but he was focused on the rest of the team.

"Ms. Legacy, are you all right?"

Her tent stood with three pegs loose, the fabric on the verge of collapse. No matter how much the biologist irritated Gemme, dread stabbed her in the gut with the thought of Luna hurt. Even though she fantasized about Luna pricking her finger to stay behind and having tentacles poke through her lush golden hair, Gemme realized the value of every life on the *Expedition*, including Luna's. They couldn't afford to lose anyone, not one strand of DNA, especially women of reproductive age. Of all people, she—the former Matchmaker—should know.

Brentwood released Gemme and sped toward the tent. Shock ran through her body as she watched and waited, smoothing over the places where the tentacles brushed her arms. Apprehension twittered inside her like the wings of a hundred moths batting against the lights in the biodome.

Brentwood threw himself down by the tent's opening, shouting Luna's name. As he fumbled with the zipper, the back flap popped open. Luna crawled out, eyes glazed over.

"She's here!" Gemme shouted at him, plunging forward into the snow. "She's all right."

Gemme offered her arm and Luna latched on, fingers shaking. As she pulled her up, Brentwood joined them. He reached out to Luna, but when he saw Gemme holding her, he withdrew his arm. "Ms. Legacy, are you all right?"

"Fine as anyone would be after getting trampled by sticky elephant jellyfish."

He laughed and Gemme wondered if she saw more concern in his eyes for Luna than he he'd had for her. Maybe she imagined the extra sparkle or the quirk of his lips, or maybe he really did have feelings for her.

A primal roar echoed over the hinterland, awakening a fear in Gemme that felt like centuries in the making, when the very first humans roamed prehistoric Earth. Her head jerked up, adrenaline coursing through her veins.

Luna's head snapped up, "What's that?"

Gemme huffed, still steaming from her thoughts. "You're the biologist."

"Something must have provoked their exodus." As Brentwood spoke, Gemme realized she didn't want to know who or what it was.

"Sounds like the laundro machines on overdrive." Luna released Gemme's arm and cringed behind the tent, leaving her to face whatever came at them. The pounding accelerated, rumbling the earth so hard an icicle fell off of Luna's tent and shattered in the snow.

"Grab what you can!" Brentwood urged Gemme in the direction of the landrover. "Let's get out of here."

"What about my tent?" Luna complained as Gemme jogged to her backpack and tent bag. "All my things, my samples —"

"Leave them." The finality in Brentwood's voice made Gemme's heart skip and she quickened her pace.

Thankfully, she'd already packed her belongings. As Gemme stuck her arm through the straps of her backpack and tent bag, another pounding racked the snow beneath their feet, making her stumble. This time it came in rhythmic thuds, like four giant hooves clomped down on the tundra. Another thunderous wail resounded over the mountains behind them.

Brentwood shouted, "Go!"

Gemme sprinted to the landrover, looking back over her shoulder to make sure Brentwood and Luna followed. Her gear weighed her down, but she had a head start and reached the hatch before they did. She threw her bags in and turned around. Her knees gave out as a mountainous shape claimed the horizon.

She squinted, making out massive, hairy shoulders, a crown of tusks poking the sky and trailing down between two enormous black eyes to a curved snout. The beast was four times bigger than their landrover and closing the distance to them fast.

"Run!" Gemme screeched.

Luna stumbled over her own feet, bringing Brentwood down with her. Gemme watched in agony as she slowed their progress and Brentwood pulled her forward, half carrying her to the landrover. The alien-mammoth charged behind them, stirring up a cloud of snow in its wake.

Strong hands pulled her backward and she realized Tech yanked her in.

"We've got to wait for them." She batted his hands away, but his grip held firm.

"I know. But we've got to save time. And you're safer inside."

Judging from the size of one of the beast's legs, she didn't think so. But she took Tech's advice all the same. She wished she could make Brentwood and Luna run faster. Waiting, nerves on a razor edge, precious seconds dragged like hours.

Tech climbed over the seat and revved the engines. The landrover roared, then sputtered out.

"Damn prototype." Tech hit the dashboard with his fist and tried again. The engines screamed as the tires lurched forward. Gemme grabbed his shoulder. "You have to wait!"

"I'm just gaining momentum. This hunk of junk's sat in the loading bay for a hundred years. Who knows if it will work when we need it to?"

"Looks like it's working now." As the vehicle accelerated, Gemme held out her hand.

"Come on!"

Brentwood handed Luna to her. Gemme grabbed Luna's arm and the biologist teetered on the platform, her toes on and her heels dangling. Gemme tugged with all her weight and pulled her in, thinking Luna weighed more than she looked. Luna collapsed on the floor, heaving as the landrover gained speed and Brentwood sprinted to catch up.

"You're going too fast!" But even as Gemme yelled at Tech, she knew it was the only way to keep them and the mining equipment safe.

She reached out for Brentwood, stretching so far she thought her arm would rip off in the wind. Her fingers brushed his, and he fell back. Behind him, the lumbering beast gained, its steaming breath pluming at Brentwood's neck.

If he stumbled and fell, the clawed paws would squash him to death. Gemme's heart sped against her chest as if it would burst through her skin and run away. She shoved her boot underneath the seat and leaned out over the rushing snow, bracing herself against the landrover's hull.

"Grab my arm!"

The hairs on the alien-mammoth's back moved of their own accord, twirling through the air toward Brentwood. His chest heaved as he leaped forward to stay out of their grasp. He grasped Gemme's arm and she clamped her fingers down around his wrist. The beast's stench overwhelmed the landrover, smelling of musky sweat and dank, moldy fur. The hairs on its back extended like a thousand arms and Brentwood ducked. The strands missed his head by millimeters.

"Pull me back in!" Gemme shouted over her shoulder, doubting Luna could hear anything over the engines. She'd lost feeling in her boot, and she wondered how long her ankle would hold before it snapped.

Brentwood grabbed her torso with his other arm. He clung to her, his legs skidding against the snow. She wrapped her arms around him and held him tightly as the mammoth hair wrapped itself around his ankles, traveling up his legs. The beast yanked and Brentwood rose up, slipping from her grasp.

Gemme shot him a fierce glance, daring him not to give up. "Hold on."

His grip tightened around her as he kicked at the strands. A piece of thermal fabric from his leg ripped off, freeing him.

Gemme yelled, "Now!"

Luna pulled her in, and Gemme gained footing in the landrover. She yanked, every muscle in her arms screaming. Brentwood fell on top of her on the floor, his weight pressing against her chest. Behind them, the hairs probed the air where he'd hung. Luna yelled at Tech, "Close the hatch!"

Tech slammed his fist down and the hatch lowered, blocking out the raging wind. She looked up at Brentwood, silence ringing in her ears. "You okay?"

He nodded, panting. "You saved my life."

Gemme smiled and quirked an eyebrow, trying to disregard the fact that he lay on top of her. "Guess we're even now, huh?"

"Yeah, but it's not over yet." Brentwood pulled himself off her and raised his voice, addressing Tech. "Open the upper hatch."

"What?" Luna shouted as she belted herself in the seat next to Tech. "Are you crazy?"

"We're not going to outrun it."

Luna twisted in her seat to confront him. "What are you going to do, ask it politely to leave us alone?"

"No." He pulled two lasers from his belt, handing one to Gemme. "We're going to drive it back."

The laser felt heavy and cold in Gemme's hand as she wrapped her fingers around it. She'd never used one in her life. Ferris had always wanted to take her to the firing range, but she'd told him a data analyst would have no use for it.

Boy was she wrong.

The hatch lifted and Brentwood climbed the seat. He stood on the head cushions, his torso poking out of the vehicle. Gemme joined him, emerging from the safety of the cabin back into the furious wind. Her hair whipped around her face and her eyes watered so much the snowflake-filled sky blurred. The beast towered over them, hairs squirming wildly. The strands rose up above their heads as its tusked snout snapped, teeth grating.

Brentwood started firing. Gemme gripped the laser in her hand and shouted, "Where do I aim?"

"Anywhere."

She clicked the safety off and pulled the trigger just as Tech swerved. The landrover bumped her backward. A shaft of light careened over the ice, nowhere near the beast. She flailed her arms, clutching onto the hatch.

"Nice shot!"

She couldn't tell if Brentwood was being sarcastic or encouraging. After all, she was a computer analyst turned ice world explorer. For someone that had sat at a desk her whole life, she thought she was doing pretty well.

She regained her footing and fired again. Each shot disappeared into the beast's gigantic hide as if they fired water drops at a lake. She aimed for its black eyes, its tusks, its toothy mouth, but nothing seemed to slow it down. The beast roared and the sound reverberated in her stomach, curdling the soy wafer she'd stuffed down that morning.

Gemme shouted over the wind, "We're making it mad."

Brentwood continued to fire. "We've got to do something."

The mammoth's head swung sideways and the beast hit the mining equipment with its crown of tusks, ivory piercing metal. The wheels on the right side came off the ground, and for a moment, Gemme thought they'd all crash into one big heap. Brentwood pulled her over to his side.

"Shift your weight."

Somehow, Tech rebalanced, and the wheels fell back onto the ice.

"That's it. I have another plan." Brentwood stopped firing and climbed on top of the landrover.

"What are you doing?" Gemme screamed her voice hoarse, scrambling to catch his arm.

He slipped from her grip. "I'm going to stop it. Just keep firing."

She watched in terror as Brentwood balanced on the metal bridge connecting the landrover with the platform of the mining rig. The landrover hit a bump, and he pitched forward, sprawling in the air before landing on the drill.

Gemme yelled down into the landrover, "Watch where you're driving. Brentwood's on the drill."

"Damned snow mounds come up outta nowhere," Tech yelled back.

She heard Luna ask him, "Are you trained to drive this thing?"

Tech didn't reply, or she didn't hear him. Either way, Gemme guessed his answer was no.

She poked her head back out, chancing a peek. Brentwood clung to the drill, pressing open the control panel and Gemme realized what he planned to do. His fingers flew over the touchscreen and Gemme waited for the drill to spin, but nothing happened. Someone tugged her leg and she ducked her head back in.

"He needs the key." Tech handed Luna a plastic card and Luna slipped it to Gemme.

"What am I supposed to do?" Gemme thought about throwing it to him, but with the wind, they'd probably lose it forever.

"You'll have to climb on there with him." Luna spoke as if she suggested Gemme join him for afternoon tea.

Biting a retort, Gemme stuck her head back out of the upper hatch. The hairs had wrapped around the drill, and the beast pulled, slowing the landrover down. The tires skidded against the friction.

Gemme slipped the card into her pocket and took a deep breath. *You can do this.*

She climbed on the roof and crawled toward the bridge using the top luggage bars as handholds. Underneath her, the snow sped away, crushed by the gigantic tires of the mining rig. If she slipped, she'd be a pancake.

Brentwood waved her back, but she lowered herself down the curve of the rear and cajoled herself into taking the first step on the bridge. Narrow enough to only walk one foot in front of the other, she balanced by holding out both arms.

She felt as though she flew on thin air as she lifted one foot, precariously poised on the other like some Old Earth tight-rope walker. A layer of ice had formed on the metal, and she probed each step with her boot before placed her full weight down. Tears froze on her cheeks, and her ears throbbed. Her lower lip split open, warm blood trickling down her chin.

You're halfway there. Keep going.

She'd never been the most graceful in her class, and now each step counted. The wind ripped through her and she leaned into it, hoping the gale wouldn't blow her away. Her breath hitched in her throat as she ran the last few steps and collapsed on the mining platform, bruising both her shins.

"What are you doing out here?" Brentwood shouted, clinging to the control console and firing up at the alien-mammoth's head.

Gemme reached in her pocket and brought out the keytag. Brentwood's eyes widened with recognition. Ignoring her aching muscles, she climbed toward him, grasping any hold she could find. He reached out and grabbed her hand, pulling her toward him. Together they gripped the keytag as if it were humanity's last hope and stuck it in the console.

The screen below them lit up as the mammoth-hair tightened its grip. The mammoth slammed down its hind legs and the engines revved as the tires screeched. The smell of burnt rubber tainted the air. A sense of sickening dread spread over Gemme as she fell into the mammoth's shadow. The beast would pummel their equipment and swallow them whole.

Gemme grabbed his shoulder. "Quickly, before we stop."

Brentwood pressed the code and the drill hummed to life, turning slowly at first. The hairs stretched until the drill ripped them out and blue-black blood sprayed over them. The beast roared, its foul breath steaming the air around Gemme. The landrover took off and she and Brentwood fell backward onto the metal grating.

He shot up and raised his laser to fire, but the mammoth collapsed on its front legs, a bald patch where the hair had been seeping blood onto the snow. It clawed at the ground, trying to gain footing, but it was losing too much blood. After a few staggering steps, the beast fell on its side.

Even though the alien-mammoth would have killed them and jeopardized the entire mission of the *Expedition*, Gemme felt sorry for its death. This planet was its home, and they were the alien invaders. Heck, they'd probably send the entire species into extinction in the next hundred years if they followed the ways of Old Earth.

"Good job, Ms. Reiner. Although I'm sad to see such a majestic animal dead, it was necessary." Brentwood shut off the drill and offered his hand and helped her up. The intensity in his eyes made her cheeks burn against the frigid air and she looked away.

"Nothing any ordinary data analyst wouldn't do."

"Trained for this in your graduate classes along with differential quantitative analysis?"

"Certainly, didn't you?" She couldn't believe the humor in her voice, especially after such a dangerous turn of events. Brentwood coaxed it out of her, calming her. With him she wasn't a boring, uptight computer analyst.

They watched in silence as the landrover circled the beast. As the vehicle ground to a halt, Gemme jumped off the platform. Covering her nose from the metallic reek of blood, she studied the beast. Some of the remaining hairs still twitched, spiraling out into the snow around it. She stared at its black eye, the pupil larger than her head. How many years had it lived on this planet before the beast met its end with humans? Did she really want to know?

Brentwood followed her, still holding up his laser. When she gave him a questioning look, he shrugged. "You can never be too careful."

Luna and Tech stumbled out of the landrover, gawking.

Gemme gestured to Luna. "How's that for a specimen?"

CHAPTER FOURTEEN
PRIORITIES

Vira's sleep pod opened before her alarm went off, revealing her dad's smiling face haloed in the automatic wake-up light.

"Rise and shine, peaches."

She rubbed her eyes, feeling as though her head was still stuck in dreams. "What time is it?"

He checked the digital clock on the lid of her pod. "I have an hour before I need to go to work. Let's see what we can do about getting you a new hoverchair."

"Really?" Excitement bubbled inside her. A new hoverchair would mean not asking Rizzy to lug her around all the time or having raw elbows from spending so much time on the carpet. Plus, she loved spending time with her dad alone.

"You bet."

He bent down and she climbed on his back, wrapping her arms around his neck. "Mom's made some breakfast if you want to take a minute to eat."

Eagerness rushed through her as if the world would end before she got her chair. "No. Let's go now. I'll eat when I come home."

"Okay." Her dad bounced her on his back, making her giggle as he carried her into the kitchen.

Her mom looked up from stirring some awful, sludgy oatmeal. "Who needs a chair when you have a ride like that, eh?"

Vira laughed, but her dad responded in a serious tone, "She needs her independence, Natalie. When I was her age, it would have driven me crazy to sit in the same spot all day."

"You were a little hellion."

He kissed her mom on the cheek. "I still am."

Laughing, they took off toward the engineering bay.

Dim emergency lights lit the corridor, and the air stung even colder than in their family unit. Vira tightened her grip, glad for her dad's warmth underneath her. She didn't feel like laughing any more. The ship was spookier than the last time she'd gone out, tracking Rizzy and Daryl before the crash. At least then the lights shone brightly, and the temperature was a steady seventy-two degrees. "When will the regular lights come back on?"

"As soon as the away team finds an alternate energy source. Don't worry; they're working on it right now. Pretty soon things will be back to normal."

Vira didn't think anything would be normal ever again. Not only were they not in space, but the Seers weren't the people she thought they were. Her dad's blind faith disturbed her.

"What if the Seers didn't want to help?"

"Nonsense." He craned his neck to see her eye to eye. "They're doing the best they can. It's their job to keep everyone safe."

And scare little girls while they were at it?

Vira opened her mouth to disagree when her dad pointed up ahead. "Here we are, Engineering Bay Six."

They passed flickering lights and ventilation tubes wheezing stale air. The portal to the engineering bay lay open, the panel fizzling like it had short-circuited. As they walked in, her stomach sank like the ship when it crashed. A line of people wrapped all the way around the room while workers scrambled behind the desk taking requests. Some of them looked like they hadn't changed clothes in days. The man standing in front of them wore a bandage around his head. Vira squirmed as she thought about his wound.

They'd never get to the front in an hour.

He cut right through two older women holding broken ionizers. They gave him a dirty look, making her so embarrassed she hid her face in his shoulder. He whispered, "Don't worry. I know the man in charge."

Her dad carried her behind the main desk to rows of machines in the back, where workers wore welding masks and used strange tools that wheezed in high-pitched noises, making her want to cover her ears. But, she couldn't because her arms were busy holding her onto her dad's back. The tangy smell of oil and chemicals tickled her nose.

A man wearing an upper officer's uniform walked in between two large pressing machines spewing sparks and her dad waved to get his attention. "Harris."

The man smiled and shuffled over, stepping through discarded metal on the floor.

"How's it going, Al? Your team holding up?"

"Yes, yes. We're doing fine. We've got the heating systems back online. Now it's a matter of waiting for the energy to start the core."

"I hear ya. I know it's hard, but the Seers' conservation methods are wise. We don't know how long it will take for Alpha Blue to find what we need."

Her dad patted her hand on his shoulder. "Hey, you know anything about the status of my daughter's new hoverchair?"

Harris gave him a wary look, making Vira feel bad she'd come to annoy him. "We're doing the best we can, but we have to work on the ship's maintenance systems first."

The muscles in her dad's neck tightened under her arms. "How much longer?" His voice grew hard and intense, like when he caught Rizzy sneaking out past curfew.

Harris's eyes flicked to Vira and then he looked away, as if it bothered him to look at her. His voice softened. "Look, to tell you the truth, she's at the bottom of the list. The Seers instructed us to finish the more promising projects, the ones that will benefit the overall colonization effort."

Her dad's skin turned red. "I see what you're saying and I'm sick of hearing about how my daughter isn't worthwhile." He jabbed his finger in the man's chest. "Let me tell you, she's brighter than half the engineers you have working here right now, and someday she'll—"

"Dad, that's enough. You're embarrassing me." Vira squeaked, surprising herself with how loud her voice was. The room quieted, and she felt all eyes staring at her like lasers. But, she didn't want her dad losing friends because of her. Her family had already suffered enough because of her disability.

Harris's face turned red, "Al, I'm just following orders."

"Sure. As we all are." He waved his hand in the air, dismissing him as he turned. "Come on, Vira. We'll find another way to get you around."

He pushed through the line. People averted their eyes like they always did when she passed, trying not to stare. Whispers followed them into the corridor.

Her dad rubbed his face and took a few deep breaths, as if trying to calm down. "I'm sorry, peaches. They just don't see how special you are."

"It's okay." She patted his shoulder, wishing he'd just think of her as a normal girl. All this attention made her worry that they'd see her real powers, and what then? No, she had to blend in more, and not having a hoverchair just made it worse. If those people couldn't rebuild it for her, then she'd just have to make one herself.

CHAPTER FIFTEEN
CHOICES

All Mestasis wanted to do was dive back into the orb. The feeling consumed her, eating her alive until she could think of nothing else. A tiny voice nagged her senses, and she pulled back from the orb, annoyed until she saw what it was: the latest causality report sent by the head nurse from the emergency bay.

Mestasis watched the names fly by like fallen stars. So many combinations of DNA lost, such a great chunk of diversity gone in one day. Failure overwhelmed her, and guilt seeped in as she thought of her selfish desire to return to the orb.

Three out of the four lieutenants had died, leaving only Miles Brentwood. Thank goodness he was the most promising one, and the leader of Alpha Blue. She'd appointed him to that position herself with no doubt of his abilities. Rereading their latest status report, she hoped the team found the energy source quickly.

The flicker of the orb distracted her. The recent reminder of her mom brought up so many memories. She'd fought to keep them buried for years and succeeded, but in the past few days they'd crept in like insidious fingers, wrapping around her brain. Seeing her mom in the orb was the last push, opening the tomb that held everything dear to her heart.

Mestasis closed her working eye and succumbed to sleep.

ॐ≪

Old Earth, 2446

You're not coming home with me, are you? Abysme stood with her hands on her hips, her long black braids falling across each shoulder to her slender waist. Behind her, the city towers of New York dazzled in a thousand pricks of light. Hovercrafts whizzed by as a lunar freighter landed on the adjacent building, loaded with minerals from the moon.

Mestasis clicked off the golden swirls on the holoscreen and their room darkened, shadows concealing her face. She knew this conversation had to happen, but the hair on her arms rose with apprehension.

I still have so much work to do, and the assessments are less than a week away.

This is the only time we have to see her. There's room on the hovercraft for both of us. I bought two tickets.

Mestasis slumped into the couch, feeling the cool plastic stick on her sweaty skin. *Next time.*

Her sister's lips curled. *Metsy, it's been years.*

Had it? She couldn't remember. Immersed in developing and honing her psychic skills at TINE, she had no time to relax and reflect on her life.

Dr. Fields wants complete cognitive electromagnetic control by graduation. We need to work harder.

Abysme pressed her hand against the wall and the lights flickered on. *We're doing the best we can. Can't he see that? We need to have a life, too, you know. We have obligations to Mom.*

Our obligations are to TINE. Who do you think pays for this high-rise apartment complete with real grown food and running water?

Abysme threw her hand up in the air. *Fine, they can have it back. I'd rather live in poverty with Mom.*

And be afraid of making rent each month, of being thrown out into the gangs?

I'm afraid our life will go by, Metsy, and we'll lose all the important moments, the reason for living in the first place.

Life can wait. Mestasis pointed out the window at the dark craters on the moon, where mining teams had stripped the surface bare. *What's going to happen when they run out of lunar REE and thorium? With the economy tanking, only the brightest and most talented will survive. Don't you see? A better life's around the corner and we're almost there.*

I don't know how you can live here with your ripe tomatoes and warm showers while Mom suffers alone.

Mestasis sighed, wishing TINE would house immediate family members along with its students. Their mom worked so hard all the time and had no money for a pass to visit them in the upper levels. Although they sent their mom food, she wanted to save all three of them, to acquire enough fortune for a rooftop flat with their own greenhouse. That was the only dream she allowed herself to foster all these years. Going back now would only distract her, making it harder to complete the final tests. How could her sister risk their future?

I can't go back. Not now, not when our graduation is so close. Don't you understand? I'm working for both of us.

Did you ever consider what I wanted?

What Abysme wanted and what was best for her were two different things. Mestasis couldn't allow her sister to choose. Besides, TINE needed them as a pair, and if Abysme left, she'd be wrecking all their futures, their mother included. She ignored her sister's question.

Promise me you'll come back.

Abysme gave her the guarded look of a caged lioness. Her mindspeak tone was bitter. *You know I always keep my word.*

Mestasis ground her fingernails into the plastic couch, making five crescent marks above the seam. She hated how she kept her sister prisoner, that she needed Abysme as much as Abysme needed her. Their close, symbiotic relationship was both a blessing and a bane. She wanted to tell her sister how much she loved her, but bitterness came out instead.

Go have fun. I'll be here, practicing, doing all the work.

Abysme didn't answer. She picked up her bags and slipped out before Mestasis had a chance to offer a real good-bye. Emptiness ached inside her and she felt abandoned, alone. Guilt trickled through her as she thought of Bysme and her mom sitting on their tattered couch in the lower levels, thinking about how *if only Metsy had come*. The three of them would be together again. One unit, a perfect whole.

She flicked on her holoscreen, burying herself in work, which was what she was good at anyway. Placing a hand on the screen, her thoughts of her mother drifted away. She pressed against the cold surface and concentrated. The electromagnetic pulses rode through her, tingling in her arms and legs. She could reach out and touch all the walls in the hundred and fifty story building. She knew on floor sixty-four, Suite A, someone had turned on an air ionizer, and on floor eighty-seven, Suite F, the coffee machine beeped.

Dr. Field's eager face flashed in her mind. Listening to coffee machines wasn't good enough. Mestasis's head throbbed as she struggled to redefine her parameters, searching for different forms of radioactive and electromagnetic waves. Being alone gave her a desperate focus, and she stretched her powers beyond the electromagnetic devices for the first time, breaching a boundary previously holding her back. She detected the presence of infrared rays given off by people. She pushed harder traveling from ray to ray in a continuous spectrum, manipulating the entire world around her.

Mestasis grinned in triumph. She'd just brought her abilities to a new level. Dr. Fields would be impressed. Using her new talent, she scanned each deck, noting any anomalies for the report. He'd want proof and it had to be exact.

One particular spot on floor twenty-one caught her attention. The heat signature produced by the thermal radiation indicated a being much smaller than a person, but two times larger than a pigeon. Besides the agricultural towers, animals had all but gone extinct. People needed the dwindling resources much more than pets. She pushed further, and an image of soft fur danced in her mind.

An animal huddled in the corner of an abandoned floor.

Mestasis froze, unwilling to believe it just as a slim ribbon of hope floated up from her heart.

She checked again. The small body had wedged itself into a pipeline. Nothing else emitted a heat signature in the room.

She had to save it.

The animal may be the only one she'd ever see and it needed her. How could she let such a helpless endangered species die? She paused, noting how low floor twenty-one was, well past the security guards, right in the middle of gangland.

She scanned her empty apartment. Abysme wasn't there to stop her, and loneliness had slowly worked its way into her heart. TINE would never let her have it, but they didn't have to know.

Mestasis stared at the door, and the plastic moved into the frame in two halves, revealing the dimly lit corridor where her sister had exited. TINE employees and students rushed by her, running to tests and meetings. She slipped down the hall, avoiding anyone's eye. Dr. Fields would ask about Abysme, and she'd have to cover, like always. Even though he wasn't psychic, someday he'd see through her lies. At least now she had a new development to offer him, something to keep them at the institute and perhaps land a future job.

Crossing the checkpoint, she flashed her ID card to the armed guards. They took one look at her status and pressed the door panel, allowing her through to the lower levels. Dr. Fields expected a lot of them, but they weren't prisoners at TINE. Mestasis made sure of that when she signed them up nine years ago.

The elevator only worked down to floor twenty-five. It slowed to a halt, the door sliding open to reveal a corridor lit by flickering fluorescent lights, half the blubs shattered. She stepped off, feeling a chill creep around her. The ventilation system didn't bother to drive heat down this far, and any warmth rose to the upper levels. Mestasis suppressed a doubt, thinking of the endangered animal. She wished her powers worked as a superhero defense. She could flicker lights, turn off a coffee machine, and tell who stood in the next room. Not enough to make a tough-as-steel gang member shake in his laser holsters.

Kicking in an old-style door with a broken metal knob, she found a staircase. She'd have to climb down the remaining four flights. Slowly stepping over the debris cluttering each step, she worked her way down. Her heel stumbled over a used light stick, snapping the plastic in two, the energy cell leaking acid on the concrete. Skirting the hazardous mess, she reached a platform in between levels and kicked a doll's head, its blue eyes opening as it bounced down each stair below her. Wincing, she waited for any sign of movement, pressing her palm against the cold concrete wall. No heat signatures registered until two floors below her, just the small huddled fur ball.

She emerged on a long-deserted factory platform. Derelict machinery cast menacing shadows around her. Stripped for parts by the gangs, the frames lay gutted. After the contractors added the higher levels, the fortunate abandoned the lower floors, each generation reaching to a sky free of smog and enough sunlight to grow food. The transport ships delivering goods and fuel only landed on top of the high rises. By the time things reached level one, there wasn't much left.

She tiptoed through the dust, leaving light footprints. The animal must have heard her steps, because a noise she'd only heard as an impersonation from the holoscreen echoed from the back corner of the room. "Meow."

Her heart melted into liquid gold. Mestasis placed both hands on the pipe, jutting out from an old air vent system. Her thoughts warmed the metal with currents of electromagnetic pulses. The nickel turned pliable under her fingertips. She coaxed the shape, drawing out the metal, widening the gap. Reaching down into the hole, she stretched her arm until fur tickled her fingertips. Carefully, she worked the small body out, scratching her arms.

Two golden eyes stared at her with sideways, oval-shaped black retinas, making the dangerous outing worth the reward. Black, white, and gold colors decorated its fur in a mottled pattern, making the kitten the most beautiful creature she'd ever seen. She hugged the tiny body close, smoothing down the fur standing up on end across its back. The animal purred, its head nestling against her.

She turned to the door just as multiple footsteps clanged up the stairway. Mestasis clutched the animal tightly and ducked behind an old plastic assimilator. She peered between the dangling metal arm and the assembly belt. Five young men entered, two carrying a large shipment container. Their hair was infused with neon green phosphorescence, the color of the infamous Radioactive Hand of Justice. They were a group with radical Robin Hood ideals making recent headlines for intercepting shipments from Utopia, the largest greenhouse in New England. What had she gotten herself into?

"Pry the lid." The man's voice cut like a razor through the shadows. Mestasis held her breath and put her hand gently over the kitten's mouth.

Two other men with lanky bodies wearing long black coats and boots strapped with flash tubes lit up the room with their footsteps. They deactivated the code sequence by overriding the manual ID keytag. A fourth man circled the perimeter, his head cocked as if he could hear Mestasis's heart thump in her chest.

She tried to calm herself and think clearly. TINE wouldn't come and look for her until the next day, if she failed to make her appointment with Dr. Fields. She needed help. Reaching out across the city, she focused and redirected her thoughts.

Abysme, can you hear me?

Nothing. Her sister must have blocked the mindspeak channel in her anger, or she'd traveled too far away to reach through thought. Dread ate a hole in her stomach. She was on her own.

The gangmen pulled bags of grapes, apples red as blood, and sacks bulging with potatoes from the container.

"How's this, boss?"

The man surveying the operation nodded, probing a grape between his fingernails. "An exotic fruit shipment. Yes, Quadrant Forty-five will be pleased."

What if they stayed there all night? Mestasis's heart pounded so hard she thought it would bounce right out of her chest and land in the tomatoes. The kitten wiggled in her hands, obviously bored and hungry. She couldn't keep it quiet for much longer.

The lookout spotted something on the floor and dragged a line across her footprints in the dust. His boots flashed as he stepped toward her hiding spot, following her trail to the plastic assimilator.

Mestasis froze, feeling her life on the brink of nonexistence. After witnessing their crime, they'd never let her live. Especially after they found her keytag and learned she worked for a division of the government. She worried about the kitten in her arms. Would they torture it? Would they throw it out the window?

Her hands sweated into its fur as the man eyed the dangling arm of the plastic assimilator. Mestasis ducked, watching through a peephole in the corroded metal frame. He had wide gray eyes like two pieces of steel, silky midnight-black hair tinged with the neon at the tips, and cream-colored skin, much lighter than hers. Too handsome to be a gang member, but that was clearly what he was.

He met her eye, his own gaze flashing with surprise, and her body jolted inside. They froze, locked in each other's gaze.

Please. Mestasis bit into her lower lip. *Please don't turn me in.*

He raised a finger to his thick lips and turned the other way. Mestasis released her breath in disbelief. Gang members were supposed to be ruthless. But curiosity filled that man's eyes instead of a hard edge.

Walking up to the man in charge, the lookout spoke with a soft and smooth voice, "We have to keep moving. We're too high up."

The leader nodded and his lackeys shoved the produce back in the container. "We'll count the rest later."

The lookout's hand rested on his subsonic laser. "I'll keep watch until the men carry the last of the containers down."

"Excellent, James. Don't linger."

The two men who had opened the container bent down and heaved it over their shoulders. The leader turned back to him. "Thank you for your protection."

James nodded, silky black hair tinged with neon falling around his face to block his profile. "I do what I can."

The gang disappeared down the stairs and Mestasis contemplated making a run for it. But the man named James had just saved her life, and she didn't want him calling out to his friends. She waited, listening to their footsteps fade.

"Tell me why I shouldn't turn you in." His voice was more amused than stern.

Mestasis gave up her hiding spot and stepped into the moonlight pouring down through the broken glass. Her body shook in survival mode, every inch of her skin tingling with oversensitivity. She could feel his heat signature from across the room, a strong, manly presence, much sharper than Dr. Fields.

"I'm not a spy. I came to rescue this kitten."

Its furry head popped up out of her uniform and she realized her biggest mistake. She should have changed into civilian clothes before entering the lower levels.

"You're from TINE?" He sounded surprised.

Mestasis kept her voice even despite the tremors spreading throughout her body. "I told you; I'm not here to cause trouble."

He stepped closer and the moonlight illuminated his face. He had a wide forehead and a sharp, broad nose. Despite his good looks, Mestasis had to remind herself he was dangerous.

James crossed his arms, his long cloak rippling behind him. "You're going to let us steal food from your rich friends and not report us?"

"They're not my friends." The venom in her voice surprised her and she bit her lip. James furrowed his dark eyebrows, studying her like a puzzle that refused to be solved.

The way he looked at her, like a spoiled high-rise princess, made anger warm her neck and she spit out her words. "I grew up in the slums, no different than you. I'm only working for TINE to get my family away from gangmen like you."

"Is that how you think of me?" He sounded amused and she wondered if he set a trap.

A kernel of anger hardened inside her. "I recognize your colors. I'm well aware of the Radioactive Hand of Justice."

He shook his head. "I'm trying to help the world, not control it."

"By stealing from the government, enacting your own laws?"

"By making life more fair for the thousands that live in the shadows of those above."

She clamped her lips down with no response. He did have a point. Although it was wrong to steal, the current system failed the majority. The government had cut aid programs before her lifetime, and too many lived in poverty and died of hunger. She was trying to save her mom and sister from those conditions by staying in the system. He was trying to save the world by thinking outside it. In reality, who made the biggest difference?

More footsteps sounded in the stairway and he gestured toward the plastic assimilator. Mestasis crouched down in her old hiding place and he stooped next to her. The room filled with men, their hair singed with red highlights. Spikes poked from their necks, the implants protruding like scales down their backs.

James clenched the metal machine arm in his fist. "Damn, it's the Razornecks."

Mestasis opened her mouth to ask who they were, but the men flooded the room, their rough voices breaking the silence. James put his hand over his laser, but she knew they were outnumbered, even for a weapon of that caliber.

He brought his lips to her ear, his breath tickling her neck. "If they find us, we're dead."

The men spread out, perching on the old equipment. They held strange tubelike glass beverages and watched the room with wild eyes.

Mestasis put a hand up to her mouth, covering a gasp. They were moonshiners, men who drank their problems away with a substance stronger than alcohol. Made from Morpheus, a chemical found on the moon, the substance brought out violence and ate the drinkers from the inside out. Highly addictive, they'd kill to get their hands on anything that would lead them to their next drink.

They became rowdy quickly, standing in a circle punching each other, while the others roamed around the room, destroying what remained of the machines. With gaunt cheeks and dilated pupils, they looked more like ghouls than men. One broad-chested Razorneck sauntered over in their direction. James slipped off his coat, threw it on top of her, and drew his laser.

"Look what we've got here." The burly man approached James with a bar of jagged metal in his hand. "Looks like a green-haired leprechaun, a do-gooder from the Hand of Justice." James stood, hiding Mestasis and she shrank back into the shadows.

Some of his companions chuckled while other spat. "I hate those guys. They think they're helping people out, but they won't share any of their profits with us."

James tightened his grip on the laser growling, "And we never will, you moonshiner crap."

Grunts of protest rang out. Mestasis's throat constricted and she struggled to breathe. She'd just met James, but she was tied to him. He did save her life.

Another one of them shouted, "Bring him here. Put him in the center circle."

James pulled the trigger, but the man had already drunk some of his moonshine, and he moved faster than any normal human. He grabbed the weapon as it flung white light into the ceiling and hauled it up in the air. James, unwilling to let go, dangled from the straps.

Mestasis closed her eyes and focused her energy. Quickly, she placed both hands on the concrete, feeling the electromagnetic pulses of the room around them, the heat signatures, and the remaining working lights. Her consciousness heightened by the impending danger, she'd never experienced so many impulses in her life. She channeled the energy and released it in a strong gush of will. All of the lights in the room flickered on before exploding above their heads, raining shards. The man dropped James, and he recovered quickly, firing warning shots with his laser.

He shouted as he pursued them, "Leave now! All of you."

Their drinks gave off a strange radioactive pulse, and she reversed it, sending it back to each glass tube with twice its force. The glass shattered in their hands, blood spraying everywhere. Cries of fear and rage erupted into the darkness. Disoriented, the men scattered, giving James enough time to work his way back to Mestasis. The gang evacuated the room as quick as they'd come, leaving a sprawling mess of glass and blood in their wake.

James pulled his cloak off her shoulders. "Are you okay?"

Mestasis secured the kitten beneath her shirt and stood, wiping her electrically charged hands on her legs to disperse the extra energy. The room swirled around her and she steadied herself, leaning on the old machine. Her powers receded and she became a normal nineteen year old once again.

Still holding his laser toward the door, James stared at her, gawking. "You did this?"

"Now you know why I work for TINE."

She thought she'd scare him away. Any man her age that was

aware of her powers stayed a clear two-meter radius away from her. But James seemed impressed. "With powers like that, you could rule TINE, never mind work for them."

Mestasis laughed for the first time that day. "I didn't know how strong they were until tonight. Besides, I don't want to rule anything. I just want to have a safe place for my family."

His expression grew serious. "Leave TINE and come join me. We have everything you could ever need: freshly grown food, running water, everything in a vast network underneath the streets."

She smiled. His offer enticed her, because it would provide shelter for her whole family that instant, instead of waiting for years to raise enough money so her mom didn't have to work. But, she could never live the life of a criminal, even if they were fighting for the lower class. She had too much to sacrifice on the higher decks. Her mother would never hear of it, and Abysme wouldn't either.

"Thanks, but I can't."

She moved to leave and he grabbed her hand, his hot fingers warming her skin. His voice was husky. "At least tell me your name."

"Metsy." She slid her hand from his grasp, studying his perfect features in the moonlight. She'd never allowed herself a sliver of romance, and the feelings she'd suppressed rose inside her like hot lava.

"I'm James. James Wilfred."

She started walking, shouting at her feet not to stop. She couldn't allow herself to become attached. "See you later, James. Good luck with your cause."

His voice stopped her as she reached the stairway. "Will I see you again?"

Mestasis froze, one hand on the doorframe. His expectation hung heavy in the air between them. She had to make a choice. She could return to her floor and forget this night ever happened, or she could risk everything to conspire with a renegade. Her conversation with James made Mestasis question how much she really trusted TINE. What if her work failed to land her and her sister successful careers? What if the government shut the program down? What if Abysme's concerns were valid? The world fell apart around them, crumbing a little more with each passing day. It might be useful to have an ally underground. Her feelings screamed inside her, and this time she couldn't ignore them.

"Depends on if you like coffee."

∽◌◠

Mestasis sighed, the memory of James filling every ounce of her body with warmth and making some parts long dead and severed feel again. She could almost wiggle her toes. As the coldness of Tundra 37 seeped back in, reality hit her hard. This frozen planet was the last place she had expected to end up.

CHAPTER SIXTEEN
WOMAN OF HIS DREAMS

"I can't continue this mission without them!" Luna whined from the front seat, reminding Gemme of when five-year-old Ferris wanted to swim in the aqua tanks with the salmon.

Tech revved the engines of the landrover, waiting for a direction from Brentwood. The old engineer had volunteered to take up the wheel, giving the Lieutenant time to rest. "Should we go back?"

Brentwood rubbed his temples and Gemme's heart went out to him. He'd gone through a lot. They all had, and the mission had just begun. "I'm not sure how far we've come escaping that creature, but I bet going back would put us a whole day behind."

Luna twisted her neck to gaze at him from the front seat. She batted her eyelashes and pleaded. "I need them. Code Beta Prime, remember?"

It sounded like nonsense to Gemme, but when Brentwood's face showed recognition, she stared at him in disbelief. Luna spoke as though the two of them had some secret language. Gemme couldn't understand what was so important about chunks of snow and tentacle goo, but she kept her mouth shut. This was Brentwood's decision, not hers.

In a resigned voice, he ordered, "Turn around, Tech."

Tech craned his neck from the front seat to meet Brentwood's eye. "You sure about this, chief?"

"Yes, absolutely." He sat back against the seat and stared out the sight panel, his jaw set in a rigid line. Gemme was tempted to ask him what Beta Prime was all about, but she didn't want to seem nosy, or overly eager for his attentions with some schoolgirl crush. And she didn't want Luna to get the satisfaction of knowing she was curious. They probably wouldn't tell her anyway. She settled into her seat and watched the snowflakes blow against the sight panel, feeling like she'd regressed back to her class years.

Tech brought the landrover in an arc around a jagged outcropping of ice. "What's the big discovery, Luna?"

Luna shifted in her seat. "Ocean life and lots of it."

The old man scoffed. "I don't see any ocean."

"It's below us. We're driving over it as we speak, kilometers of water running underneath the ice. Where do you think all those tentacled elephant jellyfish ran to?"

Gemme shivered at the thought of driving over an ocean with a layer of ice in between. It seemed almost as scary as a chrome hull separating her from deep space. Why did life have to be so precarious?

Tech shrugged. "I don't get it. The scouts said Tundra 37 had little to no known life."

Luna sounded smug. "That's because they never checked below the surface, when the findings lay underneath their feet."

"You mean this forsaken place just might prove a useful habitat in which to live?"

"If we can eat them, yes. That's why I need my sample trays. I'm trying to figure out how compatible their proteins are to our bodies. Yes we need energy, but we also need food to eat, and I don't see any apple trees spouting, or fields of golden wheat."

Golden wheat. Gemme thought back to the strange dreams she'd been having ever since the comets hit. Dreams of Old Earth. They'd seemed so tangible at the time, but sitting in the landrover with Alpha

Team Blue made her dreams feel like gibberish. She was relieved no one else could see what she experienced when she closed her eyes.

"Here we are, home sweet home." Tech parked the landrover and opened the hatch.

Gemme jumped out, stretching her legs. The paws of the alien-mammoth had decimated their camp. Luna's trays of samples lay knocked over, the small vials scattered in the snow. Luna's tent was flattened and torn, the pegs all bent out of shape. Gemme wondered if they'd get their mission accomplished at all, never mind on schedule.

Brentwood surveyed the damage, eyeing his own still standing tent. The strength in his voice gave Gemme hope. "Luna, next stop, you can have my tent. I'll bunk up with Tech. As for the samples, find as many as you can and start packing up. I'd like to leave as soon as possible. If I drive through the night, we can make up for lost time."

Tech spoke up. "I'm going to need someone to help me pry these monster hairs from the drill. I took a look at one of the strands, and the darn things are made of pure muscle. I don't want them clogging our equipment."

"I'll help." Brentwood clasped Tech's shoulder. The two of them walked to the back of the landrover. Hugging her shoulders against the brisk wind, Gemme didn't know where to start.

"Oh my poor samples!" Luna cried as she fell to her knees in the snow.

If Luna spoke the truth, her findings were just as important as the hyperthium. She'd already packed up her own belongings. Gemme sprang forward to help her. At least she'd have a task to accomplish, even if she did have to work with Luna.

Gemme bent down and picked up a broken vial and Luna gave her a questioning glance. "You're going to help me?"

Gemme shrugged. "Sure."

"Great. Thanks a million, Gemme, dear." Luna stood up, brushed off her knees, and left Gemme with the mess of samples. Gemme watched openmouthed, wondering what could be more important than collecting the answers to their future existence on this planet. Luna bent over the mess of her tent and rummaged through the torn fabric, righted an upturned tray, and started to load the vials. When she turned to Luna again, she'd pulled out a makeup kit and was applying some sort of skin cream to her face.

Gemme's frustration balled in her chest. "Luna, what are you doing?"

"Collecting my things."

"What about the samples?"

She winked at her. "You're doing a nice job, hon. Keep at it."

Gemme shook her head and picked up a few more vials filled with snow. She wondered if Luna had convinced them to come back for her personal items, and not for her research. But, no one could be that self-absorbed, right? She wished she'd volunteered to help Tech along with Brentwood. Gazing across camp, she saw them chipping away at the ice-coated hairs wrapped around the drill.

"I know you like him." Luna's voice turned cold as the frost on her boots.

Gemme paused. Did she hear her correctly or did the wind distort Luna's words?

"What?"

Luna fastened the straps on her backpack, making sure they fit perfectly over her shoulders. "I know you have the hots for Brentwood."

Gemme's heart quickened as her faced burned. She looked away, pretending to search for more vials. "I don't know what you're talking about."

Luna retrieved two vials from the ground, walked beside her, and shoved them into the trays. "I see the way you look at him, all rosy cheeked and wide-eyed."

"You must be mistaken. I—"

"He's not yours to have."

This time Gemme did look up from the snow, quirking her eyebrows at Luna. Was she kidding?

Luna stared her down with lasers in her eyes. "He's mine. I know that's why you didn't want to pair us together."

Her gloved finger pointed at Gemme accusingly. "Let me wake you to reality. I saw the ship reports on decks eighty-five through a hundred. Your computer program crashed, dear. Now it's a free for all, and I'm not letting him get away. I've had my eyes set on him longer than you've been the Matchmaker, and the Legacys always get what they want in the end."

Gemme sat in the snow utterly speechless, wondering how to respond and thinking of nothing. "Luna—"

"Shhhh. Your embarrassing secret is safe with me. Just do as I ask and I won't let him in on your little crush."

"Ladies, I trust you're almost finished."

Gemme bolted from her knees and whirled around. Brentwood, the last person she wanted overhearing such a heated conversation, approached them in a quick jog.

"Oh yes, quite finished, right Gemme, dear?" Luna's voice turned sweet again. "Gemme's just volunteered to carry the trays to the landrover for me, haven't you?"

She plopped five stacked trays in Gemme's arms. "Go on. You don't want to make us late."

Gemme gritted her teeth as the moment slipped away. She'd lost control. Luna had made her do the grunt work and got time alone with Brentwood. If Gemme called her out now, she'd look just as bad as Luna. Besides, now was not the time to bicker. Alpha Blue already lagged behind schedule, and she carried the answers to further their colonization efforts. Grumbling under her breath, Gemme left Luna with Brentwood, stumbling on her still swollen feet. How did she let the biologist get the better of her?

Luna's high-pitched laughter echoed behind Gemme as she trudged through the snow to the landrover. Her insides hardened into steel. She wished she could delete her feelings as easy as she pressed the Delete word on her touchscreen a few days ago, or that the comets had hit ten minutes sooner, preventing her from seeing Brentwood as her predestined lifemate. But deep down she knew, knowledge or not, she'd still be drawn to him like a planet to a star. Not only was he gorgeous, but he also had a sense of humor, of honor, and he made her feel special, like she was more than a boring computer analyst. Everyone talked of his looks, but it was how he made Gemme feel that drew her in.

Brentwood deserved better than Luna, stunning as she was. As the Matchmaker, Gemme could see the absurdity of their pairing. Luna would drive him crazy. She'd manipulate him, just like she manipulated her, forcing him to do all of the work his entire life. The fact that Gemme had been the chosen pairing for Brentwood burned like a hot coal in her heart. She had to show him her feelings one way or another, even if she no longer had the computer's help.

Brentwood stared at Luna, frustration brimming up. The Legacys were known for having others do their dirty work, and he couldn't have that happening on this mission, even if her family was powerful. "Honestly, you're going to make Ms. Reiner carry all those trays by herself?"

Luna laughed, edging closer to him. "She needs something to keep her busy. Besides, I don't see you helping her."

"That's because we have to talk." He leaned so close her rosy perfume tickled his nose. He knew their proximity would look suspicious, but he couldn't have Gemme or Tech overhearing, not if he wanted to follow the Seers' orders. His voice fell to a whisper. "You can't mention the code word in front of the team. If they suspect us of withholding information, it will only lead to trust issues among the other members of Alpha Blue."

The way Luna flaunted their secret mission annoyed him, and he had to put a stop to it before her actions sacrificed the main mission and before it drove Gemme away. He could feel her pulling back from him, and he suspected Luna was the cause. "What do those samples have to do with the orb?"

Luna crossed her arms in a complacent stance, her painted eyebrow arched. "Everything."

Brentwood paused to hear more, but her lips remained sealed. She had him intrigued, and she'd draw out the conversation to last as long as it could.

He gave her an admonishing look as if to say *let's not play games.* "How so?"

"So far, with the basic testing I can do out here, none of the specimens have even remotely the same composition as the orb. In fact, nothing on this planet does."

"Which means?"

"The orb is not from Tundra 37, nor is the beacon we're supposed to locate."

"You're saying that aliens, intelligent life, put it here?"

She shrugged noncommittally. "Maybe."

Unease traveled up Brentwood's back, tingling his neck. Alpha Blue trespassed in potentially dangerous territory. Who knew if these aliens wanted their device found? What if it was a weapon? What if they came back for it?

He stiffened as the picture solidified in his mind. That's why the Seers had to have the artifact and that's why they'd labeled their mission top secret. They wanted information on this species without widespread panic. The colonists had enough to worry about besides potentially dangerous alien devices. What he couldn't fathom was how they'd managed to get themselves stranded on the very same planet that held a matching artifact to the orb. Unless these aliens distributed them across the galaxy on every life-sustaining planet, the odds were steep.

Luna brought him out of his musings by clinging to his arm. "You okay?"

"I'm fine." He looked back to check on Gemme just as she turned around, catching him with Luna's fingers wrapped around his biceps. He pulled his arm away, cheeks burning like a dwarf star. He felt like a complete ass and he hadn't even done anything wrong. "I must attend to the others."

The snow crunched under his boots, hard as the stare Gemme shot him when he reached the landrover. She'd already packed and secured Luna's trays and there was nothing left to help her with. Brentwood walked over to Tech where he'd have better luck at a conversation.

Tech shifted his weight in the driver's seat. "I'm ready for another round of chauffeur, chief." A claw from the alien mammoth dangled from the rear view mirror, the tip curved like a buccaneer's blade.

Brentwood gestured to the decoration. "Trophy?"

"More like a souvenir." Tech emphasized the last syllable with a thick French accent, which made Brentwood laugh.

"Brushing up on your Française?"

"My ancestors were from Canada." He gave him a wink. "Way back in the Old Earth days, of course."

Brentwood couldn't get enough information about the Old Earth days, but now wasn't the time to learn. He leaned on the hatch. "You sure you don't want me to drive?"

"No, sir. You should get some rest if you're going to pull an all-nighter."

"Wise advice." Brentwood yearned to sit in the back next to Gemme anyway. Maybe he could squelch whatever notions she had of him and Luna for good. He climbed in, pulling the seat restraint across his chest. Gemme followed, one boot on the threshold. Just as he opened his mouth to address her, she stopped and jerked backward. Brentwood leaned over in his seat, watching as Luna grabbed her arm.

"You haven't gotten a chance to sit in front, right, hon?"

Oh no. Why did Luna insist on inserting herself everywhere he went?

Brentwood hung on Gemme's response. "No, but I'm quite content to sit—"

"Nonsense." Luna pushed past her and claimed the backseat. She belted herself in and waved her painted fingernails to the front. "Go ahead, take my seat."

"Have it your way." Gemme sounded ambivalent as she pushed past them and settled into the front seat. Disappointment panged inside Brentwood's chest. But what was he supposed to do? Order Luna to sit up front? There was no rationale to explain that. He'd be a poor leader, using his own job to win him time with the woman he admired.

He forced a smile as Luna turned to him. "Always the pleasure, Lieutenant."

"Indeed." Brentwood closed his eyes, hoping if he pretended to sleep, she wouldn't bother him.

"Onward!" Tech announced, flinging his fingers over the touchscreen panels.

The landrover took off, large wheels grinding the snow underneath them. Brentwood heard Gemme ask Tech about their course from the front seat. Although he longed to join in their conversation, exhaustion caught up with him, and the monotonous drone of the engines lulled him to sleep.

ଛ∽ଈ

His Appaloosa jerked his head with impatience as Brentwood's gaze swept up to the billowy clouds amassing on the horizon. The steed bucked and he gripped harder, the rough leather of the reins rubbing against his calloused hands. The smell of wet grass, horsehide, and old leather stung the air in a combination of scents both familiar and comforting.

"We'd best be getting home before the storm rolls in." A man with gray-speckled dark hair turned his own steed toward a vast carpet of long-stemmed grasses bowing to the westerly wind. The man wore a wool vest and cotton trousers stuffed into leather boots. A cowboy hat with a golden buckle across the front was tied to a cord under his beard. Golden swirls moved across the buckle.

Brentwood's rough shirt fell loose around his biceps, rustling in the wind against his chest. His cuffs were rolled up, and he'd tucked the hem of his shirt into wool trousers. He didn't remember putting those particular clothes on that morning, but fog covered his mind, blurring his memory.

"You joining me, Michael? The Larson family will need help bringing in the sheep, especially with Harriet's ma catching fever." The man titled his hat against the wind, the intricate etchings on concentric circles in the silver buckle catching Brentwood's eye. Where had he seen that pattern before?

"Michael?"

It took Brentwood a moment to realize the man addressed him. He could have sworn he said *Michael* and not *Miles*, but the howl of the wind muffled his words and with the storm brewing, now was not the time to question him.

"Sure, lead the way."

He kicked his spurs into the horse's flanks and his mount took off into a gallop, following the man down a dirt path cut into a hill. The grass rose up to his shins, the tips spreading into three fingers like turkey's feet.

Had he ever seen a turkey? Brentwood scratched his head, trying to make sense of his upturned world. He knew what a turkey looked like and how it tasted, but he didn't think he'd ever seen one darting through the long grasses.

"Gonna be a doozy," the man shouted over his shoulder as his horse picked up its pace. Crows black as coal cawed angrily and scattered into the sky as the horses disturbed their perches.

Brentwood searched the plains stretching across the horizon. A barn with a broad gabled roof attached to a cottage stood out in a dark silhouette. Gray smoke plumed from a red brick chimney, the scent of roasted pheasant riding the air. The sight stirred a yearning in his chest. It felt like home.

The storm rode their heels, blowing in on gusts of dank air. A pattering of rain caught up with them, light drops cooling Brentwood's forehead. They reached the cottage just as thunder grumbled in the darkening sky.

"Go on in and check on Jenna. Meet me in fifteen minutes by the crossing at Bull's Head."

Before Brentwood could respond, the man shouted a command and dug his spurs into his horse. They took off in a flurry of pale dust. Brentwood's gaze traveled along the crude logs stacked up as walls to the cottage. Deer antlers hung on the doorframe, the third ivory tip broken off into a stub. *Did I hunt that?*

The covered porch creaked as a woman wearing a paisley bonnet and an apron blue as an autumn sky stepped out. At first all he could see was her fine, brown hair as the wind stole it away from the edges of the lace. She turned, revealing eyes gray as the clouds behind him and porcelain skin dotted with freckles.

Gemme.

"Thank goodness. I thought the storm would blow in before you returned." She spoke with a slight accent, savoring the syllables in a way he'd never heard her speak before. She rushed toward him as he dismounted.

"I don't know where I am, or how I got here. All I know is you—"

She wrapped her arms around him, taking his breath away. Brentwood stood rigid as a pole in shock, his arms outstretched like a scarecrow. Every muscle in his body urged him to hold her, but somehow he thought their proximity was indecent, as if they'd only met. But he'd known her for a while. Had it been months? Years?

She moved her hands up along his neck. Her fingers trailed warmth, setting his skin on fire. She cupped his chin with both hands and pulled his face down toward hers. He molded to her body, bending to her will. She arched her head up and pressed her lips against his.

Intense need surged inside him and he pushed into her kiss. Her lips were soft and sweet like honey, and he brought his arms around her, asking for more. She pressed herself against his chest as if the crude cotton would dissolve between them.

The cloudiness in his head had cleared, and everything about the moment fit in place, as if he'd never truly lived until this day. Had his whole life before this instant been false? Finally existing in the place he ached to be, he didn't care.

CHAPTER SEVENTEEN
CHANCE

System reports flooded in, each one making Mestasis feel like more of a failure. Plants were dying in the biodome, entire species of vegetables winking out of existence. People shivered in their sleep pods, and the fusion reactor verged on collapse. She couldn't face the fact the entire colony might fail because of her errors. Ignoring the alarming impulses, she focused on her memories. The situation around her only worsened, and she hungered for escape. The orb called to her, promising numb oblivion.

ॐ~ॐ

Old Earth, 2446

"What does the mocha crème taste like?"

Mestasis fidgeted with her ID keytag as she waited in line at the Techno Expresso behind an older woman who couldn't decide with flavor of synthetic latte to choose. It was manufactured from some soybean substitute. No one had actually tasted real roasted coffee in her lifetime.

Honestly, don't they all taste the same?

Her fingernail ran along the edge, the plastic digging into the pink skin underneath. The ID strip swirled like oil underneath the fluorescent lights. As she smoothed her finger over the patterns, the golden swirls disappeared. *Interesting. It's never done that before.* The damn thing better work, because she wasn't standing in line all over again. She had a mental exercise work study to complete by the end of the weekend for both her and Abysme, and Dr. Fields expected each answer to be no less than excellent.

Had she made a mistake in coming? She scanned the rows of tables large enough to fit two cups and a soybean wafer if you didn't mind dripping coffee on your lunch. Strangers' faces yapped in conversation while others stared out the sight panel as if waiting for the end of the world. A girl wearing a TINE uniform, like herself, caught her wandering gaze and Mestasis flicked her eyes back to the older woman's latte choice, afraid to be recognized.

Would he come?

The server shot her a baleful look with hooded, indigo-painted eyelids, demanding her order. She ran her ID tag through a crack in the countertop. "I'll have a small regular."

A plastic cup dropped from a console and the server squirted dark liquid into it from a tube. She pushed the steaming beverage to Mestasis and stared at the next customer without saying a word.

"Such a plain choice for someone so special."

Mestasis whirled around, the liquid in her cup splashing onto the back of her hand.

James stood behind her holding his own dark beverage. Had he been waiting for her? Where he'd come from, she had no idea. She'd scanned the place from top to bottom before walking in.

"Being someone so special, I try not to stick out." Rubbing the place where the liquid scalded her skin, Mestasis took him in. Without the tips of neon sparking around his chin, his dark hair looked glossy. She reminded herself the phosphorescence glowed in the dark, and the fluorescent lights of Techno Expresso hid any association he had with the Radioactive Hand of Justice. In the café, he looked like any handsome twenty-something trying to make his way in the world.

He gestured over his shoulder. "I found us a table in the back."

What was she doing here? It was absurd for her to sacrifice time from her studies to meet a young man she hardly knew, a renegade at that. But at the same time, her fingers shook with excitement. She felt more alive than when she connected to the electromagnetic pulses within TINE.

Following him through the masses, she couldn't believe she had a date. She'd watched couples sitting together at the Techno Express for years, wondering how it felt to have someone to share conversation. Abysme didn't like to go out in public together because people stared at their mirror-like faces, so Mestasis always came by herself. She never thought she'd have someone to take a moment away from the world with. Not that she had a moment to spare.

She sat across from him, balancing her drink on the small table by wrapping her fingers around the curve of the cup.

He sipped his synthetic latte and tilted his angular face toward her. "I trust you made it back safely."

Mestasis's neck and cheeks grew hot, but her dark skin hid her blushes well. "I did, thanks to you."

"You saved my life too. Remember?"

She looked away, studying a hovercraft as it glided beyond the buildings and became a silver speck in the slate sky. "I didn't come here to talk about my abilities. I came to get away from them."

"I understand. We all need to escape sometimes."

She locked his gaze, searching for the real answer why they sat here together, two people from totally different worlds. The kindness in his eyes made her vulnerable, and she dropped her gaze down to her steaming beverage.

"How's your furry friend?"

Mestasis smiled. "She's doing fine. Our plastic couch, on the other hand, has seen better days."

James laughed. "I'm glad to hear it."

"You're fond of kittens?"

"You could say that. I value all life."

He looked past her to the doors of the coffee shop. "While

scavenging as boy, I found a dandelion growing out of the crack of the sidewalk, way down on the street level among the piles of garbage. It was a miracle the plant germinated underneath the concrete with almost no sunlight, fed by the acid rain. I reached down to pick it and bring it back with me, my fingers running over the hairy stem. But I knew it would only wilt and die in my cramped hiding space between the second and third floor. Instead, I cut the bottom out a plastic water bottle to shield it from the feet of the gangmen. The next day I took the few boys I knew to show them."

He looked back to her, his fingertip running along the rim of his mug. "They laughed at me and kicked the plastic shelter away." His eyes turned cold. "They trampled it. I can still remember the yellow pollen streaking the gray concrete."

"I'm sorry." Mestasis placed her hand over his. His skin was rough, his fingers calloused compared to her smooth fingertips.

James shook his head. "I'm not looking for sympathy. It was a long time ago. I'm over it." He smiled, the warmth coming back to his face. "It's nice to meet someone who values other life on this planet besides humans."

The barrier inside her crumbled. "I've always been drawn to how life used to be in the past. As a kid, my sister and I had a blade of grass in a pot of soil. We'd give it some of our water rations every day and bring it to the corridor outside out apartment where a square of sunlight would shine in the later part of the afternoon."

"What happened to it?"

"We kept it alive for a very long time, even brought it with us to TINE. I still have the pot in the apartment I share with my sister."

"What is your sister like? You had mentioned wanting a safe place for her and your mother."

Besides Dr. Fields, no one had asked her that question before. She ran her finger along the rim of her cup, thinking about how much to tell him.

"My family is loyal to a fault. Willing to risk anything for each other." Her hand burned where it touched his skin and she worried he'd sense the rising temperature, so she took it back, using it to place a braid behind her ear.

"Wow, that sounds like some family."

Mestasis smiled and sipped her coffee. He made her feel special, made her realize just how much she did have. "I'm lucky. I really am. I could have been abandoned, an orphan stuck in the system."

James nodded and slipped off his black cloak. He hung it on the back of his chair as if he thought they'd stay a long time. "I grew up in The Ministry of Mercy, and from there went straight into the gangs."

"That's probably what would've happened to me if it weren't for my mom."

James's interest in her family, the one thing she prized above all else, made her want to share more with him and her words spilled out. "She didn't mean to become pregnant. My mom's a shrewd woman. She knew how tough it was to raise a child in this world, and she had no fortune, no way to keep such an endeavor thriving. I don't know exactly what happened, but my father left when they found out she had not one but two new mouths to feed. After my sister and I were born, my mom took up two jobs, working all hours to support us. They're all I have."

"I can see why you work so hard for them."

"My mom's worked so hard for us; the recycling facility where she works has so many contaminants and hazards. It's not good for her. Every day she spends there poisons her body more. I need to get her out."

"And TINE is the only way?"

"The only way I can see, yes."

She thought he might try to ask her to join him again in the underground, but he remained silent, taking another sip of his beverage. She wondered if he'd asked her here for her powers, but he seemed more interested in who she was than what she could do. He made her feel normal.

"What about you? Do you think you've found the safest place to live? To weather the storm we all know is coming?" She noticed how the tips of his hair curved around his chin. She noticed his smooth skin trailing from his neck, down into the V-shaped neck of his shirt.

"Who knows?" He settled back in his chair, propping his boot on the ventilator by the window. "The news on the streets now is the higher-ups are building transport ships, gigantic vessels the size of small cities, able to house entire populations. They'll have self-sustaining biodomes, air filtration systems, energy cells with supplies to last generations, workout decks, schools, everything you could ever need."

Mestasis leaned forward. "You mean they're going to circle the Earth in space stations?"

He shook his head, hair falling in front of his eyes. He brushed it back carelessly. "No, they're talking about colonizing other worlds."

"How? It would take centuries to get anywhere and no one's perfected cryosleep techniques, especially for such a vast majority."

"They're going to live their lives on the ships. Imagine entire generations of astronauts passing on the genetic code to their children and their children after them, until they reach paradise planets."

"Wow." It was the best idea Mestasis had ever heard. A jolt of anger at Dr. Fields shot through her. Surely he'd had heard of such ships? Was he keeping information from her and Abysme?

It didn't matter now. She'd found out, and Dr. Fields couldn't steal the idea back from her head. The thought of the colonization ships gave her hope. If she could get herself, her mom, and Abysme on one of those transport ships, then they'd all be safe. No food shortages, no pollution, no radiation, no chemical weapons, no nukes.

He raised his eyebrows as if he read her mind. "The trick is how to get yourself on one of them. Only the super-elite with connections will have a chance."

"What do you mean? How many are they making?"

James's eyes darkened. "Not nearly enough. The majority of the population will be left behind on this dying planet, fighting for the last resources until we end up killing each other."

"No." Mestasis removed her hands from her coffee, wringing them together in thought. She didn't care if a passerby knocked her cup over. Acid was already filling her stomach and it would just add to the burn. "The world will never get that bad. Governments will always step in."

A teenage boy darted between their tables, and James held both cups as the boy slipped by. "You wanna bet? Who's going to govern when all the important politicians leave?"

"New ones will step up. The world isn't going to go to hell all in one day."

"Yeah, I bet it'll take more like a month."

"Honestly, are you that cynical?" Looking into James's face, she knew he was. And she wasn't that far behind. Even though she talked of life going on, a splinter of doubt had wedged itself in her gut long ago, and nothing she could accomplish at TINE would ever pick it out.

"You're planning on going on one, aren't you?" He leaned forward, so close his breath fell on her lips.

She quirked an eyebrow. "Maybe." Digging in her uniform, she brought out a shiny nanodisc and held it toward him. A ray of sunlight trickled down from the window, playing upon the surface in glistening radiance. He took it from her, their fingers brushing.

"What is it?"

"A code. You can send it through anything with an electromagnetic pulse." She waved her hand over to the servers in the front, "Even a coffee machine."

"What's it for?"

She smiled. "It's my number. Punch it in anywhere, and I'll know where you are."

His eyes widened. "You serious?"

She tilted her head, tiny braids falling across her shoulders. "What do you think?"

"After seeing what you did last night, anything is possible."

Mestasis shrugged as if it didn't matter. But he'd taught her anything was possible as well. Entire cities on transport ships, herself walking into a coffee shop to meet a date. The possibilities made her head reel.

She leaned back before his proximity had too much of an effect on her, before she wouldn't be able to tear herself away. "If you learn anything else about these ships, will you contact me?"

"Of course."

Mestasis dumped the remains of her beverage into a hole in the table leading to a food recycling depository. She threw her plastic cup in a bin near the wall. "Thank you. You've been a big help. You've given me hope."

"My pleasure. It's what I do for a job, remember?"

"Give people hope?"

"Or at least apples." He winked and downed the last few sips of his drink.

One question nagged at her the entire conversation, and if she didn't ask it now, she knew she'd never bring it up again. Hesitating, then forcing herself to act, Mestasis curled her finger, beckoning him closer.

At peak lunch hour, the room had grown so crowded she had to lean across the table for him to hear her whisper. His eyebrows rose in a question and he met her halfway, his face centimeters from hers. At this distance she could see the hazel flecks in his eyes and she wondered again how someone so gorgeous could be involved with such dangerous gangs. Surely some modeling company for the sight panels on the sides of the state building would have noticed him. But then he wouldn't be changing the world. "When you saw me last night, why didn't you turn me in?"

He brought his lips to her ear and her heart flitted. "Because the first time I saw you, you reminded me of what I'm fighting for day in and day out."

She pulled back to meet his gaze, fingers trembling as she held onto the sides of the coffee table. "What are you fighting for?"

"Love." James brushed his lips against hers. Everyone in the coffee shop around her vanished. The espresso machines ceased to buzz, the incessant traffic of customers halted. Nothing existed except her first kiss. She pressed her head forward, feeling the warmth from his lips travel into her mouth and down to the pit of her stomach. For a moment she forgot about TINE, about studies, about her powers, about the crumbling world. For a moment she was just a normal young woman enticed by an attractive young man.

૨~ઝ

Mestasis smiled all the way back to TINE, her cheeks aching by the time the elevator beeped on her floor. She pressed the door panel, and the walls separated to reveal a pile of luggage. Abysme sat on the plastic couch, staring at a blank holoscreen.

Mestasis froze. *You're back early.*

A current of anger rose up inside her. Abysme should be studying, preparing, making up for lost time. And here she was, doing nothing. Mestasis exhaled, releasing her frustration before she said something she'd regret. At least her sister came back, and with time for both of them to work out the next assignment together. She'd planned to work on it all day alone.

Golden swirls erupted as she clicked on the holoscreen on. Mestasis waved her sister up. *Come on, let's get started on the—*

She's gone. Abysme didn't move.

Mestasis froze as the parted walls of the door panel sealed behind her, shutting her in to a room where she didn't want to be, a reality she didn't want to face. *What do you mean?*

Mom passed away. A retrieval team took her body to the incinerators this morning. Abysme shook her head and buried her face in both hands; her body shook with tremors as she wept.

No. Surely it was a ruse, a ploy to make her feel guilty. She wouldn't put it past Abysme to fabricate lies when she couldn't get her way. Mestasis probed her sister's thoughts in denial. Feelings of grief and guilt surged through her on all conscious and subconscious levels. When she probed further, an image of their mother huddled in her sleeping cocoon, dark hair spilling out onto the floor surfaced in her sister's memory. Containers of pain meds lay strewn around her. She held a picture from when they were young girls in her sweaty hand.

Mestasis collapsed to her knees beside the couch. Why hadn't she sensed it? Had TINE blinded her to the needs of her own family?

Her twin's body shuddered as she mindspoke. *When I got home, she'd been in bed for days. I tried to get her to go to the higher floors, to scrap together everything she owned to find a doctor, but she wouldn't move. She kept saying it was too late, and without coverage they wouldn't see her anyway.*

Mestasis struggled to hold herself together. Numbness tingled through her body. The world seemed severe and empty without her mom in it. She had so many things still to tell her, so many things she didn't say. Mestasis tried to remember the last time she had seen her, and her mind came up against a wall. She had so many chances to go back, but she'd stayed each time, thinking she would make a better world for her mother. Never did she expect she wouldn't be around to enjoy it.

Mestasis felt cheated, almost betrayed. *She never told us she was sick.*

What did you expect? She worked in that old recycling plant, carcinogens seeping into her body each day. Abysme hit the couch with her fist. *You said we'd get her out of there.*

She glared at Mestasis with eyes filled with pain and hate.

Tears blurred her vision, and Mestasis wiped them back. She had to be the stronger one in times like these. *I'm sorry, Bysme. I thought we had more time.*

Time is the one thing we don't have. Abysme shot up and waved her arm over the smog-filled sky in the window. *In case you didn't notice, the world is falling apart. Flying in the hovercraft I saw gangs, right in the light of day, parading through the corridors between Quadrants six and seven. People are fighting over energy cells for their hovercrafts, and the line for fresh food stretches two buildings long. Men with lasers guard the greenhouses, and I needed to show my ID just to park the hovercraft. It's a madhouse outside TINE, and it's just going to get worse.*

Despite her shaking body, Mestasis kept her mindspeak steady. *Bysme, we'll make it through this. We always do.*

But what's the point of going on? I don't want to live in a world where you have to fight for your next meal, where a thousand people starve while I eat. I can't do it anymore, Metsy. I just can't.

Mestasis pulled herself up and strode across the room. She'd just lost her mom, and she wasn't about to lose her sister as well. She gripped Abysme's arm, yanking her away from the window. *Don't you dare talk about not living, about abandoning your work, your life.*

Abysme struggled in her grip, trying to wiggle free. *Why the hell not? What is left to live for?*

Love. Mestasis thought of James and his story about the colony ships. Resolution hardened in her chest and she held firm. *Because I'm getting us off this damn planet.*

Abysme stiffened in surprise and Mestasis pushed her point. She stared into her sister's gaze, the irises so dark they blended with the pupil. *I've found a way to get us out of here.*

❧❧

On the failing control deck of the *Expedition* Mestasis wondered if where they'd ended up was any better than staying on Old Earth.

CHAPTER EIGHTEEN
CAPTURED STAR

"In case you don't remember to chemistry class, under standard conditions, hyperthium is the lightest metal and the least dense solid element on the periodic table. Like all alkali metals, hyperthium is highly reactive and flammable, so we typically store it in mineral oil. It looks real nice when cut open, shining with a metallic luster..."

Gemme's head bobbed up and down as Tech rambled on. The tundra spread before the sight panel in an endless slate of shiny white. At first, she watched with fascination, looking for more tentacled beasts or wiry-haired mammoths, but three hours of the same horizontal ice landscape made her drowsy.

Must. Pay. Attention. Important information, vital to the success of the mission.

Glancing back, she saw Luna cleaning her fingernails, and Brentwood fast asleep, a placid expression on his face. If only she could see what occupied his dreams. Gemme turned back around and focused on Tech's words.

"Contact with moist air corrodes the surface quickly to a dull, silvery gray, then black tarnish. But we'll see what it does is this frigid atmosphere..."

She didn't get very far.

☙❧

An ant's head peeked out of a mound of sand. The antennae twitched as if detecting her. The insect emerged, crawled down the side in a wandering zigzag, and disappeared into the long-stemmed grasses. The sand swirled around it and Gemme wondered if it would sink into quicksand, but the ant continued on as the golden swirls spiraled out, shooting into the grasses like dust in the wind.

Had she fallen in the biodome?

"Oh my, Jenny, are you okay?"

Someone pulled her arm and she scrambled up into the searing rays of sunlight. Solaris Prime on Tundra 37 felt like a microscope light compared to this giant burning ball of gas threatening to blind her and bake her all at once.

"You went down so fast. I tried to catch you." The familiar woman with nutmeg hair helped her brush sand off her sundress.

"It's okay. I'm fine." No matter where she was, she was still embarrassed to have fallen on her face. The back of her jaw throbbed with pain.

"Good. Mikey's truck is pulling up right now."

She followed the woman to an antique Old Earth vehicle that looked like it belonged in a junkyard heap more than on a road. The paint gleamed red as an apple in the places that weren't eaten away with amber rust.

"We're riding in that?"

"Yeah." The woman ran up and scooped a pair of pink high heels from the back. "Don't forget your shoes."

Gemme took the pointy heels in her hands wondering how anyone could ever walk in such an absurd design. They couldn't possibly belong to her, yet the pattern of concentric circles painted on the toe reminded her so much of something she'd once owned. Bending down, she slipped the right one on her bare foot. Her toes wiggled through in a perfect fit.

The woman had already climbed in the back. "Are you coming?"

Gemme slipped on the other shoe and walked around the pickup, making sure not to touch the rusty paint, and stuck her head in the open sight panel. A young man with curly dark hair and a nose the size of a pear stared back at her. Disappointment tinged her heart. Somehow, she thought she'd recognize him.

"Mikey?"

"Dude's at the party waiting for you. Come on in."

She hesitated, one hand gripping the doorframe. Had she been here before?

"What's with you today, Jenny? You look like you ate the wrong mushrooms."

"Don't mind her, Walter; she's been spacey all morning. She gets like that when she spends too much time with her numbers."

"It's all cool, Lisa."

He reached over and popped the door loose. The metal squeaked as she swung it open. She climbed in, balancing precariously on her heels. The furry fabric of the seat felt strange underneath her bare legs as she sat down. A dangling cardboard peach wafted a sickly sweet scent from the rearview mirror.

She turned back to Lisa. "I thought you said Mikey was coming to pick us up."

"All part of the plan." She gave her a wink and mouthed, "Trust me."

Walter flicked a knob on the front panel and a strong drumbeat vibrated the inside of the pickup. A man's voice came on the speakers, "Ooh my little pretty one, pretty one. When you gonna give me some time, Sharona?"

Gemme covered her ears with her hands and Walter turned the knob again. The sound quieted.

"Don't like The Knack?"

Gemme questioned him by raising her eyebrow. He shrugged and turned the wheel. The pickup lurched forward and she braced herself against the front panel.

He gave her an apologetic smile. "Forgot to remind you to buckle up."

They rode past trees, so many of them in all shapes and sizes, making the biodome on the Expedition seem like a child's terrarium. A lake spread on her sight panel, water rippling in blue crests with a white sailboat riding the waves. Gemme's feet itched to stand on the sandy beach and wade in the shallows.

Walter pulled up in front of an old gabled farmhouse painted in fading lavender with beige trim. He parked behind another Old Earth antique with gold lettering that read Chevrolet.

"Last stop, gals. Thanks for flying 'Air Walter.'"

Gemme pulled the plastic handle and the door popped open. She followed Lisa and Walter onto the covered porch. Flowers dangled from baskets hanging over her head, and a spindly tomato plant clung to a stick in an old bucket by her feet. A black cat meowed and jumped off the back of the porch as if they intruded on its nap time.

Lisa smiled at her. "You ready?"

"Ready for what?"

"You'll see." She opened the screen door and ushered her in.

A chorus of voices echoed, "Surprise!"

People jumped out at her from either side, holding plastic cups of golden liquid. Some crouched on the staircase, and others stood the hallway waving ribbons and lace. Gemme shrunk back, bumping into Lisa. "What's going on?"

"Don't look so cross! I know it's not your birthday, Jenny. This is something much, much better."

The crowd parted, each face beaming in a smile as if she were a queen returning to her throne. She wished she knew their collective secret. She felt like an outsider trying to play a game without knowing all the rules. It was a feeling she'd experienced a lot lately.

Lisa pushed her to the kitchen at the back, where a three-tiered chocolate cake sat on a bright yellow linoleum countertop. As if those sights didn't surprise her enough, Brentwood stood beside the cake, wearing a loose-fitting shirt with palm trees and khaki shorts. A tan made his skin golden bronze, highlighting the blond in his wavy hair. He looked so good Gemme gasped air in, holding her breath.

His lips curled in a half-sorry, half-mischievous grin. "I wanted to surprise you with something big. Maybe then, you'll say yes."

She exhaled and her voice shook. "Say yes to what?"

He reached in his back pocket and brought out a velvet box. People whispered around them, poking their faces through the door. Lisa pushed them back. Brentwood lowered himself to one knee and opened the box. A teardrop-shaped diamond winked back at her like a captured star.

"We've had some pretty rough times, with you going away to NYU and me joining the police force, but we've made it through. You always believed in me, in us. I love you, Jenny, and I want you to be my wife. Will you marry me?"

Gemme didn't recognize half of what he said, but she knew the answer before he finished his last sentence. She placed her fingers over his hand that held the box. His skin burned like the sun. "Yes."

Applause filled the room in contagious happiness. Walter hollered, "Mikey and Jenny forever." But all Gemme could focus on was the warmth of Brentwood's skin underneath her fingertips. He held out her hand and slipped on the ring. Joy welled up inside her, exploding like solar flares in her chest. She didn't care if they were Mikey and Jenny or Miles and Gemme. All she knew was the sense of comfort he gave her just by staring into her eyes.

Brentwood stood and cupped her chin with both his hands, his touch so gentle, yet direct. He brought his face down and kissed her passionately, as if he could join their souls right then with his lips. She melted into his embrace and parted her lips against his, currents of passion stirring urges in her body. Nothing else mattered but here and now, this perfect moment in a universe of endless time.

CHAPTER NINETEEN
SPARE PARTS

"Please, Rizzy. If you do it, I promise I won't ever tell on you and Daryl again." Vira pressed her palms together in a triangle and beat it in the air in front of Rizzy's nose.

Rizzy looked away, leaning on her sleep pod as the fuel cell recharged. "I don't know. You're talking about breaking into Dad's private workshop and stealing his equipment. Not just lifting a cookie or an extra blanket, or even sneaking a kiss."

"It's for my new project."

"I don't care what it's for. I just don't want to get in trouble. Thanks to you, I'm in far enough as it is."

"I'm sorry I told on you, okay? I won't do it again. Dad won't even notice the parts missing. He's too busy trying to fix things in his job."

Rizzy bit her lips as if she was considering it, tapping her fingers on the pod's plastic curve. Vira held her breath. Her chest threatened to burst.

"All right." Rizzy pointed a finger at her. "But you leave my poster alone, and your days of tattletaling are over."

Vira pretended to squirt glue over her mouth. "My lips are sealed."

"Fine." Rizzy pulled out her illegal ID tag, the one that had gotten her trapped in the upper levels in the first place and waved it in the air, the shiny strip on the back glistening. "Where are you going to stash all this stuff anyway?"

Vira punched the corner of one of the panels in the floor and the metal popped up. Underneath lay a rusty compartment lined with dust. She used Rizzy's favorite expression. "I have my ways."

Rizzy gave her an appraising look and laughed. "And they think I'm the one to look out for."

Vira stared at the poster as she waited, wondering if the sorcerer would tell the Seers about her spying if he could spring right off the wall and talk. Besides Daryl and Rizzy, everyone else followed the Seers as if they were gods.

But they weren't.

They were once two human girls very much like herself.

Vira wondered what they were like when they were her age. Would they have been friends?

A plastic bin of gears, gadgets, and shiny tools dropped in front of her with a rattling *plop*. Vira blinked and shook her head, looking up at Rizzy.

"I didn't know what you wanted, so I grabbed everything I could." She put her hands on her hips. "Good enough?"

"I'll say." Vira pulled out a motor and a rounded metal beam that she could use as a steering wheel.

"So we're good?"

"Yup."

"Good. Because I'm going over to see Daryl right now, and if Mom or Dad comes back you tell them I've gone to study for colonization tests with Derva, k?"

"Derva *Legacy*?" Vira's tongue almost fell out of her mouth.

"Yeah, they won't question that, will they?"

Vira nodded. No one got in the way of the Legacys, and Derva would be an excellent study partner. She always aced all the tests. "K.

Colonization tests with Derva."

Vira didn't think Mom or Dad would be back anytime soon, anyway. They both worked so much now, she hardly saw them at all. Rizzy was supposed to babysit her. But, she didn't need her sister to look after her. She was the one that ended up looking after Rizzy.

"Have fun." Vira waved and Rizzy smiled, ducking out the door. Maybe having a sister wasn't that bad after all.

She dug through the parts scraping the bottom with her fingertips and sighed in frustration. No wheels. How was she supposed to reproduce the concentrated bursts of air that her hovercraft engines did without a decent power source?

She threw a box of metal bolts against the wall. If she was ever going to go anywhere, she needed wheels. Slumping against the wall, she bit back tears. Everything was so much harder for her than for everyone else. She'd avoided feeling sorry for herself for so long; she deserved a good bout of crying.

A whizzing sound came from the kitchen. The cleaning droid sped in, vacuuming the mess she'd made with the bolts. Its front nozzle swelled with the bolts as blue buttons flashed on its sides. Vira picked up a screwdriver to throw at it, when she noticed the shiny wheels spurring it forward.

Using all her strength, she emptied the entire container all over the floor. Pieces of scrap metal, used light sticks, and tiny drill extensions bounced in the rug. The cleaning droid beeped and turned in her direction. She held up a curled finger and wiggled it in the air.

CHAPTER TWENTY
PULSE

Mestasis's mind flicked through the latest system report with casual attention, a nagging pull from her memories stealing her focus. Mr. Reiner had temporarily stabilized the fusion core, and mechanics had repaired the hull breaches. The temperature on the ship remained stable, but the crops in the biodome still withered.

Must return to my memories.

She'd read *Romeo and Juliet* a hundred times in her spare time while driving the *Expedition*. Abysme had downloaded a bunch of classics into the mainframe before they left Earth. Mestasis knew the end, but the tragedy mesmerized her, making her relive the story again and again.

Her logical mind kicked in. *You can't change the past. You can only impact the future by acting in the present.*

Yet, an indulgent craving deep inside her rose up. *You can see James once again.*

Making sure she'd reviewed all status reports, she gave herself up to forgotten dreams.

⤜⤛

Old Earth, 2446

Dr. Fields stood before a blank holoscreen, his rigidly pressed white lab coat contrasting with the meandering wisps of the remaining gray hairs on either side of his head. In the ten years she'd known him, Mestasis thought he'd aged twenty. Perhaps it was better for them to have been born into a crazy world than for him to see it crumble around him as his youth trickled away. Although he tortured them with seemingly extraneous mental exercises, he was the closest thing to a father figure that she'd ever have. Above all else, he believed in them, even when they didn't believe in themselves.

The doctor pressed the panel and a timer appeared on the holoscreen, the numbers formed by golden swirls. "Five hovercrafts are flying in the air space over TINE. One of them carries massive amounts of uranium-235 and plutonium-239, aka a nuclear bomb. You have two minutes to detect which one before the enemy blows us to smithereens."

Abysme stood up and pointed her finger. "Not fair! We can only sense electromagnetic impulses in our building and other buildings connected to it. Not through air. It's impossible."

"Electromagnetic waves travel through air. Hypothetically, you should be able to detect it." He flicked a glance over to a mirror, where they knew a research team awaited the results of the exercise: men and women with big pocketbooks and lots of credits willing to invest in TINE. His face remained stoic as he counted off. "One minute and twenty seconds left."

"Damn." Abysme paced back and forth while Mestasis closed her eyes, feeling vibrations in the floor under the soles of her feet. The air ionizers in the room worked on maximum, and two floors down, everyone had their holoscreen on. So much noise to filter out. She tried sensing the temperature of the air on the roof, and from there, the ebb and flow of sonic waves produced by the engines of the approaching hovercrafts. It seemed as though she tugged at threads no stronger than strands of Dr. Fields' gray hair, the connection snapping whenever she pushed her mind through it.

A new pulse caught her attention, a distant tapping like Morse code. Her heart somersaulted in her chest. It was the rhythm she'd handed to James on the nanodisc. He was calling to her. She'd stood him up the next day at the Techno Express because of the death of their mother. Embarrassed and unwilling to talk about it, she'd avoided the café ever since. Mestasis had to choose: follow James's signal or complete the test and time was running out.

What if he needed her?

Her mind shot to the origin of the code, traveling underneath her feet to a corridor connecting to an adjacent building. Her thoughts jumped down several levels to a credit machine on the right wall in the hall on level seventy-seven. Just as she pulled her mind back to the roof of TINE, the timer beeped.

"That's it girls." She opened her eyes and Dr. Fields stood with an expectant, almost pleading look in his face. "Tell me which hovercraft holds the bomb."

Mestasis's stomach sank to her knees. She'd become distracted and sacrificed the exercise. Her negligence could cost TINE new investors and cost her and her sister their jobs.

"The second and third ones from my right, tail numbers EK96 and EL39." Abysme stuck her nose up in the air. "It was a trick question. There are two." Above their heads, the sound of engines roared and dissipated as the hovercrafts rose up and changed direction.

"Excellent, girls." Dr. Fields' face flushed. He could barely hold in his excitement. Of course, he thought they'd worked in conjunction. He had no idea of Mestasis's flub. Nor would he. Abysme's loyalties lay with her and not TINE.

"You may go back to your quarters and rest. That's all we need for today."

"Thank you, Doctor." Mestasis nodded to him and to the mirror. She could sense at least six bodies behind the glass, and she wanted them to know she sensed their presence, as if detecting bombs in high-speed hovercrafts fifty meters away wasn't enough. Even though Abysme had stronger talents, she felt like she'd failed and had to make it up one way or another.

Abysme followed her as she rushed into the hallway.

What were you thinking? Her sister ran to catch up. *Your mind strayed and I lost you.*

I'm sorry, Bysme. I need to meet someone.

She grabbed her arm, slowing her down. *You're scaring me. You're the one wanting us to pass these silly tests, remember? Who in all of TINE would be more important than our future?*

The person who's gonna help us get out of here.

Her sister paused at her words and Mestasis yanked her arm back and sprinted the remaining distance to the elevator. Abysme glared while Mestasis pressed the elevator panel and waited for the doors to part. *Who is he?*

I don't have time to elaborate. She didn't know how long James could stand at a credit machine without inviting questions. And she didn't want her sister to see her developing feelings for this man. *I won't be long.*

Her heart sped as she raced to the nearest corridor joining the buildings. She had rehearsed so many sentences in her head, hoping to set things right. *I'm sorry I didn't meet you. I enjoyed our last conversation. I have so much I want to ask you.* None of it sounded right.

She didn't think she could speak of her mother, the thought of that day sickening her stomach. It had been two weeks, and the sore remained just as exposed and tender as when she first heard the news. She didn't think it would ever completely heal. Yet, to be truly honest with him, she'd have to bring herself to mention it.

A line snaked out from the credit machine, running down the hall to the next building. Businessmen carrying miniscreens, women with toddlers hanging on their arms, and a few teens lucky enough to have a keytag holding credits in the first place shifted form foot to foot. She followed the string of people up a staircase, wondering why they wanted to withdraw their credits all at once.

The thought of the world collapsing rose up again and she squashed it down. Not yet. Not until she found a way off this doomed planet. The line tapered off on a balcony on the opposite side, the last person an elderly man with a muscled bodyguard painted in tattoos.

Behind them, James stood on the railing, his black cloak fluttering in the breeze. He'd tied his midnight hair in a ponytail, revealing the sleek ridges of his strong cheekbones.

He looked handsome as ever. The moment when their lips had touched came back to her in a rush. "James." She placed her hand on his boot. "Please come down."

His eyes widened as he saw her, stormy-silver like the clouds churning in the sky behind him. "I thought you wouldn't come."

"Nonsense. I gave you the nanodisc, remember?"

He leaped down, landing in front of her. Excitement flashed in his face. He reached out and pulled his hand back, as if he didn't know how to approach her.

Mestasis grabbed his hand before he jammed it in his pocket and pulled him closer. "James, I'm sorry I didn't meet you that day." Swallowing a lump in her throat she summoned enough courage to tell him the truth. Besides Abysme, she hadn't spoken to anyone about it, not even Dr. Fields. "My mother passed away. I learned the news after our conversation."

His face changed from uncertain to compassionate. "Metsy, I'm so sorry."

The facade she'd so carefully constructed crumbled and her lips trembled as tears brimmed. He brought her against his chest, wrapping his arms around her and holding her close. She heard the strong pulse of his heart beating just for her. "I tried to save her, but I was too late."

James smoothed over her hair, his fingers running down her braids to her shoulders. "You still have time to save your sister." He brought his head down next to hers and whispered in her ear. "I found the man in charge of one of the colony ships."

Mestasis pulled back to see his face. "How?"

He shrugged, still holding onto her. To the elderly man and his bodyguard, they appeared as any young couple in love. The line moved up ahead and the tattooed man ushered his ward down the steps and into the hall. James watched them leave then continued. "Connections. If you listen to people talk long enough, you hear things."

"Is he looking for people to take on board?"

"No. But he *is* looking for someone to drive it."

"What do you mean?"

"The ship itself is so complicated, so many systems must run in sync, he needs someone able to oversee all of the regulations, someone that could work with the mainframe to ensure the safety of everyone on board."

"You're thinking me?"

James nodded. "Thadious Legacy's his name, and he's already agreed to meet with you. To save your sister as well, you must convince him you and your sister work together, that he needs both of you to run the ship."

Mestasis thought back to the demonstration that morning at TINE. "That's easy. The hard part will be getting out of our contract at TINE."

"He'll pay TINE off and guarantee them a number of spots on the colony ship."

"You're sure of it?"

James nodded once. "Positive."

Mestasis's heart fluttered as her head swam with the thought of a hopeful future and most of all, gratitude. "James, you just gave me everything I wanted. I don't know what to say."

"It's not that easy, Metsy. It means being connected to the ship. Living as one until the *Expedition* reaches Paradise 18 in hundreds of years. Can you do that?"

"Of course I can, if it keeps my sister safe."

"Good." He pulled away from her and moved toward the steps. "I'll get you that appointment."

Mestasis called after him. "Wait!"

He whipped around, his face set in expectation.

"I'll negotiate to get you on there as well. After all you've done for me, I'm not going to leave you behind."

James turned to the hovercrafts whizzing by them. Her heart dropped as he ripped his gaze away. "I'm needed here. The Radioactive Hand of Justice's work will never be done. Conditions worsen every day. There's talk of war between the United Federation and the Foreign Union, besides civil unrest. You must have heard about the Mississippi drying up?"

Mestasis nodded and he continued. "Well, there's not enough water to go around. Rioters make their way here even now. Soon they'll break through the city walls."

"All the more reason why you should come with me." She took his hand. "Please let me argue on your behalf."

James sighed and his face closed up, "I'm not leaving my people behind."

Mestasis stepped toward him. With her and Abysme's powers, she had the ultimate bargaining chip. Why not try? "How many people are you talking about?"

He scanned the balcony as if he could see to the lower levels where people scrounged while they stood underneath the sun. "Obviously, I'd like to save everyone in the city, and every other city for that matter. But if I had to pick a number." He ran his hand over his long hair and pursed his lips. She'd asked him to play God, and she knew that wasn't easy.

Squeezing his hand, she gazed into his eyes and pleaded. "Just give me something I can work with."

James gazed down her cheek to her hand as it grasped his. She brought her head closer, her face tilted just beyond his lips. He bowed down and almost closed the distance. His breath warmed her mouth. "I'd say about three hundred."

"I'll see what I can do." Mestasis rose up on her toes and closed the distance, pushing her lips into his in a fierce kiss. When she pulled back from him, he pulled her back in. They stood there wanting one another, deaf to the tick of time.

When she did part from him, her voice hardened. "Set up a meeting with Mr. Legacy. I'll do my best."

❧

Ah Mr. Legacy...

If only Mestasis had known the Legacys would be the bane of their existence for the next three hundred years. She hadn't wanted to appoint Luna to the exploratory team, but as part of the contract she'd signed with Thadious Legacy, she had to favor his descendants over the rest of the crew. She only hoped the extraordinary talents of the other members outweighed Luna's propensity for greed.

CHAPTER TWENTY-ONE
CLOSE QUARTERS

Brentwood shook as someone woke him, ripping him away from the blissful fog that had claimed his mind and his heart. Luna stared at him with eyes decorated in teal shadows, looking like a galactic sorceress come to steal his soul.

"Lieutenant?"

"What is it?" He never snapped, but this came pretty close.

She took her hand off his arm as if he'd slapped it and cushioned it against her chest. "Tech says there's a massive weather front on the radar."

"What?" He shot up in his seat and the restraining strap pulled tight against his chest. "Holy Quasars." He unclasped the lock at his waist and pushed his head forward to the front seat. Gemme slept soundly, the sight of her freckled cheeks making his neck tingle with heat. Hadn't she been in his dream?

"Lieutenant, lookie here." Tech waved his chubby finger in the air to catch his attention. A fluorescent green and blue clump claimed the radar. "Sorry to wake you, sir, but we need to change course and look for shelter."

"How bad is it?" Judging for the growing plume of color, he already knew the answer.

"It's a full-fledged blizzard. The snowfall alone could smother this landrover in over four meters. Not to mention the wind."

Brentwood's chest tightened as adrenaline shot through his limbs. He'd gone from heaven to an icy hell in seconds. "Where should we go?"

"Those mountains are our best bet." Tech pointed out the sight panel at a string of ridges on the right. Even if we can't find a cave, we could blast a hole into the ice."

"All right. Let's switch seats and I'll drive. I know how to gun it and keep the vehicle in control. We'll outrun the storm and wait it out against the mountain range."

"Yes, sir." Tech ground the wheels to a halt and they pushed by each other, switching seats. Brentwood regained his composure as he secured the belt across his chest. He pushed the foot pedal and the vehicle gained speed. Where had that dream come from? He couldn't remember and he didn't have time to think back. Flurries blinded the main sight panel. The storm darkened the sky above them as it pressed in.

He watched the speedometer, fixated above a tiny symbol of the *Expedition* to the moving arrow. Seventy kilometers per hour, seventy-five. He could go up to one hundred without losing traction, but beyond that, they'd be gliding helpless on the ice. "Strap yourself in, Tech," he called over his shoulder. "Ms. Legacy, secure your seat restraint as well."

"Already done." Luna called back to him, but he ignored her. Casting a sideways glance, he saw Gemme leaning out of her seat restraint, the strap hanging loose.

"Ms. Reiner. Ms. Reiner, wake up!"

She didn't move. One look at the speedometer told him they'd accelerated to maximum performance speed. The snowflakes had grown larger, falling in clumps and collecting on the corners. He had to keep going.

"Damn!"

With one hand one the wheel and one foot pressing the pedal to the floor, he leaned over and nudged her up, exposing the seat lock in her lap. Heat traveled from his neck to his cheeks as his fingers grazed her legs. If she woke up in that instant, it'd look like he groped her.

Please don't wake up right now.

He grabbed the lock and pulled it toward him, clicking it in place. She shifted as the straps tightened, but her eyes stayed closed. Relief flowed through him until he settled back into his seat and watched the blob on the radar move in.

Snow whipped around the vehicle, blurring into streaks. Visibility lessened with each minute until the entire sight panel filled with white. Calming himself, Brentwood turned to his controls. The topography charts reported the mountain range approaching in twenty kilometers on the right. They'd driven a half a kilometer off course. He turned slightly and the tires skidded, pitching the landrover sideways. The mining equipment pulled them the opposite way, straining the metal lock hitching the platform to the vehicle. Luna screamed as the tires screeched under the pressure.

Brentwood gripped the wheel and spun it until the vehicle pointed back on course. "We'll make it!" he shouted, wondering if he reassured himself more than the others.

Gemme stirred in the seat next to him. "What's going on?"

"Blizzard." He gave her the most comforting smile he could produce. "Hold on tight."

The mountain range popped up out of nowhere and Brentwood careened alongside it, searching for an outcropping. A slab of sheer, unbroken ice sprawled for miles beside them. Brentwood watched as the arrow on the speedometer moved from sixty to fifty, then twenty as the tires sunk and stuck in the newly fallen snow. The engines roared in protest as the vehicle stopped, lodging itself against a drift.

"That's as far as we can go." Brentwood pressed the panel for the hatch. "Get out your lasers, we're blasting a hole."

"We're going out in the blizzard?" Luna shouted as the hatch opened and the howling wind barreled in, stripping them of warmth in seconds.

"Yup." Tech pushed past her and whipped out his laser, checking the charge on the energy cell. "Ready when you are, chief." His enthusiasm didn't surprise Brentwood. Tech had come up with the idea of blasting a hole in the first place.

Brentwood looked back to check on Gemme. She had her hood up, angora hair covering half her face in an adorable, yet sexy way. In her hand she held her laser, poised and ready to fire. He had a sudden urge to comfort her, to hold her close and feel the angora hair tickling his skin.

Shaking his head, he signaled to Gemme with a wave of his hand. *By the Guide, pay attention!*

She gave him a nod and he turned back to the rest of the team, screaming over the raging winds. "Set your lasers to maximum subsonic pulse. Third click down. Focus on my stream."

He fired, the white light penetrating the outer layer of ice. Each member of the team joined in, and together their lasers reinforced and steadied his stream. Steam rose from the ice as the white shafts of light burned a hole. The wind carried the steam away, revealing more and more layers of ice.

"There's no rock, it's just giant glaciers of ice." Tech shouted, face drawn as if he'd opened a present and found it empty.

"That's why it doesn't show up on the mining grid." Gemme shouted back at him. "No minerals to mine."

"I'll say."

"It will make it easier to carve out a shelter." Brentwood tried to reassure them. "Rock is harder to cut through."

They stood while the wind whipped around them, pulling at each strand of hair on his head and numbing his cheeks. Brentwood worried a strong enough gale might whip one of them away. Luna's laser dipped, slashing the bottom of the mountain with white light.

"Keep your arms up," Brentwood shouted to her. Why couldn't she follow one order correctly? Just one?

Luna collapsed on her knees. "I can't do it any longer. I'm freezing to death."

"Go back to the vehicle," Brentwood ordered. "We'll do the rest."

Luna scrambled away with tears in her eyes. Pity trickled through him. Lieutenanthood wasn't cut out for some people, but that didn't mean they weren't as important. He wished he could find a way to tell her and ease the burden of her family's expectations.

It took twenty minutes to melt a hole large enough to fit the vehicle, the mining equipment, and themselves. Brentwood's arms ached from holding the laser steady. Tech's cheeks were red as apples, and ice coated the tips of Gemme's hair. Yet, besides Luna, they held their ground. Pride surged inside him.

"Good work, Alpha Blue. Now help me dig out the landrover. We're going in."

A thick layer of snow had covered the vehicle in the time it took for them to melt a hole in the mountain. He plunged into the snow, digging out the tires with his gloved hands and cursing all their inexperience. They'd brought skin regenerators, high protein and electrolyte bars, miniscreens with a databank of information. But no one had thought to bring a shovel. His fingers throbbed, but he kept digging until he cleared the ruts of each tire.

He stood, brushing fluffy snow off the hatch. "Come on!"

Eager to get out of the cold, they piled in and he revved up the engines, gaining force to dislodge from the bank of snow. He pressed the gas and the tires skidded, lurching forward three centimeters and then falling back.

"Do you want me to get out and push?" Tech offered.

"No, that's not necessary." Flicking his hands over the control panels he selected a lower gear and tried again. The tires squealed, and he pressed harder until they found traction. The vehicle rolled forward, freed from the drift. A chorus of hollers and hoots erupted behind him as they drove into their shelter.

He glanced over at Gemme and she mouthed the words, "Good job."

Her support made him burn inside out. Even though he was a lieutenant, he couldn't ignore his feelings any longer. He wished he could get a chance to talk with her alone. How much control did she have over the pairings? The more time he spent with her, the more he realized she embodied everything he'd ever sought, and he ached to ask her if she felt the same draw toward him. If only Luna hadn't continually pushed herself in the way.

The landrover inched into cave. Headlights illuminated a glossy ceiling where the laser fire had melted layers away. It looked like they traveled through an ocean hung in suspension, water all around them but not a drop touching the hood. Brentwood marveled, feeling like a little boy in the aqua-tank room back on the *Expedition*. These walls of slick ice were galactically more stunning.

They parked at the back of the cave where the wall curved in seamlessly to the floor. Tech helped Brentwood peg up a thermal nylon tarp to block the entrance while Gemme and Luna unloaded their tents and other supplies. Although ice surrounded them, the inside of the cave was several degrees warmer than the blizzard outside. With the thermal energy cells, it would be a toasty bath.

Anchoring the last peg of the tarp into the ice wall, Tech grumbled, "Had enough snow for one day. I'm going to sleep in the vehicle tonight. You can have the tent."

"Okay, Tech." Brentwood patted him on the back. He'd driven the landrover for hours, and he deserved to get some peaceful rest. "Thanks for helping."

"No problem, chief."

As Tech snuggled in the backseat and the hatch closed, Brentwood turned to the ladies. They'd already constructed the remaining three tents while he and Tech put up the tarp. Although Luna held the last peg of her own tent in her hand, he suspected Gemme had done most of the work.

The nylon of Gemme's tent twitched as she moved around inside. Eagerness stirred inside him. Fumbling with words in his head, he walked over to speak with her. He wanted to tell her what an amazing job she'd done that day, but most of all, he wanted to ask her about the pairings, and how she chose each couple. If she felt as strongly as he did, he wanted his pairing to be with her.

Luna intercepted, placing her body between him and the tent.

"I need to talk to you."

Brentwood stifled his impatience. He didn't want to snap at her the way he did when she woke him. "Again?"

"Uh-huh. Concerning Beta Prime."

It seemed as though fate kept twisting his path away from Gemme.

Or was it just Luna? "Right now?"

"It's time sensitive information. Yes."

It took all his energy to suppress his frustration. But he was a lieutenant, and the mission had to come first. He motioned for her to join him in his tent. "Okay. If it's important."

"More important than anything else in this ice cave."

He opened the tent flap and she smiled as she slid in underneath his arm.

The thought of being alone with Luna made him squirm like he put on a shirt two sizes too small. His tent closed in on them, narrow and too intimate, yet he couldn't discuss the secret mission in the presence of the others, and the cave echoed every word. Not wanting to give Luna the wrong idea, or anyone else for that matter, he got right down to business. "What's this about?"

"While you were sleeping, I accessed the *Expedition's* database, and using the code word Beta Prime, found hundreds of secret files on the orb. It seems the scientists studying it experienced strange hallucinations and dreams, not only of memories in their past, but of times before they were born, maybe even previous lives on Old Earth."

"What are you talking about?"

"The energy from the orb stimulates parts of the cerebral cortex, and from there, energy travels to association tracts consisting of connector neurons thought to be associated with reasoning, learning, and memory."

"Hold on, are you saying that orb activates long-lost memories?"

Luna stepped closer. "Could be. There is no one part of the brain that stores memory; therefore the findings are hypothetical at best. What drew my attention was the scientists exposed to the orb reported mostly happy memories. Some said they could actually control which memories they had, bringing back the ones they wanted to relive again and again. Some found it so blissful they didn't want to leave the orb, becoming more and more reclusive. One man grew so addicted he wouldn't leave the lab. They had to stop the experiments altogether and lock it up with the Seers."

Brentwood leaned down in order for her to hear his whisper, "The question is, why? Why would an alien species design such a device? What purpose does it have?"

Luna shrugged. "I'm a biologist, not a philosopher. It may stimulate other things for the alien species, and that's just the effect it has on us. Or, they really liked their memories."

She laughed, the sound resonating a little too loud in his tent. "I'm not about to hypothesize on one of the greatest finds of mankind." She pointed at him, her finger resting on his chest. "I'll leave that to you."

He wrapped his fingers around her hand to gently nudge her away, but she brought up her other hand and caught him, gripping his hand firmly in both of hers. "That's not all."

Brentwood resisted the urge to pull away. Luna had him intrigued. Any more information concerning this secretive mission would help. Afraid to break her chain of thought, he let her hold on to hear out next words. "Yes?"

"The orb is only big enough to hold someone's mind, not their body. So the scientists could only delve so far into their memories, always leaving a part of themselves behind. This beacon that the orb points to is much larger, large enough to submerge an entire body. You could potentially immerse yourself and remain lost in it forever."

"Wow, this is all so strange to me." Brentwood felt like he floated in the belly of a giant jellyfish as the tent swam around him. Alien artifacts, old memories, temptations. His dreams came back to him, dreams of Gemme and the past. Could it be connected?

"Me, too." Luna steadied him with both her hands on his chest. "I didn't mean to upset you. Are you okay?"

He blinked, feeling dizzy. "I'm fine. I just need some time alone to think about this."

"Wait." Luna's grip on his shoulders remained firm. "There's something else I want to talk about."

He stared her down. "What now?"

"You know about the pairing machine being ruined, don't you?"

The change in subject startled him. "What do you mean?"

She smiled as if he'd just made her day. "You don't know, do you? You haven't read the reports on decks eighty-seven on up?"

He grew defensive. Even though he was a lieutenant, it didn't mean he was all knowing. "I read the survivor reports. My mission was to save the people on those decks, not the programs. Besides, I've been swamped preparing for Alpha Blue. Hull damage didn't fall under my jurisdiction."

"Well, it's gone. The pairing machine and every program that went with it. Ms. Matchmaker is out of a job. That's why she's with us, you know. The Seers had to put her somewhere."

Gemme. She was talking about Gemme. And the fact the pairing system was gone. Brentwood's head reeled with this new information. Could they choose their partners for themselves? Could he choose Gemme?

"I see what you're thinking, Lieutenant, and I'm thinking the same thing." Luna leaned in so close he could feel her body heat against him. Did she know of his feelings for Gemme? Had she talked to her?

His voice came out wispy with hope. "What am I thinking?"

Instead of answering, Luna pushed her face into his. Her lips crushed his in a firm and aggressive kiss, thrusting her tongue into his mouth. Brentwood froze in shock, jolted by the feeling of how completely wrong this whole meeting was. Light filtered in, illuminating them pressed together as the tent flap parted and Gemme peeked through.

"Lieutenant, I need to talk—"

How could he let this get so out of control? Angry and embarrassed, he pushed Luna back, ripping her lips from his as their combined spittle flew across the tent. But it was too late. Gemme had already seen their indecent kiss and her delicate features crumpled into a mask of disgust. She disappeared, tent flap flipping down.

"Ms. Reiner, wait!" Brentwood pushed past Luna, scrambling through the opening. He emerged just as she slid under the tarp into the blizzard. "No!"

Brentwood followed her, slipping across the floor of ice. He yanked the peg out and threw himself into the raging winds.

"Gemme!" He shouted as the snow stung his face. "Gemme, come back!"

Night had fallen, and he couldn't see anything in the pitch-black. He ducked under the tarp, grabbed a beacon light from the back of the landrover, and flung himself out into the frigid night.

Snow smothered the light in a thousand white, darting shafts, like swarms of moths in the biodome, blinding him to everything farther than a meter ahead. Brentwood ran along the mouth of the cave, the wind pushing him sideways into a snowdrift. "Gemme!"

How could he possibly prove Luna had pounced on him? He failed her both as a person and as a lieutenant. How could she ever respect him again?

Before the comet shower he had had his world completely under control. He hadn't realized what a small world it was, and how an infinite universe engulfed his perfect bubble. He never thought he'd have to face it until the *Expedition* crashed, revealing a world vaster than his own.

What had happened to the youngest appointed lieutenant, the man who'd graduated first in his class to so confidently lead the congregation at every meeting? Although his horizons had broadened, he was still the same man. No smaller, no weaker.

Brentwood forced himself up. He had an entire population to save, starting with Gemme.

Gemme collapsed into the snow, wondering why in the all the universe she'd just run headfirst into a blizzard. The winds tore at her thermal coat as the cold settled into the marrow of her bones, but she didn't care. The memory of Brentwood passionately kissing Luna was enough to keep her out in the dark all night. Her head felt like someone had shaken it with a molecule vibrator, and she had to get away to sort out her misplaced feelings.

To think: she'd gone in to discuss her own feelings for him. Thank goodness she'd witnessed their kiss before embarrassing herself by spewing out the indecent feelings in her heart.

Thank goodness she'd stopped her pairing with Brentwood. How could she ever marry a man attracted to someone else? Her initial instinct to touch the delete panel had been correct. All the other feelings that had come after it were obscenely wrong, and she struggled to come to terms with that fact. Now she knew why the matched parings worked so effectively. Organic romance was too messy, hurting the people involved.

"Gemme!"

Did she hear her name, or did the howling wind play tricks in her throbbing ears? She tightened her arms around her shoulders, trying to hold in her dwindling body heat. She knew she had to go back, but she couldn't face Brentwood and Luna. Not yet. She'd rather lose fingers and toes to frostbite then see them together.

"Gemme!"

There was no mistaking his voice this time. Brentwood had come out to look for her. A sudden rush of hope sparked in her heart and she squashed it. As a lieutenant, he couldn't have a member of his team die of hypothermia, whether he had feelings for her or not. He needed her to complete the mission. And so did the rest of the *Expedition*, including her parent and Ferris. Gemme knew her actions were reckless and selfish, yet she couldn't bring her legs to work. Had they frozen in the snow?

Dizziness washed over her and a heavy weariness seeped in. She realized her hands and feet had stopped throbbing. Numbness trickled through her, spreading to her face. Her eyelids felt like heavy thermal blankets.

I'll just lie down for a minute before I go back to camp.

A faint golden light caught her attention. Brentwood. Her stomach panged like a laser shot through it. Besides her gut, her sore heart was the only part of her body that hadn't gone numb. But if she slept...

No. She forced herself up. Her mind would only take her back to the field and the engagement party. She shook her head to keep herself awake. No more dreams of Brentwood. Gemme felt caught between two worlds, the harsh reality before her, and the blissful fabrication of her dreams. If she fell asleep, she'd be living a lie. She decided she'd rather have harsh truth instead.

Forcing her legs up, Gemme walked toward the light. Every part of her body shook as she struggled to wade through snow up to her thighs. "Over here."

The golden light grew stronger and Brentwood crested the hill with relief splashed in his face. Sliding down, he caught her in his arms.

"Gemme, I'm sorry. Thank the Guide I found you. Are you okay?"

Besides a bleeding heart, a sickened stomach, and the beginnings of hypothermia? Gemme nodded. "Fine."

"Come on, let me take you back to camp. I have a lot of explaining to do."

Gemme followed him, stumbling over her own feet. She hated the fact that she had to grab his arm to stay upright. She'd never put herself in such a helpless, vulnerable position again, both physically and emotionally.

They walked in silence to the cave. It didn't make sense to fight the howling wind, and Gemme had nothing she wanted to say. All she could think to do was finish the damned mission and get on with her life. Brentwood pulled back the tarp and she pushed her way through. The warm air of the cave surrounded her in a bath. Luna sat on a supply container by the lighted energy cell.

"Well, that was stupid, running out in a blizzard. I'd already told you he was mine."

"Luna, that's enough." Brentwood came in behind her. He turned to Gemme and pointed to the supply container next to Luna. "Please, sit down."

Did she have to? Luna was the last person she wanted to sit next to right now. Wondering if she could disobey a direct order, Gemme slumped down beside Luna. She felt like they were both kids in a time out, and she hadn't even done anything wrong. *Besides run into a blizzard.*

She watched as Brentwood walked over to the landrover and opened the hatch. "Tech, get up. We have a lot to talk about."

Tech poked his head out, curly black hair standing up on end. "Did I miss something?"

Brentwood's voice growled. "I've called an impromptu meeting. Attendance mandatory."

Tech's eyes widened, "Sure thing, chief." He stumbled out in his thermal fleece pajama pants. Gemme shifted away from Luna making room for him. Yawning, he plopped down in between them.

Brentwood stood in front of the trio. His hands shook, but Gemme had no sympathy.

"I'm going to go against the direct orders of the Seers. I may lose my position when we get back because of it, but there's no other way to do this and I hate keeping information from my team."

Tech scooted forward on the container, rubbing his forehead. "What's this about?"

Brentwood opened his mouth, but Luna stood, holding up a finger. "They're not supposed to know."

Gemme intervened. "Know about what?"

Brentwood gave Luna a stern look. "We should have never kept it from them in the first place."

"You're going against the Seers' orders." Luna's face turned red.

"Let them fire me for all I care." Brentwood turned back to address Gemme and Tech. "The Seers assigned Ms. Legacy and I to a secret alternate mission. We're supposed to find an alien device matching an orb the *Expedition* picked up in space hundreds of years ago. The orb is thought to have qualities that bring out someone's memories, allowing them to relive the happiest ones again and again, addicting people to its energy. Because of the danger of this news becoming a widespread panic, the Seers wanted this mission kept top secret. Ms. Legacy and I were the only ones with clearance."

The new information tickled the hairs on the back of Gemme's neck. Here it was: proof they weren't alone in this galaxy, and yet her stomach still churned with bitterness. The secret mission explained a lot of Brentwood and Luna's private conversations, yet it didn't explain anything about the kiss she'd just witnessed.

She glared at him as he continued. His words faltered when he looked at her. "My relationship with Ms. Legacy is purely professional. There's nothing going on between us, despite some of the things you may have heard or seen us do."

Gemme couldn't contain her hostility. She'd thought Brentwood was valiant and noble, and instead he snuck a kiss on the most important mission the *Expedition* offered him, and lied about it afterward. Why couldn't he just come clean? Tell them he had feelings for Luna? He was as bad as the politicians from Old Earth. "Pfft. You don't see me kissing Tech."

Tech scratched his head. "What?"

"I caught them with their faces stuck together." Gemme seethed under her breath. A small doubt that Brentwood had kissed Luna on purpose nagged at her heart and she squashed it down. "Just a few minutes ago."

Tech shook his head like she suggested hyperthium and oxygen combined to make up air. "Brentwood and Luna?"

"Enough." Brentwood interrupted them. "Luna misunderstood me, that's all."

"That's one hell of a misunderstanding," Gemme shot back.

Luna frowned. "It was pretty clear to me."

Brentwood shook his head, waving his arms to calm everyone down. "Luna, you should never force yourself on anyone, especially a higher officer. What you instigated was wrong, and would be reprimanded had we still been on the *Expedition*. But we're trapped in a cave in the middle of nowhere — "

"With possible little green men." Tech interrupted, shifting uncomfortably in his seat.

Brentwood nodded. "Yes, with possible aliens, and we have a mission to accomplish." He turned to Gemme. "I'm sorry you had to see that, and Tech, I'm sorry to have to wake you up."

Tech waved his hand. "No apology necessary, sir."

"Right. Thank you, Tech." He perused the three of them, meeting Gemme's gaze. When his eyes locked on hers, they held a glimmer of deep melancholy and pain and she wondered just what he regretted: the fact that he kissed Luna on the mission, or the fact that she caught them red-handed, or red-lipped for that matter.

Brentwood tore his gaze away and continued. "Above all, we have a mission to accomplish; two missions if you heard me correctly. The *Expedition* is relying on us and us alone. We can't bicker like this among ourselves. For decency purposes, all our conversations from now on will be held out in the open." He stared at Luna. "No more private meetings about Beta Prime. No private meetings between us. At all."

Gemme thought back to the comment Luna had made in the landrover about Beta Prime. Maybe all of their secret meetings had been centered around work. Maybe Brentwood was right? She thought about the kiss and stifled the thought. No, that lip-lock looked pretty real.

Brentwood paused when he saw her face, and faltered on his words before he continued. "N-now, get some rest. When the storm lifts, we have a six-hour drive ahead of us. Then, we'll find this alien object while Tech sets up the mining equipment."

"Yes sir, chief." Tech stood up, patted Brentwood on the back, and returned to the landrover. Brentwood stormed away into his tent before anyone could ask any further questions. Once again, the men left Gemme with Luna, alone. She moved to her tent, but Luna caught her arm.

Her eyes shone so fierce, she looked like a wounded animal about to pounce. "He's still mine, you know. He's just covering it up because you caught us."

"Good." Gemme gave Luna a curt smile before darting into her tent. "No need to push me into a recycling shaft this time. You can have him."

CHAPTER TWENTY-TWO
SACRIFICE

Lieutenant Brentwood flashed on the mainframe. Dark circles framed his eyes, and he'd pushed up his hair at odd angles. His haggard appearance heightened Mestasis's concerns. For a moment, she forgot about the pull of her memories to listen. "We're stuck in a snowstorm, but it should blow over by morning. Tech says we're only a day away from the mining site. After we reach it and get the equipment set up, we'll begin our quest for the beacon."

The beacon. A drop of sweat ran down her cheek, dangling from her chin, and dripped onto the chrome floor. Did she really want them to find the beacon?

Abysme had ordered it, not her. Now her sister lay hanging like dead weight.

A thought tugged at her mind. She could call the mission off. Would Abysme even know?

But the orb and the beacon were the only objects interesting her sister. How could she take away Abysme's last wishes?

Her heart panged. The old muscle beat feebly, but the ache was still acute. Only one thing eased the pain. *Memories. Sweet memories.*

രാ≪

Old Earth, 2446

"Excellent. I'll secure two commander seats for you and your sister and three hundred civilian positions onboard. Now, if you'll just press the touchscreen here for a digital fingerprint signature..." An older man with thick black eyebrows and a head bald as a pin hovered over his desk, leaning toward Mestasis. He looked so eager she could picture him rubbing his palms together once they'd completed the deal.

A tinge of doubt tweaked in her stomach. She paused, finger hovering over the touchscreen as golden swirls of pixels danced at her fingertips. "What about TINE, Mr. Legacy?"

"They will be well taken care of, of course. We'll offer Dr. Fields a place on onboard the ship as well."

"And James Wilfred?"

"Certainly. Granted, everyone must pass certain blood and DNA tests to ensure the health and well-being of the crew and future generations aboard the ship."

Her finger twitched above the screen, fluorescent light reflecting off her dark skin. "Routine tests?"

His eyebrows rose like two caterpillars on his face. "Yes. Harmless and practical to ensure we have a divergent supply of DNA. With the exception of you and your sister, of course."

"And what's this about favoring the Legacys throughout each generation?"

"Just a little condition I put in to ensure my descendants aren't overlooked."

"Looks to me like these arrangements destine them for lieutenanthood, among other things."

"Well, you can't be too careful, now can you? I need to know my children and their children's children will do well."

Although the bargain did favor the Legacys, it saved many others and seemed too easy, too good to be true. Mestasis thought back to the day she took a chance on TINE. Besides the distance it caused from her mother, that risk had kept her and her sister well fed and safe all this time. She'd take it again if she had the chance, and here it was: an opportunity off this doomed planet in a controlled environment complete with food, medical supplies, and everything they'd ever need. No more worrying about securing jobs or the future of TINE, no more searching for nukes in the sky. She pressed her finger down on the digital contract and the screen beeped as it read her impression.

"Wonderful! The *Expedition's* crew manifesto is now complete. We leave in two days." Mr. Legacy tilted his head, pressing a panel on his desk. The top drawer opened and he pulled out a cigar that smelled sweet enough to be made from real tobacco leaves, something Mestasis had never seen before.

"So soon?"

He lit the end of the cigar and a puff of sweetly scented smoke wafted her way. "We're behind as it is. A ship called *The New Dawn* took off three months ago, destined for Paradise 21. We'll be headed to Paradise 18, a smaller planet, but chocked full of water and greenery with only a small amount of terraforming necessary. We won't reach it in my lifetime, or that of my children or grandchildren. But at least I know my family will enjoy a safe and productive life, and that my descendants will live on."

His answer still didn't address the rush to leave. If his planet had already been secured, and they wouldn't reach it in his lifetime, why did he feel such an urgency to leave? "But why the rush?"

"Beware the things they don't tell you on the news, my dear."

She leaned forward, her fingers shaking, despite the coolness she kept in her voice. "Is the world falling apart?"

"The Foreign Union is dissolving as we speak. Wars over rivers rage in Europe, and you know about the refugees outside the city?"

She thought back to what James had told her. "I've heard, yes."

"Patrols shoot whoever gets close to the border, but the guards don't have enough firepower for them all."

Horrific images flashed through her mind and she blinked them away. "What is everyone going to do?"

"Who knows? It's not our problem, is it?" Mr. Legacy's leather chair creaked as he sat back and sucked on the end of the cigar. "I've been planning this escape for most of my life, saving credits to purchase the supplies, conducting research on paradise planets. I was lucky enough to see into the future, to make preparations. So many did not."

He reached over and clasped a tracking bracelet on her wrist. Mestasis shot him a look as if he'd betrayed her.

"You're too important for me to risk losing. This will monitor your health at all times. Nothing more. This one's for your sister. Make sure she attaches it immediately."

He handed her another bracelet and motioned for one of his guards to escort her out. "I'll send word when the preparations are complete."

She put her other hand over the bracelet as if it stung her skin and bowed her head. "Thank you, sir."

His dark eyes widened with intensity. "No. Thank you."

The guard led her through an atrium with real, fresh plants, and she resisted the urge to reach out and touch a leaf, the shiny green reminding her of the one blade of grass they had cultured as children. The memory of her mother came back to her, and she pushed it away. She couldn't deal with it, not now. Part of her felt as though she left her mother behind. She had to remind herself that her mother was gone, her body cremated, and their small apartment issued to another family, just as desperate. There was nothing left for her here on Earth.

They crossed a corridor between Thadious Legacy's building and the recycled food compactors the government had issued built in Quadrant Three. The pungent smell of stale compost and human waste wafted up from the heated vats below. The guard left her at the gate with only a nod. Eager to get out of the factory, she darted through the main lobby and into a courtyard constructed between the factory and other office buildings.

Greenhouses lined the walkway, each glass door panel locked and wired with an alarm. The energy of the security systems buzzed in the air around her, and she had to block out her tendency to connect to the electromagnetic pulses. A figure appeared between the glass domes and Mestasis ran to him, burrowing herself into his arms.

James held her close, his breath tickling her hair. "How did it go?"

"Astronomically well. I secured your three hundred seats, and a place for you, myself, and my sister."

James pulled his head back, his eyes full of awe. "All three hundred?"

Mestasis shrugged. "When the vessel carries several thousand, three hundred isn't much to ask for, I guess."

James shook his head as if he couldn't imagine it. "I never meant this to help so many people; I just wanted to make you happy, keep you safe."

Mestasis put a finger over his lips to silence him. "I know. I wanted to give you something in return. No one has ever shown such an interest in helping me, besides Dr. Fields. But his intentions lay solely to develop my abilities for TINE. Most people, that's all they see. I'm not a person, but a tool. When they see what I can do, they see endless boundaries, unlimited control, unhindered power."

"I don't." James trailed a finger from her cheek down to her neck. Her skin tingled underneath his touch. "I only see you."

Engines roared above them and Mestasis watched the sky. Five hovercrafts, all military models armed with missiles on either side flew by. TINE didn't need her to detect those bombs.

"Where are they going?" Mestasis ran in between the greenhouses to the edge of the roof. The city sprawled out before her. High-rises poked up like weeds, so close a kid could jump from one to the next. She followed the arc of the hovercrafts as she held back stray wisps of her hair freed by their exhaust winds.

James ran up beside her. He gripped the railing with both hands, staring at the horizon, his face slack. "While you were in the meeting, the Razornecks launched an attack on Utopia. They've killed all the guards and claimed it for themselves. All shipments of food have stopped. They've taken over the building as their own. I didn't think the retaliation attack would come so soon."

"So the government is just going to blow it up? Waste all that food? It's the largest greenhouse in the city. How will everyone eat?"

"There's nothing else they can do." James shook his head in resignation. "They can't let the Razornecks have it. They'll grow too strong and take over the city. It's the only chance they have to eliminate their terror cell while so many of them are contained in the same place."

Mestasis clasped James tighter. "Thadious Legacy was right. The world is falling apart."

In front of them, a plume of black smoke rose from the center of the city, mixing with the smog in the gray sky. The desolation in James's eyes made her chest tighten so hard she couldn't breathe.

James held her close, his body warmth giving her comfort against the cool, tainted air. "If so, we'll leave just in time."

≈∽

Mestasis stared at the blank white of the snow covering the main sight panel. She'd never see anything outside the ship ever again. But, in her memories, she saw the entire city where she'd lived. And most of all, she saw James.

CHAPTER TWENTY-THREE
SAMPLES

The tension in the landrover made Gemme's hairs stand up on the back of her neck. Brentwood and Tech sat in the front seats, leaving her with Luna in the back. No one spoke about the previous night. In fact, no one spoke at all. The mining site lay only hours ahead, and the culmination of their mission heightened Gemme's anxiety.

What if the first scout team reported the deposit incorrectly hundreds of years ago? What if the minerals were gone, already mined by the owners of the beacon?

And more importantly, what kind of device did the orb send them to? Who or what would be there to receive them?

Her own personal matters seemed trivial compared to the answers lying just hours away. Peering out the sight panel at the newly fallen snow, she marveled at how Tundra 37 seemed frigid, harsh, and unpredictable, and her stomach clenched as she anticipated the day to come.

The landrover plodded slower than usual. Tech had welded two metal slabs to the front bender to plow through the newly fallen snow.

The vehicle wove a path like a tunnel, and Gemme could see their trail twisting in a worm shape all the way back to the ice mountains they'd left behind.

Eventually, her mind roamed back to last night's kiss. Luna had been pushy her whole life, and Gemme had witnessed Luna's capabilities first hand by the heel of Luna's palm. An inkling of doubt festered as to her accusations toward Brentwood.

Maybe Luna had pushed herself on him. Gemme wouldn't put it past her. But entertaining that idea just gave her heart hope, and it made her feel weak and vulnerable all over again. No, it was easier to make him the bad guy, not to trust her heart, but trust her head.

"Look!" Luna squeaked, pressing her finger against the sight panel. "Stop the landrover!"

"What is it?" Brentwood sounded suspicious, and after last night, Gemme would question anything that came out of that woman's mouth. But the sheer excitement on Luna's face made her change her mind. She pressed her face against the glass. "Vegetation. A whole field of it."

Brentwood slowed to a stop and opened the hatch. Luna pushed by him and jumped out, jogging across the ice.

"Well, take me out to a black hole and drop me in." Tech shook his head. "Guess she was interested in samples after all."

Gemme wasn't as easily convinced. Maybe since she couldn't have Brentwood, she decided on the next best thing: her career. Trying to appear supportive, Gemme followed Brentwood and Tech to where Luna knelt on the ground. Thin grasses surrounded her, bending in the light wind. Gemme thought of the wheat field, but these grasses were white with a tinge of blue, so close to the hue of the snow she'd never notice them.

Luna pulled a wispy strand out of the snow crust. "This must be what the mammoths eat."

"It's not as cold here." Tech unzipped his coat. "Must be a warm jet stream blowing up from the south."

"Which would explain the melting snow and the presence of vegetation. Too bad I left my sample bags in the landrover." Luna sniffed the strand and stuffed it into her pocket. "This means there may be other species of vegetation around. If we're lucky, we'll be able to eat this as well."

"Great. I just love salad." Tech's words dripped with sarcasm. "Test the mammoth meat first, and we'll have barbecue."

"I'm going to test it all." Luna glanced at him with disdain.

Tech held up his hands. "I'm just saying you should have some priorities."

Staying out of the argument, Gemme searched for Brentwood. He stood on top of the next snowdrift waving his hand.

"Hey, guys, I think we should see what the Lieutenant wants."

Brentwood met them halfway down the snowdrift. Huffing, he pointed back to the landrover. "We're almost there. It's just over that next ridge."

"We've come to our final stop, people." Brentwood's voice had a ring of finality that sent a shiver down Gemme's back. This was it. They'd reached the end of the mission. Now her analytical skills would be tested. She wondered if she could calculate the exact dimensions and composition of the mineral deposit. Numbers and data she could do without question, but hyperthium and other minerals?

"The screen says the mineral deposit is two hundred meters away, just over this hill." Brentwood turned the landrover to the right.

"What are all those dots on the screen?" Tech sat up in his seat trying to glimpse over the edge. They were still too far down the hill to see anything.

"Don't know." Brentwood's voice was even as if he fought to stay calm. "Let's find out." The vehicle climbed slowly, tires working on overdrive to haul the mining equipment up the steep incline. Gemme's hair fell back behind her neck as her seat went from horizontal to vertical. She gripped the armrests, feeling as though they'd topple over backward.

"Sir." Tech's voice caught in his throat. "The dots are moving."

Luna spoke up. "With that alien orb, we don't know what's over there."

Brentwood stopped short of the cliff top and put the vehicle in park. "That's it. I'm going out to take a look before we reveal ourselves and the equipment over the top."

"You can't go alone!" Luna screeched.

"I'll go with him." Tech pulled out his laser and reinserted a charged energy cell.

"I'll go too." Gemme surprised herself with the determination in her voice. Waiting in the landrover would only make her anxious. She'd sat in that small compartment all day. The urge to get out and *do* something overwhelmed her.

"Well, you're not leaving me alone in here." Luna zipped up the front of her jacket, surprising Gemme. Was she finally coming around to do real work? "I'm coming too."

"Everyone goes." Brentwood brought out his own laser. "Follow me and don't make any noise. Don't shoot unless I give you a signal."

"Yessir, chief." Tech put up his hood so his face was a mass of beard and fuzzy cotton.

Brentwood cast a glance at Gemme and she nodded, tying her own hood tight around her neck. "Got it."

He turned to Luna last, his face wary as if he avoided all contact with her. "Ms. Legacy, you all set?"

"Sure thing." Luna's voice sounded less confident than usual and Gemme wondered if the threat behind the hill caused the tremor, or if their kiss had strained their relationship. She didn't have time to think further because Brentwood pressed the panel and the hatch buzzed open, stray snow flinging in to melt on the plastic seats.

Luna whispered as they stepped out. "Tech, how much mass did each dot represent on the screen. Just how big are they?"

Tech narrowed his eyes as he stared up the incline. "Big."

"Shhh! No more talking." Brentwood gestured over his shoulder and they climbed the last meter of the drift. Gemme's heart beat so fast, she thought the muscle would convulse and she'd drop dead before they reached the top. The snow sucked at her boots as if it refused to give her up.

When they got close enough, Brentwood crouched down and crawled up the edge of the ridge, peeking over the top. He waved for them to join him. Gemme followed with Tech beside her. As her eyes crested the ridge, all she saw was a dark center to a snowy valley. She squinted against the glare of the distant sun. The ground moved, a writhing mass of hair.

"Oh no." Her eyes widened despite the biting wind.

"It's a mammoth horde." Tech whispered under his breath as if he'd draw their attention from meters away.

"Why can't we go around it?" Luna asked, joining them.

"Because the minerals are located at the valley's center." Brentwood whispered beside Gemme, clutching the edge of snow with his gloves. "They're standing right on top of it."

"Why in all of Tundra 37 did they pick the one spot we needed for a home?" Luna's question came out as a whine.

"Probably warmer than lying on the ice." Tech quirked an eyebrow. "Rock is a better conductor of heat. And you saw that grass supply nearby."

"That means they won't give it up easily." Brentwood stretched his neck to see further.

"That's it." Luna slid down. "We'll have to go back and get reinforcements."

Tech shook his head violently. "We don't have that much time. The *Expedition* needs an alternative energy source, and mining and processing the hyperthium will take time. It's already taken us twice as long to get here, and we have the only landrover. Imagine how long it would take on foot if we garnered an army. Besides, I'm not leaving the equipment out here alone."

"Then you can stay here with it." Luna huffed. "I'm not going down there."

"I'll do it." Brentwood interrupted. "If I take three energy poles with me, I can set up an electrical perimeter fence while you create a diversion. It's the only way."

Luna's mouth dropped open. "That's suicide. You saw what one of them did to the landrover." She pushed past Gemme and grabbed his arm in a melodramatic gesture that made Gemme want to roll her eyes. "You're not going to risk your life."

Gemme worried about Brentwood as well, but she didn't reach out and grab him like in some Old Earth romance movie. As much as she didn't want him to go, he could make decisions for himself. He was a lieutenant, after all and they should all be following his command.

Brentwood pulled his arm away, ignoring Luna. "You three start a commotion, scare away as many as you can with laser fire. I'll sneak down and put up the energy poles. All I need is three to make a triangular defense. Once the perimeter is in place, Tech, you drive the mining equipment down."

Tech shook his head. "I don't like it, sir. I'm not even sure the electromagnetic pulse will hold them back. Won't they be able to run right through?"

"We'll set the conductors to maximum. If they cross the beams, they'll get an electric shock strong enough to stop the heart of a whale."

"Yeah, but is it strong enough to stop an alien mammoth?" Gemme wondered out loud, wanting to stop him before it was too late. "What if they have more than one heart?"

"Then they'll all stop." Brentwood winked at her and stood up. His bravery impressed her.

Brentwood walked back to the landrover and pulled out three energy poles. "Prepare your lasers. I'm going down."

Gemme's throat tightened as Tech and Luna took positions beside her on the cliff. There was so much she hadn't said to Brentwood, so much she still wanted to ask him. Her stomach flipped as she realized this might be her last chance. She'd thrown away so many chances to speak up on this mission; during the Aurora Borealis, when Luna handed her the sample trays, and so many times while driving. She wasn't about to do it again. "Wait."

Brentwood's face flashed in surprise and he gave her a questioning look.

"I'm sorry I doubted you last night."

His face softened, as if she'd touched upon the one issue he had yet to resolve in his own heart. "There's something I have to tell you too."

The tension in the air heightened as Gemme froze, her heart hammering against her ribs.

Brentwood took a long, deep breath and stared at her as if no one else existed on that snowdrift. "Gemme, ever since I found you in the emergency shafts, I knew you were special. I've been drawn to you every minute of this mission since then, and I want you to know I love you before I go down there."

Gemme's cheeks burned so hot, she'd thought she'd melt the snow around her. Her world turned upside down. It was like playing that silly child's game when they plucked petals off a synthetic flower and stuck them back on again: *Lovesme, lovesmenot, lovesme, lovesmenot.*

Beside her Luna's voice hitched in her throat, coming out as a weak cry. Tech grunted. "'Bout time."

Before Gemme could respond, Brentwood leaped over the edge.

They followed him, turning their heads to the valley below. The lieutenant skidded down the cliff using the sides of his boots. Once he reached the bottom, he held up an arm.

"Come on, gals, let's do him proud," Tech muttered under his breath. They propped their lasers up in the snow with their fingers hovering over the triggers, waiting for his signal to fire.

Brentwood crouched down, ten meters from the horde. He was an entire head taller than Gemme, but compared to those beasts, he looked like an ant and it made her heart creep up to her throat. Gemme leaned forward, resisting the urge to follow him down the incline. She could keep him safer if she covered him from above. Her finger shook against the trigger.

Brentwood's arm came down in a definite move, and Tech nodded. "That's the sign."

Tech opened fire, his shots aiming for the edge of the horde where Brentwood hid. "Aim down here. Drive them away," he shouted, and Gemme instinctively pulled her own trigger, aiming at the mass below them.

The mammoths bellowed a warning cry and the herd scattered in panic. The dark center to the valley spread thin and Gemme caught a glimpse of the gray rock surface underneath.

"Keep them away from Brentwood," Gemme shouted, pulling the trigger so hard her finger numbed. The white light didn't come out fast enough. There were too many beasts to keep at bay.

Brentwood zigzagged through the horde as if they didn't even see him. He stuck the first pole in the ground and ducked around to the other side of the valley. Gemme watched him until his blue thermal hood disappeared between two mammoths and didn't resurface. A current of fear sprang up inside her. "I don't see him."

"Brentwood can take care of himself. We've got other problems to worry about." Tech redirected his fire to a head of tusks pointed in their direction. The mammoth's coat was a shade lighter than most of the others, its hair the same color as Gemme's. It would have been beautiful and majestic if it wasn't so hell bent on killing them.

"It sees us." Luna's voice rose in panic. "It knows we're the source of the commotion."

"It can't be that smart, can it?" Gemme's fingers shook so hard she fought to hold her laser straight. Luna was the biologist. She'd know the difference between intelligence and chance.

Steam poured out the mammoth's tusked mouth as it bellowed, the sound ripping through Gemme's ears and reverberating in the pit of her stomach. The hairy hide charged toward them, barreling up the incline. It was too late to run.

"Fire!" Tech shouted. Gemme squeezed down the trigger, aiming for its head. The white shafts of light disappeared into the mass of hair. The mammoth picked up speed as if their fire fueled its anger.

"Brace yourselves!" Tech covered his head with both arms.

Before Gemme could react, the snow underneath her exploded as the mammoth pushed its head through their snow bank, throwing her through the air. She rolled down the incline, an avalanche sliding on top of her. Gemme fought to keep her head above the snow, digging her way up as the force pushed her down. Snow stung her eyes and choked her, lodging in her throat. The weight squeezed her chest and she fought for breath, gagging.

Darkness sent fear rippling through her body. Would she ever see the light again? Tossed about so many times, she couldn't tell up from down. She moved her arms through the loose snow until her hand broke through the surface to her right side, feeling clear air. Lungs about to burst, she forced her head up and sucked in breath.

The mammoth stood above her, the dank scent of wet, moldy fur clogging her nose. Her head had poked out inches from its massive paw. The blue claws curled into the snow like gnarly tree roots in the biodome by her cheek. Every hair on the mammoth's body probed the loose snow. A few ends from the paw squiggled toward her and she jerked her face away, watching the tiny muscles constrict and stretch as the hairs thrust into the snow and wiggled back out again.

Something moved behind the mammoth and Gemme saw Luna waking up a meter down from her behind the hairy flanks, her legs free of the snow.

In front of her, the mammoth waved its trunk through the air, sniffing. Gemme struggled to free herself, but the snow held her lower torso and legs like a vise grip. If she could wiggle out, she could dart right between its back legs and get away unnoticed. She clawed at the ice with her gloved hands, trying to gain traction. Meanwhile Luna watched with wide eyes.

"Luna, help me," she whispered as she reached out to her. "I'm stuck."

Luna had the same cold, glassy stare she had when she'd cornered Gemme against the recycling chute all those years back. If anything, she looked more callous. Gemme's heart beat fiercely as she whispered, fingers digging grooves into the snow. "Luna, please."

Without a word, Luna took off, scrambling up the incline toward the landrover. Gemme's lifeline snapped away, and a riptide of anger rose from the bottom of her stomach to her throat. It would only take moments for the beast to realize it stood right on top of her. Through the hind legs, Gemme watched Luna climb the snow. As she ran, her boots skidded, sending chunks of ice down the incline. One chunk bounced by Gemme's face and hit the mammoth's paw, drawing its attention away from Gemme. The beast turned and blue snot sprayed out of its trunk, splattering on the crust of snow. Gemme slammed her face into the snow as it jumped over her and stomped off in pursuit.

"Luna, watch out! It's after you!"

Luna screamed as she gained her footing back and ran. Gemme scraped together a ball of snow and threw it as far as she could to get the beast's attention, but the snowball fell short. She swallowed a lump in her throat. *She's not going to make it.*

Dread gripped Gemme's stomach as the beast closed the distance before Luna reached the landrover. Gemme wanted to shut her eyes and pretend she lay in her sleep pod on the *Expedition*.

This can't be happening.

Instead she stared as if someone had taped her eyelids open.

The beast's head dipped, exposing its tusks.

Gemme clutched snow in her fists and shouted, "Luna get out of the way!"

The hairs reached out and wrapped around her foot, pulling her down. Luna fell back into the tusks in a tangle of dark hairs and limbs.

"Noooooo!" Gemme screamed. The adrenaline flowed through her. She pulled herself up until the muscles in her arms tightened like they were going to snap and yanked herself free of the snow. At the same time, Tech shot at the beast from the top of the landrover.

"Over here, you bastard!" he shouted, making a racket with his boots on the roof.

The mammoth took the bait, leaving Luna's crumpled body alone. Gemme scrambled up. Numbed by the weight of the snow, pins pricked her soles of her feet as the blood rushed in. Working through the pain, she stumbled ahead to Luna.

The mammoth turned its attention to Tech as he fired and cursed like he'd had too much wheat beer. Hoping he could keep the beast occupied, she collapsed on her knees against Luna's huddled body. Luna's chest still rose and fell and she breathed in relief. Gemme turned her over carefully and gasped. The snow underneath her had spots of bright red. Blood seeped from five puncture wounds in her chest and stomach.

Gemme's anger cooled and her empathy stripped any remaining resentment away. "I'm so sorry."

Dragging Luna into her lap, Gemme pressed her gloves against the largest of the holes in her coat. Suddenly all the bickering between them seemed trivial and she wished she'd done more to make amends.

Coughing, Luna gazed up at her. Blood trickled down the corners of her mouth. "You win."

Shaking her head, Gemme spoke softly. "This wasn't ever a game. I didn't want to compete against you, not in school and not for Brentwood."

"But you did." Luna's voice grew weaker and she spat blood on the snow. "You beat me on every test, and now you've won him."

Gemme thought back to the conversation she'd overheard with Luna and Brentwood. Luna was right. She had taken everything from her, and she hadn't even meant to. If only they'd been friends all those years, if only Luna had pulled her out of the snow. They could have helped each other get away. Gemme could have kept her from falling. Maybe, in an alternate universe, they could have made it back to the landrover together safe.

"Luna, all I wanted was to be left alone."

Luna shook her head wearily. "It doesn't matter now." Blood caught in her throat and she gurgled. "What matters is...Beta Prime."

"What?"

Luna's breath hitched and she struggled to take in enough air to speak. Gemme put her head down to her lips. "Don't let the Seers get—"

Behind her, Tech fired at the mammoth as it pushed against the landrover, threatening to topple it sideways. Gemme reached for her laser, but she'd lost it in the avalanche. Tech fired a steady stream, but nothing stopped it. The beast ducked its head in the same motion that got Luna, and Gemme shouted, "Tech, jump off!"

Just as the tusked crown came up, Tech fired sideways pointing the laser at its eye. With one shot, the mammoth fell back on its hind legs and keeled over. The ground rumbled underneath her as the giant body hit. The hairs still writhed on its hide as the last steam of breath plumed from its pink mouth.

Tech jumped off the vehicle and ran over. "How's she doing? Is she hurt?"

When Gemme turned back to Luna, her eyes stared at the sky.

CHAPTER TWENTY-FOUR
OPPORTUNITY

Mestasis couldn't deny the orb's power over her any longer. The device glistened like a newborn star. The proximity to the beacon must have heightened its power. As the orb grew stronger, it activated regions of her brain long dormant, bringing up the memories she'd held so dear, clear as the day it had happened. The more memories it brought back, the more it lured her into its depths.

Was this only a side effect of the orb, or was this what it was meant to do? If so, how could something so special be dangerous? She allowed her mind to wander.

સ્જર્જી

Old Earth, 2446

"Meow."

"Don't worry, Calico. I'm not going to forget you." Mestasis pried the ball of fur off of her shredded plastic couch. She ran a hand over its fur, seeing odd golden swirls move on its coat and deposited the animal on the floor. Even though the kitten had already ruined the upholstery, and she'd never use it again, she nudged the animal away out of habit. "We're not going quite yet."

The kitten darted between two storage containers full of everything she ever owned, the lids popped open as she decided on last minute items to take. Thankfully, Calico had her own pet holder.

I'm ready to go. Abysme gave her a serious look from the doorway. Her own container sat fully packed by her feet. A ceramic pot painted in elaborate African tribal designs poked out from piles of clothes. It was a strange item to bring with her, taking up so much space and weight, with no use other than sentimental. But Mestasis was glad they'd still have it with them, even if the blade of grass had died years ago.

Mestasis glanced around the apartment. *I need more time.* She knew she'd forget something and miss it for the next three hundred years, or however long it took the *Expedition* to reach Paradise 18.

You're the one who wanted to do this, and now you can't? If I don't leave now, I may not find the courage again. I'll change my mind.

Mestasis froze. Who in their right mind would want to be left behind on a crumbling planet? *Why?*

Abysme put her hands on her hips. She looked mad, but her fingers trembled against her shirt. *All I ever wanted was to be with Mom. Everything here reminds me of her, and I'm afraid once we leave, I'll have nothing left.*

Mestasis shook her head. *You'll always have your memories. No one can take those away, and you'll carry them with you, wherever you are.*

Memories aren't enough. I can't talk to Mom and get a response; I can't feel her arms around me. They're only a shadow of what happened in the past.

Mestasis thought back to the day she and her sister left for TINE. The view of their small apartment burned into her visual cortex, summoning feelings as raw as the minute they left. *Memories are more powerful than you think.*

Abysme picked up her container, balancing the weight on her hip. Behind them, sirens wailed as hovercrafts flew to the city borders to keep the horde of refugees at bay. *I'll go with you on this crazy adventure, but you have to promise me, we'll never forget where we came from, that we'll never forget her.*

I promise. Plopping on the floor, Mestasis sorted through gadgets from their years at TINE. She threw out an old energy capacitor, but kept the electrolytic nanotech scanner just in case. She thought that was enough to get Bysme to leave, but her sister stood like a statue in front of the door.

It's him, isn't it? Abysme's mindspeak sounded jealous. *You're waiting for him.*

I want to make sure he makes it on board. He's the reason why we have a ticket off Earth.

Abysme stared at the door and the panels parted. *He can dock at the last minute, but I can't. I'm going on.*

I'll see you up there. Mestasis gave her a smile, thinking of how proud she was of her sister. She took a step into the unknown, a leap of faith, not only in Thadious Legacy's calculations, but in Mestasis's as well.

You'd better, because I'm not spending the next three hundred years of my life alone in deep space. Although Abysme's words teased her, her sister smiled back before she slipped out the door. The panels closed behind her, leaving Mestasis with Calico. The kitten rolled on her back exposing her white belly and stretched luxuriously.

Mestasis ran her hands over the soft fur, thankful she still had company. The apartment felt empty with all their belongings packed, and even emptier now that Abysme had left. She wondered who would live here after them and if there was a future left for TINE.

The door beeped and Mestasis jumped, startling Calico. The kitten shot upright and scurried underneath the couch. Anxiously, Mestasis parted the panels with her mind. James stood in the corridor, the ends of his black hair curving in to his square chin. His eyes shone silver as the moon and one look stole her heart all over again.

"I'm sorry I'm late."

Mestasis shot up, crossed the living room in two leaps, and threw her arms around him. "Nonsense, I'm glad to see you."

He buried his face in her braids, his warm breath moving stray strands of her hair. They held each other for a long time, neither one speaking until the silence grew like a dissonant note inside her.

His hands held her arms a little too tight. His body felt rigid. Mestasis pulled away far enough to meet his gaze. "What's wrong?"

James shook his head. "I didn't make it on the ship."

Panic and disbelief jolted inside her. She must have misheard him. "What?"

"Metsy, I'm not going with you."

Betrayal burned like laser light in her heart. "But Thadious Legacy promised me—"

"I didn't pass the genetic tests. Seems my genes carry major defects, and I have an arrhythmic heartbeat to boot. I'm a poor candidate for their genetic matching program, and the conditions aboard the ship would stress my heart."

Anger formed a hard center in her chest. She'd heard his heart, and it beat just fine. Was Thadious keeping him from her? Did he think having James aboard would distract her? All of a sudden she hated the bald man. "He's doing this on purpose."

"No, Metsy." James assured her, running a finger down her cheek. "I've felt the arrhythmia before. It usually happens when I get out of breath or climb to the higher levels. I never thought much of it until now."

Mestasis's knees weakened. She didn't want to believe him. James's grip remained firm, holding her up. He spoke with his lips against her ear. "Besides, with everything going on and thousands of people boarding, the odds of conspiracy to break us apart are unlikely. Don't blame Thadious, blame me."

She could never blame him. "I'll talk to them, make an exception for your case. Maybe they have medical advancements that can help?"

"I've already tried petitioning it. The contract is pretty clear. There's no changing the parameters. All you'll do is make trouble for yourself."

Mestasis felt trapped, forced to make a decision that would tear her apart. How could James give in to the system so easily? Why didn't he fight to be with her?

Tears flowed down her cheeks and James gently wiped them away with his thumb. "Metsy, you know I love you."

She pulled away, turning her back on him and walking to the sight panel. She'd have to choose between him and her sister. She had no doubt Abysme could fly that ship by herself, but she was the one who'd signed the contract. Besides, she couldn't leave her sister alone on a mission that she herself had chosen for them both. Her chin trembled as reality sunk in. He wouldn't budge and neither would she. This was the last time she'd see him. "Why didn't you tell me sooner?"

James sighed. "Because you'd call it off. You wouldn't go."

Would she have? Probably not. She always picked her sister in the end.

Mestasis turned back to him, somehow feeling as though she let him down. "What are you going to do?"

He walked over to the sight panel and pointed to people scurrying in the corridors between buildings, preparing for the attacks from the refugees. "Help them. It's what I do best, Metsy."

She studied his profile, trying to remember the way his chin curved, and the pure blackness of his hair. She loved his sense of valor most about him. If somehow she found a way to bring him with her, he may never reconcile the fact that he left so many behind. She'd force him to be something he wasn't, cage the hero that should save the world. Mestasis sighed, realizing she couldn't win this argument. She just never thought his honor would pull them apart in the end. "I can't go without you."

"Yes, you can, and you must. There are at least three hundred good people aboard that ship; my people, people that have fought to stay alive despite their circumstances. Guide them to a better world, Metsy. If you won't do it for yourself, do it for me."

He pleaded so intensely she couldn't refuse him. She checked the wallscreen. "We don't have much time left."

"Then let's make these last hours count." He leaned in and pulled her against him, kissing her fiercely. She wrapped her arms around his neck. Nothing was close enough. Her hands roamed over the muscles in his back, untucking his shirt. She felt around his waist, and the curves of his abs underneath his shirt as he kissed her. Each touch explored more about him, making her shiver. How could someone deem him so imperfect? To her, he was flawless.

He ducked, his arm sliding underneath her legs as he picked her up. The universe had aligned for them to have this private moment, and she lost herself in it, feeling free of any obligations or predestination. Nothing existed except the feel of his skin and the scent of their bodies intermingled. This was her paradise.

❧❦

The wallscreen beeped and a monotone voice echoed, "Incoming call."

Mestasis rose up from her bed, her head groggy from deep sleep. She hadn't allowed her conscious mind to rest that fully in her entire life; no impulses, no dreams, just blissful darkness. The world came back to her, along with delicious memories. She reached out beside her and ran her hand under cold sheets. James was gone. Emptiness overwhelmed her, spreading through her limbs until she felt cold everywhere.

Scooping up his pillow, she buried her nose in the fabric, smelling his scent. His absence caused a sharp pain in her gut, but she knew if he stayed, it would make it harder for her to leave. He'd made his choice, and now she had to make hers.

The wallscreen beeped again, insistent. Too tired to use her powers to turn the panel on, Mestasis leaned forward, making sure the blanket covered her up.

Abysme's face stared back at her in shock. Their mindspeak didn't work well on communication channels, so she spoke with real words instead. "What are you doing in bed? You're supposed to attend a formal ceremony in thirty minutes. Thadious Legacy's been asking about you. I almost snuck off the ship and came back to get you. I thought the refugees stormed our apartment and murdered you on the streets, and you're taking a nap?"

This was it, her time of choice. If she stepped on that ship, there'd be no going back. Mestasis stared at the face she knew so well, the mirror image of her own.

Abysme sighed, letting a rare glimmer of vulnerability show in the hard edges of her features. "I was so worried. I really thought something had happened to you. It made me think about things, and I'm glad you won us this chance, Metsy. I'm glad we've made it to a safe place together. I know I've never been thankful of what you've achieved for us, but I am now. I don't know what I'd do without you."

Abysme was her twin. Her other half. How could she let her down?

Mestasis realized she still hugged James's pillow. Placing it down beside the wrinkled covers, she ran her hands over the fabric one last time. Taking a deep breath, she swung her legs off the edge and stood up. The world felt rickety under her feet. "I'll be right there."

CHAPTER TWENTY-FIVE
LAST WORDS

Mammoth hairs flew over his head as Brentwood ducked and rolled under two sets of legs, thick as tree trunks. He had to keep moving to use the commotion to his advantage, giving them no chance to sniff him out. The adrenaline rushing inside him made darting through the herd easy. Even so, one misstep and he'd be one mammoth's dinner.

He'd already secured the first pole, and he only had two more to go. Hopefully, they wouldn't knock it over before he got the second one down. He needed at least two conductors to start the energy beam.

Staying on the edge of the valley, he zigzagged to the opposite side. He had to make the perimeter big enough to protect the mining area and the vehicle, giving Tech enough room to work. Too small an area would put all of them in danger once Tech drove the landrover down. He couldn't tell how far the mammoth hair could stretch. If the mammoths ruined the equipment, the animals might doom the entire crew of the *Expedition*.

An unoccupied spot of land lay exposed up ahead, protected by two mounds of snow; a perfect place for the next pole. Brentwood dashed over and pulled another metal rod from under his arm. The pole sank into the snow and he punched it down deep enough to stand up vertically. He tested the stability with a kick.

Pressing the panel on the top, he activated the second pole. A cylinder-shaped compartment rose up, exposing a ball of light and a thin, red beam cut across the snow, connecting the two poles. Encouraged, Brentwood pumped his fist in the air. If any mammoth tried to cross it, the energy would zap them dead, or at least, in theory. Heart pounding, he scanned the area. Now he had to find a place for the third pole without trapping any mammoths inside.

He looked for the easiest direction to run, but he'd lingered too long. A hulk of hair charged at him, followed by another and another. Brentwood brought up his laser and fired at the leader.

This is it. Too late for regrets. Good thing I finally told Gemme how I felt.

He couldn't blast all of them. He'd been firing the whole time and he hadn't even taken down one.

Squashing his fear, he placed himself directly in front of the laser beam. The charged particles buzzed behind him, reminding him how much power lay at his back. Death waited for him on either side. If he stepped into the beam, he'd die instantly. If he waited for the mammoths, he'd be stomped on or impaled.

Death by electrocution or mammoth tusks.

Hard decision.

Brentwood planted his feet down firmly, dropped the third pole, and squeezed the trigger.

The mammoth hair grasped out like seeking vines, reaching a meter ahead of them, as if their pounding feet wouldn't reach him soon enough. It made him stomach squirm to think of the hair finding him and crawling down his back.

Wait.

Spittle dripped from the pink mouths as their heads dipped down, revealing their tusks.

Wait.

Now! He turned, sprinted two steps for momentum, and leaped, spreading his legs out as far as they could stretch. The red laser light came closer and he willed himself higher, hoping the fabric of his pants didn't droop too far. He should have reset the configurations, narrowing the width and height of the beam.

Sprawling through the air, he cleared the laser with millimeters to spare. He hit the snow and rolled into a crouch just as the first mammoth reached the beam. The massive body jerked as it barreled into the light. The beast cried out, screeching like a pig in the livestock cells aboard the *Expedition*. A second mammoth hit the beam, then a third.

The reek of burnt hair filled the air as they writhed in the electric current. They dropped to the snow, and steam rose off their seared hides. Brentwood stepped around the end of the pole, watching the rest of mammoth horde retreat from the laser light.

"Woohoo! Take that you hairy monsters!" The last of them disappeared over the ridge at the far end of the valley, smaller beasts trailing the wake of the larger ones.

He checked the ridge, and his triumph dropped like the electrocuted mammoths, sinking into his stomach. No one was firing, meaning no one was there. Collecting the third pole, he ran across the snow.

They would never abandon their posts. Something had happened. Anxiety rose like solar flares in his chest as he stuck the third pole down and completed the triangular defense. As the cries of the mammoths receded, silence fell over the valley.

"Gemme, Tech, Luna?" he shouted, and his voice reverberated against the distant mountains.

His world stopped. What if he was the only one that survived? Thinking he put himself in the thick of the danger, he may have left his team exposed. Brentwood's hands rose to his forehead just as the rumbling of the landrover's engines ignited, producing the best music he'd ever heard. The vehicle crested the ridge and relief flooded his system.

Thank the Guide they're safe.

He shut off the laser for the bottom of the triangular defense and signaled Tech to drive down the incline. The landrover pulled in the perimeter and he followed, closing the space behind them by reactivating the beam. They may have scared the mammoths off for good, but he wasn't going to take any chances.

The hatch opened and Tech came out first, hobbling onto the snow. The man looked like he'd gone to hell and back again. Weary eyed and slumping forward, he gave Brentwood a wave. "Nicely done, sir."

Gemme followed Tech, jumping from the hatch. She ran to him and threw her arms around him, the force pushing back her hood. Her nut-brown hair ticked his chin. She calmed him like nothing else could. He closed his eyes and soaked in the moment. The close contact triggered a longing inside him and visions of a meadow and a log cabin flashed behind his lids. Was he going crazy? Or were they somehow star-destined lovers, married in previous lives? Brentwood shook the foggy memories from his head and gripped her close.

Tech cleared his throat and Brentwood opened his eyes. The older man stood behind them, his eyes dark and hooded in warning. "It's not time to celebrate."

Brentwood pulled away from Gemme far enough to look into her face. "Where's Luna?"

Gemme looked down at his chest. "She's dead."

Her words slapped him in the face and he pulled away in guilt. He hadn't even thought about the biologist in his rush to hold Gemme. What kind of a lieutenant was he? A member of his team had died and here he was thinking of romance. "Dead?"

Tech's voice was soft as he explained. "One of the mammoths spotted us on the ridge. Smart bastards, I'll tell you that. It came barreling up and tore into our hideout, causing an avalanche. The ladies went down with the snow, but I landed on the other side by the landrover."

He shook his head as if to ward out the memory. "I saw it all. The snow trapped Gemme, but Luna was free. Luna panicked and took off toward the landrover. The mammoth saw her and charged with its tusks. I'd been thrown from my laser, and it took me a while to find it."

Tech ran a hand through his beard. "I tried to distract the beast by firing from the top of the landrover. I got it away from her, but I was too late."

Still grasping what he had said, Brentwood put a hand on his shoulder. "It's okay, Tech. It's not your fault."

More like my fault. Brentwood's mind swam with guilt.

What if Tech had gone down and I stayed?

What if we'd left her in the landrover?

Second-guessing all the decisions he'd made that day, he thought of a thousand ways that may have turned out better. Luna's death loomed over his head. He rubbed his temples, trying to straighten out his thoughts.

"I talked to her before she died." Gemme spoke up, breaking him out of his trance. "She was trying to tell me something; something I think she'd recently figured out, or was keeping from us the whole time. I'm not sure."

"What did she say?"

"A lot was going on. I didn't catch everything and Luna was hard to understand with all the blood in her throat. She mentioned not letting the Seers get something."

Brentwood hadn't trusted the Seers since the crash, since he saw their hidden orb. The Legacys and the Seers went way back, ever since the very first Legacy asked the pair of them to drive the ship. They'd kept secrets from the rest of the crew for centuries. "Not letting the Seers get what?"

"Get out?" Tech offered. "The Seers are pretty old and shouldn't be wandering around."

"No." Gemme shook her head. "Before that I'm pretty sure she said it was about Beta Prime."

Tech shrugged. "She might have been talking gibberish. I know I couldn't make much sense if a mammoth's tusks poked me like a pin cushion."

"Enough." Brentwood put up his hand, his gut twisting with Tech's gruesome description. "We'll figure it out later. Right now, we need to take care of Luna's body."

He thought for a second. "Her family will want to see her body when we get back to the *Expedition*. Let's wrap her up and have a ceremony right here, say our last words, then get started on setting up the mining drill."

"Good idea, chief. I'll get the body." Tech shuffled back to the landrover.

Brentwood searched in their equipment for her thermal sleeping cocoon. When he saw her blank face dangling from Tech's arms, his stomach clenched up. She'd died on his watch. He'd have to live with that for the rest of his life. She'd had feelings for him, and all he did was scorn her, push her away. Now he could see every move she made was to get close to him. He'd been so blind. If he'd known Luna's feelings, he wouldn't have approved the biologist for the team.

No. You can't blame yourself for everything.

She'd wanted to be a lieutenant so badly, her family would have found a way to put her on Alpha Blue, even if he'd turned her down. He was the only thing she couldn't buy with favor, especially now that the matchmaking system had crashed.

"It's not your fault." Gemme came up to him as he pulled down Luna's sleeping cocoon.

"I'm a lieutenant, everything that happens on this mission is my responsibility."

She put a hand on his arm. "We all feel at fault."

He looked at her with a steady blue gaze. "You have nothing to feel bad about. She pushed everyone around, and you still helped her at the very end."

Gemme shrugged. "It's the least I could have done."

They laid Luna's sleeping cocoon on the snow and Gemme helped him slip her body in. Tech hefted her up and placed her in the cargo hold of the landrover. Gemme tucked her blonde hair back gently. "There, it's done."

The sky had clouded over during the laser fight, and now a light snow fell, covering the mammoth's footprints with a dusting of white. Brentwood brushed the flakes off of Luna's sleeping cocoon. He couldn't protect her during the fight, but at least he could make sure Alpha Blue tended to her body with care. "She'll have a formal funeral on the *Expedition*, but I feel like they have so many to deal with because of the crash, now might be a good time to say your good-byes."

Tech walked up and folded his hands in front of him. "I'm sorry I didn't get to my laser in time. Rest in peace, Ms. Legacy. You've served the Guide well." Although his speech was short, his voice was sincere.

He walked away, dragging his feet through the snow and Gemme stood up next. "Luna, I know we weren't the best of friends. I forgive you for pushing me into the recycling bin that day. I can only hope you've forgiven me. I wish I could have done more to save you. I hope your soul rests at peace."

Gemme joined Tech as he unloaded the mining equipment, leaving Brentwood to speak in private. Mixed emotions flooded his thoughts. "Ms. Legacy, Luna, I'm sorry I couldn't be who you wanted me to be. I'm sorry I wasn't there to save you. In return for your sacrifice I will finish this mission. I'll make sure Thadious Legacy's dream lives on, and the people of the *Expedition* continue. If you were trying to tell Gemme something, or warn her, I'll figure out what it was."

He closed the lid of the back hatch and watched as she disappeared beneath the door. That night he'd have to send a notification to her family. Brentwood sighed and collected his thoughts.

So much to do, and no time to grieve.

Gemme scanned the sight with Tech's miniscreen while Tech worked on the drill. Their faces shot up as he approached.

"Tomorrow, I'm going to the beacon's coordinates. I'll investigate the device linked to the orb. I have to figure out what Luna said. I must decide if we should take it back to the Seers or destroy it."

CHAPTER TWENTY-SIX
HOLLOWNESS

The *Expedition,* 2751

Mestasis hadn't allowed herself to roam back into those complete memories of Old Earth in hundreds of years, and now she knew why. Every fiber of the remains of her body panged in sorrow, vibrating in dissonance with her mission objectives. She couldn't allow her mind to wander into such dangerous territory, yet her thoughts opened the forbidden door.

What if I'd stayed behind?

Using her good eye, she gazed across the control chamber at Abysme. Ever since the crash her sister hung limp and despondent from the wires attaching her to the ceiling like a blind rag doll. Abysme had left her, and Mestasis shivered as the loneliness crept in. If she wanted her sister back, she'd have to learn more about the one thing that had interested Abysme before the ship had crashed. She had to plunge into the orb, to embrace its power and learn what it was meant to do. Yes, to help Abysme, she had to go in.

The energy from the cosmic swirls called to her, stronger than before. A repeating electrical impulse resonated from its depths, the same code she'd given to James on their first date at the Techno Express. She could remember his fingertips brushing hers vividly, and in the orb, their secret communication lived on.

But was it him?

Mestasis's mind crawled toward the orb, wary and eager at the same time. Its power had surged exponentially since they crashed, and she didn't know if she could control herself. She steeled her nerves. The last time she could barely pull herself away, and the ship needed at least one telepath at the helm. Thousands of lives rested on her shoulders, and she needed to know she could remerge to keep them safe. Rooting a part of herself within her body, she connected to the energy and allowed her mind to slip into the depths like a diver into a bottomless pool.

⃰ঌ

The light blinded her as she passed through it. Shapes formed in the distance, black figures curled in dancing poses with salamanders creeping into triangles. A single blade of grass poked through dusty soil and she reached out and ran her finger along the edge, the tip so sharp it almost cut her skin. Golden swirls of sunlight fell on her skin. She stood on a floor of concrete, sleeping blankets spread out in a row of three.

A woman wearing a grubby beige uniform hummed a song, unraveling her long braids in front of the antique mirror.

"Mom?" Mestasis's voice quivered.

She didn't turn around when she spoke. "I have a double shift tonight. Make sure your sister eats dinner."

"Mom."

This time her mother did turn around. Her dark eyes shone like brown velvet from the halo of her wavy hair, and her skin looked sleek and vibrant, high cheekbones carved into her heart-shaped face with thick lips and teeth white as pearls. Her mother's beauty captivated her and she stared, brimming with unshed tears. Here was another chance to tell her everything she'd neglected on Old Earth.

"I'm sorry I didn't visit you, Mom. I was working so hard, I thought I could give you a better home, I thought I could save you."

"My dear Metsy."

She rose from the crate and Mestasis's heart pounded, longing for her mother's arms to envelop her, to feel her love.

Her mother put a hand on her shoulder and squeezed. "I know I can count on you."

Mestasis paused. Count on her for what? To save the people aboard the *Expedition*? "What are you talking about, Mom?"

"I know you'll look after Bysme. I'll be home at 5:30 tomorrow night."

"But?" Mestasis felt oddly mute. Here she was opening her heart with everything she'd ever wished to tell her for centuries, and her mother spoke as if she'd see her the next day.

She kissed her on the cheek, her lips soft against Metsy's skin. Warmth spread throughout her face and neck. She could have stood in that moment forever, but her mom pulled her hand away. She shuffled to the kitchen and packed three soybean wafers into her old work bag.

With a wink, she took out an old plastic box and set it on the cracked plastic countertop. "Something for you and your sister to keep busy with."

"What is it?"

She smiled as she slipped out the door. "Have fun."

Mestasis remembered the box. She relived the night they'd opened the container to find a whole set of chess pieces. They'd stayed up into the next day designing a makeshift board with chalk on their floor and playing against each other until their brains felt like mush. It was one of the happier nights of her young life.

She yearned to open the container and sit with Abysme. The red coat of the king poked up underneath a crack in the lid. She reached for it, fingers dangling in the air before she jerked her arm away.

It was only a memory. Her mom had said exactly what she'd said that night, ages ago. Nothing more. Her heart tore open when she realized her words would never get through, never reach the true soul that had been her mother. But everything seemed so real. The cool countertop underneath her fingers had all the right cracks in it, her mom's hand felt just right on her shoulder. Just as she remembered it.

But that was the problem, wasn't it?

A thumping sound came from the back room. Mestasis turned to see a ten-year-old Abysme pop up from the blankets. "Did I miss Mom?"

"Yes." The sudden urge to play the night out again rose up inside her, but she squelched it down. Her sister walked by, ratty pajamas two sizes too big trailing behind her. She opened the lid, the chess pieces falling on the floor. "What's this?"

Mestasis knew her line even after all these years. "Mom left it for us."

"What is it?" She rubbed her eyes.

"A chess set."

The longer she spent in the memory, the more energy it took to remind herself of reality. She needed to find a way to get Abysme back, not play with her memory. She knew of only one way to test the boundaries of the orb, to find out what it wanted. To do so, she'd have to risk her heart being torn open all again. Mestasis closed her eyes and thought of James.

≈∽

A young teen boy brushed by her as she held her steaming cup of synthetic coffee. She watched him disappear between an old woman and her bodyguard as they waited for their coffee.

"Such a plain choice for someone so special."

Mestasis whirled around, and the liquid in her cup burned the back of her hand, creating golden swirls. The pain seared hot as the day it had happened. But she didn't care.

James stood behind her holding his own dark beverage. His presence provided sustenance for her starving soul. She soaked in his silver eyes, feeling as though she could lose herself staring into them. And she almost did.

He waited for her answer. People pushed by them, unaware of their statue figures, locked in a moment of time.

She knew what her line was, but this time, she tried something else. She dropped her cup, the coffee splattering across the floor, splashing against the feet of the other people in line. They stepped forward unaware, like ghosts.

Mestasis wrapped her arms around James and pressed her lips to his. He tasted like salt and spice, the all too familiar sensations overloading her senses. She didn't care about the *Expedition*, the crew, or Abysme. She wanted to live in this moment forever. To relive it time and time again: the heat of his skin pressed against hers, the curve of his lips. The orb held her paradise. She never thought she'd find it again. How could she give it up a second time?

Mestasis's heart gripped in her chest as she realized where Abysme was. Her sister must have attached her mind to the orb. Craving her memories, the orb trapped her in a neverland within its depths.

If she searched deep enough inside herself, she found a hollowness in the atmosphere. A blurriness at the edges of her sight she hadn't noticed before. The orb wasn't big enough to hold her there forever, to make each memory live on as real flesh and blood. But the dimensions of the beacon calling to it on Tundra 37 was.

Mestasis pulled away and looked into his face. "James, you have to help me. Abysme is gone and I don't know how to get her back. She's stuck in this orb."

James gave her a quirky smile and gestured over his shoulder. "I found us a table in the back."

"No." She pulled on his arm as he brought her to the same place they'd sat before. The seat that had once excited her now felt like a prison. James looked at her as if she'd commented on the weather. This vision was a shadow of his true self. No one surrounding her had a soul. Her heart broke all over again as she reminded herself he was gone.

Suddenly, the walls pressed in like a fist squeezing the blood out of her veins. A presence beyond the ghosts of memories lurked in the air like a disease. Mestasis searched the electronic pulses, connecting to a dark center. The presence thrived the deeper she fell, sucking at the very essence of her soul. It was old, older than she was, older than she could imagine. It wanted something; her energy, her soul? Mestasis couldn't tell. But she did sense an aching for things that could never be again. Was it the essence of melancholia itself?

❧❦

Mestasis yanked back so hard, her mind dislodged from the scene. Part of her screamed to go back, as if she'd ripped only half of herself away, leaving a fundamental part of her soul behind. Reliving previous memories was addictive, but it accomplished nothing. She had to contact Alpha Blue, she had to tell them to destroy the beacon. The cool, recycled air of the control chamber surrounded her once again as she opened her eye. She tried connecting to the communications channels, but something blocked her, pushing her back.

Computer, contact Alpha Blue. Code Beta Prime. Message: destroy the beacon.

The wires in the room tightened around her, and Mestasis fought to keep her body in control. *Status of transmission? Computer?*

The system didn't respond. The electric impulses she had sent came back at her, suffocating her consciousness as if the computer tried to blink her out of existence.

Her mindspeak barely came out. *Contact Alpha Blue.*

Something moved from the ceiling. Mestasis froze in shock. Abysme twitched like a robot come to life. Her sister's head jerked to the side, and her blind eyes stared at her with chilling calculation. *Request denied.*

❧❦

Spotlights shone on Vira as she twirled in a glittery, plum-colored gown to the center stage. The fabric glistened in the golden light like diamond dust, cosmic swirls streaming in gold along her waist. Flutes played in the orchestra below her feet as the conductor matched every pose she made with the music. She extended her gorgeous long leg in an arabesque, and the flutes rose up with a flurry of high-pitched notes.

Vira waved her wand, sparkles flying through the air and rose up, balancing on the square toes of her ballet shoes. The toned muscles in her legs catapulted her across the stage. She felt as though she danced on air with no need of wings. Her legs took her wherever she wanted to go. She pirouetted to the back of the set, where the nutcracker stood, brushed his beard with her fingers, and then slid back to the front. She finished her performance with a bow, and the dark mass of the audience in front of her applauded, throwing roses at her feet.

𝕒𝕠𝕒

"Wake up, spacehead."

Vira felt a punch on her arm and buried her head underneath the pillow, willing the dream to come back again. Maybe if she ignored her sister she'd go away.

"Mom wants you in the kitchen—pronto."

Squeezing her eyes shut, stars blossomed on the back of her lids. No stage, no sugar plum fairy dance. Disappointed, she peeked out from her pillow.

"Aw, Rizzy. You just woke me up from my ballerina dream again."

"Silly dreams aren't good for you. They fill your head with nonsense. Now, come on."

Her sister pulled her up and carried her to the kitchen. She felt like such a burden. Losing her hoverchair was all Rizzy's fault, because they wouldn't have been up on the higher decks if her sister hadn't run away to kiss Daryl.

"And your poster isn't nonsense?"

"No, that's a real story from Old Earth."

"Yeah, a real-made-up story."

"Whatever."

Her parents sat at the table with a meager amount of food spread out before them. Her mom's hair looked greasy from not being able to shower, and her dad wore the same clothes he'd gone to work in yesterday. They still had smiles on their faces, but their expressions seemed sad and forced.

"Hey sleepy eyes, breakfast is ready."

Rizzy placed Vira in her seat and she slumped down, holding her shoulders with her arms. "It's freezing in here."

"The Seers are working on getting us extra power, don't worry, peach." Her dad gave her a wink and handed her a bowl of squishy grapes and a soybean wafer.

She wanted so badly to turn the electricity on again, to have hot cooked food like scrambled eggs, but the presence behind the computer systems scared her too much to go back.

"You're not eating, dear."

"I'm not hungry." Most of the grapes were shriveled up, beginning to look like raisins. Vira wondered how long ago the bioteam picked them and if any new food was still growing. She stuffed a grape in her sleeve and dropped it on the floor for the cleaning droid. Then, she remembered she'd stolen it and disemboweled its central processor.

Her mom pleaded with her. "At least take a bite."

Vira crunched off a piece of her soybean wafer and stuck it in her mouth. She wanted to talk about something to get her mind off of the fact she was so cold her fingernails turned purple, and all they had to eat was old food. "I had my ballerina dream again."

Her mom frowned as if she didn't like hearing about it, but her dad gave her mom a stern look and then smiled at her. "That's great, dear. Tell us about it."

Vira chewed the piece of soybean wafer and swallowed before going on. Talking about her dream brought back her appetite. "I was on stage and all the people were clapping. They threw roses at my feet."

"There's no stage on the ship, or any roses," Rizzy said, obviously jealous she hadn't had a special dream.

"I was back on Old Earth, spacehead." Vira stuck out her tongue before she took another bite.

Her mother interrupted. "No one's calling anyone spacehead, today. You hear me?"

Rizzy ignored her and glared at Vira. "You're the spacehead. How do you even know it was Old Earth? You've never been there."

Vira took a breath to answer, but realized she had no clever reply. She sighed. "I just know. All the lights looked real big like antiques."

"Oh that makes perfect sense. Big lights."

"Enough girls." Their dad put down his fork with a clang. "We're all stressed-out over this crash, and we shouldn't take it out on each other." He sighed as if he didn't want to say it, but had to. "We're all having strange dreams of Old Earth."

"What?" Her mom leaned against the table. "You too?"

He nodded. "World War II, I believe, from the looks of my

uniform. From the looks of all the medals and badges I wore, I must have been a great war hero."

Rizzy crossed her arms. "My dreams are of working in some silly food store. Why can't I have cool dreams like everyone else?"

Before her dad could answer, his locator beeped. He looked down and read the message. "There's a problem in the energy core again." He shot up from his seat and gave their mom a peck on the cheek. Although he took the time to kiss her good-bye, his eyes had that strange, faraway look when things went wrong and he tried to hide it. "Gotta go, girls. Don't fight. Be good for your mom."

As he left, mom and Rizzy argued, but Vira paid more attention to the vibrations of energy coursing through the ship from the tabletop connected to the floor. As much as she wanted to shut her powers off, she could never totally get away. Everything she touched linked to the inner workings of the ship, even her sleep pod.

The ship's systems had changed while they bickered at the table. The impulses had weakened, like the vessel was dying slowly, an ill-tended plant with no gardener.

Nausea came up in a wave, the soybean wafer fermenting in her stomach. Could her powers help? She gripped the table edge with shaky fingers. The evil presence scared her too much to try.

CHAPTER TWENTY-SEVEN
DESTINY

Gemme awoke to the sound of grating metal. She opened the flap to her tent, the illumination of Solaris Prime casting a triangle of light at her feet. Even though the star's rays felt weak and distant, the brilliance reflecting off the ice-crusted snow lent her hope. Squinting against the glare, she saw the drill hanging over the exposed mineral surface, spinning so fast the twist of silver blurred.

Tech hollered in triumph from the controls. Not wanting to miss the moment the drill struck, she shoved her boots on and stepped out into the frosty morning. She walked up to the console to get Tech's attention. She shouted, cupping her hands around her mouth. "Got it running, huh?"

"Yessirree."

She guessed he'd stayed up all night working on the drill. She'd stayed up late as well, analyzing the mineral deposit using Tech's miniscreen and sending the initial calculations to the Seers. Strangely, enough, they didn't acknowledge the receipt of the information. She thought they'd at least send her a "well done."

By her calculations, they'd have enough hyperthium for generations to come. The mineral deposit spread underneath them like a glacier in an ocean, small at the top with a wide girth the farther she measured below. She still had mountains of data to analyze concerning the concentration of the minerals, and how long it would take them to process it, but she figured she'd have the entire journey back to work on her calculations. A greater purpose lay before her. They'd only completed one of the two missions, leaving the mystery of Beta Prime.

A shot of remorse stung her in the gut. Beta Prime had been Luna's mission, and now she'd take it up instead. As much as Luna had bothered her, the team felt small and incomplete without the blonde beauty. She wondered how the other members took her death. Especially Brentwood. She scanned the campsite. A small fire sizzled out, the remnants of breakfast sat in a container, and the platform rested detached from the vehicle.

"Where's Brentwood?"

Tech gazed up from the controls. "Went back to his tent. I believe he's plotting your course."

"Good." She gave Tech a thumbs-up and grabbed a bite of powdered eggs, now cold. Although she was anxious to see Brentwood, she figured she'd wait until he came out. The drill dipped in the air, the tip hovering over the mineral.

Tech shouted, "Heads up." He ran his fingers over the panel on the console, and the drill pricked the surface, rock cracking and crumbling as the point dug in. A keening wail resounded through the valley and Gemme covered her ears. A rush of relief and pride came over her as she watched the drill descend. They'd succeeded. The *Expedition* would have an alternative energy source. Ferris and her parents would be so proud.

Of course this mission didn't come without sacrifice. Every time she thought of Luna, a fresh pang shot through her chest, and the unfinished business of Beta Prime lurked in the back of her mind, casting shadows on the bright day.

Movement caught the corner of her eye. She turned just as Brentwood emerged from his tent with his travel gear packed. She wanted to run up and throw her arms around him, but after Luna's death any physical contact didn't seem right. Besides, they were on a mission to save the colony, not a romantic excursion.

Gemme refrained from running into his arms and smiled when she saw him. He gave her a serious look. "Are you sure about this?"

"More sure than anything."

How could she let him go alone? When he ran into the mammoth horde she thought she'd die watching. She wasn't about to lose him again especially after learning his true feelings. Besides, she wanted answers as well, and it seemed as though the beacon held the key to this whole mission.

"All right." His took a deep breath. "Follow me."

They walked around the console and he shouted up to Tech, "Have fun. Dig up something good."

Tech waved at them, looking like a little kid at recess time. "You too."

Brentwood leaned down to speak to her over the din of the drill. "I don't think this is going to be a picnic in the biodome."

Gemme smiled, trying to raise his spirits. "Oh really, I brought the checkered blanket just in case."

They piled into the landrover, Gemme in the passenger seat, and Brentwood as the driver. A blinking dot appeared on the radar, sixty meters from the mining site over the valley's Western ridge. Brentwood's face turned rigid, the muscles in his jaw clenching.

Gemme put a hand on his arm. "You don't have to do this. We could tell the Seers the beacon was inaccessible, or destroy the whole site with lasers from meters away. Tech and I won't say a word."

He shook his head, fingers gripping the wheel so hard his knuckles turned white. "No. We need answers. What if these aliens come back? What if it's some sort of weapon they'll use against us? What if there are more of them?"

Settling back in her seat in silence, Gemme knew he was right. The potential knowledge gleaned was worth the risk. She watched his profile as he drove head first into the unknown. "You're the bravest man I've ever known, and I'm proud to be by your side."

Her words softened his features and he turned to her, green gaze sparkling. "I'm proud to be by yours."

The landrover careened through the snow, unhindered by the mining platform. A week ago, Gemme would have shaken in her boots, but this mission had taught her to embrace chaos, that life wasn't all preplanned, and some amount of chance was okay, necessary even to grow. Most of all, she'd learned to let go.

Brentwood turned to her. "How do you feel about the pairing system being gone?"

It was a loaded question, and she sighed, thinking about where to start. If she were going to tell him she'd deleted their match, now would be the opportune time. She couldn't keep it from him forever, especially if she wanted their relationship to develop into something more.

"At first I hated it. I thought I couldn't go on without my job as the Matchmaker. I valued organization over chaos, predestination over choice. When the ship crashed, my world shattered."

"You don't seem so shattered now."

"No." Gemme smiled, thinking about why. "I guess I realized that there's more to life than analyzing data. Sometimes you have to let go before you really find the truth, before you find yourself."

He scratched his head, suddenly bashful. "What I'm getting at, Gemme, is that I want to know what you think of us together?"

His question hung in the air between them like a tantalizing promise. She took a deep breath. "The day of the comet shower, I was up in my office doing matches. That's why you had to rescue me from the top floors."

Brentwood nodded. "I remember."

Gemme swallowed. "I saw our names together. We were supposed to be paired."

Brentwood's face fell in shock. "Why didn't you tell me?"

"I thought you were in love with Luna. Besides, it would have come out as desperate seeing it didn't matter anymore, and I had no proof."

Brentwood shook his head. "I can't believe it. All this time..."

"There's more." Gemme played with her glove, tugging on the index finger. "When I saw our pairing, I couldn't believe it. Luna had just come in asking to be paired with you. She tried to bribe me with a ticket to visit the Seers, and I denied her. When I saw my name next to yours, I thought everyone would think I'd hacked the system and chosen you for myself. I was afraid of being called a hypocrite, of losing my job."

She closed her eyes, afraid to see his reaction. "I pressed the delete panel. I denied our own pairing."

Brentwood sat speechless, his face a mask. She couldn't tell if he felt angry, hurt, or betrayed. She continued on, "I didn't think I deserved you. After I pressed delete, I regretted it so many times. My actions haunted me during this entire mission."

"Oh, Gemme." He reached across the seat and took her hand. "It must have been horrible, knowing we were supposed to be paired and seeing me with Luna. I'm sorry I let it her behave so badly. I'm sorry I waited so long to tell you how I felt."

"I'm sorry I didn't tell you in the first place." Her hand shook in his and she squeezed, holding his fingers tightly. "Can you forgive me?"

"There's nothing to forgive. You didn't even know me then."

She settled back and took a deep breath. He'd lifted the secret weighing down on her this whole mission. She'd shunned the notion of organic romance for so many years, and now she believed in it wholeheartedly. She'd want him even if the computer had deemed them incompatible.

Brentwood's voice came out soft and tentative, "Would you press delete now?"

Gemme looked away as her cheeks heated up. Maybe it was wrong to pair people in the first place. "No, I wouldn't."

His hand burned so hot in hers, she thought they'd steam up the whole landrover.

"I wouldn't either."

"So what are we going to do now that the pairing isn't valid?" Gemme asked, her voice shaky.

He turned toward her, intensity in his gaze. "We make it happen by ourselves."

Gemme bit her lip feeling like a teenager all over again and Brentwood smiled, returning his attention to the path ahead. "I wonder why the computer paired us together in the first place?"

"Pairing is determined by genetic history. It's designed to prevent inbreeding—"

"Yes, I now that. But do you think there's more to it? Do you believe in destiny?"

She'd gone a long way from believing in analysis and numbers to placing her faith in chaos and chance, but to go as far as to think fate intervened in the computer's choices...she couldn't say. "I'm not sure."

Before he could respond, the radar beeped, signaling their approach to the beacon.

Gemme leaned over to see farther out the sight panel. The landscape was eerily barren, twists of flurries rising up like mini tornados across a sheer sheet of ice. "I don't see anything."

"It must be underneath the snow." Brentwood pressed the main control panel. The hatch lifted and he jumped out. He offered his hand, helping her out of the landrover. "I wish we brought shovels."

"Next time we drive to the middle of nowhere and dig up another alien beacon, we'll be prepared." Even though Gemme joked, tension sizzled in the air around her. Her ears rang like someone struck a high-pitched tuning fork, and the resonance sounded just beyond her hearing capacity. She felt like they'd traveled to the end of the world, or the beginning of all things, depending on which way she looked at it.

"How far down?"

He shrugged. "A meter, two meters at most."

"Then let's start digging."

She knelt in the snow and punched the crust until the ice broke. Brentwood found two buckets in the landrover, and they used those to scoop the snow and throw it into a heap beside the landrover. They dug until Gemme's nose ran and her cheeks numbed. She had to go back to the landrover for breaks to warm her fingers and toes. "Do you think the aliens might still be around?"

Brentwood shrugged and looked around at the barren landscape. "They never came for the orb. Scientists dated it back thousands of years. Seems to me the owners are long gone."

They were a meter and a half down when she brought her bucket down for the next scoop and hit something hard with a *thunk*.

Brentwood's gaze shot up. "That's it." He jumped next to her and helped her brush snow off the surface. Her heart beat so fast, she felt the heated blood pumping through her veins. A crystal surface shone in the sun's light, oily swirls dancing across the top. They dug farther, revealing a chest a meter tall, and wide enough to stash all their equipment. Gemme ran her gloves over the smooth surface as Brentwood dug around the base. Symbols of all shapes and sizes were carved into the sides.

She traced the symbol of a cross with an oval on top. "It's like an ankh, the Egyptian symbol for eternal life." As her finger traced the symbol, a shiver ran up her spine. The only people she knew that seemed to live forever were the Seers, and their quality of existence always made her cringe. She'd rather die than have people connect her to a machine.

Brentwood pointed to a figure eight on its side, "And here's the symbol for infinity."

She pointed to a ring-shaped geometric figure, the area between two concentric circles. "Over here there's an annulus, the Celtic symbol for eternity."

"But what are these?" Brentwood pointed to strange etchings of oval faces without eyes, and four-fingered hands holding curved objects.

"I have no idea." She thought back to all of her history classes, but no references surfaced. "I've never seen them before."

"Neither have I." Brentwood clapped his gloves together to shed the layer of snow around his fingers. "Can you help me heft it out?"

Gemme crouched down next to the chest. "It looks heavy, but I'll try."

She dug her fingers underneath the bottom. Surprisingly, the crystal seemed like it weighed mere ounces.

"This doesn't make sense. It's too light."

"I'm not complaining." Brentwood smiled. "On the count of three."

"One."

"Two." She joined in, her voice sounding stronger than she felt.

"Three!"

They heaved, raising it over their heads. Once they cleared the top, they pushed the crystal chest onto the snow. Brentwood climbed out of the hole and gave Gemme his hand, helping her up.

Circling it suspiciously, he crossed his arms. "The data suggested living matter. The Seers called it a biological anomaly made up of collagen and protein."

She shrugged. "We could have used Luna's help right now." Both fell silent. Would Luna have enjoyed this? Probably not. She would have stayed in the landrover.

When Gemme touched the symbols, the golden swirls gravitated toward her fingers. Every time she pulled her hand away, the colors dissolved, remerging at the corners of the lid. A sudden urge to see what lay inside came over her. Her entire life lead here, to this chest on the farthest region of Tundra 37.

"The only way we're going to understand it is if we open it."

Brentwood nodded reluctantly. "I'll pry off the lid." He walked back to the landrover and pulled out one of the tent poles. Jamming the end underneath the lid, he forced his weight down on the pole. His face strained as he pushed. Gemme joined him, placing her weight on top of his.

"Doesn't look like it's going to budge."

Right after he spoke, the pole gave way, and the lid popped off, landing with a gush of air on the snow. White smoke rose from the inside, dissipating into the coldness. Brentwood gave Gemme a questioning glance and she nodded. They approached the chest, her heart beating faster with each second.

A mumbling of voices wafted up from inside. Gemme froze as fear gripped her feet. Something was in there, something alive.

Brentwood put a finger over his lips and Gemme strained her ears to hear the voices. She expected some type of exotic language, but she could make out words like *angle* and *degree*.

"It can't be," she whispered, "They're speaking English."

She took a step forward and slapped her hand over her mouth as she recognized Ferris's voice. At first it sounded like he talked gibberish. As she tiptoed closer, his words became clear. "How do you find the sine and cosine when they just give you an angle measurement, like 240 degrees?"

Gemme quickened her steps and leaned over the chest. The bottom seemed endless, stretching out beyond the snow underneath the crystal to an alternate dimension. Inside, she saw Ferris sitting on her family's plastic couch with his miniscreen in his lap.

"It can't be." Gemme leaned in further. "Ferris?" She called his name but he didn't look up. Instead she heard her own voice echo out, "When the angle is 240 degrees, it falls in the third quadrant, where all the sine and cosine angles in that quadrant are negative—"

"Gemme," Brentwood spoke beside her, bringing her back to reality. "What do you see?"

She rubbed her eyes and tore herself away to look in his direction. Even as her eyes lost contact, the vision urged her to come back, to see what happened next. Her answer was so ridiculous, yet she couldn't lie. "My brother, Ferris. He's talking to me about his math exam, the one I helped him study for seven years ago. I know it's crazy, but that's what I see. You don't see it?"

"No."

Her spirits dropped as confusion spread through her. Maybe she was losing her mind. Snow blindness, isn't that what it's called when you've been exposed for too long? But it didn't cause hallucinations.

Brentwood spoke softly, "I see my mom trying to feed my brother vegetables. I'm talking to him, trying to reassure him there's going to be a dessert in the end."

She spoke through her fingers over her mouth. "What are we seeing, then?"

Brentwood shook his head as if he couldn't believe it. "What the scientists saw: our past."

"Miles," Gemme used his name for the first time. "The chest, it's asking me to touch it, to go inside."

Brentwood took in a ponderous breath. "I feel it too. I can't resist it. I need to know, to go inside."

Suddenly, her mind shot back to the mammoth fight, and Luna lying in the snow. "When Luna was dying, she'd tried to warn me not to let the Seers have it. What should we do?"

"We test it out first. See if there's anything dangerous in there. If so, we destroy it."

Gemme stared into his gaze. "I don't want you to go alone."

He took her free hand in his and his fingers curled around hers. "We'll go together."

CHAPTER TWENTY-EIGHT
ETERNITY

Gemme held her breath as they stepped into the chest. A luminous glow of golden swirls enveloped the sky, increasing in intensity until it blinded her, leaving blossoming splotches on the back of her eyelids when she shut her eyes. A fierce current of wind blew around them, roaring in her ears. She clutched Brentwood's hand tightly. If this was the end, then at least she'd be with him.

The wind gained force, whipping her hair around her face and jerking her coat sleeves until she thought they would rip open. She focused on Brentwood's hand, his grip firm like a pillar of stability. The wind tapered off into the sky above them, leaving them in silence. She cracked opened her eyes just a sliver, not knowing what to expect.

Snow, snow, and more snow. Endless white. Tundra 37 spread out before them in all its stark bleakness. She licked frost from the corners of her mouth and tasted frigid air on her tongue. Her breath plumed. Disappointed, she searched for the sides of the chest around her feet, but boundless snow stretched out for miles.

"That's it?"

A tentacled beast crested the snow mound beside them and flung itself down, sliding on the icy surface. When it got to the bottom, it scampered on its many paws toward a crack in the ice ahead. A glinting light reflected off its back and Gemme recognized her miniscreen. Another tentacle clutched the picture of her and Ferris. Anger rose inside her. The stupid beast still had her belongings, but now she'd get them back.

Gemme broke into a sprint, making a beeline for the hide of tentacles. Maybe she could reach it this time before the beast catapulted off the edge. Her fingers brushed the sticky tendrils, but the miniscreen vanished in the jellylike substance deep within the hide. She grabbed a tentacle and held on, feet trailing in the snow, while she thrust the other hand into the gooey mess. Her fingers brushed the sleek surface of the screen before strong arms pulled her back. The beast disappeared, her belongings sinking with it into the chasm of ice water below.

"Whoa! You almost went over again."

"I nearly had it this time." Gemme struggled in his arms before her skin prickled with a sense of déjà vu. She turned around to face him. "What's going on?"

"We're reliving a memory." Brentwood scanned the landscape. "We must be, because your things wouldn't be in such good condition after all this time had passed. And what are the odds that we'd find the exact same beast by the exact same crack."

Gemme shook her head. "I don't understand."

"Neither do I."

The world blurred around them until the snow grayed to resemble the inside of the *Expedition*. They sat huddled over the air vents. Alarms wailed, and the air sucked at them from behind. Brentwood pointed at a drop to the corridor below.

"We have to get out of here. Give me your hands and I'll help you down."

She slipped her hands into his, and she remembered. *We've done this before.*

Brentwood gave her a questioning frown.

"Don't you see, we're still in the chest."

"You'll have to jump."

"No."

He stared at her as if she'd lost her mind. "The upper decks are losing pressure. We can't stay here much longer."

Gemme cupped his face in both her hands. "This isn't real."

His hands wrapped around both of her wrists. "Feels pretty real to me, now let's go."

She wouldn't budge, even as he tugged her hands off his face. "It's a memory. The ship has already crashed."

"You must have a concussion. I'll have a medic examine your head once we get to safety." Metal crunched above them and the ceiling warped in.

Gemme ignored their surroundings and stared into his eyes. "Miles, listen to me. We're on Tundra 37, team Alpha Blue, mission Beta Prime."

"Beta Prime?" He blinked and shook his head. "What am I doing? Where are we?"

Gemme gave him an encouraging smile. "We're in the chest."

He blinked. "You're right. I got caught up in the moment and—"

Before he could continue, sparks flew all around them. The ship crashed while they sat in the air shaft. For a moment she thought *she* was the one who was delusional. Maybe they'd gone back in time, or her mind had concocted the future. Who knew the boundaries of this chest? Now they would both die because of her. She buried her face into his shoulder and his hand cradled the back of her head. The noise of crunched metal filled her ears until she could think of nothing else. Then, silence, as if someone had pressed the pause button on a wallscreen.

"Surprise!"

People shouted at her from all directions, some waving blue streamers and others blowing on noisemakers in her face. She tumbled forward and grabbed a railing to the stairs, feeling real oak underneath her fingertips. Where was she?

"Miles?"

A man with a pear-shaped nose grinned, half-chewed piece of candy sticking out of his mouth. "Mikey's in the back, waiting for you."

Gemme stumbled forward, elbowing her way through the crowd. She remembered snow, and her colony ship, but this domestic environment was foreign to her. Following the hallway, she saw pictures of people on the walls; an old couple on a porch, a girl riding a horse, a graduation ceremony. They were all vaguely familiar, but no names came to mind.

A tiered cake rested on a linoleum table in the next room. When she rounded the corner, she saw Brentwood on his knee. "Thank goodness I found you."

He stared up at her, confused. "I don't know what I'm doing here, Gemme, but I have this."

He opened a velvet box. A diamond sparkled like ice under Solaris Prime. She pulled the ring from the velvet liner and placed it on her finger.

"Whatever the question is, I say yes!"

People cheered behind them, but Brentwood rose and turned away, distracted.

"What is it?" Gemme grabbed his arm.

He rubbed his temples. "This is another memory, it must be. It feels so real. I can almost remember buying that ring."

"But this isn't even our lives."

Brentwood's mouth quirked up in the corner. "Maybe it was."

Gemme's head reeled. "Are you suggesting we've been together in past lives?"

"Look around you, Gemme. What do you see?"

A banner hung from the doorframe with the phrase Jenny and Mikey forever painted in red. Jenny and Mikey, Gemme and Miles. Maybe the computer hadn't calculated their pairing at all, maybe fate had chosen long before their parents birthed them on the *Expedition*. She could go crazy thinking about the ramifications.

"I want to go back," Gemme pleaded, taking his hands. This memory land played with her mind, tantalizing her with just enough to keep her interested, to make her forget their mission and the people she cared about most. If she spent too long in it, she'd lose herself, reliving old memories for all eternity.

"Just a few more minutes." Brentwood's eyes shone bright. "I want to know more."

If she left without him, she'd lose him in the chest. Besides, a part of her wanted to know who she was, where she'd came from, and why Brentwood stood by her side. Gemme wrapped her hands around his and closed her eyes. "Bring it on."

The air crackled above her head. Gemme opened her eyes to gray skies churning in a brewing wind. She stood on the porch of an old log cabin looking upon soft meadow stretching to the far horizon. She tried to comprehend so much vegetation and resources, wondering how humanity could have floundered all of it.

A jolt of lightning cracked the sky in half. Gemme stared, waiting for another as a deep rumbling shook her stomach. The humidity in the air covered her like a blanket, clinging to her many layers of aprons. She wiped he forehead with her sleeve. Her tightly strung knee-high boots hugged her calves, and she staggered in them before she got used to the feeling of her muscles cramped. She jumped off the porch and waded through the long-stem grass. The stems tickled her elbows.

"Miles!"

Her voice didn't carry well over the wind. Gemme contemplated leaving the log cabin, but no other landmarks stood on the horizon, and if she left, she'd risk never finding him again. No, this time he had to come to her.

She climbed the steps back onto the porch and pulled open the wooden door. A warm fire cast a flickering light inside, inviting her in. She slipped through the door, smelling spices. A caldron brewed a thick stew with chunks of carrots and meat and she picked up the ladle and stirred. Steam rose up to the brick chimney. Hopefully, he'd smell her cooking and come home.

A loom sat in the far corner displaying a half-done purple blanket threaded with yarn. Gemme ran her hands over the fabric, wondering if she'd done this, and what it was for. Her fingers paused over the undone weave work. On her left hand, third finger, she wore a thin band of gold. A wedding band.

A horse whinnied from outside and Gemme stumbled to the door. Dark clouds had brought rain, and it pelted down, misting the horizon. A figure riding a spotted horse galloped through the meadow, cutting a line in the parted grass. She recognized the broad shoulders and the way his head tilted down just a bit. Excitement shot through her.

Yanking back on the reins, Brentwood pulled the horse up beside the porch. Gemme threw herself down the stairs. The sky opened up and rain poured, cooling her forehead. She tore off her bonnet and the water trickled down the sides of her cheeks.

He dismounted and walked toward her, and she ran to his arms and nuzzled against him.

"Isn't this wonderful?" He spoke into her ear as he held her. "Our own little paradise."

Gemme gazed up at him. "How many of our lifetimes have we been together?"

His face was steadfast and sure. "All of them."

"How do you know?"

"I can feel it."

A connection that lasted past the grave, a love that lasted forever. And she had it. Gemme gazed up, watching the raindrops fall on his mouth. Her cheeks flamed with his proximity and her desire. Brentwood must have seen it, because his eyes held such longing, such intensity. He leaned down and pressed his lips against hers. She tasted cool rain on his mouth and pushed into him, wanting more.

"Wait." He pulled back, gasping for breath. "Not now."

She moved her hand up his chest, feeling lean muscle. "Why? I have a warm fire going in the cabin and hot stew."

"Sounds delicious." He smiled and she wondered if he even thought of the soup. "But we can't."

Her heart tore with need. "What do you mean? There's no one here for kilometers around. It's just us."

"The *Expedition*. They need us."

A flash of bright snow and bone-chilling air seared her memory. Why would she want to go back there? "Can't we stay just a little while?"

"No, Gemme." Brentwood pulled away from her. "If we stay, we'll never leave. At least I know I won't."

Realization flooded her system and this place no longer felt like home. "That's what the chest wants, isn't it?" She bit her lip. "It wants to keep us here, but why?"

"Who knows? I don't want to stay around to find out." Brentwood challenged the sky. "We want out." As if in answer, another streak of lightning webbed out in all directions, spreading through the sky and vanishing in a second. This time the rumbling came much sooner.

Golden swirls spread through the sky. Gemme tugged on his arm, suddenly anxious. "The storm is getting closer. We have to go inside."

"That's what it wants." He closed his eyes and held her close.

She buried her face in his chest, the winds picking up speed around them, whipping her hair. "How are we going to find our way out?"

"The chest is only so big. We're probably still standing in the same place right now while our minds travel. It's an illusion. It's not real." He put his hand on the back of her head. "Close your eyes, Gemme. Think about Tundra 37, think about your brother and the others on the *Expedition.*"

She did as he said, imagining Ferris, not as a teen studying for his math exam, but as a full-grown young man in the present. She thought of her parents, performing their jobs in a crashed ship that would never fly again. They needed her. She had to go back.

࿊

The atmosphere changed from hot and humid to frigid and dry. Icy air wrapped around her and she peeled open her eyes. She stood in the chest with Brentwood, solid crystal beneath their feet. They stepped out together onto the snow. Brentwood retrieved the lid and slipped it on. The cosmic swirls eddied around it, then dispersed.

"Why would the Seers want it?" Brentwood said, disgusted.

Gemme shrugged. "Maybe they want to study it, protect us from whatever it is? Maybe they don't know what it does."

"Or maybe they do."

She froze, giving him a meaningful look. He spoke treason. Knowing Brentwood, for him to say such a thing would mean he had more to go on than just a hunch. She heard him out.

"When the ship crashed, the Seers were unresponsive. I went to check on them."

Gemme gasped. "Face-to-face?"

He nodded. "Much closer than I would have liked."

He shook his head as if trying not to remember with too much detail. "When I got to the control chamber, everything was damaged. I found one of them unconscious on the floor and plugged her back in. The first thing she asked for was her sister. I didn't know if the ship could survive without both of them, so I frantically looked for the other one. I found her sister hanging from the ceiling, also unconscious. After pressing a respirator to her face, she woke up asking about the location of the beacon. You'd think she'd ask about the ship's status, or the number of survivors, but no, she'd distinctly referenced the beacon. Come to think of if, her sister interrupted right after and sent me away, as if she didn't want me to notice her sister's slip."

"You mean the beacon the chest gave off here on Tundra 37?"

His eyebrows rose. "I can't think of anything else."

Gemme flicked a glance over at the chest. "But why would such a chest be important to them?"

"Maybe they miss their former lives. I know I'd go crazy hooked up to a machine for three hundred years, wouldn't you?"

"I don't know." Anger hardened in her stomach. "They're supposed to put us as priority. They're supposed to protect us."

Brentwood nodded sadly, "I know. To lose faith in them would be to lose faith in the entire system. This is all speculation. I'm not even sure what to believe. All I know is it's suspicious they'd crash land us on a planet that has a corresponding beacon to the orb in their chamber."

Brentwood's voice grew firm. "I say we take the chest back to the *Expedition*."

"What?" She spread her arms through the air. "Are you out of your mind?"

Brentwood shrugged. "Maybe I am. But if we take it back, we'll know just what they wanted it for. We'll know who to trust and who's in it for their own good."

"What if they're both in it for their own good?"

"Then they'll get stuck inside."

"But who's going to run the ship?"

"We'll find a way. Do you really want those twins overseeing operations if they sacrificed all those lives for their personal gain?"

Gemme sighed. "I guess not. No."

"Then, are you with me? I could use your help."

"I'm always with you." Gemme stepped toward him and reached out for his hand. "Isn't that what we've learned from this?"

He took her hand in his. "Only if you want to be."

She spoke with conviction. "I do."

CHAPTER TWENTY-NINE
US

Brentwood drove like he transported hazardous material as he carefully maneuvered the landrover with the chest inside back to the mining site. Every bump and turn he calculated carefully so the lid didn't open, even a crack. They'd tied it down with rope, but who knew how much it took to hold the powers of the chest back. Even now he felt it's beckoning like the chest tugged on a string tied to his gut. Gemme kept glancing back over her shoulder, making him even more uneasy.

"What's wrong? Is it moving?"

She shifted in her seat as if she were uncomfortable. "No. Shivers keep crawling down my spine. It holds so many answers, maybe even answers to the mysteries of the universe, yet I know how much danger is involved. I almost lost myself in there. I almost lost you. Even now it calls to me and I have to force myself to ignore it. I don't think my mind would be able to handle all of the truths it holds."

"Me neither. That's why we shouldn't leave it alone with the Seers. We'll make them open it with us present."

"How are you going to do that?"

Brentwood patted his laser. "If it comes to it, then laser negotiations."

Gemme gave him a nervous look. "Like with the mammoths."

Regret panged in his chest and he winced. "Hopefully, this time no one will get hurt."

They rode the rest of the way in silence. Brentwood thought of all the possible situations that might play out with the Seers and the chest, and wondered if he could manage running the ship without them. The systems necessary for survival were primarily the energy distribution and the air ventilation. They didn't need to steer the ship through space any more. How hard could that be?

Probably harder than he could have guessed. He was never good at computers, and electrical wiring made as much sense to him as the chest. Brentwood realized he gripped the steering wheel too tightly, and relaxed his fingers. Maybe someone like Tech could rewire the systems. Or maybe he was wrong about the Seers, and they had the crew's best intentions in mind.

The vehicle crested the snow mounds surrounding the valley and the mining site came into view. Tech had the drill in full force, the equipment shining like a new tool in the rays of Solaris Prime. The sight gave Brentwood a small measure of comfort. At least his first mission had been successful. No matter what happened with the Seers, they'd have more energy to survive.

Tech jumped off the mining rig and ran in their direction when they approached.

"How much should we tell him?" Brentwood took in a ponderous breath as he parked the landrover. "I don't want the old man worrying too much."

"Someone's got to know in case the whole situation turns bad." Gemme placed a stray lock of hair behind her ear.

"Okay, we tell him everything then."

Gemme nodded. "I think it's best."

When the hatch opened, Tech stood there with an expectant look on his face. "Find anything good?"

"We found something, all right." Brentwood jumped out, eager to stretch his legs, and Gemme followed. "But we think it'll do more harm than good." They explained to him what had happened, leaving out the details of their romance.

"Does it really show you the past?" Tech leaned inside to peek at the chest.

"All the way back into former lives on Old Earth." Gemme answered. "But I'd be careful if I were you. You could get stuck reliving old memories and forget about the present. We almost did."

"Don't worry 'bout me." Tech inched back from the landrover to join them. His face paled like he'd seen another mammoth horde lurking in the back of the vehicle. "Made too many mistakes. Hell, I wouldn't go back to my past if someone paid me with all the wheat beer on the *Expedition*."

Brentwood laughed, but he didn't sound lighthearted. His face turned serious. "We think that's what the Seers want."

Tech sobered from his joke quickly and adjusted his collar as if the thought choked him. "You're going to take it back to them?"

"That's the only way we'll know what they truly want and if they value the crew of the *Expedition* more than their memories of the past."

Tech patted Brentwood on the back. "You've got a heavy duty, my friend."

"Don't worry about us." Brentwood reassured him. "We'll figure out this chest business. Just keep mining that hyperthium. You have the most important job out of everyone."

"Speaking of hyperthium..." Tech pointed to two large containers beside the mining platform. He had a sparkle in his eyes. "I've got a shipment to take back with you."

"Already?"

"Yessir. Tell them there's more where that came from. A whole lot more."

Brentwood's chest warmed with pride. "Excellent, Tech."

Tech waved off his accolades. "I was nervous for you all. Couldn't eat, and you know how much I love to eat. So I figured—keep myself busy until they get back."

"Looks like you did more than keep busy." Brentwood smiled.

"Job well done."

They loaded the containers in next to the chest. Brentwood thought the added weight against the crystal would keep it from rolling around in the back. He turned to Tech. "Great job. I'll send more workers your way when I get back."

"I could certainly use some help. It would speed up the process. And my wife, I bet, wants me back soon." Tech pulled on the end of his beard. "So you guys won't stay for dinner?"

Brentwood shook his head. "I want to straighten things out and move on. Besides, the chemists on the *Expedition* could start processing the hyperthium right away, and we should bring Luna's body back as soon as possible."

Tech extended his hand. "It was an honor working with both of you."

Brentwood shook it first. "You too, Tech."

Gemme took his hand next. "Stay warm."

"Yeah, I wouldn't want to melt my beard, now would I?" He gave her a wink before walking back to the drill.

"What was that all about?" Brentwood whispered to her as they jumped in the landrover.

She laughed and rolled her eyes, a playful gesture he hadn't see her do before. "An inside joke."

They rode for the remainder of the day and into the night until their headlights cut through darkness. Without the drill and the mining platform, they made excellent time, and he estimated they'd reach the *Expedition* within the next day.

Brentwood parked the vehicle and turned to Gemme. "Shall we make camp for the night?"

"Sure. I know I don't want to sleep in the landrover with Luna's body and that chest."

"Okay, I'll get the tents." Brentwood pressed the panel for the hatch.

"Tents?" Gemme emphasized the plural.

Brentwood paused as the hatch opened behind him. "What do you mean?"

"Why do we need two?"

Brentwood's heart sped up. She asked him if they could stay together, in one tent. She'd already hinted at it in the memory in front of the log cabin, but that felt like a distant dream now. In fact, they hadn't ever really kissed in reality, only in the chest. Faced with the harsh truth of Tundra 37 and the chest, he hadn't thought of whether or not they'd sleep in the same tent.

"I thought for reasons of propriety—"

"Look around us." She waved her arm across the sight panel. "There's no one here for hundreds of kilometers around. What we do is our business." She studied the depths of his eyes, her gaze intense and warm. "It's just us."

He touched her cheek. "Are you sure?"

"All my life I've been shy; I couldn't speak up when the Luna pushed me down the recycling chute, and I couldn't tell you we were paired together. Ferris had told me before I left there was more to life than numbers. He was right. I was afraid to come out of my shell, to think outside the box and take chances. The comet shower, Tundra 37, this mission, they all forced me to grow. I'm not shy anymore."

Gemme met his gaze. "In other words, yes."

Brentwood realized he'd been holding his breath, and he exhaled. She'd changed so much, but he had as well. "On the *Expedition*, I thought I had life figured out."

Gemme nodded and he smiled when he thought back to his own naivety. "Then I met you, and it was like someone splashed me with cold water and woke me up. I was tongue-tied. You made me feel vulnerable, and I wanted to know why. After the ship crashed, the Seers assigned me to Alpha Blue. When I saw your name on the team, I felt excited, but also scared. I was heading into unknown territory, and I feared I'd fail the team and the *Expedition*. But most of all, I was afraid I'd fail your expectations."

"You didn't." Gemme assured him, taking his hand. "You exceeded them."

Brentwood wondered how he could deserve such a marvelous woman. "Life can change in an instant. I saw that with the ship and with Luna, and it shook me up. But you calm me. You give me focus. It's the bonds we've built with each other that hold us together when things get rough."

He rubbed the palm of her hand with his fingers, heat rising inside him. "Our bond is so strong, it's lasted over centuries. That's why you threw me off when I met you. Part of me knew we were destined to be together. I want you too, Gemme."

He leaned in and kissed her tenderly. Her lips softened against his, and she pushed into him, demanding more. He responded, his hands traveling across her shoulders to her neck. This time *she* pulled back, gasping for air. She spoke, almost breathless. "So let's go set up that tent."

CHAPTER THIRTY
TEMPTATION

Bysme, let me go. Mestasis struggled to move, every impulse blocked by her sister's wrath. Abysme's temper raged, and harnessing her hatred gave her unequalled power. She had always been the stronger telepath, which had been a blessing until now. She'd thought Abysme had lost control, but she'd gained every last ounce of it while Mestasis drifted off into memories. She should never have allowed herself to go back so far and linger for so long.

Abysme's blind eye widened and she writhed in her restraints. *The beacon draws near.*

Forget the beacon. I've been inside the orb, and there's nothing there but temptation. Mestasis's mind shot up every channel she could find, but she ran against dead ends. If no one looked after the ship, the systems would fail. She had to convince her sister to let her go.

Abysme continued, oblivious to the ship's imminent danger. *Everything is there. You, me, Mom. We're together.*

She sounded like they'd already died and gone to heaven. But there were thousands of people's lives resting on theirs. Mestasis forced herself to concentrate and think of a tactic that would penetrate her sister's delirium.

Remember the oath we took to protect the ship and all the colonists?

Abysme squirmed as if she didn't want to remember. *I've been a slave to this ship and its crew for so many years. Don't we deserve our freedom?*

Mestasis remained silent. She had a point. But she'd signed away their freedom hundreds of years ago in Thadious Legacy's office. In return they received extended life and power. But, to use that power to achieve their own ends at the expense of the crew was unthinkable. This wasn't her sister talking, it was the orb.

Bysme, let the orb go. It's only an illusion, a trap.

Abysme shook her head. *I don't care what it is. When Alpha Blue brings back that beacon, I'm going in.*

Mestasis balked, feeling her grip on her sister slide, tearing a hole in her heart. To be deceived or forced against her will was one thing, but Abysme knew what she did was wrong. She flung herself headlong into temptation, and she didn't care who she plowed down in her path.

Vira tossed in her sleep pod, banging her elbow against the side. She wanted to fall into a deep sleep and enjoy her ballerina dream all over again, but a sense of jittery uneasiness crept over her like spiders under her blanket. The strong presence pulsed on the other side of the systems, searching for her.

As the ship grew weaker, the presence grew stronger, like it sucked the vital life of the systems to support its own demands. She sensed it in every vibration. It wanted control, and it hated the fact that an intruder had spied. If it caught her, it could keep her soul stranded in the neverland of the electric grid while her body fell into a coma.

She wished she could shut off her powers. In fact, she wanted to get rid of them altogether. All they'd done was cause her problems, and she knew she couldn't keep them hidden forever. Smoothing her hands over her blanket, she tried to convince herself to fall asleep. Somehow, she knew the presence couldn't find her in her ballerina dream. When her conscious mind dozed, she was safe.

Vira hid her head under her pillow. She hadn't meant to spy. She was just trying to keep her family safe. But somehow, she didn't think her excuses would matter. It would only be a matter of time before it found her out and then everyone would know about her powers. They'd take her away and her poor parents would never be happy again.

An ugly question reared its way into her head.

What if she was the only one who could save the ship? What if she could stop it?

Vira shook her head and ignored the answer. She wasn't ready to be a hero. The other men on the *Expedition* were working on the energy. Her dad said so. They'd figure out a way to stop it, and then her mind could roam free. She hugged her blanket to her chest. All she had to do was lie low and wait.

CHAPTER THIRTY-ONE
SACRIFICE

The hunk of crushed metal poking out from the horizon grew larger, igniting nervous jolts of energy in Gemme's limbs. She gripped the armrests of her seat, wondering how a place she'd called home her entire life could look so ominous.

"I don't see any deck lights on." Brentwood squinted out the sight panel as they approached. She wanted the comfort they'd given to one another last night, but the warmth of their tent seemed a lifetime away, like the cabin on the prairie. Drawing strength, she assured herself that with their love they could handle anything the Seers threw at them.

"Maybe the Seers are conserving energy?"

"Or maybe they ran out and the energy core has failed." He narrowed his eyes, his jaw set in a grim line.

Gemme took his hand, the touch of his skin against hers now familiar, but still just as exciting. "We've brought the first shipment of hyperthium. Whatever it is, we'll fix it, okay?"

"I hope it's something that *can* be fixed."

Skidding in the snow, they pulled up to the back hatch. Icicles two times longer than Gemme clung to the hull in deadly stalactites. Snow coated the entire chrome ceiling, piling up as if the landscape had claimed the ship for itself. The hull looked more like a mountain than a ship that only days ago had flown through deep space.

Brentwood pressed the communications panel. His voice was gritty, like he hadn't spoken all day. "Alpha Blue requesting entry."

Gemme gave him a nervous look and they waited in silence as she struggled to calm herself. What if everyone was dead? The Seers hadn't responded to her communications concerning the hyperthium, and she hadn't heard from Ferris in days.

"Entry granted. Requesting status of Beta Prime." Even though it was a sign of life, the monotone voice sent a shiver across her shoulders.

"She didn't even ask about the hyperthium." Gemme smoothed her shaky hands over her thermal pants.

Brentwood's eyebrow rose. "Exactly."

He drove forward, speaking into the microphone on the control panel. "Beta Prime located and secured. Requesting an audience."

The Seer responded quickly. "Request granted. Report to the control chamber immediately with Beta Prime." Gemme wondered if she detected a hint of eagerness in the otherwise emotionless voice.

The doors retracted slowly, revealing a dark and empty docking bay. Gemme had expected an audience and a grand parade, Alpha Blue in its entirety lugging great bins of hyperthium behind the landrover to thunderous applause. Instead, she returned to a ghost ship. "No one's here."

He shrugged. "Probably isn't worth heating this part of the ship, so I bet the Seers directed the workers elsewhere."

The hatch opened to silence and the occasional bang of metal as an icicle cracked off the hull. Gemme jumped out and scanned the empty docking bay. The doors rumbled as they closed, leaving them in shadows. She had to warn Ferris, but she didn't want to drag him into anything dangerous. Clicking off her locator, she joined Brentwood at the control panel.

His fingers brushed the touchscreen. "I'll send for a team to unload the landrover."

Gemme felt like the Seers manifested in every chrome plate,

watching them move, hearing them speak. She whirled around, searching the shadowy ceiling and hugged her shoulders. Without the distant light of Solaris Prime, the bay felt frostier than the ice world outside. "Should we wait for them?"

Brentwood shook his head. "I'll leave a message saying we're checking in with the Seers and to tend to Luna's body. I'd like to avoid any questions about the chest."

"Okay. Let's get out of here before everyone shows up."

They rounded the vehicle and Brentwood pressed the panel for the back hatch. The chest rested between the hyperthium containers like a pearl among stones. The cosmic swirls moved underneath the crystal, collecting on the side that faced them as if drawn by their presence.

"Do you think it remembers us?" Gemme asked as Brentwood pulled it forward.

"Who knows? We'll keep the rope tied around the lid just in case." He tugged the chest out and Gemme took the other side, marveling at the lightness. For something that held so much, the crystal weighed as though it held nothing at all.

Brentwood gestured over his shoulder. "I know a private corridor that will take us to the Seers without running into anyone. Come on."

She followed him to the back end of the loading dock. He typed a code into the panel, and a secret portal dematerialized from the wall. Gemme watched in fascination.

"It's an old escape route," Brentwood explained while balancing the chest on his knee as he positioned his hands around the sides for a better grip. "For the Seers. They were to be kept alive at all costs, even in the event of a ship failure. The Seers had their own escape pods. They could control the other pods from deep space using their mindspeak to organize an emergency landing on a suitable planet. Once biologists and doctors connected them to the mainframe, they abandoned the escape plan. Now the Seers can't survive without the ship, so it doesn't matter."

"It matters to me." Gemme tried to ignore how the swirls twisted around the place where her arms touched the chest. "How come I didn't know about this?"

"Confidential. Only the Lieutenants know."

She narrowed her eyes. "How much more do the lieutenants know that I don't?"

Brentwood smiled, surprising her. "Not much. I'm sure you as the ex-matchmaker have your own little secrets."

Gemme smiled. "Maybe a few." She was tempted to tell him about the hypergene secret, but she'd have to go into great explanations, and she decided now was not the time to further complicate matters.

Brentwood sighed. "To tell you the truth, I didn't even know about the beacon or the orb until just a few days ago."

"So much has changed in so little time." Overwhelmed, the darkness of the corridor pressed in on her while the chest's innate glow beckoned. She tried not to focus on it, but her eyes kept returning to the elusive shine.

"I know one thing that hasn't changed at all in centuries."

He stole her attention from the chest and she flicked her eyes up. Brentwood checked over his shoulder as he walked backward and then turned to her with a lopsided, boyish smile on his face.

"What?"

"Us."

Gemme almost melted onto the chrome floor on the spot. Her knees weakened and she struggled to keep the chest level. "I'm glad that hasn't changed."

"So am I."

As much as she feared the chest, its powers had brought her and Brentwood together like nothing else could, and she couldn't deny the visions it presented them. Even now she wondered just how far back in time their previous lives stretched. Did they exist in the medieval era? At the rise of the Roman Empire? The roped holding the chest loosened and a sliver of green caught her eye underneath the lid. If only she could peek in and see what the crystal was trying to tell her.

"We're almost here."

Brentwood's voice roused her from her trance and she yanked her head up. They stood in front of an elevator shaft.

"This will take us right to the main control deck." He studied her passionately. "Are you ready?"

Embarrassed by her sudden urge to look inside, Gemme wanted to ditch the chest as soon as possible. "More than ready."

"Let's finish this." He elbowed the panel, but the screen remained black. Gemme's heart crawled into her throat while they waited. "They must have cut the power to the elevators."

"I'm not lugging this up ten flights of stairs."

Just as Brentwood spoke, the portal dematerialized, and the elevator panel set to deck sixty-seven. Gemme stumbled back and almost dropped the chest. She whispered under her breath, "They know we're here."

Brentwood shrugged as if he wouldn't let the Seers ubiquitous powers scare him. "Guess that solves that problem."

They stepped onto the platform and the elevator rose to the command center at the helm, ushering them so quickly, Gemme could feel the pull of gravity weighing her down. Misgivings nagged her. She never thought she'd have to see the Seers, never mind confront them. "What do they look like?"

Brentwood tapped his toe while the elevator brought them up. "Wires, machines, and missing parts." His shoulders moved as if a chill crept across them. "Be prepared."

She didn't know if anything could prepare her for this moment.

The elevator beeped, and the portal dematerialized into a dark corridor lit only by sparks from frayed wires. They stepped carefully over the debris from the crash.

"Nothing's changed since I was last here." Brentwood kicked part of the ceiling panels out of their way. "Either they haven't allowed anyone up since, or no one's overseeing the operations."

"We need this ship running, Gemme." He gave her a serious look as if to warn her about the fragility of the Seers, and how important they were. She knew the risks they took in bringing the chest, but Brentwood was right about determining their motives. She'd rather piece the parts of the ship together herself than have two crazy twins at the helm.

"I'll do everything in my power to uphold that." Gemme kept her reply general. She didn't want to speak so openly about their intentions. Who knew what the Seers heard?

The portal dematerialized to the main control chamber as they approached and cool, regulated air flowed out, chilling Gemme's cheeks. Wires hung from the ceiling like dead foliage in a forgotten forest, and she ducked to avoid their broken ends. Some of the loose cables brushed her head and shoulders as they parted their way into the dark room, sending shivers down her neck. She stumbled over a pile of debris. The chest pitched, but Brentwood held it up as she regained her footing.

The glow from the orb on the floor illuminated the main sight panel ahead of them. Thick snow piled up against the glass, covering the helm. The ship must have crashed head first into a snow mound. She wondered how long it would take to shovel themselves out and reminded herself it wasn't necessary. The *Expedition* would never fly again.

"Place it down here." Brentwood instructed. They crouched low to the floor before setting the crystal chest down as gently as they would a baby's cradle.

Rustling came from the ceiling behind her. Gemme craned her neck and stumbled back, falling over the chest onto her butt. Two fragments of human beings hung in suspension, like two giant spiders with eight thousand long wiry legs.

Leave us. The skeletal face on the left jerked up, two blind eyes lolling. Although her lips didn't move, Gemme heard her voice clearly in her head. She looked to the other one, but her torso was rigid as a robot. The other twin had one dark eye that looked almost normal, and in it Gemme saw a tremendous amount of fear and pain.

How could the biologists leave them like this?

Brentwood gave her a reassuring nod as he offered his hand to help her on her feet. Gemme grabbed his hand and forced herself to keep her ground beside him.

He spoke up. "No, we stay."

The blind one tilted her head. *You would disobey us?*

"I'm here to protect you." Brentwood's voice was firm. "This chest holds the past; it sucks you right in and tempts you to stay until you forget everything going on in the real world. It's not safe, and I suggest we destroy it."

No! Her voice roared in their heads. Gemme's hands shot up and she squeezed her palms over her ears.

Leave the chest with us.

Brentwood's hand hovered over his laser. "We're not going anywhere."

Wires rustled behind them like mice scurried underneath the chrome floor. Gemme whirled around as a thick cord poked through the metal grating at her feet.

Brentwood shouted, "Look out!"

She kicked at the cord as it extended toward her and climbed up her leg, coiling around her calf.

"Miles! Help!" She screamed as it pulled her to the floor. Brentwood fell beside her, wires and cables winding around his arms and legs. Her fingers dug around the coil to yank it off just as a cable shot out from the wall and wrapped around her wrist. A plastic tube, thick as her arm snuck up behind her, slipping along her neck.

Gemme struggled to breathe. The tube would so tightly, any movement would choke her. Brentwood grunted beside her as he struggled against the restraints holding him down.

Her heart squeezed to see him debilitated. "Are you okay?"

His eyes were bright with adrenaline. "Can you reach my laser?"

A wire held her hand inches away. She wiggled her fingers. Her pointer grazed the cold surface of the holster. "I almost have it."

A cable shot up, wrapped around the barrel, and dragged his laser into the bowels of the ship.

"So much for that." The muscles in his face strained as he fought to find a way out.

The blind Seer lowered herself to the floor. One by one, the wires connecting her to the ceiling broke loose. Gemme's heart pounded. Would she come over and suffocate her with the tube?

The Seer glanced once in her direction, blind eyes intense, and using the wires and cables, slithered toward the chest.

Bysme, please. Please don't go. This voice sounded different, deeper. Gemme saw the other Seer blink her one good eye. A tear trailed down her pasty cheek.

Why didn't she do something? Gemme wanted to shout at

Mestasis to stop her twin, but then she saw what was happening. The Seer's body was rigid because the tube running into her spine had been pulled halfway out, pink liquid dripping to the floor.

You've kept me here long enough, Metsy. I've always done what you wanted us to do, and what's it gotten us? Trapped in the same room for hundreds of years, waiting for a planet we'll never be able to enjoy. Don't you get it? Once we reached Paradise 18, we'd be done for. The ship would be abandoned and we'd be left to die. I want out, and this chest will let me live my life all over again.

Gemme wondered how she could hear their mindspeak. At this point, the Seers must be shouting so loud to one another that they didn't care.

What about the people we swore to protect?

I'm done living for others. It's time I lived for myself. Her voice dripped bitterness.

Mestasis twitched, trying to move without the body fluid to enable her atrophied muscles. A joint in her neck snapped as she turned her head to her sister. *You steered the ship into the comet shower, didn't you? You wanted to land here, all for the chest.*

Abysme dragged herself forward, unhindered by the accusation. *I've been planning it for years. Ever since we found the orb. I'm not going to let you or anyone stop me.*

You've gone crazy, Bysme. Let me go. Let us help you.

Abysme approached her sister and the loose wires around her torso wound around the links keeping Mestasis in place. One by one, she yanked them out, disconnecting her sister from the system. Each broken connect racked her sister's body with a shudder. *You will join me. I'm in charge of our futures now, and we're going into the chest.*

Stop! If you do this, we'll both die.

The ship's shot to hell. We'll die anyway. Why not pass on in the comfort of our mother's arms?

Mestasis yelled, her eye burning with intensity. *I gave up James for you, for us to have a safe life together.* Pain filled her voice, making it quiver. If Gemme weren't tied down, she'd run to comfort her. She looked to Brentwood, but he busied himself squirming in his restraints to find a weakness.

And now you can see him again.

He's not in there, Bysme. No one is! They're your own memories, pulled from the recesses of your mind. James, our mother, all the people in our past died hundreds of years ago. There's no way to get them back.

They're real to me. Abysme yanked more wires loose. *You said you've always known what's best for us. I stood by and let you make all the decisions, and I've had it with being passive while opportunities for true happiness passed us by. Now, I know what's best. We're going in.*

Mestasis's dark eye turned on Gemme, pleading with her to help. Gemme stared back at her and shook her head. Her sister was gone. She'd totally lost it. How could Gemme possibly right her sister's wrong? Undo all of the death and devastation she'd caused? There was no way.

"We've got to do something," Brentwood whispered as he struggled, his face turning red. "She's going to kill them both. We need at least one of them at the helm."

He was right. Mestasis hadn't done anything wrong, and she could still help them save the ship. Lights flickered above them as the last twin disconnected from the system. Warning alarms wailed in the control chamber and down the hail, echoing one after the other. The ventilator above them shut off, the familiar buzz dying to complete silence.

Pushing her thumb into the palm of her hand, Gemme popped the digit out of her knuckle. She bit her lip as the streak of pain shot through her arm. Then she pulled her hand free.

Too distracted by disconnecting her sister, Abysme didn't notice her escape. With her free hand, Gemme unwound the tube around her neck and pulled her legs from the coiled wires. She moved to help Brentwood, but he shook his head and flashed his eyes at the scene behind her.

Gemme whirled around. Abysme had disconnected Mestasis and dragged her limp body to the chest. Gemme threw herself across the floor and landed on top of her, the wires on the Seer's back poking into her stomach like a porcupine's quills.

Aaaaaah! The Seer's voice screamed in her head as Gemme wrapped her arms around her. The torso writhed beneath her, layers of old skin flaking away underneath her fingernails. Wires lunged at Gemme's face trying to poke out her eyes, but she buried her head into the Seer's back held on, stopping Abysme from reaching the chest's light.

The reek of dead skin and decomposition gagged her. Gemme had feared the Seers since her childhood, hoping she'd never had to meet them face-to-face, and now she sprawled on top of one, the Seer's thin wisps of gray hair tickling Gemme's cheek as they wrestled. Everywhere on Gemme's body, her skin crawled.

But she had greater problems than her worst fear come to life. The wires scratched at her back, tearing into her thermal coat. It would only be a matter of time before the frayed ends ripped through the outer layer to her skin. One look at Brentwood told her he wasn't able to help. She took a chance and released an arm to swat the wires away.

There were too many to keep at bay, and they scratched her arms leaving thin ribbons of blood. Abysme squirmed out from underneath her, and Gemme lost her grip, her sweaty hands slipping down her back.

The Seer's wires reached toward the light. Anger welled inside Gemme as she thought of all the people Abysme had inadvertently killed. People she'd sworn to protect. Now, the Seer wanted to run away, leaving them all here on this frozen, forgotten planet to pick up the pieces. Gemme grabbed her main spinal tube trailing behind her and yanked her back. "No you don't, you selfish bitch."

Abysme turned and hissed, white eyes wide as two moons.

"Gemme watch out!" Brentwood shouted, his voice hoarse with alarm.

The wires flew through the air, trying to pierce Gemme's body. She ducked and caught one in her hand, inches from her throat just as another shot through her pants leg and grazed her calf.

Gemme collapsed to the floor in pain, but she wouldn't release the tube. The Seer crawled toward her on her wire limbs. Gemme scurried back, favoring her leg. The blood ran in a streak across the chrome. Abysme gained on her, squirming up her legs to her chest.

Wincing, Gemme expected a wire to impale her or shoot through her gut, but the Seer stopped inches from her chin.

Abysme's face contorted into sheer surprise, toothless mouth opening wide. She whirled around just as a wire moving against the rest plunged through the air above her and stabbed her in the back and through the heart, protruding out of her chest.

Gemme froze in shock and glanced behind Abysme to her sister. Mestasis lay on her back, head rolling to the side. The Seer's voice resonated in her head. *You and Lieutenant Brentwood have the love that I once had. Don't ever let it slip away.*

Mestasis had saved her by murdering her own sister. Gemme stared at the Seer in shock.

Mestasis's black eye leaked a stream of tears then shut.

CHAPTER THIRTY-TWO
THE MOST IMPORTANT

Vira's miniscreen flickered and she smacked it against the floor. The blue liquid in the energy cell had run out an hour ago, and it was her last one.

"Come on, don't die on me now." Teachers had temporarily suspended classes until the situation with the *Expedition* stabilized, but when she was stuck learning geometry again, she wanted to have her proofs completed.

Besides, doing homework kept her mind off all her problems. She was sick of not having what she needed: her hoverchair, fresh food, and now energy cells. How were they supposed to live on Tundra 37 without all those things?

She minimized the glow of the screen and her undone proof flashed on. She scanned the last line before the miniscreen powered down and went dead. Guilt came over her as she thought back to all those hours wasted playing Star Quest.

Vira pressed the start panel over and over and nothing happened. Pounding her fist into the floor, she slumped against the wall in her room. Now what was she supposed to do?

"Mo-om!"

No answer. Vira shouted with the full force of her little lungs. Her voice echoed in her room and died away. Mom must have left to take Dad dinner. He never came home anymore, working long hours in the energy core, trying to keep the ship going.

The dim lights flickered around her, the room alternating between blindingly bright and black as deep space. Vira covered her face with her hands. When she pried her palms off, she was plunged into darkness.

"Rizzy?"

Was her sister playing pranks again?

"I know that's you, so cut it out."

No answer. She pushed her useless miniscreen off her lap and dragged herself to the kitchen. The carpet left burns on her arms, so she'd developed the technique of anchoring herself with an elbow, then pulling her weight forward arm over arm. Slow but sure. Isn't that what her teachers had said about the *Expedition*'s progress? Vira was overcome with melancholy. Well, not any more. The ship would never fly again.

The icy chrome floor chilled her belly as she entered the kitchen. A half-eaten soybean wafer stuck out from the edge of the table, but other than that, no signs of life.

How could they leave her alone? Air wheezed over her head as the main ventilator shaft shut off. The silence of stagnant air reminded her of when the ship first crashed. Vira's face squished up as she held back her tears. She sniffed, wiping her eyes on her pajama cuffs and tried to calm herself down. *Someone will come home soon.*

An alarm wailed down the corridor outside their family cell and she scrambled up, heart beating out of control. A shorter, more insistent sound beeped a warning followed by an automated response. "Engine failure in fifteen minutes. Core shutdown imminent. Evacuation procedures commence."

Vira held her breath, not wanting to believe it. The ship was dying and she was alone.

She crawled underneath the kitchen table and curled up in a ball.

She couldn't hold the tears back any longer, and they ran down her cheeks, wetting the front of her favorite pajamas. But soiling her pink jammies didn't matter, because if someone didn't stabilize the energy core, they'd all be dead.

She bit her lip until it hurt. After feeling sorry for herself, she wondered if there was a way she could help. If she could channel the remaining energy, she could connect to the ship and find out what was wrong. Maybe she could fix it. She thought back to Rizzy's poster, the mage staring her down as if demanding her to use her powers. She'd done it before with the air ventilator. Controlling an entire ship would be more complex than one air ventilator, but at least she could try. Vira paused, hands hovering over the chrome floor, fingers shaking. If she reconnected to the systems, the evil presence would find her.

Metal banged as the hull adjusted to the changes in air pressure. Vira cringed, thinking of her parents, Rizzy, and even stupid Daryl. As much as she hated them at times, she wanted to see them again and sit together at the dinner table as a family, eating fresh food and calling each other a spacehead. If her dad couldn't fix the problem, and the Seers didn't care, it was up to her.

She held her breath and pressed her hands against the floor, feeling all the connections still alive within the mainframe branching out. No conscious presence presided. In fact, the systems ran blindly, each program terminating when their cycles completed with no new orders issued. No one was in charge at all.

Vira shot up. If she wanted to save the *Expedition*, she'd have to reach the control chamber where she could access each system at once from the main console. The heartbeat of the ship weakened, and she didn't have much time before the spark keeping the energy core running flickered out.

She crawled back toward her room and popped open the secret floor panel. Her scooter, made from old parts and the cleaning droid sat, almost finished. She didn't have a steering wheel, or a seat to hold herself up, but she could hold on and drive it with her mind like she was able to turn on the ventilator.

She activated the scooter and rode it to the front portal, stopping before the chrome. She couldn't reach the panel for the portal, so she ran her hand along the wall. The wavering current of electricity tickled her fingertips, and she shot it up to the panel before it flickered out. The portal dematerialized, and the scooter propelled forward, pulling her with it.

People ran through the corridors so fast, they didn't notice a girl lugged by a makeshift scooter at their feet. An older woman cried and a young man screamed for help inside his family cell. Guilt weighed on her as she ignored them and whizzed by, clinging to the scooter. She could only save them by reaching the control room.

The scooter dragged her to a back elevator, grander than any of the ones she'd seen before with double sets of portals, the frame painted in a filigree of loopy designs with two pairs of dark eyes staring over each portal. She pressed her hand to the wall. The wires ran dead for several decks. Probing deeper, she drew a current directly from the dying core to get the portals to dematerialize. The particles disappeared and she nudged the droid ahead with her mind. It wheeled her over the platform.

Her heart raced as the elevator rose, thumping in her hears. What if the Seers set a trap to catch her? A jolt of anxiety shook her body. Would they really sacrifice the ship and risk lives to catch a spy? She had no idea. But the energy core had destabilized. She could feel the tension brimming as the radiation permeated the inner shield. Getting caught was a gamble she'd had to take.

The portal dematerialized to a corridor cluttered by debris. It looked like no one had walked there since the ship crashed, and a shiver crept up her back. The scooter sputtered as it led her off the platform, the small green lights on the nose dimming.

"Come on you space bot! Not now."

The buzzing of mechanics inside its belly clicked off as it powered down. Vira checked the energy cell, and the blue liquid in the tube had run out. An ethereal shine emanated down the long corridor from what could only be the control room. She was so close. Climbing off the scooter, she pulled herself forward a foot at a time.

Scrambling over Abysme's body, Gemme reached Brentwood, ripping wires from his arms. The grooves left ugly patterns on his skin. "You okay?"

He nodded and stared beyond her shoulder. "Help Mestasis."

From what she'd seen, it seemed like a lost cause, but Brentwood was right. The Seer had to come first, and if she could do anything to get her back, she would. Gemme ran over to Mestasis and cupped her wrinkly face in both hands. Her skin felt dry and cold underneath her fingertips. "Mestasis, wake up."

The Seer lay limp in her arms. Gemme shook her and her head twisted to the side. Hesitantly, she laid her hand on her chest: no heartbeat. The finality of the moment hit her like a laser in her stomach. She turned back to Brentwood. "I think she's gone."

"Plug her back in, restart her heart."

Wishing she had some sort of medic skills, Gemme turned the Seer over and pushed the spinal tube further into the input hole in her back. Pink liquid dribbled into her body, but Mestasis's limbs hung lifeless. No matter how much Gemme jiggled the tube, only a trickle of liquid flowed. Around her the ship's sirens wailed as the systems shut down one by one. An automated voice rang out, "Warning. Engine failure in fifteen minutes. Core shutdown imminent. Evacuation procedures recommended."

"By the Guide." Brentwood's face paled as he struggled with his own restraints in panic. "I didn't think losing them would cause a core failure. I had no idea."

"Probably wouldn't have if the ship was in better shape." Gemme knew that made no difference now, but she didn't want the fate of the entire ship resting on Brentwood's head. They'd made the decision together, and now they had to fix it.

Gemme tried again to wake Mestasis, jiggling the tube she'd attached.

"I brought her back before." Brentwood pulled his leg from the wire clump and stumbled over. He checked the tube, then turned her face to him. "Metsy, please come back to us."

"She's dead." Gemme's voice broke on her words.

"She can't be." Brentwood pressed on the Seer's chest in rhythm and blew air into her mouth. "Come on, Metsy. We need you."

"I can do it." A small voice rang out behind them and they whirled around. Gemme recognized the girl she'd talked to in the safe zone after the comet shower had hit the *Expedition*. Sweat ran down the girl's forehead, dripping off her black curls, and her cheeks flushed red with exertion. Sprawled on her belly, she must have dragged herself all the way there.

"Vira, what are you doing here? You should be evacuating." Brentwood's voice was stern.

Gemme's mind turned back to that day in the emergency chamber. Vira had more control of her world than she let on, and the things she knew about Gemme were impossible unless she had secret access to the systems. It all fit into place like a grand puzzle, and Gemme couldn't believe she hadn't seen the connection before.

Vira was the first person on the *Expedition* to inherit the Seers' abilities. Although the Seers themselves had no children, scientists had implanted random crew members with their eggs. The Seers had no knowledge of these experiments. Only the Matchmaker for each generation knew, and they tried to produce a crew member with the Seers' unique abilities. There was no time to explain this to Brentwood, so he'd have to trust her. Gemme gave him a knowing look. "Let her try."

Brentwood spread his hands in a helpless gesture. "What can she do? She doesn't know CPR."

"Help me lift her." Gemme climbed over the debris and sprinted to Vira. "We're taking her to the main console."

"You mean let her run the ship like the Seers did?" His mouth fell open and he had to clamp it back up. "She's just a girl."

"She can do it." Gemme gave Vira an encouraging smile as she picked her up. The girl shook, but her face was set in determination.

Vira's voice was strong. "Please, give me a chance."

Gemme carried her over the debris, holding her close to her chest. She spoke into the girl's black curls. "You can fix it. I know you can."

The automated response echoed on the intercom, "Ten minutes until core shutdown. Evacuation recommended."

"All right." Brentwood helped Gemme over the debris to the center of the control chamber. Placing their hands around her waist, they lifted her to the ceiling where the Seer's had hung for generations. Vira grabbed the loose wires, wrapping them around her arms and closed her eyes.

Gemme sent all her positive energy through her arms into the girl. *Please Vira, you're all we've got.*

The alarms trailed off, and the lights dimmed to blackness. The white shine of the chest illuminated their faces in a ghostly sheen. Silence settled over the control chamber and Gemme could hear her own intake of breath. The chill crept in, crawling over her body and settling in her bones. She felt like the final ember of a fire before the winds of Tundra 37 blew out the last flickering flame.

Is this how it would end, she and Brentwood, holding the final hope of a dying civilization at the end of a frozen world? She looked into Brentwood's eyes like she'd probably done for generations, always finding solace in the green flecks. He was her home, no matter if they were on Old Earth, on the *Expedition*, or Tundra 37, and the last thing she wanted to see was the warmth his eyes held for her.

Light, brighter than Solaris Prime, gushed around them. Had the core had exploded? Gemme shut her eyes, still holding onto Vira. What if they failed? The girl, and all the other children on the *Expedition* wouldn't live long enough to have a full life. Deep melancholy sickened her stomach as she realized their mission would fail not only Thadious Legacy's vision but also mankind. If only the Seers' powers hadn't been exploited for so long. If only they'd found Vira's abilities sooner. A hundred *if onlys* flitted through her mind, none of them correctable in the last seconds before the core's explosion engulfed the control chamber.

The bright light faded. Gemme breathed in and loosened her grip around Vira's soft pajamas. Gemme wiggled her toes in her boots. She was still alive. The fluorescent lights above them flickered on, and she saw Brentwood, triumph in his eyes.

"Engine core stabilized. Evacuation procedures unnecessary." Vira's high-pitched voice echoed over the intercom. Like the Seers, her lips didn't move as she mindspoke. Her voice was calm but childishly joyful. "Everyone return to your cells."

"Amazing." Brentwood shook his head, peering up at her. "She rebooted the system."

Above them, Vira clung to the wires like the ship was an extension of her arms. Her eyes remained closed, a placid expression on her features.

"How did you know she could do it?" Brentwood whispered.

"She inherited the Seers' abilities," Gemme whispered back, afraid to disturb her. "She has the same hypergene the Seers have."

"But how? The Seers had no children."

Gemme winked. "Just like the Lieutenants have their secrets, the Matchmakers have their own."

She thought he'd smile at her teasing, but Brentwood looked furious.

"What's wrong?"

"When the comet shower hit, and I was looking for survivors on the upper decks, the Seers directed me away from her. They didn't think her life was crucial enough to risk losing me. I disobeyed direct orders and saved her anyway."

"How horrible." Gemme couldn't imagine choosing between a disabled little girl and a lieutenant. She could never be a Seer. Even if she had their powers, she couldn't calculate life so cold and rationally. Maybe it was such decisions over the years that made Abysme go crazy. Or maybe she was crazy to begin with. Gemme hoped Vira could handle the enormous responsibility of their job. She'd be there to help the girl every step of the way. "She sure proved them wrong."

Brentwood smiled like a proud parent. "She's the most important of us all."

CHAPTER THIRTY-THREE
ICE PRINCESS

"Looks like you found more than hyperthium on your mission." Ferris leaned against the portal to Gemme's cell with a self-satisfied grin on his face. He wore his navy blue engineer uniform proudly. His new job assignment processing hyperthium fit him well.

"What do you mean?" Gemme paused, snapping the last buttons on her uniform. She checked herself in the mirror and straightened her ponytail.

"Lieutenant Brentwood? Of all people?"

Her fingers froze with her hair halfway through the elastic loop in her hair. Had he seen them holding hands? "I wanted to wait until the ship was stable before telling anyone. How did you know?"

Ferris chuckled and entered the room. "I have my sources."

Her cheeks flushed with mild embarrassment. She'd have to get used to the idea of other people knowing about her relationship with Brentwood. At least they wouldn't suspect her of setting up their pairing with the matchmaking system. They'd fallen in love the organic, old-fashioned way, and it thrilled her. Looking back on the past few weeks, the freedom of choice was superior to anything the computer could conjure based on genetics and analysis. To go from standing by the computer's choices and defending her job to discounting the entire system was a stretch, and it showed Gemme how much she'd changed these past weeks.

"So you're going to find your own match as well?" She turned the question back on him with a teasing look.

Ferris shrugged. "I guess I'll know when the time is right."

Gemme checked the wallscreen, feeling spoiled because they'd had full power for three days now, thanks to the first hyperthium shipment. "Speaking of time, the ceremony's supposed to start any minute."

"I'm waiting for you," Ferris reminded her. "Got to look perfect for Brentwood, eh?"

"Shut up." She threw a bath towel at his head and pulled the rest of her hair through her ponytail.

Ferris ducked and offered his arm. "If I may."

"Only if you'll behave." Gemme laughed, and they left her cell for the docking bay at the rear of the Expedition.

Newly fallen snow glistened as the back panels of the *Expedition* rumbled open, and the bright rays of Solaris Prime shot in. Gemme stood on the top of the staircase with Brentwood at her side, watching the balcony fill with all of the families on the *Expedition*. Through all the destruction and desolation, there were still so many left to follow in their ancestors' footsteps. They hadn't failed Thadious Legacy after all. Mankind would go on, rebuild, and endure on Tundra 37. Maybe someday they'd even build another ship and try again for Paradise 18.

The landrover pulled into the bay lugging several containers of hyperthium behind it, and some bales of a new wheat-like plant that scientists had deemed edible after finding the strand in Luna's pockets.

A wave of fondness came over her at the sight of vehicle. She'd spent so many days and nights with it, it was like running into an old friend. The crowd roared in applause, and their excitement fluttered Gemme's stomach.

The hatch opened and Tech jumped out, his beard was a great deal longer than when Alpha Blue took off on their mission, and Gemme was glad he'd finally have some time to rest at home. People chanted his name. His wife stood rigid in the front row, looking as if she'd rather cuff him on the head than give him a welcome embrace.

"About time he came home," Brentwood shouted over the applause. "I ordered him to last week, and he said he still had containers to fill."

"Bet his wife thinks the same." Gemme clapped as Tech bowed. Behind him, men pushed the hyperthium forward onto hovercarts for processing.

"I hope it's enough to keep us going." Brentwood caught Tech's eye and saluted him.

"Oh, it's enough." Gemme raised her eyebrows. "Enough for generations to come."

"That much?"

Gemme looped her arm around his. "For sure."

The crowd hushed as the portal to the corridor behind them dematerialized and a grand silver in the sun emerged with wires trailing behind it. As the chair floated to the edge of the stairway, Vira's face came into view. She looked much older than her years, and Gemme knew she'd gone through a lot these past weeks.

"She's like the princess of Tundra 37." Gemme stood on her tiptoes to get a better view.

"The ice princess," he replied with a curve of his lips. "She's a sign of hope for all of us."

"So far, she's doing pretty well," Gemme said. "After all, the first order she gave was to lock up that chest."

"Personally, I would have made you a lieutenant first." Brentwood squeezed her arm.

"Well, that order came next." Gemme ran her fingers over her own silver lapel pin, her instant connection to the girl. She looked forward to mentoring her as she and Brentwood led the crew into the new phase of their lives.

Vira gazed in their direction and nodded to them. Gemme waved and gave her an encouraging smile. They'd gone over this speech three times that morning. She knew Vira would speak well.

The little girl's voice boomed over the masses. "Congratulations to Tech Dougherty and his mining crew."

Applause rumbled through the bay, filling Gemme's ears. She caught Ferris's eye in the crowd standing by her parents and winked to them. They waved back before turning to Vira. The girl raised her small hands up and the applause settled down.

"And congratulations to all of you who have worked hard to successfully get the *Expedition* back online. Architects are planning new buildings, and under Lieutenant Brentwood's instructions, I've sent a team to locate an appropriate place for our colony." Her voice rose up, thundering in the high ceiling of the docking bay. "Tundra 37 is ours."

The cheers rumbled around her, and Gemme turned to Brentwood. He winked at her and her neck flushed up thinking about the time they'd shared. She had to refocus on Vira's speech. Even though she knew every word, she wanted to hear it spoken in this moment, from Vira's lips.

The girl's voice grew somber. "We've earned it with much sacrifice and hard work."

Gemme thought about Luna, and all the others who gave their lives for this vision, all the generations of Lifers who lived in the confines of the ship so they could walk on a real world, underneath their own sun.

Vira gestured toward the Solaris Prime. Her voice gained strength, and Gemme recited the words with her, whispering them over the crowd, wishing for the other Lifers to catch onto her hope and believe it. "But this is only the beginning. Go now and carve your own paths in our new world."

ACKNOWLEDGMENTS

I'd like to thank my agent, Dawn Dowdle, for believing in my manuscript and finding such a wonderful publishing company. Also, thank you to Liz Pelletier and Heather Howland at Entangled Publishing. Thank you to Kerry and Stacy, my eagle-eyed editors who worked so hard to polish this manuscript and find more depth in every plot strand, making the orb so much more than just a ball of golden swirls. My beta readers come next: the best sister in the world, Brianne Dionne, and my mom, Joanne, for giving me support and intriguing insights. My awesome critique partners deserve numerous thank yous: Cherie Reich, Theresa Milstein, Lisa Rusczyk, Kathleen S. Allen, Lindsey Duncan, and Cher Green. My flute teacher and life mentor, Peggy Vagts, comes next, for encouraging me to pursue writing and flute as duel dreams. And lastly, my husband, Chris, for allowing me the time I needed to work on edits, do research, and most of all, write.

BIOGRAPHY

Aubrie is an author and flutist in New England. Her stories have appeared in *Mindflights*, *Niteblade*, *Silver Blade*, *A Fly in Amber*, and several print anthologies including *Skulls and Crossbones* by Minddancer Press; *Rise of the Necromancers* by Pill Hill Press; *Nightbird Singing in the Dead of Night* by Nightbird Publishing; *Dragontales and Mertales* by Wyvern Publications; *A Yuletide Wish* by Nightwolf Publications; and *Aurora Rising* by Aurora Wolf Publications. Her epic fantasy is published with Wyvern Publications, and several of her ebooks are published with Lyrical Press and Gypsy Shadow Publishing. When she's not writing, she plays in orchestras and teaches flute at Plymouth State University and a community music school.

http://www.authoraubrie.com
http://authoraubrie.blogspot.com

www.ingramcontent.com/pod-product-compliance
Lightning Source LLC
Chambersburg PA
CBHW031001260626
47169CB00002B/652